CORR

Books by the same author

The Tears Series:
A MILLION TEARS
THE TEARS OF WAR AND PEACE
SILENT TEARS
TEARS UNTIL DAWN

The Nick Hunter Adventures:
CHAOS
DÉBÂCLE
HAVOC
MAYHEM
RETRIBUTION
TURMOIL

http://www.henke.co.uk/home.html
henke@sol.co.uk

Corruption

Paul Henke

To Carole,

Best wishes!

Paul Henke

Methuen

Published by Methuen 2019

1

Methuen & Co
Orchard House
Railway Street
Slingsby
York YO62 4AN
www.methuen.co.uk

First published in the UK in 2012 by
Good Read Publishing

The right of Paul Henke to be identified as the Author of
this work has been asserted by him in accordance with the
Copyright, Designs and Patents Act 1988

Methuen & Co Limited Reg. No. 5278590

A CIP catalogue record for this book is available from the British Library

ISBN 978 0 413 77813 0

Printed and bound in Great Britain by
Clays Ltd, Elcograf S.p.A.

'Yes, please. White, no sugar. Thank you.'

Andrea went through to her own office. This was the first time she had been there and stopped in surprise. It was large, there was a desk in one corner, a filing cabinet and other cupboards along one wall as well as a table in the middle of the room capable of seating half-a-dozen people in comfort. The right hand wall was lined with a bookcase filled with European Union Treaties and volume after volume of regulations created over the years of the EU's existence. From the three windows opposite the door she could see over the roofs of Brussels. Like the remainder of the furniture to be found in the Parliament buildings, it looked and was expensive. The waste of public money stuck in Andrea's throat, although she admitted to herself many of the large accountancy practices were almost as bad.

Dumping her briefcase on the floor, she sat down at her desk. Miss Phillips entered and placed the coffee with a plate of biscuits in front of Andrea who smiled her appreciation. She took out a pad and pen from her briefcase and began to re-examine the list she had made of things that needed doing. She had been working for a couple of hours when her secretary buzzed through.

'Is it alright if I go for lunch now, Miss Nelson?'

'Yes, that's fine. I'll have things for you to do when you get back.' Glancing at her watch she saw it was 12.30.

Andrea worked on. As was often the case, she immersed herself in the job in hand and lost all track of time. There were no interruptions, no phone calls, no one knocking on her door looking for her. She heard the door to the outer office close and she realised her secretary had returned from lunch. She glanced at her watch and frowned. The woman had been away for nearly two hours.

Andrea pressed a button on the intercom and said pleasantly, 'Miss Phillips, will you come in here, please?'

The woman entered. 'Miss Phillips, please take these,' she handed over the pages she had written, 'and type them up.' All this was said in a pleasant tone but then her voice hardened. 'For the record,

I expect my secretary to take one hour for lunch. No more. Do I make myself clear?'

The woman looked discomforted and nodded. 'Yes, Miss Nelson.'

'Good. As long as we understand each other I am sure we will get on famously. I have been looking at the staff list.' She handed over another sheet of paper. 'I want to meet these people at the times I have stated. Starting in ten minutes.'

'Yes, Miss Nelson.'

The first person on her list, her deputy, Herr Hugo Reiner, was fifteen minutes late. The remainder of the afternoon continued in the same way. At 5pm she was expecting the fourth person on her list to appear, even though by then they were running very late. She never appeared. On the hour she heard chairs moving, an increase in the noise made by a room full of people and in two minutes the room was empty. The last person she saw walking out of the door was her secretary. She had left without as much as a goodnight.

Andrea sat down at her desk and put her head in her hands. The work ethic of the public sector compared to the private never failed to astound her. This, however, was bordering on the ludicrous.

Slowly over the next few days she began to make her mark on the department. She was always first in and last to leave. Some of the statistics she learnt didn't surprise her – they shocked her! There was virtually no proper accounting for the billions of taxpayers' money sent to the European Commission each and every year. What there was proved to be farcical. If ever pigs had their noses in the trough, she thought, then the people who worked at the EU Parliament epitomised it.

One of the first facts Andrea learnt, although nobody had bothered to tell her before she accepted the job, was that the Parliament's internal auditors had refused to sign off the accounts for almost 20 years. There had never been independent auditors appointed in all that time. The scale of the job confronting her suddenly felt overwhelming. The level of absenteeism for spurious excuses, the tardiness of arriving for work and the lengths of breaks taken was mind numbing. How was she going to change the culture she was facing? Having been in the job for two weeks, she knew she needed to stamp her authority on her department. To help her do so, she arranged a meeting with her deputy at 14.00.

At 14.30, in a temper, she was about to ring through to Reiner's office but decided to visit his office instead.

She walked along the corridor, entered his secretary's office, smiled and said, 'Is Herr Reiner in his office?'

The woman looked at her, startled. 'Yes, but he's busy.'

Andrea frowned. 'We have an appointment.' She stepped the few paces across the room to the door opposite. She knocked, reached for the handle, turned it and pushed. The door wouldn't budge. She turned to the secretary who was looking worried.

'Is he in?'

There was no response.

'I just asked you if he was in.'

The reply was in rapid French.

Andrea stepped to the desk and replied in equally rapid French. 'So he's in. Please unlock the door.'

Her use of French startled the woman. 'I cannot. There is no key. You have to turn a small handle on the inside.'

Andrea berated herself. Of course you did. She had the same lock on her office door.

She went back to the door and knocked on it. There was no reply. She knocked on it again. Still nothing. She began to get worried. 'Is he ill?'

The woman shook her head. 'I . . . I don't know.'

Knocking again, even harder this time and still with no response, Andrea became worried. She went back to the outer door and looked at the various people at their desks. One was a large man, somewhat obese, who was sitting at his desk idly turning over pages in a file.

Andrea walked across to his desk. 'Come with me, please.'

He looked up, startled.

'I need your help.'

Nodding, he got to his feet, still not having said anything and followed Andrea back to the locked door.

She stepped aside. 'Break it open.'

'What?'

'I said break the door open. I think Herr Reiner might be ill. There is no answer when we knock on the door.'

The man shrugged and put his shoulder to the door. Nothing happened so he tried harder. On the third try the door flew open and he stumbled into the office.

Andrea was on his heels. Herr Reiner was lying on a couch situated along the left wall. He propped himself up and, in German, groggily asked, 'What's going on?'

Andrea stopped in surprise. Turning to the man who had helped, she said, 'Thank you. Please leave us.'

The man went out, a sly grin on his face.

With her hands on her hips, she glared down at Reiner who had just swung his feet onto the floor. The smell of alcohol mixed with bad breath permeated the room.

'What the hell do you mean by this? What do you think you're doing?' Andrea had to fight with her emotions not to be yelling at the man.

He replied in German, a look of equal anger on his face.

'You speak English fluently,' Andrea said. 'I would appreciate it if you used it.'

The reply was again in German.

Andrea turned to the door where his secretary was standing and said, 'You are fluent in both languages. I want you to translate.'

Before the woman could say anything Reiner said something to her which caused the woman to close her mouth, a sullen look on her face.

Andrea was getting impatient. 'Well?'

In response she received a shake of the head and the secretary said, 'I . . . I cannot. I . . . I . . .' she stopped speaking.

Reiner lurched to his feet. Unsteadily, without a word, he left the office. Andrea watched him go to the men's cloakroom.

She suddenly became aware that every member of staff was looking at her. She hesitated a moment as to whether to stay where she was or return to her office. She decided to go back to her office. Turning to the secretary, she said, 'Tell Herr Reiner I expect him in my office in fifteen minutes.'

He didn't appear. Her working relationship with Reiner was destroyed and obviously could never be put right. That was when she received another of the many shocks she had so far experienced. She discovered it was impossible to get rid of Reiner. Far too many senior managers enjoyed long, liquid lunches.

2

As Richard Griffiths sat looking at his wife across the kitchen table he knew that he had failed. He acknowledged that some of their problems were down to him. But he had tried hard, very hard, to make things right. They had been married just eleven months and a few days. Even at the beginning things had been rocky. Which wasn't surprising after what they'd been through only a short time prior to their nuptials.

Richard felt the old memories stirring as they often did when he was in an introspective mood.

It had started with the death of his first family. They had planned a holiday in the States, a holiday they had been looking forward to – he with a great deal of contented satisfaction, the twins and Ellen with loads of excitement. It was to be Christmas with a difference. At first, Phillip and Lucy had taken some convincing that Father Christmas would know where they were and deliver their presents. Even so, it had been necessary to visit the grotto in the shopping centre and make sure the message was passed on.

His wife, Ellen, and the twins – just six years old – had been the centre of his universe. Then came that fateful day. Richard had been called away to the Gulf of Mexico for a job that would last only a couple of days at the most. As soon as it was over he would join his family in Colorado for Christmas.

When the plane with them onboard was blown out of the skies his world had collapsed. He had fought depression and despair until finally he had his life back on track. He then moved heaven and earth to exact revenge on those responsible. He had only been partially successful. That was when he had met Victoria. Common sense finally prevailed and he gave up his quest. By then it had been too late and the Islamic fundamentalists responsible for the original atrocity came after him.

On the day of their wedding the terrorists struck with catastrophic results. People were killed and Victoria kidnapped. It had taken all Richard's guts and determination to find the terrorists, kill them and rescue Victoria. After further problems, one being Victoria's psychological damage, they had finally married. It had been hard going at first, but he had been determined to make it work. It was fine for a few months but then things started to go wrong. Little things at first, such as complaints about his absences and their lack of a social life. Victoria had nothing to do but hang around the house all day. Richard had encouraged her to take up charitable work but she had found one excuse after another not to.

The more complaining she did, the more he retreated into his shell. Then came his promotion to Managing Director of Griffiths and Buchanan Offshore. The company was a division of the international holding company, Griffiths and Buchanan plc, which had been started by his great-grandfather – Sir David Griffiths – early in the twentieth century. His shareholding in the company made him wealthy while his ability got him the job – one that he loved.

In theory, the promotion should have meant more time at home. In practice, he used it as an excuse to stay away for longer periods. Victoria accused him of having an affair which he denied while at the same time offering all sorts of proof that he wasn't. Nothing he said or did satisfied her.

Now this.

It was Saturday morning, the time was just after nine o'clock and they were having breakfast together.

Victoria, he acknowledged to himself, was beautiful. Her blonde hair framed a wide mouth and hazel eyes that had been capable of penetrating to his soul. Even the small scar on the left side of her mouth, virtually unnoticeable, received as the result of a car crash when in her teens, he found endearing. She was dressed in a white blouse and tight shorts in deference to the warm weather.

She had her head bowed, not looking at him, toying with the mixture of fresh fruit in the bowl in front of her. Richard knew she was aware of his gaze but she chose not to acknowledge it.

'I'll be back from the office around two o'clock. Why don't we go down to the coast, walk the promenade, even go swimming?'

Finally, she looked at him. In her soft American accent, she replied, 'I don't want to.'

In exasperation, he asked, 'What do you want to do then?'

Her answer surprised him. 'I want to go home.'

'I thought this was your home!' They had bought the house a few weeks after getting married. It was terraced and described by the estate agents as the epitome of Georgian elegance, situated off Belgravia Place, in the heart of London. The five en-suite bedrooms, the study, lounge and large, well equipped kitchen, spoke of wealth.

Now she looked up at him. Her gaze was harsh, her mouth determined. It was a look he had encountered before, though not with quite so much anger.

'This place?' She flung her spoon down onto the table. It bounced and slid onto the floor. They both ignored it. 'I hate it here! Hate it! The spectre of your first wife and the two . . .' she paused, about to say something she would regret later, but instead, managed to say, 'the twins, hovers over us. I can't stand it!'

Richard knew she was lying. There were no photographs of Ellen and the twins to be found anywhere except in his office. There he had a large photograph on his desk and an album stowed away in a drawer. Whenever he required solace he would take it out and idly look through it. Though he had done so less and less as the days and weeks turned into years.

He nodded in acknowledgement. It was time to grasp the nettle. Standing, he threw his napkin onto the table and said, 'Fine. I'll speak to the lawyers and start divorce proceedings. We can stop this charade once and for all.'

The look she gave him was one of spite, tinged with relief. 'I want a settlement. A substantial one.'

About to tell her to go to hell, he changed his mind and nodded. 'One million pounds will be paid to you when you sign the divorce papers and a further million when the decree absolute is issued.'

Victoria was about to make a derisory comment when Richard held up his hand. Standing, he added, 'It's up to you. You can have the money or we can spend the next few years in court.'

The wind was taken from her sails as common sense prevailed. She knew he was right. She nodded, relief now etched in her face.

Then she surprised him. 'I'm sorry Richard. I really am.' She shrugged. 'I didn't want this to happen. It just . . . .just crept up on me.'

Richard nodded and said in a quiet voice, 'I know. I'll take a few things and stay in the company flat. I'll leave you to pack and take anything you want.'

Victoria nodded and said softly, 'Thank you.'

He left the room. Going upstairs, he threw a few necessities into a grip and went back down. In the hallway he picked up his briefcase. At 6ft 1in, with broad shoulders, he had the black hair and the dark brown eyes of the Griffiths family. He was 36 years old, an ex-Royal Naval diving officer who still worked out in the gym. His craggy features made him interesting rather than good looking, but there was something about his smile and the look he unintentionally gave that women found appealing. Even so, apart from the few years before he had met Ellen he had been faithful to both his wives.

Dressed in a light grey suit with a white shirt and his dark blue, naval club tie, festooned with the Royal Naval crown, he left the house. There was a spring in his step. It was as if a weight had been lifted off his shoulders. He was actually looking forward to his day. Although it was the weekend, he was going to be tied up with a conference call most of the morning as details of the China deal were hammered out. The Chinese were tough negotiators. But then, so was he. It was the sort of battle he relished.

Richard spent the morning on conference calls with personnel all across the globe. He had agreed a deal with the Chinese to supply one of the company's giant tugs to tow an American oil exploration rig from the Gulf of Mexico to an area about 200 miles off Shanghai. The rig was one of the few in existence capable of working at these depths and the tug, Goliath, one of the few vessels capable of dragging it through the potentially rough seas they could expect to encounter. A daily rate as well as an estimated time of arrival had been agreed. For every day earlier that the rig arrived on station then B & G would receive half a days' hire costs. The crew would share in the extra profits.

Richard knew that a generous incentive was always a good way to get the most out of the company's workforce.

It was nearly two o'clock in the afternoon when Richard finally stood and stretched. He acknowledged that he had been delaying going back home to collect a few more things he had realised earlier he needed. He wanted to avoid another row with Victoria at all costs and thought it best to let her know he would be returning if only for a few minutes. He rang the house but there was no answer. He thought about phoning her mobile but decided against it. Instead, he hurried outside and grabbed a taxi. With luck, he could be there and gone before she returned.

Paying the cabbie, he went up the steps to the front door and went in, calling her name. To his relief, silence greeted him. He went upstairs and grabbed a suitcase which he packed with shirts and a grey suit. Lugging it downstairs, he was headed for the front door when he noticed an envelope on the side table in the hall with his name on it.

It was in Victoria's handwriting. Picking it up, he tore it open and read :-

Richard,

This is to say goodbye. I have packed the things I wish to keep and am taking them with me. The remainder please give to a charity shop.

I am sorry that things have turned out the way they have, but there is nothing to be done about it. We cannot control our feelings or our hearts.

Have your lawyers send the necessary papers to my parents' place and they'll make sure I get them.

I wish to get everything done and dusted as soon as possible, something I know you will want also.

I wish you a long and happy life.

Victoria.

Richard scanned the letter once more, screwed it up and went into the kitchen where he threw it into a rubbish bin. Despite his feelings earlier in the day, the letter touched him – she had been through so much. A mixture of guilt and regret washed over him. Thoughtfully, he crossed over to the coffee maker and busied himself putting beans and water into the machine. He acknowledged to himself that action was needed. The first thing was to sell the house. Even in the tough market that had the country by its throat the place would sell easily. He was in a part of London where the rich wanted to live.

While the coffee filtered through, he took his case and grip back upstairs, unpacked it and turned to leave. He paused, collected together his sports gear and went back downstairs. He forgot all about his coffee as he grabbed his car keys and went out the front door. A couple of hundred yards away was a row of garages. He aimed the remote at one of them and the doors slid open. Inside were two cars. One was a Range Rover 4x4 while the other was an Austin-Healey 100 Four, manufactured by British Leyland in the 1950s. Richard had seen it advertised in a magazine a few years earlier. The sentence "some work required" was an understatement. He bought it for peanuts and spent a fortune getting the car restored to its original beauty. He had made one concession to modern technology – he'd fixed a sat-nav to the corner of the windscreen.

He started the engine, drove out into the street and zapped the garage door shut. The gymnasium he used was in St Katherine's Dock. He drove with the roof down, the sun beating on the back of his neck. As was usual when driving in London, he hardly managed to get above 20mph.

He parked in a nearby multi-storey, raised the roof of the car, went outside and wandered over to the old, listed building where the gymnasium was located. At reception he collected a locker key and went along to the changing room. Then, in the main hall, he watched for a few minutes as men, and some women, faced each other, bowed and attacked. Others were already in the middle of a bout of Bartitsu.

The art of Bartitsu was a British invention. It combined the best elements of boxing, wrestling, fencing and savate – a French discipline where both hands and feet were used.

Richard had taken up the sport only ten months earlier and admitted that due to lack of practice he was merely adequate at it. However, Bartitsu was a great way to deal with stress even if it meant attacking a dummy or another person. After sparring with his instructor, Richard usually had a few bruises.

A couple of hours later he showered and left, feeling better for the work out.

3

Sitting in her tiny apartment, five kilometres from the Parliament, a glass of white wine in her hand, Andrea acknowledged to herself that the job she had undertaken was more difficult than she had expected. She had met with the heads of the five units that made up her department, along with more junior personnel, questioning them about what was needed to improve matters. She had tried to keep the interviews positive. She hadn't pointed out the flaws in the accounting system, the missing hundreds of millions of euros, the squandering of money on an unimaginable scale. Early on, she had acknowledged to herself, if a company, private or public, operated in the same way, its directors would have been in prison long ago.

At one meeting she had asked a middle manager about the lack of double-entry book keeping.

He had sighed, blown out his cheeks, looked uncomfortable and shrugged.

'Well?' Andrea had asked. 'It's a simple question.' She had not received a satisfactory answer.

Two months into the job and she was thankful her contract was only for two years. That should enable her to sort out the mess, install proper accounting procedures and give her enough time to ensure they were working properly. After that, she could go back to doing something that wouldn't send her blood pressure sky rocketing about twice a day. Cynically, she admitted to herself, twice a day was a good day. Normally, it was more like half-a-dozen. She drained her glass, thought about a second, decided to leave it and went to bed.

The following morning, she had a meeting with members of the Directorate-General for Budget. It was in the Justus Lipsius building, an imposing steel and glass giant of crass flamboyance, built at five times the original budget. But then, as Andrea discovered, being over budget was normal for the European Union. Five times over was more than acceptable – it was the norm. Often the figures were more like eight or nine times, and even these huge amounts were never questioned. Vast sums were unaccounted for. MEPs and commissioners had been leaving their posts as multi-millionaires with no explanation as to where the money had come from. More to the point, as far as she could tell, there hadn't even been an investigation into their accumulation of such wealth.

There were 12 members of the Directorate in the room, seated at a horseshoe table capable of seating 30 people at least. She felt like a prisoner on trial about to be cross examined by prosecuting council.

'We've invited you here to give us an update on the progress you're making,' said Jacques Dupuis, sententiously.

Standing behind the chair that Jacques Dupuis had indicated, Andrea looked along the line of sombre faces. They were all on the opposite side of the table, staring at her. They each had a cup of coffee in front of them with plates of biscuits scattered along the table.

Glancing around, she spotted the usual coffee machine in a corner of the room. Swinging her briefcase onto the chair, she walked across the room, saying over her shoulder, 'Good morning.' She summoned up a smile from somewhere.

Then her smile turned into one of real enjoyment. The looks on the faces of the others almost caused her to burst out laughing. She took her time pouring the coffee and adding milk. Behind her she could hear the rustling of papers, the restless movement of bodies unused to being challenged. However, there was nothing they could do about it. Apart from Budget Director General Jacques Dupuis, she was the most senior person there.

She was about to take a plate of biscuits but changed her mind. In spite of her display of bravado, she had a tight knot in her stomach.

She sat down at the chair next to her briefcase, took an appreciative sip of her coffee and asked, 'What would you like to know?'

'We would like to ascertain what progress you have made with creating and implementing new procedures. As we discussed originally, we need a system that will be more acceptable to the tax payer. One that shows true democracy at work. Efficient and, more to the point, plain and simple for all to understand.'

Andrea doubted that no matter how plain and simple she made it, less than one in fifty people in the EU would be able to understand it and less than one in five hundred would care or take any notice.

'First of all,' Andrea said, 'the computer systems you have are totally inadequate for the job they should be doing.'

'Rubbish,' said a woman sitting next to Dupuis. 'The system has only been in use for eighteen months. If anything isn't right, it is the competency of your department when it comes to using it.'

Not knowing what she would be asked, Andrea had arrived with her briefcase packed with files. Opening the case, she flicked through them until she found the one she wanted. She extracted it, opened it, looked down and then back at the woman.

She smiled at her and then said, 'We haven't met, but I assume you are Frau Eva Bachmeier?'

The woman nodded. 'That is correct.' She looked to be in her middle fifties, her blonde hair showing grey at the roots. She had once been attractive but the years of using too much makeup and eating too much of the wrong food had taken their toll. Even so, she was elegantly dressed, her designer jacket and white blouse, testimony to the fact she didn't skimp when buying clothes.

Andrea looked at the file again though she knew its contents all too well. 'The company which supplied the software is called Kaufmann International. Am I right?'

'Yes,' said Dupuis answering for Frau Bachmeier.

'The price paid for the system was nearly five million euros.'

'If you say so,' Dupuis frowned at her.

'The system is virtually worthless as it is totally inadequate and not fit for purpose. Furthermore, I have been checking the shareholding of the company.' She looked at the German woman who squirmed in her seat. 'It is one hundred percent owned by BLC Capital which is registered in the Cayman Islands. BLC Capital has, as its major shareholder, a Mrs Anne Naismith. Mrs Naismith's maiden name is, of course, Bachmeier and is your-sister-in-law. BLC Capital has another company called BLC Pensions which pays two hundred euros into your current account and . . .'

'This is ridiculous. The money I receive is a tiny pension for a job I had . . .'

Andrea interrupted. 'You did not let me finish. Apart from what goes into your account a further ten thousand euros are paid monthly into an account belonging to your daughter who lives in the UK. In Hull, to be precise.'

Frau Bachmeier shook her head. 'How dare you investigate my daughter! It is outrageous! Her affairs are no concern of yours.' Then, on the verge of hysteria, she added, 'You cannot know this. You cannot!'

'Of course I can. The UK Government has spent years trying to stop this type of fraud where off-shore bank accounts and off-shore registered companies are used. Most attempts have failed, especially when they are trying to deal with large conglomerates. Unfortunately for your family, you don't have the resources to do the same.' Andrea looked stonily at her. 'You, Frau Bachmeier, have a twenty percent holding in the company while the rest is owned between your sister-in-law and your brother.' Before the woman could say anything, Andrea slid out a sheet of paper and pushed it in front of her. 'This is a copy of the shareholding details I got from Companies House in Britain. You can see precisely what I mean.'

The woman looked sick and then blustered, 'It is true I have a share holding but it did not influence in any way the decision to buy the software.'

It was obvious from the look on the faces of the others at the table that they didn't believe her. However, nobody looked at the woman; they continued to stare at Andrea who, in turn, was looking at Frau Bachmeier.

Frau Bachmeier suddenly sat up straight and said, 'I did not make the decision to buy the software. It was made by a member of your department.'

'That is correct,' said Andrea. 'It was done by Herr Reiner. However, that is of no consequence. I have here a copy of one of the regulations that states quite clearly that no company or business may supply any service or product to the Parliament if any member of staff is in any way connected to said company or business. Would you like to read it?'

There was silence around the table.

After a few seconds, Dupuis said, 'That is all very well but we should continue.'

Andrea looked at the man in astonishment. 'You have to be joking!'

'What? What?' said Dupuis, not only surprised but disconcerted to have his authority questioned.

'There is no way that this meeting is going to proceed with Frau Bachmeier here. Not only do I insist that she be expelled from the room but I expect action to be taken against her for fraud and theft.'

Dupuis looked at Andrea for a few seconds and then turned to Bachmeier. 'Please leave.'

The woman stood up, glared at Andrea and stalked from the room. As murmurings and comments sounded around her, Andrea looked in surprise at Dupuis. She couldn't believe it. 'Wait a moment. You should call security and have that woman escorted from the building. She should be suspended while a full investigation is carried out and if what I say is found to be true, she should be sacked and criminal proceedings should be implemented.'

Dupuis, stroking his moustache with some agitation, shook his head. 'I,' he emphasised by tapping his chest with his forefinger, 'will decide what is to happen. Let us proceed.'

About to make another protest, Andrea changed her mind. However, she wouldn't be letting the matter rest.

'Then let me say that we urgently need a new software system. One that is suitable for the job. There are a number of them which I have identified. Based on our requirements, the most expensive is one and a half million euros, while the cheapest is just under the million. Training and presentations on the systems will be extra, though from the figures I have been supplied with, I don't think it will be unreasonable.'

There were a few nods from the others at the table, whilst Dupuis merely scowled and continued to stroke his upper lip.

'The next matter is far more serious. The most basic requirement when keeping accounts is to use double-entry bookkeeping.' Seeing the look of puzzlement on some of the faces she couldn't hold back a sigh. 'Let me explain.' She decided to be pompous. 'In the thirteenth century, Venetian merchants invented a new form of bookkeeping. It was formalised by an Italian monk named Luca Pacioli around 1500 in a book called *Summa de Arithmetica, Geometrica, Poroportioni et Proportionaltie.*'

Although she was enjoying the look of irritation on the others' faces, Andrea decided to cut to the chase. 'It is the simplest of systems. To reduce the likelihood of fraud and outright theft the system recognises that every financial transaction must have a source and disposition. This means that every financial transaction is shown by the equation Assets equals Liabilities plus Owners' Equity. Which means every transaction creates two entries, a debit and a credit. Do you follow so far?'

She waited for them all to nod. She was aware that there were at least four different languages spoken between the attendees and had been surprised that there had been no translators present. She learnt later that practically everyone in the Budget Directorate spoke excellent English.

'Good. A change in the assets' side is called a debit which is mirrored by a change in the equities' side, and is known as a credit. If entered correctly, the books will balance as the credits will equal the debits.'

She paused. The looks on the faces of the people in front of her was one of utter boredom. She hoped she was about to change all that.

'The software is so bad that after entries have been made they can be changed. As there is no audit trail the alterations cannot be identified.'

'Then how do you know that changes have taken place?' One of the people at the table asked.

'That's a fair question. The answer is, because of the sheer scale of the fraud and thefts that have taken place where people haven't actually bothered fiddling the books. There's an arrogance with the people committing these actions that . . . that beggars belief. If it is possible to make the alterations then there is no doubt that in too many cases that is what's being done.'

'That suggests dishonesty amongst the Commission,' said Dupuis.

Andrea managed not to look astonished at what he had just said, but couldn't help asking, 'Are you on the same planet? Have you any idea how much money we are talking about?'

'I won't be spoken to in that manner,' said Dupuis, his anger turning his face crimson.

'Look,' said Andrea, becoming equally angry, 'we are talking about hundreds of millions of euros in outright fraud and theft and billions wasted through further fraud by end users. And that's with me barely touching the surface of what's going on. If we are to control the vast sums of money that pass through this Parliament each and every year then we need radical changes and improvements. Which,' she added with a great deal of asperity, 'was why I was hired in the first place.'

The meeting continued with Andrea bringing out point after point. It was obvious that she had been meticulous and painstaking in collating the information. As far as she was concerned, every issue was a damning indictment of the way the European Parliament was organised and run.

In the middle of the afternoon there was a break for coffee. Two women appeared, pushing trolleys with fresh coffee, tea, cold drinks and local pastries. The men and women of the Budget Directorate stood up, stretched and went across to the trolleys to get some refreshments. Nobody went near Andrea. Some cast looks at her but she chose to ignore them. Although she could have done with a cup of tea right then she decided not to bother. It would have been too embarrassing to collect a cup and stand and try and make small talk with people who evidently didn't want to speak to her. Or maybe, she suddenly thought, they had been told not to fraternise with her. She looked across at Dupuis who was standing with his back to her.

In spite of the enjoyment she'd had from some aspects of the afternoon, overall, she was worn to a frazzle. For a moment, she thought of resigning – just walking away. However, even as she thought it, she knew she couldn't. The whole mess needed fixing. Honesty needed to be brought in to the Parliament. All she needed to do was find people in the Parliament who would be willing to clean up the mess. Surely, she thought, there were enough people she could call on to make it happen? If so, how was she going to identify them? She couldn't exactly put an advertisement in a newspaper – *Wanted. An honest employee working in the European Parliament.*

The meeting recommenced.

'I have one other important matter to bring to your attention. Last year's closing balance for the accounts did not compare with this year's opening figures. In all my time in the world of accountancy I have never seen anything like it. Over three hundred million euros discrepancy.'

'Is that three hundred million more?' piped up one of those present. Some of the others chuckled unconvincingly.

Andrea turned her gaze on the man. She bit back the retort she was about to make and instead said, in a scathing voice, 'Either would be equally bad. However, the money is missing.'

Dupuis came in then. 'How can you be sure?'

This time, she couldn't avoid venting her spleen. 'Look, I am reading from the last set of unsigned audited accounts. There is a statement on file that they will not be signed off due to the serious irregularities to be found in them. There is, however a final balance as you'd expect. That is the number that should correspond to the opening balance for this year. It doesn't. So why is that Mr Commissioner for the Budget Directorate?' It was the only phrase she could think of using without actually calling him a thieving liar.

The barb struck home. His anger was etched deep on his face. As was always the case in situations like the one they were in, words had to be used carefully – insults obvious but not overt.

Dupuis said, 'To date, Ms Nelson, you have brought us no solutions only problems. It was to solve those problems that we hired you.'

Before he could continue, Andrea interrupted him. 'I have told you what needs doing as well as how to do it. I won't sit here and take the rubbish you're spouting.' She reigned back on her tone. She was in serious danger of overstepping the accepted line of politeness. 'I have put everything I have told you in writing and I have a copy here for you. I shall have copies made and sent to each of you,' she looked along the line. 'Furthermore, I shall have a copy delivered to every MEP and commissioner so that they all know what the situation is and what I am trying to do.'

Dupuis blanched. 'Wait a moment Ms. Nelson. Let us not be too hasty. I think it would be best all-round if we solved the problems in-house, so to speak. I am sure you must agree.'

'I do not wish to embarrass the Parliament in any way,' said Andrea, 'but I will not be bullied.'

Andrea could see that the smile Dupuis managed to summon up was a strain, but he did reply in an even and calm voice, 'That is not what I intended. I think we all agree that to keep matters in-house is in the best interests of the European Union.'

There was one thing Andrea had learnt since arriving at the

Parliament. If backed into a corner, the good of the European Union was always the mantra used to hide something either untoward or, more often, illegal. The good of the EU was sacrosanct. It was the epitome of the driving force that was uniting Europe, creating a large, stable economy and stopping any more wars on the Continent.

The first two objectives Andrea had yet to make up her mind about. The last one made her spit blood in anger. What about NATO? What about the million Americans, soldiers and airmen, who stayed in Europe after the war? Which American President said they'd come to Europe twice, they wouldn't be coming back a third time? They'd be staying. She was paraphrasing but the Yanks had stayed and faced down the USSR, not the Europeans – apart from the Brits of course, even though the country was bankrupt.

Then, when was it? Andrea had a head for remembering virtually anything connected to numbers. The 19th of the ninth in 1946. Winston Churchill had called for a United States of Europe to ensure future peace in a broadcast made from Zurich. He had called on a reconciliation and partnership between France and Germany, the two countries whose enmity had fostered two world wars. She wondered what he would think of the corrupt mess that had been made of it.

Shortly after that the meeting was closed. Looking at her watch, Andrea realised why. In spite of not finishing the agenda, it was fast approaching five o'clock in the afternoon.

She returned to her office. Her secretary was still at her desk, working. During the months a subtle change had come over their relationship. There was no question of Maud taking extra time away from her desk. She frequently worked during her lunch and stayed late whenever Andrea did.

'Maud, don't hang around here. You get off home. Your mother needs you.'

Andrea had learnt that Maud's mother was living with her. She was a semi-invalid who seemed to need a great deal of attention and frequently phoned Maud with one demand or another.

'That's okay, Miss Nelson, I've plenty to do here.'

Andrea looked at the clock on the wall. 'I tell you what, there's a bottle of white wine in the fridge in my office, why not come and join me for a drink?'

Maud looked startled for a moment and then nodded. 'I'd like that. Let me close down these files and I'll come through.'

Andrea went into her office, dumped her briefcase alongside her desk and crossed to the fridge hidden inside the wooden cupboard next to the coffee machine. She took out a bottle of Chardonnay, unscrewed the top, found two wine glasses and poured the wine.

She was about to return to her desk when she changed her mind and went and sat on the easy chair with the low table in front of her. Maud came in and Andrea waved her across.

Her secretary sat down tentatively on the edge of her seat and reached for the glass.

Andrea smiled and raised her glass. 'Cheers.'

'Cheers,' Maud replied.

Both women took appreciative sips.

'How did the meeting go?'

Andrea shook her head. 'Unbelievable.' She proceeded to tell Maud all about it. When she had finished, Andrea said, 'You don't seem surprised.'

Maud sighed. 'I'm not. It's what's been going on for years.'

'Then why hasn't anything been done about it?'

'It's too ingrained. May I speak frankly?'

'Of course. I wouldn't expect anything else. More wine?'

Maud held out her glass, Andrea topped it up and then poured some more for herself.

'When you first came to the department I wasn't sure what to expect. I thought you were one of the lapdogs put in to do the bidding of the bosses in this place. I came to realise that you weren't. That you were,' she looked embarrassed for a moment and then said, 'that you were, are, honest. That you had come in with the intention of doing a proper job.'

'That now seems to be a tall order.'

'It is. I believe in the ideal of the European Union,' Maud was becoming more animated, leaning forward, a gleam in her eyes. 'But in order for it to work we have to have an honest system. You're the person best placed to achieve that. I don't know how you'll do it, but it must start with you and this department.'

Andrea nodded slowly but then said, 'I'm not sure I can manage it.'

'Well, we have to try.'

Andrea looked a little surprised at the use of the word "we" while Maud sat back a little, embarrassed.

'I didn't mean we, I meant you.'

'No, I won't get anywhere without your help.' It was Andrea's turn to lean forward, excited at the possibility of what they could do. 'We need to amass enough damning information which we can release not only to the press but to the sovereign governments of the EU countries. I know we'll identify those members of each government who will use the information properly. Who support the ideal but not the structure.'

'Yes,' Maud was also sitting forward, excited by the thought. 'I . . . I can help.' A look of determination passed across her face. 'I already have a great deal of information on a flash drive which I can copy and let you have. It needs work to put it into some semblance of order. Time lapse and subject matter being the two obvious ones.'

'Right. What if you make a start in the morning? Meanwhile, I'll also begin to collect information and do the same with anything new that crosses my desk.' Andrea looked pensive for a moment, 'I think I'll give more work to certain individuals in the department and watch them manipulate what they learn to suit themselves. They will give added credibility to whatever we come up with. What we need is the sort of evidence that will result in prosecutions. It will be through the courts that the truth will come to light.'

4

For Richard, the months passed in something of a blur. Work demanded a great deal of his time. Time he was more than willing to give. Work kept his mind off his personal problems, though he was the first to admit his problems paled into insignificance when compared to those faced by many people in the world. The European debt crisis had little effect on B & G Maritime. Their customers were worldwide. China had no industrial or economical problems. Neither did Argentina nor India. All three countries' economies were booming and all three had a continuous need for B & G Maritime's services.

His lawyers took care of his divorce and he sold the house for a profit. Not one to accumulate personal property, Richard gave much of his belongings – household goods and the like, to a charity that supported servicemen who needed both medical and financial help. He moved into the company flat, hung some of his clothes in the cupboard while leaving the bulk of his belongings in the trunks they were packed in.

The flat was near South Kensington Underground. It had three en-suite bedrooms, a living room, large kitchen and a separate dining room. It was well stocked with the paraphernalia required to live in reasonable comfort though most of the items found in the property had never been used.

Richard took possession of the largest bedroom whilst those visiting London on company business used one of the other bedrooms.

Most of the time he spent abroad. Travel, he told himself, helped to broaden the mind. More significantly, he admitted, it helped to assuage his feeling of loneliness. Not that he missed female company. He had plenty of it, even if it was only meaningless relationships which helped to kill a few hours or a few days. Each time, he ensured the woman didn't get the idea of there being a long term relationship, which suited him admirably.

*   *   *   *

Jules Fournier was Third Secretary at the French Embassy in London whose job covered a multitude of tasks. He was to inform the French government about changes in British policy both home and abroad, to defend his own country's foreign policy positions with the British and to help organise official visits of French dignitaries to the UK.

He was 44 years old, of medium height and weight, with brown hair going grey at the sides. His eyes were brown and he had a round cherubic face that often looked as though he was sucking on a particularly sour lemon. It was acknowledged by the good and the great of the French Diplomatic Corps that the man had reached a grade above his level of competence. Unmarried, he had no immediate family and few, if any, friends. He had grown increasingly bitter over the years, hating his job, hating the people around him and terrified of what the future held.

Fournier was also the temporary assistant to the military attaché, Colonel Paul Cuzin, a man in his early fifties, tall and thin, he was always immaculately dressed, whether in uniform or civilian clothes.

The Colonel had been passed over for promotion and was a man eaten up by bitterness. He would be retiring in just over a year. His ex-wife and three children didn't speak to him. That was another cause of his eroding anger. So he'd had an affair, so what? Many people had affairs. It was the nature of things. Monogamy wasn't natural – for either sex. He had tried to explain that to his sons and daughter a year after he and his wife had parted. They had just reached the end of their teens and he figured they would be of an age to understand. He had underestimated the damage his wife could do drip feeding her hatred of him into their receptive ears.

That had been five years ago and he hadn't spoken to them since. His mistress had long since lost interest in him and gone onto pastures new, while he had turned to the bottle to seek solace. It hadn't worked. In fact, all it had done was to earn him two unofficial reprimands for his conduct and one official one. That was when it had been made clear to him that he would not get a further promotion and that he should retire at the first opportunity.

Ironically, although they had similar thoughts, similar feelings, neither the Colonel nor Fournier realised how the other felt. They were both too tied up in their own misery to take notice.

Spring was in the air and Colonel Cuzin was at the Pussycat. It was a sleaze of a place where the drinks were overpriced but the women were cheap. He was sitting next to a blonde who had brown roots, surgically enhanced breasts and wore too much make-up. He was nursing a half pint of beer and a small whisky, while she had what was euphemistically called a Singapore Sling, her fourth. Instead of gin, fresh pineapple juice, Cherry Heering and Benedictine, the drink was made from watered down gin, bottled pineapple juice and soda water to create the foam. Plenty of ice hid the taste.

The music was loud and far too modern for his taste. He had been sitting there wondering what to do. Should he go upstairs with the woman for the next 15 minutes or so, or get the hell out of there and go back to the embassy?

He didn't notice the man until he sat opposite him and held out his hand across the table. He yelled, 'Victor Gillespie. I think we've met before.'

Cuzin took his hand but shook his head. 'No, I don't think so.'

'Yes! Wait a minute.' Appearing to be thinking, he sat up straight, snapped his fingers and pointed at him. 'An Italian Embassy cocktail party, three months ago?'

Cuzin thought for a moment. He had been at a cocktail party at the Italian Embassy around then, so they must have met, even if only briefly.

'Could be,' Cuzin recalled.

'Listen, old chap, what do you say we get out of here and go somewhere else?'

Cuzin frowned. He wasn't sure. The girl beside him squirmed and somehow contrived to have her blouse slip and show more cleavage, if that was at all possible.

'We can go to the Screeching Parrot.'

Again, he hesitated. The place was expensive.

'It'll be my treat. I had some good fortune today. I'll tell you all about it. Come on, it's better than this dump.' Gillespie suddenly laughed out loud. 'Don't worry, I'm not trying to pick you up,' he almost had to yell. 'The Parrot has a better standard of, shall we say, clientele? Come on. I've nobody else to go to the ruddy place with.'

Standing up, Cuzin nodded. 'Let's go!'

The woman said something that he didn't quite catch but guessed it wasn't pleasant. The two men left, grateful to get out into the quiet of the night and the drizzling, March rain.

'That's better,' said Gillespie. He was a big man in every sense of the word. Tall with broad shoulders, his posture helped to hold in his thickening waist line. He had thinning fair hair, an angular nose and thick lips.

As they walked along, Cuzin asked in a slurred voice, 'What's this good luck you had?'

He had been expecting something like a win at the horses or dogs or something equally contrite, but instead was told, 'An uncle died six months ago with no will. I was the next-of-kin. However, there was so much money involved, family crawled out of the woodwork demanding a share. I learnt today that all other claims had been thrown out and I get the lot.'

Cuzin had to ask, 'How much?'

'Two million.'

'Euros?' Cuzin couldn't keep the surprise out of his voice.

'Pounds. So let's go and spend some of it.'

The rest of the night had been something of a blur. They'd had too much to drink, mainly Champagne at £100 a bottle of inferior stuff, and ended up at Gillespie's place with two women who were paid to stay the night. They were expensive and Cuzin was too drunk to enjoy his.

He had woken late with a hangover and left the flat without making too much noise, not wishing to disturb Gillespie.

A week later, Gillespie had phoned him on his mobile.

'How did you get this number?' Cuzin demanded.

'You gave me your card.'

Cuzin didn't remember doing so, but he'd been so inebriated it was more than possible.

'Do you fancy another night out? At the Parrot again?'

'Eh, sorry, Victor, but its way over my budget.'

'Never mind your budget. It's on me again.'

'I'm not sure. I don't like to accept charity.'

There was surprise in Gillespie's voice when he said, 'Charity? It's not charity. You're not going to believe this but they found some more of my uncle's estate. Another hundred grand which I intend spending. So come and help me.'

The Colonel didn't think to ask him about friends and acquaintances. As the weeks passed, accepting Gillespie's hospitality became easier.

On the morning of their eighth evening out, when the two young hookers they'd brought back to the house had been sent on their way, Gillespie asked, 'Would you like to make some money?'

Cuzin looked surprised. 'How?'

They were sitting in the kitchen and combined dining room of Gillespie's tastefully and expensively furnished two bed-roomed flat on Alderney Street. They had glasses of orange juice in their hands, croissants warming in the oven and coffee dripping through a filter.

'You know I only come back here at weekends.'

'Certainly.'

'I am on a special retainer from the European Parliament.'

'What sort of retainer?' Cuzin frowned. 'I thought you didn't need any money.'

'I don't, but I'm not going to refuse it if offered, now am I? It's money for old rope. I'm paid on the understanding that should I learn of anything that can be considered, shall we say, an impediment to the Parliament forging ahead to create a United States of Europe, then I would pass the information up the chain of command.'

Cuzin looked at Gillespie with surprise, which rapidly turned to a frown. 'I don't understand. What sort of information?'

It was Gillespie's turn to frown. 'Anything. A banker being against the euro will, shall we say, have his collar felt?'

The words meant nothing to Cuzin so he just shrugged and looked blank.

Gillespie didn't bother elaborating. This was, after all, about the money. 'Look, Paul, I have been authorised to pay you five thousand euros as a retainer.'

Cuzin protested, 'But I've done nothing to earn the money. I have nothing to tell you. Anything I hear is common knowledge discussed openly between staff or at public events either in the embassy or at other locations.'

'This money is in case you learn something of value or of interest.'

'I'm not sure,' shaking his head, Cuzin looked doubtful.

'Well, if you can turn down a monthly retainer of five thousand euros for doing practically nothing . . .'

'Monthly? Did you say monthly?'

Gillespie kept the smile off his face. 'Naturally. You didn't expect anything else, did you?'

'I, er, I'm not sure. I thought it was a one-off payment.' He made an obvious statement followed by an equally obvious question. 'If I have any other income I have to declare it to my superiors. How do I ensure the correct tax is paid?'

Gillespie's smile was beatific. 'It is paid into an offshore account and is tax free.'

Whatever he'd been expecting it hadn't been that. He had assumed that there was some sort of mechanism for making such payments legally as the money would have to be accounted for. Then he had a second surprise.

'Your retainer is payable from the 1st of January.'

'But it's March.' Cuzin stated the obvious.

'Which means fifteen thousand euros are payable to you now.'

In front of Gillespie was a folder. He opened it and took out a sheet of paper. 'This has details of the bank you can use. You see it's in the Bahamas. This is their e-mail address. They will set up an account on your behalf, arrange passwords and the like. You tell me the account number and the transfer will be made immediately.'

Cuzin was thinking furiously. Being in the military, one lesson had been drummed into him. If something looked too good to be true then it probably was.

'Well?'

Drumming his fingers on the table, Cuzin said, 'Let me think about it for a few minutes.'

'Take as long as you like. With retirement only nine months or so away I would have thought sixty thousand euros would go some way towards making your departure from the army that much more comfortable.'

That was pretty much what Cuzin had been thinking. He didn't owe his superiors anything. Besides, the European Union Parliament was paying so it had to be legitimate. Taxation was something else altogether. The thought jolted him. Perhaps it wasn't the European Union. Perhaps it was some sort of criminal organisation. But no matter how he looked at it he couldn't see what they had to gain by paying him such a large amount. At least, he thought, large by his standards. Tax free meant he was being paid almost as much as he earned as a Colonel.

Gillespie opened his laptop and said, 'Here. Try it and see. He quickly got the website of the bank up on the screen, pressed a few buttons and turned the computer towards the Colonel. Cuzin hesitated and then typed in his e-mail address and other details he was being asked for, including an eight letter password. He confirmed the password, pressed send and watched the screen.

'Let me get us a coffee and we'll see what happens,' said Gillespie.

Both men took milk and sugar. While Gillespie busied himself, with his back to Cuzin, he was smiling. It was always easy. The money was too tempting.

It took less than two minutes. 'Mon Dieu!' Cuzin exclaimed.

'What is it?' Gillespie turned from the percolator and placed the mug of coffee in front of the other man.

'According to this I now have fifteen thousand euros in my account.'

Gillespie looked over his shoulder and said, 'That was only to be expected.'

Ever cautious, Cuzin asked, 'How do I know it is really there? How can I be certain this isn't some sort of trick? A scam?'

Again, it was not uncommon to be asked the question. The answer he gave was the same on each occasion.

'Instruct the machine to transfer money to your bank either here in England or to your bank in France, if you have one.'

Cuzin nodded. He went back to the site of the Bahamian bank and typed in the appropriate instructions. He transferred the money in English pounds. Next, he went to the website of Lloyds TSB and quickly accessed his account. Even as he watched his overdraft went from nearly £2,000 to a credit amount of over £3,000.

'Satisfied?'

He was more than satisfied. He was ecstatic. He nodded.

The payments were made without fail. For the next three months,

Cuzin felt guilty that he had nothing to tell of any interest or importance. He tried offering some of the garbage he heard but Gillespie wasn't interested and told him not to bother unless there was something of real importance to tell. Cuzin stopped saying anything and merely accepted the money, which suited Gillespie. After all, he wanted the Colonel for the big one at Christmas.

There had been no inheritance. No dead uncle. Just a very healthy monthly payment to his account, also in the same bank in the Bahamas. The only difference was the amount. In Gillespie's case it was a hundred thousand euros a week for which, in his opinion, he worked hard. There were, after all, many Cuzins around the UK he needed to corrupt – those men and women who, at every opportunity, sang the praises of the European Union. People whose mantra was how beneficial it was to have a single Parliament able to represent the nearly 500 million people across Europe, a figure that exceeded the USA by some 200 million. China was another matter with a population of over 1.3 billion. It was accepted by all those in both political and financial power that China would emerge as the world's greatest super power in the next decade or two. It would be greater than the USA and the EU but both continents had at least to try and rival the Chinese. Hence the propaganda extolling the idea of a united Europe.

In early December, Gillespie and Cuzin had just enjoyed a particularly entertaining weekend when the operation was first raised.

'Paul, you will be leaving at the end of February. Have you given any thought as to what you intend doing?'

'Er, no. That is, I thought things would continue much as they have done. You know, with my retainer.'

Gillespie shook his head. 'I am afraid it doesn't work like that. Once you leave the army your usefulness will be at an end.'

Cuzin was gutted. He looked shell shocked. For some reason he had assumed the payments would continue. He had no plans. What in hell was he to do?

'There is something,' said Gillespie, thoughtfully.

'What?' the Colonel asked eagerly.

'You're a soldier. Have you ever killed anyone?'

Cuzin frowned. 'Yes. No. That is, I haven't killed anyone up close although I was in Iraq for three months.'

Gillespie let the suggestion of Cuzin being involved in front-line operations hang in the air.

'So you have no compunction about doing so?'

Looking uncomfortable for a few moments and then deciding it was a hypothetical question, he replied, 'Of course not. I am a Colonel in one of the finest armies in the world.'

Gillespie let the man enjoy his delusion and said, 'How would you like to retire with five million euros in the bank?'

Frowning, Cuzin looked at the other man with half closed eyes and said, 'Is this some sort of a game? I don't understand.'

'There's nothing to understand. Would you like five mill, yes or no?'

Cuzin chuckled. 'And who do I have to kill for such a large sum of money?'

5

For Richard Griffiths, Christmas was a dilemma. The world was virtually his oyster, but he couldn't decide what to do, where to go. One option was to fly out to the Seychelles and meet his parents who were on a world cruise. As their only child he knew how worried they were about him even though he kept assuring them everything was fine. Diving in the Seychelles or skiing in Switzerland. Those were the two options he'd short-listed after giving the matter a few minutes thought.

Richard was rarely if ever, indecisive. Taking out a £1 coin he decided to flip for it. Heads the Seychelles, tails Switzerland. He flipped, caught the coin and placed it on the back of his hand. Tails. He grinned, Switzerland it was.

He hit the internet for Grindelwald. It was an area he'd been to many times in his teens. He and his cousin, Nick Hunter, were similar in age and had skied together regularly – equally enjoying the evenings' events after their strenuous exercise on the piste. It seemed a lifetime ago.

That was an idea! He'd see if Nick was free to join him. He phoned Rosyth to be told that Hunter was away. Richard assumed that it was some assignment or other. Richard phoned Hunter's parents in Balfron in Stirlingshire.

'Auntie Sian?'

'Hullo, Richard. To what do we owe the pleasure? As if I can't guess.'

Richard grinned. 'Do you know where he is?'

'As usual, no.'

'But you can text him?'

'Certainly.' His aunt didn't tell him that actually they texted General Macnair, the boss of TIFAT – The International Force Against Terrorism – to contact their son. It was irksome, but both Hunter's parents understood the need for security.

'Have you any idea when he'll be back in circulation?'

'Sorry, none whatsoever. Although he did indicate he'd be back by Christmas.'

'Good. I wanted to ask him if he'd like to join me on a trip to Switzerland.' From the silence with which his message was received Richard knew his aunt wasn't enamoured of the idea. But he understood why. They rarely saw their son, in spite of the fact that HMS *Cochrane*, Rosyth, where TIFAT was headquartered, was less than 40 miles away.

He hastened to add, 'Not over Christmas itself. I was thinking between Christmas and the New Year. For a week or so.'

Sian Hunter thawed somewhat. 'I'll try and get a message to him.'

'Thanks. How's Uncle Tim?'

'Fine. You know what he's like. He's writing a thriller.'

'Is it any good?'

'Let me put it this way,' she lowered her voice, 'he should stick to writing facts.'

Richard chuckled.

'What about you?' his aunt asked. 'Is everything okay? Is the divorce settled?'

'Yes, thanks. The decree absolute arrived a few weeks ago.'

'What was the delay?'

'The American lawyers tried to wrest more money from me.'

'And did they?'

'No. I basically told them to get stuffed. If they wanted a fight they'd get one. My lawyers told them that they could keep matters tied up for years. The other side finally saw sense.'

'What about Victoria? Do you have any contact?'

'No. It's like she never existed.'

'I am sorry.'

'It can't be helped. Life moves on and I've no complaints. To be honest, things are far better now she's gone. I was trying to make things work when there was little chance of it.'

'Not an uncommon thing to do. I think we all hate failure in whatever form it takes,' said Sian.

'Have you heard from Mum and Dad?'

'Yes. We received a postcard last week. You know what your mother's like when it comes to modern technology. She's a Luddite to her core. She hasn't caught up with Skype yet.'

Richard smiled. On that philosophical note they said their goodbyes. Two days later, Richard received a text from his cousin. Nick was on duty over Christmas but could make it for the 30th December until 4th January. If that was okay then Richard was to go ahead and make the arrangements.

Going back onto the internet, Richard made the bookings. Having decided he didn't want to spend Christmas in the UK, he booked a room for himself from the 23rd December to the 4th January and one from 30th December until 4th January at the Grand Hotel Regina. Each one had a double bed with panoramic views. Ever the eternal optimist, he hoped the double beds would be needed.

*   *   *   *

Andrea Nelson was bone tired and in need of a holiday. Every day was a battle. Not only was she fighting other departments, particularly the Budget Directorate, but also many in her own fiefdom were being obstructive. She knew what the problem was, of course. It was easily identified. The staff had settled into their comfortable niches and didn't like to be prodded into doing something new.

Whenever she asked about the new accounting software she was informed of one problem or another. All were spurious but contributed in delaying the installation of the new system. It was making her angrier by the day. She knew her reaction to what was going on was causing her undue stress and so she took to using a local gym and swimming pool a couple of times a week. She vented her anger using the running machine, lifting weights, swimming a few dozen lengths and then trying to relax in the steam room.

There was another major issue she was fighting. It beggared belief that directors of a department, who were making purchases of goods and services, spending vast sums of money, were the same people who signed off on the payments. They were authorising their own spending. It was unheard of! Again, when she brought the issue before the Budget Directorate with the solution to the problem, she was told it would be looked into.

Finally, the new accounting software was signed off and work would begin in December. Her satisfaction lasted only a few days. The implementation team, consisting of eight people, were not meeting until the middle of January. She realised that the system was basically to be implemented by a committee. She knew what that would mean – they'd be lucky to see it installed within 12 months.

To add insult to injury, that day Andrea discovered that Frau Eva Bachmeier had not been dismissed nor had she been arrested for fraud. Instead, she had been sent to a post in Luxembourg on an increased salary. Disappointed at this news, Andrea left work early, had an extra long workout in the gym and when she got home drank a bottle of white wine. Her excuse to herself was that as it was Friday, there was no need to get up early the next morning.

As she opened her eyes Andrea groaned. She regretted having drunk the bottle of wine the previous evening. She wasn't used to it. It was just past six o'clock and still dark outside so her planned long lie-in seemed a forlorn hope as she was wide awake. She tried to get back to sleep but tossed and turned for twenty minutes until she gave up, threw back the duvet and climbed out of bed. The room was cold as she didn't like sleeping in a warm bedroom. She went through to the bathroom where it was warm, ran a bath and looked forward to a quiet day at home.

Breakfast consisted of a glass of orange juice, a bowl of cereal and a mug of coffee. She switched on the TV and watched the BBC news. It was all doom and gloom especially in regard to the European Union, the euro and the tottering economies stretching from east to west.

She watched the riots taking place in Athens and parts of Spain and listened to the reports about soup kitchens and the level of suicides in Greece. She shook her head in sorrow and anger. She knew that anybody over 40 years of age in Greece was unlikely to get their lives back on track. If the economy of the country did recover it would be fifteen even twenty years before the right level of benefits trickled down to ordinary people trying to make a living. They would be working until the day they died. Looking at the facts, it was very unlikely that a state pension would be introduced, but if it was, it would be a miniscule amount.

She remembered her support of the European dream when it had all seemed to make sense. Then a few years ago, as the EU began to unravel she had become sceptical. She sipped her coffee and thought to herself that the scepticism she felt was now shared by a majority of the people in Europe. The only ones who continued to believe in a United States of Europe were some politicians. Abraham Lincoln's quote crossed her mind. *You can fool some of the people all of the time, and all of the people some of the time, but you cannot fool all of the people all of the time.* Which, she was now aware, was precisely what many of Europe's politicians were trying to do. On top of that, of course, came the thousands who were enjoying the gravy train that the EU had become.

Shaking her head in irritation, she told herself – resign, get the hell out and go and find another job. But that wasn't the solution. She had wanted the job. She liked the notion of fixing financial problems. The thought of what she would be able to do had genuinely excited her.

Now here she was, stressed like never before and wondering what she was doing in the rats' nest called the European Parliament. The fact was she hated to give up on anything. She came to a decision. Someone had to shine the torch of truth on the quagmire that was Brussels and Strasbourg. She was a lone voice battling against a giant of incompetence, mismanagement and outright fraud tinged with a great deal of corruption.

She sighed, switched on her computer, checked her e-mails, deleted most of them and replied to a few. Nursing another coffee she stared at her computer screen and acknowledged to herself that she needed a break. Apart from a few days here and there she hadn't had any real time off since arriving in Brussels eight months earlier.

Right! Two weeks in Switzerland. Skiing, being pampered and perhaps late nights if she could just meet the right fun-loving and interesting man. One thing she was sure of – she wasn't looking for any lasting relationship.

She looked for the most opulent hotel to be found in the Bernese Alps, an area she had never skied in before. Grindelwald looked ideal. Plenty of blue and red ski runs. She trolled through the list of hotels finally settling on the Grand Hotel Regina. Before she could change her mind, she booked herself in from 22nd December to 4th January. Thinking about it, she realised that it would be the longest break she had taken since her student days. She hoped she wouldn't be bored.

* * * *

Colonel Paul Cuzin wasn't a man to be easily shocked. Now, he was shocked to the core. In spite of never having seen active service, he could easily envisage what a bomb could do. Hollywood showed the scene often enough. At first, he had thought Gillespie was joking. Then, at some point in their conversation, he came to realise that the man was deadly serious.

'Victor, you want me to take in explosif plastique,' in his agitation, Cuzin had resorted to speaking French, 'and blow up the embassy?

With people in it? During the cocktail party?' There was no disguising the shocked horror in his voice. It was the reaction Gillespie had been anticipating.

'Paul, there will be a few deaths. So what? Think of the money that will keep you in luxury for the rest of your life, and at what price? Virtually nothing.'

'How you can say it is virtually nothing when so many people will be killed and injured is . . . is beyond me. You cannot be serious.'

'I am serious. What we are being asked to do is nothing in comparison to what it will mean. It will help to create a pan-European defence force which will take us a step closer to a politically United States of Europe.' When it came to the subject of Europe, Gillespie was a true believer. Unusual in such a man, he was a fanatic on the subject. It just so happened, the wealth creation side of it made it doubly attractive to be a part of the greatest event ever to take place in Europe. Which, he told himself, just like so many others did, included the two world wars. 'You are like me. We have had many discussions on the benefits of a United Europe. The world power we would become.'

'I cannot see how it will help to create a Europe wide defence force.'

'Trust me, it will.' He had no intention of telling the good Colonel that this was going to be just one of many such acts. All designed to foster and cement the idea that working together, properly, would help to prevent terrorists from entering Europe. Would help to protect their borders from illegal immigrants as well as fundamentalists who wished them nothing but serious harm. With each attack the EU propaganda machine would burst into life and demand a unified force. Public opinion needed moulding, steering, shaping. The long game had been played and had proved to be highly successful over the decades. Now it was the short, sharp action that was needed to bring about the final goal.

Cuzin shook his head. 'I don't know. I don't think I can do it.'

'Paul, it's not difficult. The explosives can easily be smuggled into the embassy.'

'You forget the new detector machines. They can easily find any plastic that is being taken in.'

'No, they can't.'

'What do you mean they can't? I've seen a demonstration. The machines are highly effective.'

'Oh, I'm sure they are. What you haven't seen is a new plastic polymer which completely hides any trace of the PE. I've watched it being tested with the same machines that are in the embassy. In fact, they are the same machines found in the majority of Europe's embassies as well as our airports.'

'What if terrorists get their hands on this new polymer? What then?'

Gillespie smiled. 'After one or two disasters, new machines will be installed across the whole of the continent.'

'That will cost hundreds of millions.' Cuzin couldn't keep the surprise out of his voice.

'Precisely. More employment, a great deal of money circulating around Europe's economies and an opportunity to show how effective Europe is when it comes to fighting terrorism.' He didn't add that the opportunity for fraud was huge and to be welcomed by all those involved with that end of Europe's business.

'I still don't know. I need more time.'

Gillespie nodded. 'Fair enough. Let me know tomorrow. Say we meet back here at eight. We can have a drink or two and later on go to a club.'

'I'm not sure about that. But I will come and give you my decision but then I'll return home.'

The two men shook hands and the Colonel left. He had a very worried look on his face.

Gillespie watched him go. He didn't particularly like the man and his time with him had merely been business. Even so, he did feel a pang of regret at what he was probably going to have to do.

Reaching for the phone, he pressed a button and speed dialled the number of a man who lived locally. It was answered almost immediately.

'Jaak? I may have need of your services.'

* * * *

Cuzin walked with his head bowed, his shoulders hunched. He'd aged ten years in as many minutes. To blow up the embassy? To kill innocent people? People he knew?

He straightened his shoulders, ignoring the rain that was seeping down the back of his collar. No, the Colonel told himself, he would not do it, he could not do it. He would tell Victor that the idea must be abandoned. Better to live in poverty than to exist with his conscience eating away at him for what he'd have done. He may not live in luxury but he would have sufficient to get by on. Then there was always something he could find to do. Perhaps join a security company in some managerial position. After all, such companies were springing up all over the world.

Yes, that's what he would do. He'd tell Victor tomorrow that he had made up his mind, he wouldn't do it. Then he had another thought. Surely, his duty was to prevent it happening? Not just refuse to be the one who actually carries out the crime. Not just a crime, he thought, an atrocity. He told himself that was what he had to do. He would warn Victor not to do it. That he would be arrested and tried and probably sent to prison for the rest of his life.

By the time he reached the corner of the next street he couldn't prevent himself from thinking what it meant. Five million! He could go wherever he wished. He could live in luxury for the rest of his life. He could settle down. Find a wife. His thoughts grew excited. Go to Thailand. Perhaps take himself a young bride there, someone docile and obedient. His thoughts galloped away and then came back to earth with a thud. It was no good. He couldn't do it. It wasn't in his nature. He was an officer in the French army. He had integrity and honour. He would tell Victor as much. Then there was another fact to

57

take into consideration. If he refused to carry out the attack then it wouldn't take place. It couldn't. There wasn't anybody else. That thought gave him solace.

Arriving home, he drank a large brandy and soda in one long swallow and went to bed. Sleep eluded him and the night passed slowly. It was still dark when he finally gave up trying to sleep and climbed out of bed. His tiny flat was warm. He liked the warmth and kept his central heating running continually. He had the barest of furniture and very little food. He either ate at the embassy canteen or at a local restaurant.

His one luxury was his coffee machine and while he pottered around his kitchen with the machine gurgling, he came to a decision – absolute and final. He would tell Victor that the attack could not go ahead. That he would report the matter to his Ambassador and to the embassy security people. He would assure Victor that he wouldn't name him. He would tell them that he had heard an attack was planned.

As he sat at the table, he placed his cup in front of him and his face in his hands. That was ludicrous. Where had he heard it? How had he heard it? When had he heard it? Who had said it? What language? What colour was their skin? Were they Muslims? If so, did he think the embassy was targeted because France had banned the wearing of the burka in public? Which was probably what would be claimed should the attack go ahead. Fundamentalists were ideal scapegoats for many of the sins committed in the world – something the terrorists encouraged. It helped to spread fear, loathing and distrust in the West.

The interrogation, which was what it would be, would be long and tedious. He knew how these things worked. It was inevitable that he would slip up. It couldn't be helped. A mistake here, a wrong word there. His interrogators would leap on any discrepancy and his story would quickly unravel. His affairs would be investigated, his life closely examined. Then they would check his bank account and see some of the money he had transferred from abroad to his UK account. They would demand an explanation. Then would come the admission of his payments from the European Union. No matter how much he had told himself it must be legal if the money was coming from the EU, he knew it wasn't. Self delusion was a powerful tool when you wanted something badly enough. They would tell him that the European Union did not make such payments. It was an honourable institution that was close to becoming the Parliament of the whole of Europe. Bribery and corruption was not, in any way, associated with the organisation.

He would be arrested. Of that there could be little doubt. His head was swimming. He had no idea how long he sat there but finally he knew what he needed to do. He had no choice. If it meant being imprisoned, then so be it. Even if it meant being stripped of his rank and losing his pension, somehow he would manage. He could live with all of that. What he couldn't live with was his conscience should the attack go ahead.

Putting on his overcoat, he left the warmth of his flat for the wind and the drizzling rain of London. He found himself down by the Thames and sat on one of the cold benches that lined the pavement. Later in the day he would phone Victor Gillespie and tell him of his decision.

'I see,' said Gillespie, looking at his watch. It was just coming up to lunchtime. 'And there is nothing I can say that will change your mind?'

'No, Victor, I won't do it. I will not say anything to anyone.'

Gillespie sighed. 'It is a shame, but if you have made up your mind, then that is that.'

'I beg you, don't try and do this terrible thing.'

'Without you it is not possible,' lied Gillespie. 'Let us meet again after the new year.'

With sincere relief in his voice, Cuzin said, 'Yes. I would like that.'

'You still have three months to your retirement so do not worry.

The payments will continue until you leave and after that, who knows? There must be something a man of your talents can bring to the table. Leave that with me. I'll see what I can do.'

The relief in Cuzin's voice was palpable. 'Thank you, thank you, Victor. I appreciate it very much.'

Gillespie broke the connection. He was a forward thinker. A planner. Which was why he was held in such high esteem by his bosses. He could always be relied upon to get the job done. The fact that he didn't have an ounce of compassion in his body also helped him to achieve his objective.

He used the phone again. 'Jaak? Where are you?'

In a heavy accent, Jaak Kivi replied, 'On the Embankment.'

'What is he doing?'

'Nothing. He is sitting looking at the river. He was using his phone a few minutes ago.'

'That was to me. Is everything in place?'

'Naturally.' Kivi was affronted. He considered himself to be a true professional. He was an Estonian and in command of the UK's enforcement team. He prided himself on his reliability and that of his two colleagues. To date, they had been used six times in two years and had never failed. Three had been deemed accidents and two unsolved murders and one a terrorist attack. On that occasion eight people had died and many more had been injured. Even so, they had carried out their allotted task.

'You know what to do. I leave it to your discretion. If it looks as though he is about to use his mobile then you need to take him out. Understood?'

'Yes.' Kivi broke the connection. Kivi was short and stocky, with a round face, small eyes, and a broken nose. His head was shaved and he was rapidly developing a double chin. He enjoyed eating in fast food restaurants, eating English fish and chips and drinking real ale. None of which was any good for his waistline or his general health, a fact his wife nagged him about relentlessly. He had been a professional wrestler back in his own country participating in a sport with very few rules. Unlike the West, where wrestling was fake – a choreographed dance between two so-called fighters – in Estonia men had been known to have their eyes gouged or their ears bitten off. In Kivi's case, he had suffered the latter, losing the lobe of his left ear. His opponent was left with a broken back and would never walk again.

Thinking of his wife, he speed dialled her. 'Reet?' He spoke rapid Estonian. Very few people would be able to understand them even if they were overheard. As it was, nobody was near him or her. She was seated four benches along from Cuzin, an umbrella in her hand, held at an angle, hiding her face from the Colonel. Her disinterest in him all too obvious should Cuzin notice her.

In shape and size, Reet was virtually a mirror image of her husband. She too had a round face with small eyes but in her case, her nose was straight, thin and hooked. Her brown hair was cut short, though it was hidden beneath a headscarf. She was constantly battling with her weight and as a result ate only healthy foods. It didn't seem to do much good as she became heavier, year after year.

The third member of the team wasn't with them. His name was Peeter and he was their son. At 22 years of age he had shown himself to be very good at what they did. Just then he was somewhere in Europe skiing, taking a well earned break. It was, Kivi liked to say, a family business.

'Yes, Jaak.'

'It's on.' He looked both ways. The Embankment was deserted. Thank goodness for the rain.

'I will go now.'

His wife stood up and walked towards the Colonel. When she was between him and the wall, she paused and looked south across the river. She knew that Cuzin would inevitably look at her. It was the nature of things. There was nothing and nobody else to look at from where he was sitting.

Kivi approached silently, directly behind his target. He looked both ways once more, glanced over his shoulder, took the final step to the bench, drew his silenced Heckler & Koch P7 and put a bullet into the Colonel's head. The specially modified 9mm Parabellum cartridge entered the back of the skull and stopped somewhere in the brain. As a result, the gore and blood wasn't as bad as it would have been if the bullet had exploded through the front of the skull. The lack of mess wasn't important on that occasion but sometimes it was, hence the specially adapted bullets. The body was thrown from the seat. Kivi stepped around the bench, put his hands under the Colonel's arms and easily hoisted the body back onto the bench.

His wife picked up Cuzin's umbrella and shoved the handle down the front of his overcoat, arranging it so that the back of the head was hidden. Anyone coming close would see immediately that something was wrong. In that weather and probably being British the chances were nobody would go near him.

Mrs. Kivi slid her hand through her husband's arm and moved closely to him, sharing his umbrella, her own folded up. Slowly they walked away. They would go to Blackfriars before they took the Underground.

As they walked, Kivi took out his phone. It was answered immediately. 'It is done.' He didn't wait for an acknowledgement but simply broke the connection.

6

Five days before the cocktail party, Gillespie met the man as arranged. He showed him what he needed to do. 'Do you understand?'

Jules Fournier, Third Secretary at the French Embassy nodded. His excitement and anticipation was tinged with fear. Nervously, he said, 'I have never handled explosives before. Are they safe?'

Gillespie held his temper intact. 'Let me show you something.' He picked up the plastic container shaped like a flying disc. It was roughly 9ins in diameter and 1in thick at the centre. It tapered to less than a 1/4in at the edges. The bottom was flat with a sheet of paper covering it. When this was peeled away, the adhesive found underneath would stick it to virtually any surface. The shape meant that the brunt of the explosion was downwards.

He lobbed it into the air and as it was landing kicked it against the nearby wall. Fournier flinched. Picking up a second device, Gillespie threw that onto the floor with all his strength. By now the Third Secretary's face was chalk white.

'It is perfectly safe. Now, let me show you how to set the timer. Picking up another bomb he twisted it and the bottom came off exposing a simple recess. Next, he picked up a small timer off the table and said, 'You press here, move this dial, press again and you see that light?'

Fournier squinted at the faint red light. 'Yes.'

'That means it's armed. That is the time it will explode so you can set one of these for up to twenty-four hours before you want it to go off. Got that?'

It was child's play and Fournier croaked. 'I understand.'

'You then insert it into the recess like this.' He slotted the timer into place. 'Here, you do it. Set it for 21.00 hours.'

Fumbling with the timer, Fournier set it, slipped it into the slot and said, 'Like this?'

'Good. You know where to place them?'

'Yes. I am sure that they will be well hidden.'

Nodding, Gillespie said, 'There is one more thing. Do you ever wear a waistcoat?'

'Occasionally.'

'Good. Take this.' He handed over a thin strap with a pouch in the middle. 'You put the explosive in here,' he slid one of the discs in, 'tie it at your waist and hide it under your waistcoat. The bomb sits in the middle of your back and with your coat open cannot be seen. Here, try it.'

Fournier did as he was told and looked at himself in a mirror. The explosives behind his back couldn't be seen. With a waistcoat, the strap would also be hidden.

'Do we need all eight bombs?'

'Yes. Four to do the job and four to deter the bomb squad.'

Deter was an innocuous word used instead of kill, or murder or any other word that meant the deaths of innocent people.

'Now listen. The second four you must set at different times. The first four you set for 21.15 hours. The first of the other four you add five minutes to the timer, the second another fifteen, the third yet another fifteen and the fourth you add an hour and a half. That will stop the bomb squad from getting too close.' He didn't add it would heighten the drama, increase the tension, and make a terrible incident infinitely worse. 'Is all that clear?'

'Yes.'

'Another thing, it must be 21.15 hours as his so-called Royal

Highness Charles and his wife will be arriving fifteen minutes earlier. They are never late.' He spoke disparagingly.

The man nodded, then, clearing his throat, asked, 'Paul Cuzin. The Colonel. Did you have anything to do with his death?'

Gillespie looked perplexed. 'Me? I didn't know the man. All I know about it was what I read in the newspapers and heard on the news.'

Fournier narrowed his eyes. There was one part of him that wanted to believe the answer, while another screamed at him that Gillespie was lying. It was all too much of a coincidence.

'How can we be sure the explosives won't set off the detector? I only have to be found with the stuff on me to spend the rest of my life in prison.'

'I shall take one in.'

'You?' Fournier looked at Gillespie in shock.

'Naturally. I need to prove how ineffective the detectors are. I shall be wearing it like I showed you. I shall have an appointment with you tomorrow at say, ten o'clock. Are such appointments common knowledge? Made public somehow?'

Shrugging, Fournier replied, 'Sometimes, but usually only if anyone else needs to be there. Apart from that, no.'

'Right. When you get back to your office put me in your diary. What about secretaries? Do they need to know?'

Fournier shook his head. 'You can't come at ten o'clock, I have a meeting with the Ambassador to discuss the cocktail party. It shouldn't take long. It will be better if you come at twelve o'clock instead.'

'Midday it is.'

'What reason will you give for visiting the embassy?'

'You deal with the European Union. I am thinking of investing in France and wish to discuss the possibility of loans and grants from the Parliament.'

'Investing in what?'

'Does it matter?'

'Yes. I may easily be asked what you're doing there when I'm getting myself a coffee or having lunch. Idle chatting, that's all.'

Gillespie frowned and then snapped his fingers. 'Just the thing. Building energy efficient offices and houses out of metal containers. It's a new industry which is ideal for presenting to the EU. You and I are planning some sort of presentation. Whatever. I'll leave that to you.'

Fournier nodded. 'I've heard of it.

'After I've shown you how easy it is, you will take the other discs into the embassy over the next few days and put them where we agreed. Is there anything else?'

Shaking his head, Fournier said, 'I don't think so.'

'Right. Take this.' Gillespie handed over a bag. 'It has the explosives and the timers. I shall be at the embassy in the morning as near to twelve o'clock as possible.'

The two men shook hands. Fournier returned home and let himself in. Before he did anything else, he stood in his lounge and poured himself a large vodka which he drank quickly. A second one he sipped. He placed the bag in the cupboard next to the front door and proceeded to get drunk on vodka and lager.

The following morning, he walked to the embassy, trying to clear his head. He entered through the main door and crossed to the staff security point. Placing his briefcase on the conveyor belt, he stepped through the detection arch.

'*Bonjour*,' the guard greeted him.

'*Bonjour. Comment allez-vous*?' Fournier asked, lifting his briefcase. He didn't wait for a reply. He was too nervous. Once upstairs, he sat in his office, his head in his hands, composing himself. He saw that his hands were shaking slightly. He put it down to the alcohol.

The next 40 minutes dragged slowly. At 09.55 he went along to the Ambassador's office. The arrangements for the event were discussed in detail, with the First and Second Secretaries as well as Fournier present. Fournier could barely concentrate although he tried to participate.

The meeting had gone on longer than he had expected. At 11.45 the Ambassador said, 'The Metropolitan Police have been on to me about the death of Colonel Cuzin. They appear to be no further forward but insist it's terrorists who are responsible. They claim that they will get the people who carried out the murder but it will take some time. For now, the body has been released and we can deal with it.' The Ambassador spoke in an indifferent voice. His dislike of Cuzin was well known. 'Jules, please make the necessary arrangements to ship the body back to France.'

'Yes, sir.' At that moment his personal bleeper sounded. The Ambassador scowled at him.

'Sorry sir. A rather important businessman has come to see me. He quickly explained what about, glad that he and Gillespie had discussed the matter.

'Excellent,' the Ambassador smiled. 'Pull out all the stops and make sure the business is not established here in Britain.' As with his attitude to Cuzin, the Ambassador's dislike of the British was known amongst certain members of the staff. It was a fact that was carefully disguised when in public.

The three men were dismissed and Fournier went downstairs. There was a queue of people at the public security point wishing to see an official. The staff security point was now used by those who had actual appointments.

Gillespie was standing close to the security detector as though he didn't have a care in the world. Over one arm was his overcoat, in his other hand was a briefcase.

Seeing Fournier, Gillespie walked towards him with his hand out-stretched. 'Monsieur Fournier, a pleasure to meet you again.' Shaking hands, they exchanged pleasantries and started up the staircase.

Entering Fournier's office, Gillespie slipped off his jacket and waistcoat, took the strap from his neck, handed over the disc and put his clothes back on. From his briefcase he took the timers and handed them over.

'Satisfied?'

Fournier nodded, unable to speak for a few seconds. When he did it came out as a croak. Clearing his throat he tried again. 'Yes.'

'Let us discuss my business in more detail.' Seeing the look on Fournier's face he barely managed to keep the anger from his voice. 'What if someone enters? We need to be able to show why we are meeting.' Gillespie went through what information he had lifted from the internet. Although it was a convincing display, nobody came in.

After an hour, Gillespie announced that he was finished and Fournier escorted him down to the entrance. He then returned to his office, sat at his desk, leant back and placed his hands, fingers interlocked, on his head. It had gone like clockwork. Like clockwork, he repeated to himself over and over. Excitement was rapidly replacing the fear he had been feeling.

*   *   *   *

Over the course of the next few days Fournier stored the eight explosives in a locked cupboard in his office. Then, on the morning of the cocktail party, he put on his usual dark grey suit with waistcoat, a white shirt and maroon tie. He let himself out of his flat and stepped into a day that was cold and blustery but dry. Arriving at the embassy, he passed through security and went up to his office.

Once inside, he did something unusual. He locked the door and sat at his desk. Suddenly, he was swamped with a mixture of doubts, guilt and fear. He licked dry lips with a dry tongue. He inhaled deeply. He exhaled slowly. He got his pounding heart under control and his breathing back to normal. It was time to place the explosives.

Removing the first one from the cupboard, he set the timer for 20.50. This was twenty minutes earlier than instructed. The reason for that was very simple. He was supposed to be at the party and needed to be on time. If he arrived late, questions would be asked. Serious questions. He could easily find himself in the spotlight of suspicion. He would time his approach to the embassy so that he was near the corner of William Street when the bombs exploded. There, he would be protected from the blast. If Prince Charles was early, all well and good. If he was punctual, then he would survive. Whichever, Fournier told himself, he would have earned his money.

He placed the disc in the pouch and tied it around his waist, under his waistcoat. He didn't bother with the neck-strap. He wouldn't be carrying the explosives for long. Leaving his office, he passed a number of people as he walked along the corridor, heading for the lift. He couldn't help wondering if any of them would survive the blasts.

Pressing the button, the lift appeared, the doors slid open and he stepped inside. He went down to the basement. He stepped out of the lift, walked across to the cold store and tugged the door open. The back of the room was an outside wall. Nervously, he twisted the pouch around, took out the frisbee, peeled off the paper on its base, reached behind a rack of vegetables and placed it against the wall. One shove and it was securely fixed. He stood back and looked from all directions but couldn't see any sign of it. He walked out and back to the lift. It was still there; he stepped inside and pressed the button to the first floor.

Two men walked towards him. One flashed a badge which Fournier was unable to read. 'Monsieur Fournier, we are from the Police Nationale, Internal Affairs, and have been sent across from Paris. We would like to ask you a few questions.'

*   *   *   *

Richard poured himself a glass of white wine and stood in the kitchen, wondering what to do that evening. He wasn't one to sit and watch television and debated with himself whether or not to go to the reception being held at the French Embassy.

Taking out his mobile he scanned through the telephone numbers and found the one he wanted.

'Pierre? It's Richard Griffiths.'

'Richard, my dear friend. What can I do for you?' Pierre Duverger was the First Secretary at the embassy. His English sounded as though he had spent his teenage years in Eton – which had been the case.

'I was wondering if it would be in order for me to come to tonight's reception? I know I sent an apology but I find I'm at a loose end.'

His friend laughed. 'Okay. There's someone coming I would like you to meet.'

'Oh? Not business I hope.'

'Certainly not. There are two sisters, one of whom I am very interested in. I needed someone to take care of the second one and you fit the bill nicely.'

'Hang on! What's she like?'

'Very attractive. I assure you.'

'Yeah. I remember Marseilles. That cocktail party you invited me to. The two sisters, remember?

Duverger chuckled. 'Yes. But at least she wasn't a dog.'

Richard sighed. 'True but not far off. Okay. I'll take her off your hands.' Then he added, 'Perhaps, if she's attractive enough.'

Again, his friend laughed. 'Let's just say that she's more than adequate for you. Trust me. You won't be disappointed.'

'Incidentally, anything further about the murder of your military attaché?' Richard asked.

'Some, but not much. The cameras show a man and a woman. However, due to the rain and their umbrellas, it's impossible to identify them. We have Internal Affairs over from Paris. It seems that Cuzin had some unexplained sums deposited in his bank. They've been interviewing people who knew him all afternoon. Have you seen today's papers?'

'No, why?'

'It's being claimed that the attack was by Muslims. That a team of killers had entered the country to carry out the murder.'

'That's ludicrous. Who would insert a team and all that entails to kill an army Colonel attached to your embassy? The waste of resources and the risks involved are far too great to justify such a move. On top of that is the fact that very few, if any, Muslim women are involved in this sort of attack. We know they are now being used in more suicide bombings but that's different.

'We agree. Your Commissioner of Police has just been on the phone to my Ambassador saying much the same thing. However, the media, as we all know only too well, will invent a story if they can't ferret out the truth.'

'Amen to that,' said Richard. 'Okay, I'll see you later.'

* * * *

To Fournier, the two men appeared bored, as though they thought it was a waste of time. The questions they asked were perfunctory, ticked off a list they each had in front of them. They had offered him a coffee which he had declined, while the two men drank the stuff on an almost continuous basis. The result was frequent pauses while one or other of them went to the toilet. Although Fournier managed to appear relaxed, he stayed hyper-alert, terror only a couple of degrees beneath the surface. Finally, after 45 minutes, he was thanked with a nod and dismissed.

He sat for an hour in his office trying not to shake. He thought back to the interview. The questions had been about Cuzin. They had made it clear that they were trying to build a picture of the Colonel in an effort to discover why anyone would want him dead. All he'd had to do was stick to the truth. Even so, it had taken every ounce of concentration not to show the nervousness tinged with fear that he was feeling.

He finally got himself under control. It was then that he began to analyse his thoughts. Truth to tell, he was excited. It was unlike anything he'd felt before. The aftermath of what his actions would mean, he expunged from his mind. He wouldn't think about it. Even so, idiotically, the first part of Newton's third law came to mind.

To every action there is always opposed an equal reaction.

What would be the reaction to what he was going to do? One thing was certain, Cuzin would be forgotten.

The year was winding down. Christmas was only a few days away and people were looking forward to returning home to France, or have relations come to the UK. The cocktail party would signal the end of the working year for all but a skeleton staff. There was joy in the air. The embassy was officially closed for business and people were coming and going almost in a random, purposeless manner, chatting and exchanging greetings, as well as an occasional gift.

Fournier was pretty much ignored. Placing the explosives where he needed to was child's play. Nobody took any notice of him. Even so, he took his time. He spread the task throughout the day, setting the timers at the time he had decided.

At 17.00 he left the building to go home. He was filled with anticipation of what the next few hours would bring.

* * * *

It was a black tie affair and, glass of wine in hand, Richard went upstairs to shave, shower and change.

Just on 20.35 Richard decided to walk. A stroll of just over a mile would be very pleasant as it was a dry, crisp, calm night. The weather forecast had been for snow that afternoon.

He headed towards Knightsbridge, walking past the German Embassy in Belgrave Square, taking his time, thinking about what he was going to do in the future. All year he'd been too busy but now he needed to make a few decisions. The first one was to buy a place of his own. He'd contacted various estate agents and told them what he wanted. There was one flat he liked the look of just around the corner from where he was now living. Three bedrooms was probably over-the-top, but what the hell. It was end terraced with a garage attached. The garage was more expensive than a four-bedroomed house in the shires but that was the price you paid to live in that part of London. First thing in the morning he'd instruct his solicitor to go ahead and buy the place.

His tardiness saved his life.

He was approaching the embassy when he paused and put his hand in his pocket. He drew out the gold embossed card, ready to show it at the door. Having declined the invitation, his name wouldn't have been on the list of guests that was checked off at the entrance. Even with the card, if your name wasn't on the list, you wouldn't get in. Duverger would have fixed that. As always, the threat of terrorism caused problems to the simplest of activities. It was a fact of life that people had come to accept.

He was a couple of hundred yards away watching chauffeur driven cars and taxis depositing the great and the good when the first explosion occurred.

The blast was of such severity that even at that distance Richard tottered backwards and landed on his backside, his hands behind him saving him from any serious injury.

The screaming started and the yells for help thundered through the still evening air. Richard sat where he was for a few moments and then struggled to his feet. His thoughts were to give help to those injured. He was about to run towards the shattered front of the building when the second blast occurred. This time, the explosion threw him off his feet and he landed heavily, his head hitting the pavement. He lay there dazed for a few seconds before sitting up. He groaned and reached behind his head. It hurt like hell. He brought his hand up in front of his face and though the world was swimming, managed to focus on the blood.

With a groan, he staggered to his feet, using a railing next to him to stand up. A wave of dizziness wafted through him and he gagged, feeling sick. He stood still for a few seconds as his eyes came back into focus and he could see again.

What he saw was utter carnage.

His brain began to clear. Slowly Richard approached the shattered building. After he had left school he had gone to Dartmouth Naval College and from there he went on to train as a bomb and mine disposal diving specialist. After eight years he had resigned his commission and joined G & B Maritime, a move he had never regretted for a minute.

Now his training kicked in. People were running to help and he tried to call out to stop them. The prospect of booby traps was all too likely. His voice came out in a croak and he felt dizziness and nausea sweep through him. He stopped, held onto the railing and gagged. At the second heave he vomited. There had been very little in his stomach so it was mainly bile and wine that erupted from his mouth. After a few seconds the feeling passed and he began to feel a little better. He did his damnedest to ignore the throbbing headache he was developing and started across the street.

'Get back,' he shouted. 'Get back.' He was waving his arms.

People stopped and looked at him in surprise.

One man yelled at him, 'There are people trapped in there. We've got to get them out!' He turned back to the embassy and continued to approach the rubble.

Richard yelled, 'Stop!' The man kept going. 'There may be booby traps! Don't you understand? We need the bomb squad here before we dare go near the place.'

That caused the man to pause and look back at Richard. The possibility of further bombs finally penetrated the man's mind and he too yelled at others who were heading towards the building, to stay clear.

The prospect of more explosions halted everyone in their tracks and they started to move back. Above the noise of creaking timbers and the occasional brick and stone falling loose could be heard the sounds of people yelling for help in various languages.

The third explosion blew bricks, stone and rubble into the air. People close to the missiles were injured. One man had his skull crushed when a chunk of stone landed on him. The crowd turned and ran, jostling each other, pushing to get away. Richard stayed where he was. He reckoned he was far enough away not to be in any danger.

In the background could be heard the sound of sirens and a few seconds later fire engines as well as squad cars began to fill the street.

Trained to deal with situations like the one they were facing, the authorities quickly established some semblance of order around what was left of the embassy. Hoses were run out while the police put up boundary tape to keep people back.

To the right of the building a thin cloud of smoke was rising and was quickly extinguished. A small army of people were gathering, including the bomb squad. Richard stood at the police tape and watched as they climbed into their protective gear. He had a great deal of admiration for the three men and, he noticed, one woman who were kitting up. Their protective clothing rarely, if ever, proved effective as was shown in Afghanistan and other trouble spots around the world. These were, Richard acknowledged to himself, amongst the bravest people anywhere in the world.

It was just then that the dogs arrived. The animals were trained in sniffing out explosives. They could cover an area of potential danger more quickly and more effectively than the machines that had been invented to do the same thing. With a sense of smell around 2,000 times greater than a human's, the contribution made by the dogs in finding explosives was vital.

The four dogs were all Labradors. They were already sniffing the air, tails wagging, eager to get to work. Their handlers settled the dogs down and moved slowly towards the rubble.

The calls for help had slowly faded though there were still some muffled yells coming from under the wreckage. The first bomb was found ten minutes into the operation.

The dog handler took one look, saw the timer ticking down with what appeared to be less than two minutes to go and yelled at the top of his voice.

'Out! Out! Less than two minutes! Shift it!'

Nobody questioned him. Nobody hesitated. The dogs and their handlers moved as quickly as the wrecked building would allow. Twisted ankles, even broken legs were risked as they clambered over the rubble.

The bomb disposal team had been waiting at the edge of the wreckage and they too, moved back. The first handler reached the road and ran, his dog barking, tail wagging, thinking it was all part of the game.

The second and third handler also reached the road and rang like hell. The fourth one wasn't so lucky. He and the dog were at the edge of the rubbish when he stepped on a stone, it rolled under his foot and he went flying. His dog stood next to him. She had her tail curled under her body and was whining while licking his face. It was as though she was telling him to get up.

The man pushed himself to his feet, took a step, groaned and went down. It was at that moment the second booby trap went off. Being on the ground helped to save the man's life. Bricks and stones fell around him but none did any serious damage. The dog wasn't so lucky. A chunk of stone landed on the dogs back and broke it. She yelped, went down and lay there howling, piteously.

Her handler pulled himself to the dog and cradled her head in his lap, stroking it gently.

'It's alright, old girl. It's alright.' His eyes filled with tears and started rolling down his cheeks.

The bond between the handlers and the dogs was powerful. It was built on mutual love and understanding. The two worked together and played together. For the dog, it was fun and games until their harnesses went on. Then it became work.

The other three approached slowly. They all knew only too well what their colleague was going through. One of them knelt by the injured animal and took a close look.

'Her back is broken,' he said in a gentle voice.

'Get something to deaden her pain,' said his friend. 'From the ambulance.'

The man stood, went away and came back a few moments later with one of the ambulance crew.

'I'll do it,' said the paramedic. So saying, he removed a vial and syringe from a bag he had slung over his shoulder, filled the syringe and injected the dog. After a few seconds she stopped whimpering.

'Thanks,' said the dog handler to the paramedic. He looked at his three friends. 'You'd better get back to work' he said. 'I'll take her back to the van.'

Nodding, the three handlers and their dogs went cautiously towards the embassy. The next device was found five minutes later and made safe by the bomb squad.

The other bombs were found in quick succession and dealt with. An hour after the first explosion, the all clear was sounded and the work of finding the injured, the dying and the dead, began.

Body parts were found along with corpses that had been crushed, some beyond recognition. Three men and one woman were rescued uninjured while a dozen or so had to be rushed to hospital. The rescuers worked in short shifts. A great deal of care was needed to ensure walls and floors didn't collapse as the rescue services carried out their work.

Hardened though they were, some members of the rescue services vomited when they found body parts lying under the rubble.

Richard saw no sign of his friend Pierre Duverger and he assumed the worst. Time passed in a blur. His head was aching and still seeping blood. Finally, around 22.30, he pushed his way through the throngs of people who were packing the street and made his way back to the flat.

Once there, he took a shower and then sat in the kitchen with a large whisky and soda in his hand while holding a few sheets of kitchen roll to his head.

Lifting the glass, he saw that his hand had a slight shake to it. The intended sip turned into a few gulps before he replaced the glass on the table. Closing his eyes he couldn't help asking the question. Why me? Why was I spared when I could so easily have been in the embassy or close enough to it to have been killed? Richard knew it was a question that would be asked by many people that night. There were others asking it from the opposite perspective. Why him? Why her? Why couldn't they have been late and missed the blast? Why? It was such a small word that held such huge implications whenever it was asked.

Richard took another drink of whisky. Taking his hand from behind his head, he checked for blood. The wound had stopped bleeding.

He wasn't sure how long he sat there, but eventually he realised his glass was empty. He contemplated getting another but decided not to bother. He made his way upstairs and went to bed. He was asleep in seconds.

7

The five men were seated around a table in the private dining room of a three star Michelin restaurant in the 17th arrondissement of Paris. The restaurant on the Rue Jouffroy was world famous and reservations had to be made weeks in advance. That didn't apply to these men. They expected and received special treatment.

Four of the five were commissioners in the EU Parliament. Each, in his own way, had a satisfied look on his face. These were the men who had given the job of Accounting Officer and Budget Execution Director to Andrea Nelson for a period of two years.

A tall, thin man with an angular face was the first to speak. His name was Peter Waterfield. He smiled at the other four as he looked around him with some satisfaction. He couldn't help enjoying a flashback. He had been appointed three years earlier. The circumstances of his appointment were known to just a few senior people in the Labour Party, but many theories abounded. He had been thrown out of the UK Parliament for corruption not once but twice, yet he had still landed one of the most lucrative jobs in politics. His third wife had just left him which was another reason for his feeling of contentment.

He glanced at the man sitting on his left, Jacques Dupuis, who, as usual, was stroking his upper lip while next to him sat a German, Gunther Friedmann. He was short, only 5ft 5ins, but what he lacked in height he made up for in weight. Rotund was the polite way of saying he was fat, thought Waterfield. The man was bald, except for a fringe of grey hair and had a heavily veined, bulbous nose – testament to his heavy drinking. He also liked his food – the richer and stodgier the better. However, Waterfield was the first to admit, behind Friedmann's avuncular manner was a sharp brain devoid of any compassion. Surprisingly, he was contentedly married. Waterfield had met his wife on numerous occasions. She was equally fat, loved the same food and was renowned for being even more ruthless than her husband. In effect, a perfect match. Those who knew the Friedmanns described their marriage as having been blessed by the devil. All three of their children, two boys and one girl, had jobs in the Parliament, attached to their father's department.

Waterfield looked across the table at Enrico Maimone. His name had its origin in Sicily, where his family came from. There was a rumour that he was connected to the Sicilian Mafia. He was 6ft tall, slim, with black hair, a moustache and blue eyes. He was considered good looking, his numerous affairs testament to the fact that women found him attractive. A chain smoker and an alcoholic, at 40 he was the youngest of them. As they were occupying a private dining room, he was allowed to indulge his nicotine habit. The highly effective air-filtration unit helped to keep the atmosphere clear of cigarette smoke.

Waterfield glanced at the last man at the table. He was Irish by the name of Patrick O'Flynn. He wasn't a commissioner but a judge at the Court of Justice. He spoke with a cultured English accent but when it was called for, his Irish brogue was predominant. He had a petulant mouth, shifty eyes and thinning brown hair tinged with grey at the sides. Waterfield knew it was often said of the man that he displayed the demeanour and mannerisms appropriate to a judge. In short he was a pompous ass. O'Flynn had become a past master at getting people acquitted of crimes such as serious fraud, albeit at a heavy price. Now, Waterfield told himself, the judge, like the rest of them, was in the big league, in fact the biggest. On a personal level, all Waterfield knew about him was that he had a family consisting of a wife and two boys who rarely spoke to him. Hence they remained in Dublin.

The five men were all dressed alike. Black suits, white shirts and stripped ties, albeit of different colours. Whenever they had meetings like the one that evening, Waterfield couldn't help thinking that they looked like actors pretending to be bureaucrats at the first night of a new show. Actors, however, usually had an air of uncertainty about them. They, on the other hand, were supremely confident in what they did. He acknowledged to himself that they virtually controlled the European Union and how they did it was simplicity itself.

When he had first arrived at the European Parliament he had been astounded by what he had found. Laws were written by the unelected Commission in secret. They were handed to a committee of five for vetting and any amendments. From there they went to the Chamber and were presented to the elected Members of the European Parliament. The laws then went through "on the nod" as it was called. There was virtually no debate and few, if any, changes. The MEPs could delay a new law but they couldn't stop it from eventually being passed. Political commentators across Europe all agreed on one thing. There was no democracy in the EU – it was a sham.

Waterfield knew that he and the other three commissioners at the table had been responsible for more laws being passed than any other group. Most of the laws were to the detriment of the Union but had helped to make the five of them rich. Thanks to the level of fraud in the EU Parliament, each of them had made millions from one fund alone. This was the Structural Fund, which was meant to regenerate the poorer parts of the continent, such as Sicily. He knew that in the past, on the island, tens of millions of Euros had been siphoned off by the Mafia. That was considered small change.

With the disasters now taking place in world economies and particularly Europe, buying or selling vast numbers of shares in a volatile market meant that those who knew what was about to happen could benefit from it – and they knew. They had each amassed a

81

substantial fortune which, Waterfield knew, was going to grow significantly over the next few years. This was due in part to the Chinese and to the complete mess surrounding the euro. The threat of further unrest within Europe's sovereign countries had focused the minds of all five men. They had no doubts that a pan-European security service was required and the final moves to achieve it were now being made. The first of these moves had been the destruction of the French Embassy in London.

Two waiters appeared with a trolley of food. They had chosen a set menu of seven courses. They lingered over the meal, enjoyed every morsel while they plotted. The vintage wines they had chosen each cost what the average European earned in a week.

A television had been wheeled into the room before they had arrived. Picking up the remote control, Waterfield pointed it at the end of the room. 'Shall I?' he queried.

Dupuis answered for them. 'Yes, do. It will be interesting to hear what is being said.' His smile widened. 'They will be running around like, what do you say, headless chickens?'

Waterfield nodded and smiled in return. 'Not only will they be running about like headless chickens and blaming everyone from Islamic Fundamentalists to left wing activists, people will be demanding the recall of national parliaments. There will be demands for a pan-European solution to a Europe wide problem. Even the British will want action.' He nodded. 'As we know, it is the nature of things.' He didn't need to add that such events played right into their hands. The subtle guiding of the Parliament over the last 30 years or more was nearing its goal. 'Now, is there any further business?'

The other four men shook their heads.

'In that case, I'll ring for the waiters and have the table cleared,' said Maimone. Standing, he crossed the room and pressed the button next to the door. Less than a minute later, two waiters appeared. The table was quickly cleared and a fresh trolley of drinks was brought in and placed alongside the wall.

Gunther Friedmann stood up and went across to the well-stocked trolley. On it was everything from a vintage port, a superb Madeira, a vintage brandy and an incredible 50 year old malt whisky. 'What will you have?'

Waterfield and Maimone chose the port, Dupuis the brandy while O'Flynn and Friedmann took the whisky. He placed the appropriate glasses in front of each man and the bottles on the table. They could help themselves.

Waterfield pressed the button on the remote while they each poured their drinks. When the television came on they ignored their drinks, their eyes glued to the pictures being shown.

A news reporter was standing with a microphone in her hand, facing the camera. 'The devastation is unlike anything since the twin towers. The fire has been extinguished and now the long and laborious task of finding if anyone is still alive has begun. You can see the arc lights that have been erected, casting deep shadows that could be hiding further bombs. We know that the terrorists who carried out this atrocity frequently leave booby traps behind to kill those trying to rescue people trapped in the rubble.'

As the woman droned on, trying to find the right words, the five men raised their glasses in salute and smiled further.

They watched the television for a few more minutes then Waterfield said, 'Right. Let us get on with our work. Expenses for the operation in Britain?'

'As we expected,' answered Maimone, 'a total of one million euros in actual payments and we had the cost of the flat and other incidentals.'

'Good,' said Waterfield. He shook his head as though in wonderment and said, 'How in hell those two idiots at the embassy thought they would be getting five million is beyond me.'

'Greed,' said the judge, 'is a powerful factor when it comes to self-delusion.'

The others nodded.

'First, the agricultural subsidies,' said Waterfield. 'Jacques?'

'Before we deal with that,' Maimone said, 'have we sorted the problem of the American Embassy in Madrid?'

'Yes. I had word only today,' replied Waterfield. 'A fleet of cars will be used. As we agreed, it will be the third target sometime in the new year.'

'Do we know how many cars?' O'Flynn asked, intrigued.

'I believe it will be eight. The cars will be packed with as much explosives as possible. Two at each target point, with the second going in two minutes after the first has exploded. We know that the first car in each case will be stopped before getting as far as the walls. However, the blast will cause huge damage and with luck will enable the second car to get closer still. Whether it does or not is almost irrelevant as the second blast will add massively to the damage and the death toll. Now, can we get on? Jacques?'

Dupuis opened the file in front of him. 'The Common Agricultural Fund. We have convinced the media and many MEPs that we have the situation under control and that we have reduced subsidies from fifty-one percent to forty-six percent. As further legislation appears on the statute books we will reduce the percentage even more.'

'But in reality?' asked Friedmann.

'In reality, we have managed to increase the amount by two percent. That's thanks to the new olive growing subsidies.' He chuckled. 'The amount of money being paid out means that most of Europe is covered in olive trees.' Shaking his head in wonderment, he went on, 'How on earth nobody has recognised the fact and tried to do something about it is beyond me.'

'Stupidity and inertia,' said Maimone.

All five men chuckled.

'What's happened about the flax?' Waterfield enquired.

Dupuis shook his head in sorrow. 'There's nothing we can do about it. As you all know, after we increased the subsidy for flax to five times that paid for other cereals, many farmers in different countries increased flax crops. Spain was the greediest. They increased the area of land used for growing flax from just over 1,800 hectares to more than 9,000, a five fold increase in five years.'

The others nodded. They knew all this. What they wanted to know was how the situation affected their profits, as they referred to the fortune they were each making.

Dupuis was a pedant and would continue giving his report along the lines he had set for himself. 'The flax is of such inferior quality that there is no market for it. Furthermore, as OLAF was closing in,' he was referring to the European anti-fraud organisation, Office de Lutte Anti-Fraude, 'some flax producers panicked and burnt down seven significant flax warehouses across the country.'

Waterfield looked at the others who were becoming impatient, just wanting the bottom line, not listening to the background of events, most of which they knew anyway. However, the French Commissioner continued in his usual fashion. He had a reason for doing so. He had a pleasant surprise for them.

'As you know, Miss Loyola de Parra, who until recently was the Spanish Agricultural Minister, had a moment of inspiration when she blamed the Common Agricultural Policy for giving the subsidies in the first place. She said she and her department were merely looking after the interests of Spanish farmers, which, after all, was her job. The Spanish press backed her all the way, pointed the finger of blame at members of her large staff though none were named and the scandal quickly faded away as they always do. OLAF has dropped the matter and Miss de Parra has now been appointed as commissioner for transport and energy, the second largest budget in the European Union.'

'Yes, yes,' said Waterfield, unable to hide his irritation any longer, 'we know all this. We got her the job. Now get on with it.'

Dupuis said, 'Due to OLAF's interference, we have lost nearly one million euros in income.'

'What!' said O'Flynn, 'That much?' In reality, it was a relatively small amount as far as the coffers of these men were concerned, but even so, they were not happy. They were never happy at any loss, no matter how trivial.

'I am afraid so. However, I have some good news. Some very good news.'

'It had better be very good,' said Waterfield. The loss of 200,000 euros, his cut, rankled with him.

'I had a private meeting with Anicka this morning,' he paused.

The others sat up straighter, their interest suddenly alight with anticipation – they hoped.

'She has agreed to join us. However there is one condition.'

'And that is?' asked Friedmann.

'She wants two million euros. She described it as a joining fee.'

The other men at the table said nothing for a few moments as they pondered the demand. In reality, there was nothing to think about, Waterfield decided. It had taken nearly two years of slow, tedious probing to get to where they now were. Fraud and corruption were so prevalent across the European Union that to investigate and prosecute all those involved was a task beyond imagination. With many, it was small things – such as accepting invitations to a meeting at a luxury resort, travelling first class and staying in five star hotels, with everything paid. Or receiving a case of vintage wines for Christmas, or a gold Rolex watch, or an expensive painting by an up-and-coming artist. Waterfield knew the list went on and on. For the vast majority, who were accepting the largesse, it amounted to little more than peanuts. If challenged, the recipients would claim it as their due, their right. So ingrained into their psyche were these thoughts that they believed it themselves. Hence, if they were ever asked, they would insist that they were doing nothing wrong. It was merely the price of doing business in the European Union. When an honest broker came onto the scene and suggested that the corruption was worse than a banana republic, they were quickly disabused, worn down by the counter arguments, or more often than not, persuaded to join the club. It was, they acknowledged to themselves, a highly satisfactory arrangement.

For them, the vast sums being distributed across the continent were inconsequential. It merely bought them what they wanted – real power. The combination was heady, invigorating, all-encompassing. They saw themselves as emperors without crowns and behaved as such. What was more, their next few moves would be their crowning glory. The bombing of the French Embassy was the beginning of the operation, planned like a chess game, always thinking a dozen moves ahead.

One such long term move had been the recruitment of Anicka Kadlec to the inner circle. It had been a long and slow process for obvious reasons, but they had got there. What a coup! The head of OLAF working with them, the Director General herself!

The previous man had been Austrian. He was known to be a man of integrity and honesty and an investigation into his background seemed to confirm the fact. Anicka Kadlec was a Czech with a somewhat murkier history but that was built more on innuendo than proven fact. Even so, there had been enough to suggest she was approachable which had proved to be the case.

'She has already cost us a million euros,' growled Enrico Maimone.

Dupuis shook his head. 'First, the amount is of no consequence and secondly, she had no option. The hyenas were sniffing around and had to be gotten rid of.' The hyenas in this case were two journalists who had come across a story that may not have made the front pages but would probably have been extensively investigated and reported. If that had happened, there was no telling where it might have ended. Furthermore, the scam was a fairly low key affair, but still lucrative.

Local councils and government departments across the European Union put out tenders to buy office equipment and consumables. Once a company secured the order, they found excuses not to deliver the goods in the tender, but offered alternatives which were always more expensive than the quote. Inevitably, the new price was agreed, the bribes paid and everyone was happy. Taxpayers were the exception but as they had no idea this scam was being perpetrated every day, they were happy in their ignorance.

'Thanks to her, there have been no questions asked and no investigation,' said Maimone, emphasising the point by holding his finger in the air. 'The whole issue has gone away a lot quicker than we could have hoped.'

'True, true,' the others nodded and murmured.

The reporters had ceased their questioning when paid a significant sum of money. How much of the million euros went into the pockets of the reporters, the men in the room neither knew nor cared. All that mattered was that the issue had been dealt with. The Director General always knew if an investigation was to take place and had the power to stop it. If she couldn't stop it, then there were steps that could be taken to minimise any damage. Forewarned was forearmed.

'What about the latest operation?' asked Dupuis.

'What about it?' Waterfield frowned.

'Does she get briefed? Should she be involved?'

'No!' replied Friedmann, 'It is too soon. She may find it a step too far and renege on our deal.'

'It is too late for that,' said Maimone.

'No, it isn't,' Waterfield looked thoughtful. 'The scale and the scope of what we are doing are such that she could ask for, and receive, immunity from prosecution.' His next words were ugly. Words avoided by the five of them. 'Fraud is one thing. Mass murder is quite another.'

They didn't look at each other. They squirmed. Even hardened, egocentric, psychopaths like them did not like such harsh words being used. The actions they were taking they justified under a cloak of self delusion, such as it was good for the economy or good for the people of Europe. It was another but vital step towards that goal of all goals – political integration. They used language such as "more people were killed in car accidents in a week," or "more people died of cancer in three days" and so on. It was self-justification without end and as they trod the path to their goal, it just so happened they became immensely wealthy.

After a few moments, O'Flynn asked, 'What is the total earned from the CAP for the last twelve months?'

'We have siphoned off ten million.'

'Euros or pounds?' Maimone asked.

'With the state of the euro and the dollar I thought it best we deal in pounds.'

'Good,' said O'Flynn.

'Thank you,' said Waterfield now turning his gaze on Dupuis. 'Jacques, the regional development fund?'

'Excellent, as always. After all disbursements, we have netted eight million. Euros that is. Matters are in hand to convert to Chinese yuan.'

'That's very good,' said Friedmann. 'I am also converting some of my assets into Argentinean pesos, as a precaution.'

The meeting continued as one fund after another was briefly discussed. After all, none of them needed or wanted any details. They were only interested in the bottom line.

It was close to 10.00 pm when they were finished.

'Right,' said Waterfield. 'Everything is running pretty much as normal. We have two more pieces of business. Let us start with a unified military.' He paused, almost salivating at the thought of what it would mean. He could see that the others were enjoying similar reactions.

A single European military force where all purchases of all equipment were centralised and distributed across Europe meant a fund of staggering proportions. The opportunity to siphon off funds made what they'd done so far seem like pocket money by comparison. They had amassed so much wealth that they wouldn't be able to spend it in three lifetimes, but they still wanted more.

To date, there had been three debates in the EU Parliament on the creation of a single military force. It had taken a great deal of effort but finally things were moving in the right direction. Senior officers across the European Union were supporting the idea. Except, of course, Waterfield admitted to himself, the British. Their military didn't trust Europe for many reasons both historic and current. However, that distrust wasn't without a great deal of justification, as the near past and the present proved. When any military action was required, it was inevitably led by the Americans and backed by the British. Other EU forces were shamed into helping, often with hardly more than a token presence. With a combined military, however, each country would be able to hide behind the shield of a democratic decision made by the whole of Europe. They would be able to tell the Yanks to go to hell and fight their own wars without Europe.

At last, Waterfield said, 'We have one final item.'

They all glanced around the table at each other. They knew what was coming.

'Unfortunately, we cannot allow the Accounting Officer and Budget Execution Director to continue in her post. She has to go.'

They all nodded.

'It must seem like an accident,' said Friedmann.

'Naturally,' replied Waterfield. 'I shall make that clear to Mr. Kowalak and leave matters in his hands. However, I must emphasise, that may not be possible. Operational decisions are made on the ground.'

There were further nods all round. When all was said and done, the objective was more important than the means.

'Let us enjoy a nightcap before we adjourn,' said Friedmann. 'I think we deserve one.'

The others smiled and reached for the bottles.

8

Richard had woken in something of a daze. His head hurt like hell, and his mouth was tinderbox dry. For a moment he couldn't think where he was until it seeped into his brain that he was in his bed. The memories came flooding back.

With a groan, he climbed out of bed and went into the bathroom. His reflection in the mirror confirmed the fact that he wasn't at his best. He shaved and took a long shower. His head had stopped bleeding and with two Aspirin the pain had reduced from debilitating to manageable.

Down in the kitchen, he helped himself to cereal before switching on the television. It was tuned to the BBC. The events of the previous evening were being picked over.

'It has been confirmed that there are twenty three people dead and at least twenty injured. Some are serious, others have minor injuries. The bomb squad and special branch have been searching the site looking for clues as to who was responsible. In the meantime, a number of organisations have claimed responsibility. Muslim fundamentalists from the Middle East to Sub Saharan Africa are all claiming to have carried out this atrocity. There has been rejoicing in Iran and parts of Pakistan as well as Somalia and Saudi Arabia. However, as yet, there is no indication as to who was

*responsible. This is Leon Fox, outside the French Embassy.
Back to you in the studio Phyllis.'*

Richard picked up the phone. He had a couple of calls to make. He was
about to ring his parents when he thought better of it. They hadn't
known he was going to the event in the embassy and decided it would
be wiser to keep it that way. His mother would get on at him to see a
doctor and get checked out which was a waste of time. As she would
only worry he would have to give in and he wasn't in the mood.
However, there was one person he could talk to. Someone who would
understand what he'd been through and his reticence to contact his
parents. He speed dialled his cousin in Rosyth.

* * * *

It was the middle of the afternoon and Nick Hunter was sitting in his
office, his feet on his desk, looking out of the window towards the
River Forth. He was a Commander in the Royal Navy, attached to The
International Force Against Terrorism, TIFAT. When he was offered
the opportunity to join TIFAT he had been on the point of resigning
his commission. With military cutbacks in general and the scrapping
of ships in particular, he saw few, if any, prospects for staying in the
RN. Now with there being more Admirals than ships the whole structure of the Royal Navy had become a farce. To add insult to injury, for
the first time in its history, the Royal Navy had fewer ships than the
French. It was a fact that rankled with many serving personnel.

He thought back to the beginning. The excitement of going to
Dartmouth Naval College; the incredible competition between those
who aspired to become naval officers; the surprising drop-out rate of
those who decided not to stay the course; then the passing-out parade.
The guest of honour, the man taking the salute, had been Prince
Charles, an ex-naval officer and a very popular one at that.

After passing out, it took the best part of another year to qualify as
a Mine Warfare and Clearance Diving Officer or MCDO.

He had loved his time as second-in-command and then command of a minehunter. That was followed by a staff job and then he was offered the appointment to TIFAT. It would mean front-line anti-terrorist work where his skills could prove to be useful. He'd jumped at it, finding general service in the Royal Navy no longer exciting or demanding. As soon as he joined TIFAT he worked at honing his already considerable skills to a lethal level.

Now he was third in the chain of command. His boss was General Malcolm Macnair, while the second-in-command was Colonel Hiram B. Walsh, an American on secondment from the 1st Special Forces Operational Detachment – Delta.

TIFAT had been formed a few years earlier and was made up of mainly special forces personnel from all across the world. It was recognised as one of the toughest and most efficient organisations to be found anywhere. Essential when the ability and viciousness of the enemy was considered. Their mandate had been extended to include certain organised crime syndicates but on the whole it was terrorism they combated on a worldwide basis.

That weekend he was the Officer of the Day and was required to remain onboard HMS *Cochrane*. Although *Cochrane* was a shore establishment, it was still referred to as a ship. This was a legacy from the days when it had been a naval base. Due to the cutbacks it had been due for demolition but TIFAT had come along and rescued the place. Unusually for any military organisation there was nobody below the rank of Sergeant. The experience and ability of the men there was way beyond what was expected of any military force. These were the elite of the elite and when that included the SAS, SBS, DELTA, SEALS *et al*, that was saying something. As a result, the officers and NCOs shared the mess and bar.

He had been surprised to hear from his cousin that morning but after hearing what had happened he understood why Richard had called. A near death experience was best handled by talking to somebody. Somehow, it reduced the trauma. When you came close to death like he had on a number of occasions, it reminded you of the frailty of life, of how tenuous it could be.

He was contemplating going for a run and a workout when his phone rang.

Swinging his feet to the floor he leant forward and pressed the receive button.

'Hunter.'

'Commander,' said his boss, 'can you spare me a minute?'

Hunter grinned. Spare me a minute was a euphemism for get yourself in here straight away. 'I'll be right there, sir.'

He stood up. With dark hair, almost black, wide shoulders, at 6ft 2ins he looked like his cousin, Richard Griffiths, albeit he had dark blue eyes. He was wearing black trousers, a white, open necked shirt, dark blue sweater with the three gold stripes proclaiming his rank.

He stepped out of his office and along the corridor to a door at the end. Knocking, he entered and closed the door behind him. There were two men sitting there, his boss, General Macnair and someone he recognised instantly and was surprised to see.

'Ah, Nick, I think you know Sir William Summers.'

Hunter nodded at the short, round man who had risen to his feet. His cherubic smile hid one of sharpest minds to be found in the security services anywhere in the world, albeit also one of the most cynical.

They shook hands.

'Good to meet you again, sir,' said Hunter. 'Congratulations on your knighthood.'

Summers nodded. 'Thank you. I'm not sure I deserved it. It just comes with the territory. It's good to see you again Commander and congratulations on your promotion.

'Thank you, sir.'

As Summers was head of MI6, Hunter was intrigued as to why the man was there and so close to Christmas as well.

'Coffee?' The General asked, nodding at the percolator sitting in the corner of his office.

'I'm fine, thank you, sir.'

'Take a seat.' The General indicated the chair at the head of the table. 'I asked Sir William to wait until you joined us before he briefed us.'

Hunter nodded.

The two senior officers were facing each other across the table and had mugs of coffee in front of them.

'We have a problem,' began Summers. 'Clive Owens and ourselves have been working for some time on a very delicate situation.'

Owens was the head of MI5. There was a distinct territorial barrier between the two organisations. MI5 dealt with security matters in the UK, while MI6 was responsible for all matters foreign.

'As you know, Commander,' he then smiled, 'may I call you Nick? Commander is too formal.'

'By all means, sir.'

There was no suggestion that Hunter should refer to the head of MI6 other than formally. There were, as always, certain barriers that weren't crossed.

'As you are aware, in the past the liaison and more importantly, the exchange, of information and intelligence between MI5 and ourselves has been less than adequate.'

As always, in spite of being the head of MI6 and spending most of his working life in the forefront of the fight against terrorism, Sir William Summers had learned the use of double, even triple talk. It was needed in case an enquiry was ever called – usually as a result of a grave error by the establishment – then different interpretations could be put on the words and phrases. It was known government wide as "Civil Service Speak".

Seeing the look on the faces of the other two, Summers stopped for a moment. 'Sorry. What I should have said was that the sharing of intelligence has been poor at best and downright obstructive on occasions. It has led to security failures that have had serious consequences. You both know what happened with the Underground bombing. We knew it was in the offing thanks to a contact in Pakistan. When we passed the information on it was done in such a way as to protect our source, thinking he would be of use in the future. MI5 misinterpreted the information and acted too late. A mistake, the consequences of which weren't just a drop in share price. We are now working closely with Five. A committee of three people from each organisation has been looking at something that came to light by accident about a year ago. Quite frankly, we were so shocked by what we found that we began to look at it in depth.'

'Into what?' Hunter asked, as always impatient to get to the core of a problem.

'You know that there are many rumours about the corruption to be found across Europe due to the European Union Parliament.'

'It's been going on for years,' said Macnair. 'It's been said often enough but the European governments choose to ignore it.'

'That's true. That's at the heart of the problem I want to discuss with you.'

Frowning, Hunter said, 'Sir, what's going on in the EU is hardly anything to do with us. Fraud and corruption is for local police forces. Anyway, doesn't the EU have its own agency, or department, whatever it's called, for investigating fraud across the EU?'

'It does and I appreciate your point. Normally, I would agree. There is nothing to concern us. Perhaps that's the wrong word. I should say nothing for us to become involved in. However, what we've uncovered goes way beyond fraud and corruption.' Summers paused for a drink of coffee. 'We have proof that there are acts of terrorism being ordered by individuals from within the EU Parliament.'

Both Macnair and Hunter looked astonished. To give himself time to think, Hunter got to his feet and stepped across to the coffee machine. Lifting the jug he waved it at the other two, both of whom shook their heads. He poured out the coffee, added milk and returned.

'That's a serious allegation,' Hunter said, before taking a sip of his drink. 'What is the proof?'

Sir William frowned. 'I will fill you in on this proof, but I have to emphasise, it is not the sort we can use in a court. It has also been a long and slow investigation. Both Clive and I have had to be very cautious about how we proceeded.'

'Why?' asked a puzzled Hunter.

'We were told in the beginning to back off. That the EU was moving forward, political union was on the horizon and nothing was to stop it.'

'This comes from a Conservative government?' Macnair couldn't keep the surprise out of his voice.

'Yes. That's because the Liberal Democrats want it.'

'I thought,' said Hunter, 'that they were backing off.'

'Only in public. Behind the scenes they're pushing hard. It's why Labour is becoming more supportive of the idea almost daily. With the Lib Dems on their side, in a coalition, then they'll probably get back into power. You know about the cries to create a unified army, navy and air force?'

'Yes,' replied the General. 'Which in turn will take political union that much closer.'

'It's being done step by step, even if the majority of the British people don't want it,' said Summers.

Hunter said, 'According to the polls, we want our country back, but right now that seems to be a tall order.'

'True. However, there are political parties across Europe demanding the same thing. The majority of Europeans want to return to the common market which was the agreement we signed up for.'

The political lecture they were receiving wasn't new. Sir William was only covering old ground that had been discussed over a few drinks on many occasions.

'It's contrite, but the saying by the first Baron Acton, *Power tends to corrupt, and absolute power corrupts absolutely. Great men are almost always bad men."* applies in this case. However, things came to a head a couple of months ago. Do you remember Colin Sayers? A Conservative Member of Parliament for a constituency in Norfolk?'

Hunter frowned and shook his head. 'I can't say I do. Why?'

'He was screaming blue murder in the House of Commons for something to be done about the unethical practices and the downright dishonesty to be found in the EU Parliament. He was told on numerous occasions to desist, to find some other cause to fight. But he refused. He died in a boating accident when canoeing on Loch Lomond during a weekend break.'

'Sorry, it doesn't ring a bell,' said Hunter, tugging at his right ear lobe.

'You were out of the country at the time,' said Macnair. 'By the time you got back it was done and dusted and of no interest except for the by-election in his former constituency.'

'We are fairly certain he was murdered though we have no hard evidence. The Strathclyde Police were beginning to think so as well when suddenly they changed their minds. It was the oddest thing. The Strathclyde Assistant Chief Constable pulled the investigation and wrote it off as an accident.'

'And you're sure that wasn't the case?'

Summers shrugged. 'We can't say that with any conviction but it rang alarm bells. MI5 took a quiet look. Unfortunately, it wasn't quiet enough. Clive was hauled before the Parliamentary Intelligence and Security Committee and was told in no uncertain terms that not only was he to drop that specific case but was not to get involved with any other that was connected to European Union matters.'

'Isn't that overkill?' queried Macnair.

'Of course it is. Normally, if there is something odd going on and alarm bells are ringing, the necessary intelligence is gathered, processed and action taken by the appropriate agency.'

'But it still wasn't something for MI5 to get involved in,' said Hunter.

'True, which was why he was trying to keep it quiet. Clive was looking for info that would enable him to go back to Strathclyde and show it hadn't been an accident. He'd kept things as quiet as possible yet still the Parliamentary ISC learnt about it.'

'Which means there's a leak,' said Macnair.

Sir William nodded glumly. 'Not just a leak, but whoever it is, is clearly pretty senior. He's narrowed it down to half-a-dozen people, thinks he knows who it is and is convinced he will know for sure by the new year.'

'Will he be able to do anything about it?'

'Not if it's the person he thinks it is. She's too well connected and too senior. She's also in line to take his job when he retires.'

'I take it,' Hunter said, 'you've come here personally to try and make sure nobody knows you've been in contact?'

'Correct. I'm on a short break fishing in Scotland. Just for a few days starting yesterday. I left instructions that I didn't want to be contacted unless it was in an emergency.'

'Doesn't last night constitute an emergency?' Macnair asked.

The head of MI6 sighed. 'It does but it's really a job for Special Branch and Five. I pointed that out and told them I'd be back tomorrow.'

'They wouldn't have liked that,' said Macnair. He didn't need to spell out who "they" were. Britain's political elite were already making loud noises, saying a lot, achieving nothing. 'So what do you want us to do?'

'Your mandate far exceeds ours as we've acknowledged in the past. I know there are some in government who are trying to get it changed but thanks to the Americans and somewhat unusually, the Russians, that isn't happening.'

'Not yet,' said Hunter.

'As you say, not yet. Right now, you can do things we can't. Your armoury is far more, shall we say, flexible than ours? You also have skills my people don't possess.'

The head of MI6 didn't need to say what they were. Every front-line person at TIFAT was well schooled in unarmed combat, using explosives, firing virtually any type of weapon ever manufactured, breaking and entering without leaving a trace, carrying out surveillance operations and myriad other skills needed to do their job. Most importantly of all, they could act without being hamstrung by too many rules and regulations, all of which were designed to protect the guilty under the banner of human rights. TIFAT's successes had been significant. Many terrorists had been eliminated, along with those people who backed them either financially or with indirect aid.

Hunter acknowledged to himself that the West had finally reacted. In the language of Shakespeare's *Julius Caesar*, it had been a case of, *"Cry havoc, and let slip the dogs of war."* Security services worldwide were being reined in to the detriment of the law-abiding public. No vigorous cross-examination of a prisoner even if the authorities were certain that person had valuable information, which could help to save lives. Hence TIFAT. They were the dogs of war but even they were slowly, yet surely, being kennelled.

Opening his briefcase, Summers took out a blue file and placed it on the table in front of him. 'There are two levels at which things are happening. Do you remember about ten months ago a European official by the name of Bruce Cash was killed in a car accident? It made all the papers and news reports for a couple of days.'

'Wasn't he in charge of the audit of the European Union?' asked Macnair.

'Correct. It was Cash who reported on the massive fraud that was taking place. I should say frauds. He had led his team for twelve months, putting together damning evidence against some MEPs and a substantial number of commissioners.'

Hunter nodded. 'I remember. It was an accident.'

'It was no accident. He was a man of great integrity and I must say great bravery. He put his findings in a report which was given to a man by the name of Peter Waterfield. He's a commissioner who is responsible for the Internal Audit, Administration and Personnel Commission. As a result, he wields a great deal of power.'

'It sounds an impressive title,' Hunter stated.

'They all have impressive titles. It makes some very inadequate people feel important. Some of them consider themselves above the law and think they can do as they like. Waterfield is a particularly vile individual.'

'Then arrest him,' was the logical statement made by Hunter.

'We can't. We have no real proof. It's all done with smoke and mirrors. It is nearly twenty years since the European Union Parliament was audited. If this was a company, publicly quoted or private, the directors would have been arrested long ago and would have spent a considerable time in prison.'

Hunter looked at Sir William through half-closed eyes. 'Are you saying this man Waterfield had something to do with Cash's death?'

'We're fairly certain he ordered it.'

'I knew things were pretty bad but this is unbelievable,' said Hunter.

Sir William shrugged. 'I know, but it is happening. The question of fraud has been raised many times. Whenever it is, we get statements such as, "It isn't true. There are errors, but that is inevitable with a budget as large as the one the EU is operating." They use such arguments all the time. Anyway, Cash took his report to Waterfield who took it from him and threw it into a drawer of his desk. Cash was told to forget about it and he in turn threatened to call a press conference. Waterfield responded by threatening him with disciplinary action on charges of not complying with staff regulations because Cash had approached the Court of Auditors as well as the Parliament itself via certain Members of the European Parliament without the proper authority.'

'So you're saying they had him killed,' said Hunter. 'How sure are you?'

'Pretty sure but I want you to help us find proof.'

'What for? We don't take people to trial,' Macnair shook his head.

'I don't want it used in a court of law. I want you to have proof before you take any action.'

Macnair and Hunter exchanged glances before Hunter said, 'You want us to double check whether or not he's involved.'

'If this man is ordering the deaths of innocent people,' said Macnair, 'we'll deal with it. What about the fraud side of things?'

'We're pretty certain he's part of the conspiracy with a number of others. Don't be under any misapprehension, these people wield enormous power. This is secured by their access to what are virtually unlimited funds. It is European taxpayers' money but they treat it like it's their own.'

'What sort of figures are we talking about?' Hunter asked.

'Hundreds of millions, quite literally.'

Hunter looked suitably surprised. 'I take it this is a question of cut off the head and the rest will die?'

'Not quite. Cut off the head and we may manage to get some semblance of control. We may even be able to get an audit completed and others arrested.

'There's something else, sir, isn't there?' Hunter was looking at Summers.

'How very astute of you. I was about to come to that. TIFAT operatives are the most capable people when it comes to self-preservation. How should I put this? You don't hesitate.'

'Don't hesitate to do what?' Hunter asked.

'To shoot first. Across Europe there are teams of men, usually three strong although there are some women also, who we know are referred to as enforcers. They are mainly Estonian and Slovakian. If anyone steps out of line a team is sent in to ensure it never happens again. The first time they pay a visit they issue a warning. There is no second warning.'

'How do you know?' asked the General.

Sir William Summers' tone grew heavy. 'I had two agents working on it.'

'Had?' said Hunter. 'How did they die?' he asked.

'A car accident in the middle of the night on the A10 motorway near Brussels.'

'What happened?' asked Macnair.

'The report shows they were speeding, hit an oil patch, lost control and smashed into a very large trailer lorry going the same way.'

'But you don't think so,' suggested Hunter.

Summers lifted his shoulders with the palms of his hands turned upward and said, 'I honestly don't know. Knowing the two agents I doubt it. Seeing the evidence, I must accept it.'

Silence, like a fog, permeated the room.

'Before they died, they managed to find out a few things. It's all in here.' He opened the file. 'We don't have a lot to go on. Have you heard of a man by the name of Jakub Kowalak?'

'No. He sounds Polish,' said Macnair. 'Who is he?'

'He is Polish. We believe he's the person responsible for recruiting and supplying the teams of killers.'

'How sure?'

'Pretty sure. Over the last few years his name has come to light on numerous occasions.'

'Why not arrest him?' Hunter asked.

Summers clenched his jaw and pursed his lips. 'We did try a few years back. I've read the file. A number of witnesses went missing while others changed their testimony. This is the man.' Summers slid a photograph across to Hunter. It showed the head and shoulders of a man of obvious Slav ancestry, with a slab of a face, heavy jowls and grey hair. 'We believe there are at least fifty people in his organisation. So far, none have been arrested and charged with so much as a speeding offence. We think they've been responsible for at least thirty deaths, possibly more, and God alone knows how many beatings and threats.'

'If they've been operating for so long,' said Hunter, 'and done so much, they would have come to the attention of Interpol before now.'

'That's true. I said that none have been arrested so far, that's because as soon as the police have started any form of investigation to arrest any of them, they vanish. We're certain it's back to Estonia and Slovakia but once they've gone there's no finding them. We have another lead. Let me show you these.' He took out some photographs and slid them across the table.

'The man you see here calls himself Victor Gillespie. In fact, his real name is Donald MacGregor.'

'Scottish?' Hunter asked.

'As English as they come. He's based in London. I can't be sure, but I think he may have had something to do with the attack on the French Embassy.'

'You think? You don't know?' Macnair asked.

Summers shook his head. 'No, I don't. You know what intelligence work is like. A bit of information here, a bit there. His name has come up on a number of occasions and when I put it all together I decided it was time to take a closer look at Mr. MacGregor.'

'Do you know where we can find him?' Hunter asked.

'We have an address in London. It's a rented property belonging to an offshore company in the Bahamas. Oh, all legal and above board, it's just we're unable to trace the actual owners.'

'Is council tax paid on the place?' asked the General.

'Regular as clockwork. Also from an off-shore account.'

'Okay,' said Hunter. 'We'll start with him. Is that alright with you, sir?' he looked at Macnair.

The General nodded. 'Yes, but we'll wait until after Christmas.' Before Summers could protest, he went on, 'We're not rushing into this. Our mandate may say one thing but from what you tell me we could be walking on very thin ice. I want more intelligence. Everything you've got and that'll take time to sift through. Right now we're a skeleton staff which will be further reduced in the next twenty-four hours.'

'It's waited this long,' said Summers, 'a couple more weeks won't make much difference – just as long as we clean out the stables.'

Hunter leaned back in his chair and said, 'Like Hercules and the Augean Stables?' suggested Hunter.

Summers nodded.

'Don't forget, after doing the job, he was double-crossed.' Hunter put his hands behind his head and interlocked his fingers.

Sir William Summers said, 'We shall have to ensure it doesn't happen in this case.'

On that note they agreed to continue the meeting the following morning and adjourned to the wardroom. A drink was called for.

*   *   *   *

Richard Griffiths had slept most of the afternoon. When he awoke he switched on the television to see what was happening. As he listened, he recognised what was being said as the usual claptrap following a terrorist attack. He tuned it out as he went into the kitchen and made himself scrambled eggs on toast. He returned to the living room and watched the television while he ate the simple meal and sat back with a mug of tea. He got caught up with what was being shown on the screen.

Phyllis Nesbit, the same presenter who had been on at breakfast, had three guests on the sofa. She glanced at the Conservative MP, the Labour MEP and the BBC's political commentator, Adrian Staples.

She opened the proceedings. 'Welcome, gentlemen. Let me begin with you, Adrian Staples. Do we know the names of the dead as yet?'

Shaking his head, Staples replied. 'No. They won't release the information until after the families have been contacted. What we do know is that the Ambassador and his wife are both dead, as is Pierre Duverger, the First Secretary.'

Richard groaned. He hadn't seen that much of Pierre, but when they had met they'd always had a good time.

'Are we any further advanced in discovering who is responsible for this atrocity?

'No, Phyllis, they are still working on it. There is one peculiarity that has arisen. A dead body has been found around the corner from the embassy. In one of the gardens on William Street.'

'Oh? Do we know who it is?'

'Yes. The body has been identified as that of Jules Fournier, a Third Secretary at the Embassy.'

'How did he die? Surely he was a long way from the blast.'

'That is correct. He was shot twice in the back and his body was dumped in the garden. It was hidden behind a rubbish bin, though still easily spotted.'

'So when was the body found?'

'Two hours ago, apparently. The statement has only just been released.'

'Is there any connection with what happened to the Military Attaché?'

'It's hard to tell, although the *modus operandi* is similar.'

'Any word as to how the explosives got into the embassy?'

'At first, it was thought that the outside caterers who were used to supply the provisions for the cocktail party had been responsible.'

'But this isn't the case?'

'It doesn't appear to be.'

'Do we know anything about the catering company?'

'Not much. We have been told that their premises have been raided. It has been emphasised that the company has been put through a stringent security check once a year for the last five years or more and has been found to be clean.'

'Has anyone been arrested?'

'To the best of our knowledge, no. We are waiting on further announcements by the police.'

Phyllis swivelled her chair a few degrees. 'Bruce Middleton, as the Conservative MP for the area where the explosion took place, do you have anything to add?'

'Yes. The French should have implemented the standard procedures required at such an event.' His tone matched his words, pompous, supercilious and over-bearing.

'Mr Middleton, with all due respect,' a phrase used when the last thing that was going to be used was respect, 'How do you know that they didn't?' Then she had an afterthought. 'What are standard procedures in a case like this?'

Middleton had little idea what they were and so he did what he always did when he painted himself into a verbal corner like the one he was now occupying. 'You know only too well and don't need me to tell you. There are systems which all embassies have in place, to ensure an attack like the one we have just witnessed doesn't happen. These systems I am not going to spell out as they must be kept secret.'

Phyllis didn't bother to question him further on the matter. She knew he had no idea what he was talking about. She continued, 'Is there any indication as to who is responsible?'

'We don't know for a fact but it seems obvious that it is Islamic fundamentalists,' said the MP.

'How can you be sure of that?' asked Phyllis, although she knew it was inevitable that Muslims would be blamed.

Middleton continued, 'That is the word coming back to me from the police.'

She didn't ask what word? There was no way he could have any more information than that already gleaned by the broadcasters. In fact, he would certainly have had less. Still, she wasn't going down that road. The point of having these guests was to create controversy and encourage debate.

Continuing to speak in an exasperated tone that implied he was addressing an idiot child, Middleton said, 'Who else would wish to carry out this appalling crime? This is why we need a pan-European defence force. One united organisation to fight illegal immigration and hence terrorists coming into Europe. If we did have, nothing like this could possibly have happened.'

How such a force would help the battle against terrorism nobody said or questioned. It was a mantra that was being expounded more often in Governments across Europe.

'Bruce Middleton, Conservative MP, thank you.' She swivelled her chair a few more degrees. 'Mr Neil Canter, as Labour MEP for the area what are your thoughts?'

Canter had been elected by a margin of less than a hundred. It was a blip in the forecasted results that still had the political pundits baffled.

'First of all, I would like to express my deepest condolences and concern for the victims and their families. I agree with my colleague here,' he spoke in a calm and rational voice, hiding the fact that the two men detested each other, 'we need a thorough and comprehensive investigation, so that we can establish what happened and put into place the necessary measures to ensure it doesn't happen again.'

Phyllis Nesbit put a frown on her face, as though not understanding the comment. 'I thought that was all taken care of following 7/7. If I remember correctly, Labour announced that measures would be taken to ensure nothing like it ever happened again on British soil.'

'Ah,' said the MEP, 'that's the point I'm making.'

'What point?' Her frown was deeper and this time not contrived.

'The embassy isn't British property. Technically it belongs to the French. Hence they are responsible for their own internal security.'

'Come now, Mr Canter, surely the responsibility is a shared one?'

'Not on the actual premises it isn't.'

She turned her attention back to the MP. 'Mr Middleton, do you agree that security of embassies is in the hands of each country?'

'It's not a question of whether I agree or not. It's a question of fact. Embassies will not have us on their premises or in their grounds.'

'Why is that?'

Shrugging, Middleton said, 'It's the way it has always been. Of course, the whole question of co-operation would be mitigated with our embassies representing the European Union and not individual countries. This would be further enhanced with, as I have already stated, a pan-European military force. Then we can get our special security services working more closely to ensure nothing like this ever happens again.'

'Thank you.' Having Middleton on the programme had been a deliberate ploy. They all knew the tack he would take. He never missed an opportunity to further the cause of a united Europe. It was an objective shared by many who worked at the BBC as had been shown over the years by the careful selection of interviewees and those invited onto political panel programmes to express their views.

Phyllis put her hand to her ear and pressed. The voice came over more clearly. She paused and then looked at the camera. 'We are going over live to Number 10 where the Prime Minister is about to say something.'

*   *   *   *

The screen changed. Richard only half listened while he made some coffee. He was still finding it hard to come to terms with the fact that he had almost been killed. A few more paces would probably have been enough. Pouring milk into his coffee he sat back down, his hands wrapped around the mug.

He sat for a minute or two and then began to tune in to what the Prime Minister was saying. At first, the words washed over him while he told himself whatever the man said would be a lie. After all, he was the man in opposition who made a cast iron guarantee that he would hold a referendum as to whether or not the United Kingdom should stay within the European Union. After the election he claimed that such a referendum had been held in 1974 or 1975, whichever it was, and hence there was no need for a second one. Richard, being pro-Union, didn't mind. What he objected to was the fact that the man, Britain's Prime Minister, could treat the population with such contempt as to lie, expecting to get away with it.

Richard continued to pay attention. 'This vile, cowardly act will be investigated to the utmost of our ability and resources. Rest assured, we will catch those responsible and they will suffer the full weight of the law.'

Richard tuned out again disillusioned at what he had heard.

The Commissioner of the Metropolitan Police was then introduced and he said much the same thing. As always, reading between the lines, nobody had a clue at that moment as to what had happened. Painstaking procedures would uncover most if not all of the facts. However, it would take time.

9

Hunter ran five miles before breakfast and completed a work out in the gym. His breakfast was porridge oats, followed by a couple of boiled eggs washed down by sugarless tea. He handed over the duty to his relief and joined the two senior officers in Macnair's office.

With fresh cups of coffee in front of them, Summers started the meeting. 'Let's get back to the EU itself. We have a number of people liaising with police forces across Europe who are working the legal end of things. They are trying to amass enough evidence which can be used in court. However, ourselves and the various forces are being hamstrung by OLAF at every turn. Oh,' Summers waved his hand as though brushing away a fly, 'OLAF makes all the right noises. They promise reports that are never forthcoming. They also argue that there is too much scaremongering and exaggeration of the problem,' he paused.

'And?' Hunter queried.

'If anything, it's being understated to a massive degree.'

'Sir, I'm sorry, I still don't get it. What do you want us to do? Track down these enforcement teams,' never one to beat about the bush, he continued, 'and kill them?'

Summers shook his head. 'Tracking down all these people and dealing with them one by one would take far too much time and effort when you have or will have other operations to contend with.'

'In that case, what do you want us to do?' Macnair repeated the question.

'These teams only work for money. Nothing else interests them.'

'That goes without saying,' said the General.

'So what happens if we cut off the source?'

'They'll vanish back into the cesspools they've crawled out of,' said Hunter.

'Precisely. Now, every indication points to the fact that there is a controlling body at the top of the pile. A body of men and possibly women who are responsible for what's happening. Suppose we are able to identify these people, this cabal, what do we do about it?'

The two military men exchanged glances. Neither answered.

'Arrest them,' said Macnair.

'That seems reasonable to me as well.'

'Suppose we do. Suppose we find the evidence we're looking for? What then?'

'I don't understand,' said Hunter. 'Get the evidence and take them to court.'

'There's a far bigger consideration.'

It was the General who replied. 'Of course. The political implications will be enormous, catastrophic. If proof was given to the courts of the scale of what was happening then the whole edifice would crumble. The EU wouldn't just fail it would shatter.'

'There wouldn't be another opportunity for a hundred years to bring Europe together, if ever.'

'Granted,' said Hunter, 'but a lot of people know how things stand. How rotten it all is.'

'Thinking it, even knowing it are two different things to having it established beyond a shadow of a doubt. The vast majority of people are happy in their ignorance. Let's face it, life is tough and most people have enough to contend with in their day-to-day lives. Even an orderly exit from the EU is far better than the implosion that would occur if all this got out.'

'I can see that,' said Macnair. 'Hence the reason you need us.'

'How have we allowed things to get to this state?' Hunter asked. The question may have been rhetorical but he got an answer.

Sir William shrugged. 'A combination of many things. Political ideology is, without doubt, the driving force. Then add to that the potential for wealth and power and it becomes a heady and almost unstoppable bandwagon leading to where we are today. It only takes a few individuals to begin the process. In effect, to start the rot. It gradually takes hold. The months and years have slipped by and the poison has slowly but surely been spreading across the continent. What happens when people complain? One of the first accusations made is that the person trying to talk sense is described as xenophobic. That's coupled with racism and bigotry.'

Hunter nodded. 'I guess you're right.'

Summers blew out his cheeks and sighed. 'We're floundering. We are facing a situation that has never existed before and, to be honest, we don't know which way to turn.'

'That's one hell of an admission,' said Hunter.

'I know. It's one of the reasons I've delayed coming here. I have spent months trying to work out what to do. If we can identify the top echelon of leaders and get rid of them, we might be able to get somewhere. If we can significantly reduce the flow of money being used illegally we might just start making inroads into the whole mess.'

Macnair said, 'It sounds to me as though you're not convinced we have much chance of success.'

Summers looked at the papers on the table in front of him, staying silent for a few seconds before replying. 'I'm not, but I've decided to tackle the problem before I retire, as afterwards it'll be too late.'

'Surely the problem needs solving through the ballot box?' Hunter asked.

'In the long term of course it does. You'll get no argument from me or anyone else who believes in democratic principles. However,' Summers leant forward and stabbed the table with his right index finger, 'it's getting started that's the big issue. I think that poverty will run wider and deeper across Europe and floating on the top will be a new aristocracy. Bureaucrats who contribute nothing whatsoever to where Europe needs to go in the future.' He paused, seeing the doubt in the eyes of the other two. 'Our worldwide competition isn't Scotland versus England or the UK versus France. It's holding our own in an economy that really stretches around the world. Where there are industries operated by hard-working, committed people who are dragging themselves out of poverty. I don't need to spell it out for you. Look at China, India, Brazil plus a dozen other countries continuing to rise in world markets. That's our competition. Europe and America is saturated with goods and services it doesn't actually need or want. The politicians are lying to us about the mess we're in, which is what they always do. Not only do we have corruption and fraud on an unimaginable scale, there is also what I call legal fraud. How is it possible for senior employees, as well as elected officials, to retire with enough capital coupled with a very generous pension, as to be deemed millionaires? I know I keep using the word, but the whole system is bowing down under the weight of corruption.'

'Do you want us somehow to try and stop further integration of the EU? Is that it?' Hunter queried, frowning. 'If you do, I don't see that we can.'

The look of shock and horror on Sir William Summers' face told its own story. 'Good Lord, no. That isn't our concern. That's the business of the electorate, the ballot box and the politicians. No! All I am saying is, we must clean up the system and get rid of the crooks. We have to let proper democratic principles solve the political issues.'

'Good,' Hunter nodded.

Hunter and Macnair sat in silence for a moment or two, then the General said, 'Well, Commander, what do you think?'

Hunter looked from one to the other and then nodded. 'There's a lot of truth in what Sir William says. We know that. If we could clean out the ... the stables, then there is a possibility that the system could be made to work the way it was always intended. The way people dreamt of decades ago.'

'I must make something clear,' said Summers. 'I'm pro-Europe. I have spent my life fighting for this country and, by extension, for Europe. If we do end up with a single government in the centre then so be it. I am not commenting on the politics of the situation. I *am* commenting on the reality of what we face if Europe is to survive in anything like its current form.' He paused then added, 'Does that make sense?'

Macnair replied, 'Yes, it does. Is there anything else you can tell us?'

Summers shook his head. 'I'm sorry, no.'

Macnair and Hunter exchanged glances.

'Nick?'

'Yes, sir. I think after what Sir William has told us we need to do something. We can't just let Europe rot even if we don't agree with the politics.'

Macnair looked pensive, drumming the fingers of his right hand on the table. After a minute or so he nodded. 'I agree. William, leave whatever you've got and we'll take a close look at it. Christmas is only three days away so I suspect all of Europe will be grinding to a halt and that will include the EU Parliament.'

Summers smiled, looking relieved, like a weight had been lifted from his shoulders. 'You've no idea how much I appreciate this.'

10

After seeing the head of MI6 away from the base, Hunter asked, 'Has Isobel left yet?'

'I'm not sure,' replied the General. 'I think she's due to leave this evening.'

Isobel Sweeney ran the Information Technology department for TIFAT. She had a team of 15 operators; two of whom, short, fat Leo with powerful glasses to deal with his myopia and tall, skinny Gareth who could consume more calories in a day than three average people and not put on an ounce of fat were near geniuses when it came to anything to do with computers.

They had been known to hack into national databases, security systems and banks all over the world. They had liberated more funds from crooks and terrorists and distributed them to good causes than was imaginable. All of which they achieved without leaving any trace.

'I'll go over to the section and speak to her. See what we can find out about this character MacDonald,' said Hunter.

'I'll come with you.'

They grabbed their greatcoats and stepped out into a cold, blustery day. It was, as the BBC had said earlier, a typical Scottish day in late December. The two men crossed the parade ground and approached the IT department. Hunter used his code to unlock the door and they entered.

The room was long and low and filled with computers. The systems at work in that room were amongst the most powerful to be found anywhere in the world. This was due mainly to the efforts of Isobel, Leo and Gareth. The General always reckoned that if the two men had been criminals they would be filthy rich and unknown.

The room was looking festive with Christmas decorations and a party atmosphere pervaded the place.

On seeing the two senior officers, Leo said, 'Better watch out. Here comes trouble.'

The room was virtually empty of staff as most had left the day before for a fortnight's leave. The skeleton crew on watch were about to pack up though two people would be on duty throughout the holiday.

'Hullo, General, Nick,' Isobel smiled at them both.

'Afternoon, Isobel,' said Macnair, returning the smile.

'Hi, Isobel, Leo, Gareth.' Hunter nodded to them.

'We've got something for you,' Macnair began. 'Any chance of you taking a look? Or are you about to go?'

'Only for lunch. I'm not leaving until Tuesday. Believe me, Christmas Eve is early enough to get to my family,' Isobel said. 'Three days there and I'll be climbing the walls and heading for the sunshine.'

'Where are you going?' Hunter asked.

'No idea. I'm going to decide on the day I leave.' Isobel was well known for her whims and had often entertained the others over a drink with where she went and what she did. Though she was an attractive woman, she never seemed to have a man in tow. When asked, she usually replied that she hadn't found one to entertain her when not between the sheets.

'What about you guys?' Hunter asked Leo and Gareth.

'Same. Then I'm going to Gibraltar,' said Leo.

'And I'm going to Disneyland in Florida,' said Gareth. 'My girl-friend's daughter wants to go.'

'Rubbish,' said Leo. 'It's Gareth who wants to go. The girlfriend's daughter is just an excuse.'

The two, who were close friends, began bickering until Isobel called them to order. 'Right. Good. Now then, gentlemen, what do you want us to do?'

'This afternoon,' Hunter replied, 'we'd like as much information as you can find on a man by the name of Donald MacGregor. He also has the alias of Victor Gillespie. Anything you can find will be useful.'

'Is there anything you can tell us?'

'We have this address. It's owned by an off-shore company.' Hunter handed over a post-it note.

'Okay.' Isobel turned to the other two. 'Set it running, will you? The system can work over lunch.'

It was a mere five minutes later that the group of them left the building and made their way to the self-service canteen in the main building. There were few tables in use, as most of the staff had already left for Christmas.

However, there were two men Hunter wanted to speak with. 'Sir,' he turned to the General, 'I'm going to talk to Jan and Phil. I'll be taking them with me.'

Macnair replied, 'I thought you might.'

With a tray of cottage pie and fresh vegetables, Hunter joined the other two. He greeted them with the words, 'We've got a job.'

Jan Badonovitch was a senior NCO with the Russian Spetsnaz and had been with TIFAT from the start. He was 5ft 8ins tall, broad shouldered and as tough as they came. He also had a wicked sense of humour though it was often kept buried in his psyche.

Phileas Peabody was an NCO from the famous American SEALS – the elite of the elite, SEAL TEAM 6. He was tall, 6ft 1in, and lean and could run a marathon at a speed that would rank him in the top dozen or so runners in the world. He claimed that being black gave him an edge when on night time operations – he didn't need face camouflage. He had only joined the team recently, replacing one of the team who had been killed during an operation in Europe.

'What is it?' Badonovitch asked eagerly. The prospect of spending his leave in Rosyth hadn't been appealing and he'd debated with himself whether or not to head south to a beach and some sunshine. He and Peabody had just been talking about the prospect.

As they ate, Hunter brought them up to speed on what was required of them.

Both Peabody and Badonovitch had questions and the three men sat together for over an hour discussing what they had to do and what gear to take with them.

Finally, Hunter pushed back his chair and stood up. 'Let's go and see Isobel.' After stacking their plates and cutlery they went outside and across to the IT department.

They found Isobel standing on her low dais, leafing through a print out. 'Ah, the three Musketeers,' she joked. 'I take it you two are in on this op?'

'That's an affirmative,' Miss Sweeney, Peabody replied.

'Phil, I've told you before, the name is Isobel,' she smiled.

'I'll try and remember, Miss, sorry, Isobel.'

'Have you got anything?' Hunter asked.

'MacGregor did military service. Five years in the SBS.' Isobel was referring to the Royal Marines Special Boats Service. It was an organisation that bred tough men – or at least moulded them.

'Only five years?' Hunter asked.

'He was thrown out. It says for insubordination but looking closer I would say he started some sort of fight with an officer. Put the man in hospital. He also appears to have a reputation for hard drinking.'

'Did he do any time?' Hunter asked.

'Only waiting time. Ten days and he was out.'

'What happened then?'

'He dropped out of sight although he turns up like a bad penny from time to time.'

'How do you mean?' Hunter frowned.

'He became a mercenary. His name is mentioned on odd occasions.'

'Anything serious?' Peabody queried.

'One incident in Angola. He appears to have killed a man. The son of a member of the Angolan government. MacGregor got out by the skin of his teeth. Using his military records we got his National Insurance number. That enabled us to get into the Inland Revenue database. The last time MacGregor paid any taxes was nearly five years ago. The address you gave us is, as you said, owned by an off shore company registered in the Bahamas. That in turn is owned by a company in Hong Kong.'

'Do we know who owns it?' Hunter asked.

'MacGregor,' said Leo, pushing his glasses back up his nose.

'Like Summers said, there's more than enough to take a close look,' Hunter stared at the screen. 'An area like Shacklewell may not be extortionate but it does require a pretty good income. I'll speak to the General. We can put a few things in place before the holidays and follow up in the new year. I'll hand the duty over and we'll head south for a couple of days. Jan, Phil, you two go down to the armoury and get us Glock 19s plus silencers.'

With an overall length of 174mm it was a compact weapon to carry but with the same stopping power as the 17 which had an overall length of 225mm. Even the modified silencer, which did an adequate job, only added 40mm to the gun. Weighing 600g it was also relatively comfortable to carry.

'Also get the new bugs.' He was referring to the new parabolic microphones. Although less than 5mm in diameter they were highly efficient. The receiver had new filtering circuitry as well as a Digital Sound Processor which meant there was no buzz and hum in the background. The bugs were voice activated and had enough power in them to last up to seven days. The system was micro-technology at its best. They transmitted to a receiver placed within 500 metres which in turn transmitted back to computers in Rosyth. Information could then be filtered out and anything of any relevance forwarded to the teams.

Returning to the office block he went up to Macnair's office. Normally in the outer office was stationed a PO Wren (Writer), who was the General's secretary, but she had already left for the fortnight.

Knocking on the door, he rejoined Macnair. 'Sir, I'll hand the duty over and we'll head for London this afternoon. Find a hotel and take a wander around MacGregor's patch. See what we can find.'

Macnair nodded. 'Okay. How long will you be gone?'

'I don't know. We'll make it back by Christmas Eve. This is by way of a recce. We need to know if the address we have is where he actually lives, otherwise we'll have to start all over again. With luck, we'll also be able to bug the place.'

The General leant back in his chair. 'Don't forget your weapons ID cards. The last thing we need is for any of you to be banged up over the festive season.'

'Once was enough.' He was referring to an operation they'd had going down in the southwest. An overzealous Police Inspector at Plymouth arrested two of TIFATs men when they were involved in a tricky and dangerous operation. It had taken the General two days to sort the mess out by which time their target had done a bunk. Since then, appropriate warrant cards were carried when any weapons were part of their equipment – which was almost all of the time.

Hunter glanced at his watch. 'We should be away in the next half hour or so. We'll take the train from Edinburgh and hire a car once we get there.'

Hunter left the office and returned to his cabin. He changed out of his uniform and threw what few items he needed into a grip. Then he went down to the front door where he found the other two already waiting. Badonovitch handed over the silenced Glock and Hunter put it into the special pocket that had been sewn into the left side of his jacket. The gun sat snugly, hidden from view but easily and quickly accessible. A staff car drew up, they threw their bags into the boot and climbed into the car.

At Waverley, they picked up three first class tickets. It was 16.15

when the train pulled out of the station, all of three minutes late. Dusk was falling fast and snow began to drift gently down.

Almost as soon as the train started a trolley appeared offering complimentary teas and coffees as well as snacks. The menu on the table showed that a hot meal would be served from 17.00.

Halfway to London Hunter's phone rang. It was Isobel.

'We've had a bit of luck,' she began. 'We've managed to have a good look at the area MacGregor lives in and we've found a pub come hotel opposite to where he lives. It's called the Shacklewell Hide and from its website looks reasonable enough. Good enough for you three, anyway.' There was no mistaking the smile in Isobel's voice. 'MacGregor's flat is about eighty yards away. We've been into the local council's database and identified the plans for the place which we're sending to you now. He's on the second floor.' There was a pause, and then she added, 'That's it, you've got them.'

'Book us into the hotel, will you?' Hunter asked.

'I've already done it. I told them you wouldn't be arriving before half past ten and they said that was okay. I've also booked a car at King's Cross with Europcar, a BMW 3 Series.'

'Thanks, Isobel.'

'We've also been into every airport departure system in the UK for the last week and into the new year and there are a number of MacGregors booked on various flights but no Victor Gillespie. Of the MacGregors there's only one Donald and he's seventy-five and from Portree in Skye. Of course, MacGregor could easily have half-a-dozen more aliases.'

'What about the ferries and the trains to the Continent?'

'We're working on that but, as you can appreciate, it's a much bigger job. I'll call you later.' With that, Isobel broke the connection.

Hunter took out his iPad and looked at the plans of MacGregor's property. It was in a four storey building with two en-suite bedrooms, one bigger than the other, a large lounge and kitchen/diner. He showed it to the others.

'Nice place,' commented Peabody.

The train was delayed twice. The small amount of slack allowed for in the timetable was quickly eaten up and they didn't arrive at King's Cross until just before 22.00. There they picked up the car and were soon crossing London. The snow hadn't followed them into England and the night was clear and cold. The car had a sat-nav system and Hunter typed in the postcode for the Shacklewell Hide. He then followed the route he was given.

The roads were busy even at that time of night. They passed a 24 hours superstore where the car park was full. With three days still to go to Christmas Hunter guessed people were avoiding the last minute panic buying that gripped people at that time of year.

In Shacklewell, they parked just along from the entrance to the pub, almost opposite the building where MacGregor's flat was situated. It was just on 22.47 and loud and raucous music was coming from inside. The usual gaggle of men and women were standing outside the door, drawing deeply and hastily on their cigarettes. Hunter was always amused that satisfying their nicotine addiction was more important than freezing in the bitter cold.

They booked in and were directed to the third floor where they had adjoining en-suite rooms facing the road. A quarter of an hour later the three of them stood at the bar with pints of real ale in front of them. They did little more than take occasional sips as they were unsure how the rest of the night would unfold. It was late night opening until at least 01.00 and the place was packed. As a result, Hunter nearly didn't see him. Then the crowd opened for a second and there, sitting at a table on the other side of the room, was Donald MacGregor. He looked a lot older than his service photograph but unmistakable nevertheless. He had his arm around the shoulders of a woman giggling drunkenly alongside him.

Hunter turned his back and leant against the bar. 'MacGregor is over in the corner, at the far side of the room. He's got a woman in tow.'

'You sure, boss?' Badonovitch asked quietly.

'Yes. I'm going out to the car.' Looking around, he added, 'He's by the door to the left. Take a look. If he makes a move for the exit, let me know.'

'Where are you going?' Peabody asked.

'Over to his place. I'll set a few bugs. This is a good chance, while he's otherwise occupied.'

Hunter returned to the car. It was now bitterly cold and he pulled his fleece lined collar up around his ears. Opening the boot, he found his tool bag and rummaged inside. He found what he needed, removed a lock-gun, slipped it into his pocket, closed the boot and crossed the road.

There were no other pedestrians. Even those desperate for their nicotine fix had gone inside as the temperature continued to fall. The promised deep freeze was hitting with a vengeance.

The front door had a simple Yale lock. Hunter slid out the thin, flat blade on the gun and pushed it into the lock which lined the mechanism in place. Using his thumb, he pressed a button on the right side of the handle and the gun vibrated in his hand. Two more blades shot out, filled the keyhole, flicked back and forth and in seconds the lock was turning in his hand. He pushed the door open, paused and then waited for the hydraulic system at the top to close the door slowly.

He was in a foyer. There were no lights on and Hunter was grateful that the place wasn't fitted with movement sensitive light switches. Half-a-dozen paces ahead he could just about make out a staircase and on his right a lift. On the left was another door to the ground floor flat. From what he could see around him it appeared to be pleasantly decorated. There didn't appear to be any cameras but even so Hunter kept his collar turned up. He took the stairs two at a time to the next floor and there in front of him was the door to MacGregor's flat.

The lock was more substantial than the one at the main entrance and Hunter had to change the attachment on the front of the gun.

Still, in less than a minute the door was unlocked and he slipped quietly inside. He found himself in a hallway. On the left was a coat-stand with a couple of jackets hanging from it as well as an umbrella in the stand. On the right was a wall mirror with an occasional table beneath it on which was a pair of gloves.

There was one door, directly in front of him. At that moment his phone went, he took it from his pocket and saw it was Badonovitch.

'Yes?'

'Get out boss. Now.'

No explanation. Hunter didn't need one. He stepped back through the door, pulled it shut and as he did so he heard the door down below being slammed open. No lights came on. Hunter took the next flight of stairs at a run and stopped just around the corner. By craning his neck, he could just see the door to the flat. MacGregor appeared and what Hunter saw caused him to reach under his coat and slide out his gun. He watched as MacGregor pushed at the door to his place with his left hand while in his right he held an automatic of some type. What was also interesting was that the gun was fitted with a silencer.

Hunter also took out his own silencer and fitted it while he watched MacGregor looking around and then upwards. Hunter was in shadow and didn't move. Although it was nearly pitch dark, Hunter was aware that even the slightest movement might lead to detection. He watched MacGregor's gun-hand. If the man began to move it to point upwards, Hunter would shoot him.

MacGregor turned his attention back to his door. He pushed at it harder but it didn't move. Reaching into a pocket, he took out a key and quietly slipped it into the lock. He stood facing the wall alongside the hinged side of the door. He paused a few seconds, turned the key and slammed the door open. He was greeted with silence. He stayed where he was for a few seconds and then knelt down before looking around the corner. Hunter watched as MacGregor crabbed inside and vanished from sight.

Hunter stayed where he was. MacGregor took the best part of ten minutes before he reappeared. Hunter figured the man had methodically searched the place. It was proof, if any was needed, that MacGregor was a very careful man. Hunter watched him as he stood by the front door. He appeared to be looking down at the carpet and Hunter realised he was listening.

In Hunter's estimation the man's professionalism went up a notch or two. MacGregor didn't hurry. He waited patiently, but that was something Hunter was also good at. Hunter stood like a statue, careful not to rustle his clothes, breathing slowly and evenly. The noises of the night began to permeate the building. The sounds of laughter, faint music and unintelligible yells wafted across from the pub. A car passed slowly along the street.

MacGregor must have stood there for at least five minutes before he closed the door to his flat, put his gun under his coat and started back downstairs. Hunter stayed where he was. He heard the front door open and close. A minute or two later his phone vibrated in his pocket and he took it out. It was Peabody.

'He's just walked in, boss.'

'Thanks Phil. I'll be over in a few minutes.'

Twisting off the silencer, Hunter slipped it into his pocket and placed the Glock in its holster.

He went quietly downstairs and just as he reached the bottom he said softly, 'Jan? Where are you?'

A cupboard door under the stairs swung open. 'I'm here, boss.'

Hunter grinned. He hadn't known Jan was there, he had just been certain he would be. 'How did MacGregor know I was here?'

Badonovitch replied, 'He took his phone out of his pocket, looked at it and left like a bat out of hell. I followed. The door hadn't closed properly when I got here. I followed him up and when I saw him back out of his flat nipped in here.

'OK. You stay here and I'll go back.' Hunter was hoping that when the alarm went off again it would irritate MacGregor rather than have him rushing over again.

Hunter bounded up the stairs, used the lock-gun, took out three bugs, paused, twisted the lock and moved as fast as he could. Through the door ahead and he was in the lounge. He placed one bug under an occasional table. Across the room was the master bedroom. One bug went behind the headboard. Seconds later he was in the kitchen and stuck the bug under the serving counter that separated the kitchen from the dining area.

He started for the front door, paused and placed a fourth bug under the false mantelpiece and then felt the vibration on his mobile. He went straight out, closed the door behind him and took the steps upwards, back to where he'd been. Only this time he went up another floor and sat on the top step. He waited patiently, his silenced gun in his hand.

The routine was much the same as the first time only MacGregor didn't take so long before returning to the pub.

When they finally left the building, Hunter asked, 'What does a silent alarm system tell you, Jan?'

'That he's not interested in frightening people away, but more interested in catching them. He also drinks a lot, boss. He bought two large whiskies and two half pints of lager in the time you were away.'

'Which makes him particularly dangerous. I'll check the receiver in the car.'

11

Andrea Nelson took the train from Brussels. It went via Luxembourg and Strasbourg before heading south for Basel. From there she travelled to Bern where she changed trains. So far it had been a very pleasant journey. She had decided to treat herself and was travelling first class where the service was as good as could be found in a five star hotel – what she was hoping for when she got to Grindelwald.

There was a twenty minute wait in Bern before she caught the train for Thun and Interlaken. The scenery was spectacular, particularly once she was travelling alongside the Thuner See. Arriving at Interlaken, she had fifty minutes to wait for her connection so she dumped her bags in the left luggage office and wandered around the town. It was just coming up to 3.00pm on a cloudless day, the sun pleasant, the air brisk. It had all the hallmarks of a perfect Christmas holiday, weather-wise anyway.

The town had a feel about it that could only be found in the Alps. It was picture-book perfect. She stopped at a restaurant and sat outside, ordering a coffee and a pastry, enjoying the feel of the sun on her upturned face. She made a mental note to buy sun-block before she went up the mountain. It was so pleasant that she lost track of the time and missed the train so she killed time wandering around the shops. Finally, she bought the sun-block and returned to the station.

She was lucky to get on the train, as it was packed solid and she had to stand next to the door for an uncomfortable thirty-five minutes. The sun was setting fast and the train line was already in deep shadow. However, craning her neck she could see the top of the Schwarzhorn over on her left, about 10 kilometres away, reaching the best part of 3,000 metres into the sky.

The stress of the last eight months began to fade. She felt anticipation at what lay ahead and decided she would have a quiet time, enjoy being pampered by the staff at the hotel and do some gentle skiing. The train arrived at the resort and she was glad to step out onto the platform.

There was a trolley with a small sign on top. It announced Grand Hotel Regina. Andrea went across and two youngsters took her suitcase and placed it on the trolley. She gave her name, they ticked it off a list and announced that her case would be delivered to her room while she checked in.

Andrea left the station and headed towards the hotel which was only a couple of hundred metres away. The entrance was grand, the welcoming smiles effusive and the ambience of the place soothing.

As the key card to her room was handed over, the receptionist said, 'Madam, there is a folder of information in your room. If there is anything you require, please don't hesitate to contact the desk. It is manned twenty-four hours every day.'

'Thank you.' As she turned from the counter she almost bumped into a tall, black haired man. 'Sorry,' she smiled.

He smiled back in a way she found interesting, to say the least.

'That's OK.' He spoke in a deep voice, his accent home counties English.

She liked his smile but told herself to buck up. Somebody like that was bound to have a woman in tow.

As she walked away she felt as though his eyes were drilling into her back and she looked behind her. He was ignoring her and standing with his back to the room, talking to the concierge.

Berating herself for being so childish, Andrea headed for the lifts and dismissed him from her mind.

* * * *

Richard Griffiths stood at reception and wondered if the woman he had just seen was alone. If she was, then the holiday was already beginning to look promising. She was the third woman he had seen who he would be delighted to entertain.

He signed in, gave an imprint of his credit card and went through to the nearest bar. The Regina bar boasted live music but not until 8.00 o'clock in the evening. He slid onto a stool in front of the bar and ordered a Pear Schnapps and cold beer chaser. It had been years since he'd drunk Schnapps and he was looking forward to it. One healthy sip and he realised why it had been years. He left the glass, finished his beer and thought about the woman he'd nearly bumped into. If she was on her own, being so attractive, he thought he had better make a move sooner rather than later.

He went up to his room and unpacked. The room was large, had a comfortable couch and chairs around an occasional table as well as a king size bed near the windows that opened onto a balcony.

Richard stretched and yawned. It had been a long day. He had driven from London, taking a day and a half. It was the sort of thing he enjoyed doing. He'd prevaricated as to whether to take the Austin-Healey or the Range Rover. Commonsense told him to take the 4-wheel drive; his sense of adventure told him to take the sports car. Commonsense had lost out. The night before he'd spent in Reims, at a pension near the town centre. It had been adequate, clean and acceptable for one night. Aching slightly, he decided a swim and sauna would soon sort out the kinks.

A few laps of the swimming pool, followed by thirty minutes in the sauna and he found he was dozing off. Back in his room, he threw himself on the bed and drifted off to sleep, waking with a start just after 8.00 o'clock. He quickly stripped off, showered and dressed, putting on a white dress shirt, open-necked, a dark blue single-breasted jacket and grey trousers. His shoes were black and heavy duty. He was planning to take a stroll through the town after dinner.

He returned to the bar where a four-piece band was playing some gentle film music. It was ideal for the ambience of the room.

This time, he settled on a malt whisky with a drop or two of water. He sat at the bar, leaning with his back against it, propped up by his elbows and scanned the room. It was half full with couples of all ages. There were one or two families with youngsters but nobody sitting alone. After a few minutes he turned back to the bar, took a few sips of his drink and picked up the menu. There were two. One was for the elegant Grand Regina Restaurant, while the other was for a side bar that specialised in traditional Swiss dishes. He decided on the latter.

As he turned, the lady he'd seen earlier at reception walked up to the bar and stood only a metre away. She smiled at him, turned to the barman and asked for a white wine – a Swiss Fendant du Valais.

She was standing at the bar alone. She was ordering her own drink. He watched as she signed for it. She turned towards him and smiled again.

Richard stepped closer and held out his hand. 'Richard Griffiths.'

'Hullo. Andrea Nelson.'

Richard gazed into her brown eyes with their enchanting green fleck and admired her. She was, he decided, quite stunning.

'I hope you're enjoying the view,' she said, with an impish smile.

Richard reared back like a startled stallion and realised how rude he'd been to look at her in that way. He decided to take the bull by the horns. What the hell – he was only going to be there for a fortnight.

'Sorry. Are you on your own? Or are you waiting for someone?'

'I'm on my own. I am not waiting for anyone and I shall be here for the next two weeks.' Smiling, Andrea added, 'What about you?'

Richard's grin widened, if that was at all possible. 'Ditto, ditto and ditto.' He felt a pang of conscience at the thought of Hunter but quickly dismissed him from his mind. He had no doubt his cousin would be doing the same thing if their roles were reversed.

'What do you do, Richard Griffiths?'

'Me? I work for an off-shore company that supplies tugs to drag oil drilling platforms around the oceans.'

'Sounds interesting.' If she was being sarcastic her tone didn't suggest it.

'What about you?'

'I am afraid my job is far more tedious. I'm an accountant.'

Richard couldn't keep the surprise from his face. 'An accountant? I would have thought you did something far more glamorous.'

Andrea smiled. 'Such as?' Then she added, 'And anyway, who says accountancy isn't glamorous?'

'Well . . . that is . . .' he grinned again. 'You're absolutely right. What do I know? So who do you work for? Yourself? Private practice? Large company? Who?'

Looking at him pensively for a moment she had made up her mind before coming on the holiday that if she met anybody she would say she was in private practice. Whenever she told someone she worked for the European Union she usually had a tirade along the lines of how wasteful the whole thing was. How debilitating for all business as more laws came into being, strangling the life out of free enterprise and wealth creation. She didn't want to put up with that on this vacation. She wanted peace and quiet, so she lied.

'I'm in private practice. My own little business. Come and go as I like. Anyway, that's enough about work. Let me buy you a drink.' Andrea indicated his empty glass. Her's was still relatively full.

'No, it's okay, thanks. I've had enough whisky. I'll have some wine with my dinner. Speaking of which, will you join me?'

She looked thoughtfully at him for a few moments before nodding. 'I'd love to. Where shall we eat? The main restaurant, the Jagerstube or shall we go somewhere else?'

'The Jagerstube has about all that I want.'

Andrea smiled. 'Me as well.' She picked up her glass and said, 'Shall we go through?'

Richard nodded and realised he was relishing the evening ahead in a way he hadn't for a long time.

*   *   *   *

Conducting a surveillance was virtually an art. Too much time spent in one place, too much attention on one person and it didn't take long to be noticed. This was especially true if the target also knew how to conduct such an operation and as far as the team was concerned, MacGregor probably did know.

Hunter went up to his room while the other two stayed in the bar nursing their beers. He set up the recording equipment and then phoned General Macnair to bring him up to speed with what had happened.

'Good work, Nick. I'll check with Isobel in the morning that she's receiving the transmissions.'

'Right, sir.' Hunter returned to the bar and said, 'Drink up. We can't stay here without fresh drinks.' He turned to one of the girls behind the bar, 'Miss, three more pints of the IPA, please.'

When they were placed before them, Hunter picked his up and said, 'Cheers.' Badonovitch and Peabody did the same.

It was well after 01.00 before the staff began to call "last orders" and then "time". Badonovitch and Peabody left immediately while Hunter stayed a little longer. Customers began to thin out and he watched MacGregor leave, supporting the woman with him who was now fairly drunk. Watching them go, Hunter was grateful that they didn't need to listen to whatever the bugs picked up. Only relevant information would be passed to them.

Breakfast was full English – bacon, eggs and all the trimmings. It and the coffee were excellent.

Mid-morning they took a call from Rosyth telling them the woman with MacGregor was leaving. There was no suggestion of her returning anytime soon. Throughout the day they kept watch, two hours on, four hours off. They photographed anyone entering or leaving the building and sent them to Rosyth. The day crawled past. MacGregor stayed in his flat listening to classical music.

The following morning, Hunter received a phone call from Rosyth. 'Hi, Isobel.'

'Morning, Nick. MacGregor was on the phone a little while ago telling what sounds like a friend that he's staying in London. He described it as having peace and quiet before the new year.'

'Is that some sort of code or is it for real?'

'We can't tell but I'd say it's for real. A code would be more than a little over the top.'

'Hmm. Whether or not, we can't be too careful. He might be up to something. If he is responsible for what happened at the French Embassy and has other attacks planned, now's a good time of the year to carry them out. Our guard is down and we bask in the notion of peace on earth and goodwill to all men.'

'My, my, Commander, such cynicism. But I think you're right.'

'Leave it to me. I'll talk to Jan and Phil and let you know what we decide to do. Is the General in?'

'Gone for a walk. Christine is here. She'll be taking him back to her place later on.'

'Okay. Thanks Isobel. I'll phone you later.'

Hunter knocked on the doors of the other two and they left the pub for a stroll around the area. Hunter told them about his conversation with Isobel.

'It's okay, boss,' said Badonovitch. 'Phil and I already decided we'll stay here. Christmas is just another day. If we weren't on an operation we'd be at Rosyth twiddling our thumbs.'

'What about somewhere to stay?' Hunter asked.

Peabody replied. 'I already talked to the landlord, just in case. He said it was okay. They're open the whole time and can fit us in no problem.'

The fact that the two men had already enquired about the possibility of staying came as no surprise to Hunter.

'Besides, boss,' Peabody added, 'the beer and the food's better here than in the mess.'

'Thanks fellows. In that case, I'll let the General know and I'll leave in the morning.'

The day was a boring repeat of the previous one.

The following morning, Christmas Eve, it began to snow, getting heavier as the morning passed. Trains were still running on time when Hunter left at 09.45 for King's Cross.

The snow affected the traffic and by the time he crossed London and returned the car he just managed to catch the 13.00 for Edinburgh. It had been due to arrive at 17.25 but was an hour late. He caught the train to Stirling departing at 18.34 with just a few minutes to spare.

It was a crisp, bright night without a cloud in the sky and he enjoyed the ride. The train was packed with revellers going home or visiting friends and family for the festive season. He took a taxi from the station out to Balfron, a sleepy village in the west corner of Stirlingshire. His parents' house was opposite Shearer's garage, and on arrival he found the house to be alive with lights and music.

*　　*　　*　　*

Richard was enjoying himself immensely. He found, as he always did, that the chase was to be savoured. Andrea was excellent company – intelligent, knowledgeable and witty. His clumsy attempt two nights earlier to get her into bed had been adroitly swept aside but it had just left him more determined than ever. Besides, he told himself, he'd been expecting too much on a first date. Richard had loitered around the hotel, used the pool and sauna, taken a doze, gone for a walk, visited a few bars and returned to the hotel to meet Andrea for dinner. It had been another pleasant evening with a similar outcome to the night before.

This morning they had met for breakfast before going down to the ski shop where they got kitted out with skis for them both and boots for Andrea, as Richard had brought his own. The day was overcast, but there was no wind so it wasn't unpleasant, even though the temperature was around minus six degrees.

The area was packed with jostling, laughing people, some carrying skis, some wearing them while others had a snowboard slung over their shoulders. The snowboarders were the people who walked with a superior air and gave the impression that skiing was beneath them – that snowboarding was the real game in town. They were the people who went off-piste, took risks and lived life to the full – a fact they frequently pointed out.

As usual, queuing was a bore. They finally made it onto the ski lift after nearly 20 minutes. They sat on the bench seat, a metal bar running across their waists, the skis on their feet supported by a further bar. The scenery was awesome. Ahead towered the Kleine Scheidegg, one of Europe's most famous mountains for skiing.

'When you do something like this,' said Richard, 'it's as if the stresses and strains of the last few months have peeled away. You can forget your worries and immerse yourself in the sheer enjoyment of the here and now.'

Andrea laughed, 'I know what you mean. And it'll stay that way until the day before we're due to return home and work. When reality rears its head and you have to start thinking about what the future has in store.'

'Which is why,' said Richard, craftily, 'we should make the most of the here and now. Enjoy life while we can. Before it's too late.'

Looking at him, her head on one side, a wide smile showing how much she was enjoying herself, Andrea said, 'Too late for what?'

Seeing the cloud that passed across Richard's face she stopped smiling and said, 'Sorry,' she touched his hand, 'I don't know what I said, but I didn't mean to upset you.'

Richard shook his head and conjured up a smile. Christmas was the time of the year where he felt the loss of his first wife and their children the most. Though it was true the pain was receding and was now merely a dull ache.

'You didn't. I'm having a great time, and from where I'm sitting,' the seat reached the summit and the bar was pushed up, 'it can only get better.'

Andrea laughed as they flung themselves off the seat and gently skied to a halt a few metres clear of the lift. A hundred metres away was a large and busy taverna, packed with people calling out to each other, laughing, drinking and smoking.

Richard looked at his watch. 'It's just coming up to eleven o'clock. How about a coffee?'

Andrea nodded. 'That sounds like a good idea. Though I'll have hot chocolate like only the Swiss can make. I've been looking forward to sitting here in the open air, enjoying the views and drinking a hot chocolate for about a month.'

'Then so be it.' Richard pushed down on the release lever behind his ankle, slipped off one ski and then the other.

Andrea did the same and they walked up to the restaurant. They did as everyone else had done which was to jam their skis, with sticks, in a mound of snow and walk onto the balcony to find a table.

Service was quick. Andrea made appreciative noises about her chocolate while Richard enjoyed his coffee.

'Are you ready?' Richard asked when they had finished. 'It's time we hit the slope.'

Andrea nodded ruefully. 'I guess so. I can't procrastinate any longer.'

'I hadn't realised you were,' he said, in some surprise.

'Well, you said you hadn't been skiing for a while and I've been putting it off as well. Shall we?'

They clamped their skis back on and set off on the gentle part of the mountain that led from the restaurant to the actual slope. He hadn't been skiing for a number of years and had forgotten how much he enjoyed it.

As he watched Andrea, a few metres in front of him, he was suddenly aware of how graceful she was. She hit the top of the slope where the edge dropped away and paused, looking back at him.

Before he reached her and before he could say anything she said, 'Race you to the bottom.' With that she flung herself over the edge and headed straight down the slope.

Richard was taken by surprise for a second or two but then

launched himself after her. He bent his knees, put his skis close together and bent forward. Andrea stayed ahead as they shot past several floundering skiers. After all, they were on a blue run. This was for beginners and those not so adept at skiing – which was what Andrea had implied.

He jinked left and right, aimed down a particularly steep section of slope and came up alongside Andrea. They were just two metres apart, the ice hissing beneath their skis, smiles plastered on their faces. They were back where they had started less than five minutes after leaving the restaurant.

Richard laughed out loud. 'What gave me the impression you couldn't ski well?'

Andrea looked at him in innocent surprise and said, 'I can't imagine.'

'Mmm. I think we'd better find a red slope.'

They had a late lunch and skied red slopes until just before sunset. It was then that Andrea announced she'd had enough for the day and that it was time to return to the hotel.

Richard decided to use the Steam Room for a while, to sweat out his aches and pains while Andrea said she was going for a doze.

They agreed to meet in the bar at eight o'clock.

*   *   *   *

Richard was down early and had already enjoyed a glass of white wine when Andrea arrived. She looked stunning. She had on a low-cut black dress that clung to her body and reached to below her knees and over that she was wearing a cream coloured, single breasted, short coat.

Richard managed a somewhat crooked smile and after a few seconds said, 'You look ravishing.'

Andrea smiled back and said, 'Why, thank you, kind sir.'

'A drink?'

'White wine please. A Swiss Fendant.'

The dinner that evening was a sumptuous buffet. The quality and the range of food were astonishing. They had reached the cheese and biscuits course of the meal when Andrea, looking sheepish said, 'I have a confession to make.'

'That sounds ominous. Don't tell me you're married.'

Andrea shook her head. 'It's a lot worse than that,' she said, trying to bring some levity into what she was about to say. 'I told you I'm an accountant, which is true. However, I'm not in private practice. I work for the European Union Parliament. Can you forgive me?'

'What for? Telling me a white lie about your job?'

'No, silly. For doing the job I do.'

Richard burst out laughing, and then Andrea did the same.

'I'm glad I told you. I don't know why I didn't in the first place. I just get fed up with having political debates with people as soon as they find out what I do for a living.'

Richard shrugged and said, 'I have distinctly other interests for the next ten days.'

The music started as a gentle background sound which later in the evening became more raucous and livelier.

At midnight "a Merry Christmas" was exchanged with many other visitors and approximately an hour later Richard and Andrea became lovers.

12

Christmas day was a rehash of Christmas Eve.

They skied two red runs and ended up on the other side of the mountain, where they had lunch. It was there that Richard noticed the two men for the first time. He put it down to the fact that Andrea was an extremely attractive woman and men liked to look at her. He dismissed them from his mind.

Looking towards the east, Richard said, 'See the cloud building up? It's coming this way. Let's hit the slopes and get back to the hotel before it gets here.' He shivered. 'Brr, the temperature is falling.'

'OK! I'll race you,' Andrea said with a laugh, jumping up from the table and stepping across to her skis.

'Oi! That's not fair. I still have to pay,' Richard protested, gesturing to the girl who had served them. He stuffed a 50 francs note in her hand, told her to keep the change and hurried away. As he left the restaurant he dropped his glove. Bending to retrieve it, he was convinced one of the men had used his mobile to take a photograph of Andrea. Then he dismissed the notion as idiotic. He was placing his skis on the ground as Andrea started down the gentle slope towards the piste.

Richard pushed hard on his sticks and reached the edge of the piste, launching himself over without a pause. He glanced back. The two men he had noticed were in turn hurrying to get to their skis. It wasn't much, but Richard had been in a few difficult situations in his time. More accurately, in downright dangerous situations and alarm bells were now ringing in his head.

He had been slaloming left and right 30 degrees, following in Andrea's path, but now he bent his knees, tucked his sticks under his arms and aimed straight down the slope. The piste was relatively quiet as many people were either enjoying a long lunch, or were sleeping in their hotel.

He got within ten metres of Andrea and yelled, 'Head straight down!'

'What?' She looked back over her shoulder at him as he closed the gap and was now less than five metres over her shoulder.

'Andrea, now listen. This is deadly serious. We appear to have picked up a couple of men who are following us.'

'Who?' She instinctively looked back, swerved and came down in a tangle of skis and sticks.

Richard stopped next to her in a flurry of snow. 'Are you okay?'

'I think so.' She lay still for a moment and then tentatively climbed to her feet. Her right ski had sprung free, the safety lock working as intended. Stamping her left foot to make sure the ski was still firmly in place she bent and replaced the right one.

'What's this about being followed?' She looked up the slope but saw only a dozen or so skiers criss-crossing the slope.

'I may be wrong but I don't think I am. Let's get off this slope and back to the hotel.'

Andrea looked speculatively at Richard, nodded and then set off straight down the slope. They were neck and neck when Richard called out, 'I know it sounds ludicrous but I'm pretty certain they were interested in you.'

'Who?' The scepticism was evident in her voice. She couldn't help thinking, 'What do I really know about him? What's his game?'

'Andrea, there were two men watching you at the restaurant. When we left in the rush we did, they also ran for their skis.'

'It could be a coincidence.'

'It could be, but I don't think so. Look, is it possible they're journalists?'

Frowning, she asked, 'What makes you think that?'

'Well, you know. Being who you are and all that.'

'Who I am?' She couldn't keep the surprise out of her voice. 'I'm nobody as far as journalists are concerned. Hell, nobody knows me except my immediate superiors and my department. They, whoever they are, are more likely to be interested in you than me.'

Richard yelled, 'Not a dog's chance.' He grinned sheepishly, most of his features hidden beneath a scarf he'd wrapped around his chin and neck – the temperature was falling and the mist was rolling in by the minute, 'I'm probably wrong in that case. Maybe they decided to move quickly for the same reason as we did with this blasted mist rolling in.'

'Race you to the bottom,' Andrea called out with a laugh.

They dismissed the notion of being followed and concentrated on their skiing.

Richard won by a short head. 'I'll claim my reward later,' he grinned at her. 'How about one more circuit, before the weather gets too bad.'

'Okay by me.'

The gondola was virtually empty and they climbed on board. Looking down, as the cabin swung into the sky, Richard saw the two men arrive at the station. They bustled forward, skis in hand, for the next cabin.

Stepping closer to Andrea, Richard said in a low voice, not wishing to be heard by any of the other people there, 'Look, I know you'll think I'm crazy but I think those two men are interested in us for some reason. I've been wracking my brains for a reason they might be after me but I just don't see it.'

Andrea shrugged and said, 'I told you what I do. Who'd be interested in me?'

'What if,' Richard spoke slowly and pensively, 'they are trying to get some sort of dirt on you? Something they can hold over you for some reason?'

Andrea shook her head decisively. 'There are more affairs going on in that place than you can imagine. Those with families in Strasbourg wait until they get to Brussels and those with family in Brussels wait for Strasbourg. And that's people with husbands, wives and children. Me? I've already told you, I'm nobody. So it's a pointless exercise. No,' she shook her head decisively, 'there are far bigger fish to fry than little old me. People who could be blackmailed, for one. I couldn't be because I have nothing to hide.'

Richard sighed and nodded. What she had said made perfect sense. 'You're right. I must have imagined it.' He nodded out the right side of the cabin, 'The weather is closing in fast. We'll hit the slope and then it's back to the hotel where I'll think of things we can do to entertain ourselves.'

'Oh?' Arching an eyebrow she smiled, 'And what do you have in mind?'

Grinning in return, Richard said, 'You'll have to wait and see.'

They alighted at the station, put on their skis and headed down the slope. Looking back over his shoulder, Richard saw the next gondola arrive and the two men climb out. One of them pointed down the slope at him and Andrea.

Turning back to look down the slope, he yelled out, 'Come on, I'll race you,' and they both shot off down the slope.

A full-bodied massage each was followed by a doze, a swim and the use of the sauna. During that time, Richard saw nothing of the two men and he was beginning to think he had imagined it all.

For them, dinner was in the Jagerstube where they had cheese fondue, washed down with tea without milk or sugar. Afterwards, they enjoyed a bottle of white wine. After such an invigorating day on the slopes they went to bed early. This time it was to sleep.

On Boxing Day, after a lazy and leisurely breakfast, they sat with a cup of coffee next to the window leading to the terrace. It was snowing hard. They both had a brochure of the hotel showing its services and activities which were all designed for one thing – to ensure the guests were pampered.

'What do you fancy?' Richard asked.

'I'm definitely going to use the solarium as well as the spa and health club. You?'

'The fitness centre to kick-off with and then I'll take it from there. I need the exercise.'

'You must be joking,' Andrea said in mock horror.

Late morning they took their kit and went their separate ways. Once Richard got to the fitness centre he changed into shorts and t-shirt and went in to use the machines. He started with the running machine and kept up a steady pace for ten kilometres. He always found that when running it was a good time to think. The two men he'd seen on the slopes were niggling at him but he could make no sense of it. Andrea was right. Who on earth would be interested in either of them? Even so! He followed the run with a series of sit-ups, 20 at a time with a pause in between until he'd completed 100. The last 20 he did slowly, keeping the strain on his stomach muscles. Another 15 minutes lifting weights and he was done. He'd worked up a sweat and was feeling very satisfied with himself.

From there he went into the steam room where he found Andrea. They were alone. They sat side by side and after less than ten minutes they agreed they needed to go upstairs. They ended up in Andrea's room.

That evening, Richard wore a single breasted, cream coloured lounge suit, with an open-necked, maroon shirt. He went down to the bar where he ordered a whisky and soda. At that moment, Andrea joined him. She was wearing a floor length, blue, off-the-shoulder dress, low cut and the same jacket as the evening before.

'You look gorgeous,' Richard said.

'Thank you, very much.'

'Ah! Yes. I've been meaning to tell you that my cousin is coming here on the thirtieth.'

'Oh? Male of female?'

'Male.' Then he added hastily, 'You'll like him. He's a good laugh.'

Smiling, Andrea said, 'I'm sure I will.'

'I hope you don't mind. I mean, we'll see him on the slopes but we won't be spending much time with him.'

'Its okay, Richard, honestly.' She then put into words what they'd both been aware of since the start. 'This is a holiday. A holiday romance, if I can dignify this interlude with such a word. Come the fourth of the new year we'll be going our separate ways.'

Richard shrugged, slightly uncomfortable before he nodded. 'Yes. You're right.' He raised his glass, as did Andrea, and they clinked glasses. 'Let us eat, drink and be merry,' he stopped with the Ecclesiastes part of the quote, he didn't finish the Isaiah phrase – for tomorrow we die.

Richard and Andrea loitered over their dinner. They shared a fondue bourguignonne of tender sirloin steak and a selection of sauces that were delicious, eaten in an intimate atmosphere.

The music and the dancing were fun.

Just after midnight they were walking off the dance floor when Richard saw the two men sitting in a booth near the door. One of them was staring at Andrea and didn't appear to be taking any notice of him.

At that moment the music stopped and a short intermission was announced. They were only a few metres from the booth where the men sat. The man looking at Andrea said something in a foreign language and the other one glanced over his shoulder at them. He said something sharply to his companion who immediately looked away and began to fiddle with the glass of beer in front of him. Then the man picked up a shot glass, drank its contents in one and followed it with a swig of beer.

Richard had heard the voice but hadn't understood what was said. The language sounded Russian or something similar, eastern European, at any rate, and set off alarm bells ringing in his head.

Surely, he thought, they must be journalists. Even as he said it to himself, he knew it wasn't the case. There was something frightening about them. A deadness that made his skin crawl. It was also, he told himself, ludicrous imagination.

As they went up in the lift, Richard said, 'Let's use my room tonight.'

'Okay. Any reason?'

'No. Just for a change.'

'Richard,' Andrea tucked her arm through his, just as the lift arrived on their floor, 'one thing I love about you is the fact that you appear to be incapable of lying.' Then she added hastily, 'Not that I love you.'

'Oh, I can lie alright, that is, if I have to.'

'Well, I haven't formed that impression. So why are we using your room when lots of your stuff has found its way into mine.'

Richard sighed and then said, 'I don't know. Those two men we saw on the piste were down in the restaurant and I didn't like the way they were looking at you.' Then he added hastily, 'Not that you don't look beautiful, of course.'

'Too late,' she punched his upper arm playfully. 'Anyway, they could be staying here and so it wouldn't be unreasonable for them to be in the restaurant listening to the music.'

'I know. I've been telling myself the same thing. I just have this feeling. Idiotic, I know. But I can't help it.'

'In that case, if it'll help you to sleep better, we'll use your room. Let me get a few things first.'

They stopped at Andrea's room, she threw a few items into a plastic bag and they went along to Richard's room. Once there, he poured glasses of white wine.

'I know I'm sounding a bit melodramatic but let's be careful until my cousin gets here,' said Richard.

'Why? What can your cousin do?' Andrea was intrigued.

'Have you ever heard of TIFAT? The International Force Against Terrorism?'

'Of course. I think they're based in Scotland.'

'Correct, Rosyth to be precise. Nick's a Royal Naval diving specialist, handles all sorts of bombs and explosives.'

Frowning, Andrea said, 'What you used to do?'

'Correct but for me that was a few years ago now. He not only kept it up but he was persuaded to transfer to TIFAT. He's third in command. If anything is going on he'll sort it out.'

'You have a lot of faith in this cousin of yours,' Andrea smiled.

Richard took the statement seriously and said, 'Yes, I do. He's one of the toughest people I know. Yet,' he hesitated, and then added, 'he has a considerate streak in him. He can be very kind.'

'You make him sound like . . . like some sort of saint.'

Richard burst out laughing and then replied, 'Hell no. He has a nose for trouble, or a penchant for it, I should say. He's always in one scrape after another.' Richard was silent for a few seconds before asking, 'What's your job?'

'What do you mean?' Andrea took a sip of wine.

'You told me you work in the European Union Parliament and that you're an accountant and we left it there. So what exactly do you do? I know you said you didn't want to talk politics so if you tell me to mind my own business. I won't mind.'

'It's not exactly politics. I don't mind telling you. My title is Accounting Officer and Budget Execution Director.' Seeing the blank look on Richard's face she went on to explain. 'I run the department responsible for auditing the finances of the Parliament.'

'It sounds like a big job.'

'I suppose it is at one level. However, the EU dream has turned into a nightmare. The vast majority of Europeans are beginning to have a very poor opinion about the place. People are beginning to wake up to the fact that it costs a vast sum of money to run with little or no benefit. It is an organisation built on sand.' She paused and then added, 'Corruption is endemic on a scale that is unimaginable.'

'I know things are pretty dire, but you paint a gloomy picture.'

Andrea sighed and said, 'It is.' She leant forward and placed her glass on the table in front of her. 'Actually, do you mind if we do talk about it? I know it's a bore but there are things happening that need

146

sorting out and I don't know what to do. Maybe talking to you will help me to decide.'

'Sure, I don't mind.'

Andrea lifted her glass and took another sip of wine before replacing it on the table. 'I've got to the stage when all I can do is go public with my findings and damn the consequences.'

Richard snapped the fingers of his right hand and stuck out his index finger. 'Sorry, I didn't mean to be rude. But the man who had the job before you, a Dutchman? Poul somebody or other?'

Andrea nodded. 'Poul Zimmermann.'

'He was killed wasn't he?'

Nodding, Andrea said, 'A hit and run involving a white van. Whoever did it was never caught.'

Richard frowned and asked, 'Wasn't there some sort of scandal involving the man?'

'Yes. Photographs were found that showed he had a mistress, that he was spending a great deal of money on her and that he was embezzling from the Commission.'

'I remember now. Wasn't there a huge fuss that it was all a set up?'

'Correct, well remembered.'

'I was on a tug dragging an oil rig across the Atlantic. Listening to the news and downloading newspaper articles was about all the entertainment I had for a couple of weeks.'

'I think he was murdered and the information given to his family was fabricated. His wife didn't believe any of it and she began to make a great deal of noise about the whole affair. So what happened? She was given a very substantial pension and the problem ceased to exist.'

'How can you be sure he was murdered?'

'I can't be sure but its little things that suggest it. It's the way the whole affair was handled. It's the corruption that's going on all the time as shown in the accounts I'm trying to audit.'

'Look, if what you say is true,' then he added hastily, 'and I believe you, shouldn't you just quit? You could well be in danger if those two men are any part of it.'

Andrea looked uncomfortable and then said, 'You could be right. I just didn't want to believe it.' She shivered. 'I'm suddenly quite scared.' She lifted her glass and took a gulp of wine.

'Good. That's the right reaction. People who say they're not scared are lying to themselves and to those around them which makes them a liability.'

'What should I do? Go to the police?'

'The Swiss police?'

Andrea nodded.

'And tell them what? That you think two men want to harm you? Want to kill you? How ludicrous does that sound?'

Slowly she nodded. 'I take your point. Maybe I should just return home.'

'Then what? I don't want to read in the newspapers or hear it on a news broadcast that the Accounting Officer and whatever the rest of your title is, was killed in a hit and run accident, or was shot, or knifed.'

'So what should we do?'

Richard liked the fact that she had changed from I to we. 'Be careful, until Nick gets here. We can tell him what's happening and if anyone can take care of things, he can.'

'Man and superman?' She raised her eyebrows.

Richard said, 'Something like that. Now, tell me stories about what's going on in this den of iniquity known as the European Union Parliament.'

'Alright. Did you read the *Daily Telegraph* article published earlier this year?'

'About what?'

'The heading was the Scandal the European Parliament tried to keep secret.'

'No. If I did, I don't remember it.'

'One of the jobs we managed to do as internal auditors was to find huge breaches in the control of payments made by the vast majority of the EU's officials. Did you know there are over seven thousand of them?'

Richard looked suitably surprise. 'That many?'

Andrea nodded. 'What we found was that staff who claimed expenses, which is just about all of them, are the same people who authorise the payments. We discovered that officials were being paid twice or even three times for the same expenditure a lot of which they weren't entitled to in the first place. Then it gets worse.'

'Worse? How on earth can it get worse? If that was happening in a company heads would roll.'

'It gets worse because the audits have been kept secret from MEPs. Only fourteen senior MEPs who constitute something they call the Bureau have seen the reports. And they've had to sign a confidentiality agreement stopping them from disclosing what they contain.'

'Surely they have an obligation to make public what they know.'

'Of course they do. I have already told members of the Bureau precisely that and, in a nutshell, they're frightened.'

'Of what?'

'The fraud is so wide and deep, MEPs see themselves being dropped by their parties and that is something they do not want. They are currently riding the richest, most generous gravy train that has ever existed, which is saying something.'

Richard nodded. 'I take your point. Do you want some more wine?'

'Please.' She held out her glass, Richard poured the wine and then topped up his own glass. 'There's an anti-fraud department within the parliament called OLAF which stands for the Office de Lutte Anti-Fraude. They released a statement recently saying that the disclosure of any fraud to the public would disrupt decision making.'

'That's absurd. Something should be done.'

'That's just about impossible. I'm sure there's some small group of people at the top but who they are and what actual jobs they have I've no idea. But I intend finding out,' she said with spirit.

'Be careful, you can't just go wading in. You've no idea what you might find.'

'It's my responsibility.'

'No. That's where you're wrong. If it's as bad as you say it is then it's everybody's responsibility. The EU ideal looks good on paper but something, we agree, has gone badly wrong. Just think of the mess we could be leaving behind for future generations. I agree something needs to be done, but it will take more than one person, that's for sure.'

'You can't possibly know but I've found irregularities totalling over five hundred million euros.'

'Over how long? Ten years?' Richard was astonished at the amount.

Andrea was silent for a few seconds, rolling the stem of her almost empty wine glass between her fingers, and then shook her head. 'No, in the last twelve months.'

Richard was lost for words. The sum was staggering, beyond imagination.

'There is no audit trail for many of the contracts awarded to different companies and what's more, many of those companies have family members and friends working in the Parliament.'

'But surely there are others who can help you to do something? To sort out the mess?'

'Of course there must be, but who? I've spoken to senior staff in my department, staff in departments responsible for procuring everything from paperclips to new computer systems and either the people I spoke to didn't want to know because they're part of the whole thing or they're scared of the consequences. You know, I've trawled through the audit reports going back almost twenty years. Not one set of accounts has been signed off due to the level of fraud uncovered. If the total is added up the sum is enormous. And remember, that's just what I can identify. In my estimation, I'm looking at maybe twenty percent of the total. If so the figures become truly frightening.'

'I think you have an impossible, and possibly dangerous task,' Richard concluded.

14

Peter Waterfield hated Christmas. All the ludicrous fanfare, the enormous waste of money, the over indulgence, the myth about a man born 2,000 years earlier and the utter nonsense the festival had become thanks to a jolly fat man who lived at the north pole and gave presents to the children of the world. It left him feeling utter contempt for all those who indulged.

He also wasn't keen on the cold and so he had flown to Bermuda where the skies were blue and the temperature hovered around 18°C. He was alone, which was also what he liked. He was in the middle of negotiating his divorce but his wife was proving obdurate. He was beginning to contemplate the use of one of the enforcement teams. Only in her case there wouldn't be any of the usual warning of a second chance such as the one given to others who stepped out of line.

His hotel was the luxurious Fairmont Southampton, where he had taken a suite on the top floor. It was large and anonymous, just the way he liked it. He'd been going there off and on for a few years, usually whenever he was between marriages. As a result, he had developed a working arrangement with one of the doormen. For a reasonable price the doorman ensured suitable night time companionship. No drinks, no dinner, no overnight companions, just 30 minutes or so. Always the girls had a couple of things in common. None were above the age of 18 and they were all well endowed.

He had seen a photograph of the girl who would be joining him later and he was looking forward to the encounter. He was standing on the balcony to his room, a rum and coke in his hands, thinking about going down for dinner when his mobile beeped. It was a text and read, *The woman has company. The man's name is Richard Griffiths. He is a businessman from London. They have separate rooms. Is collateral damage acceptable?*

Waterfield sent back a one word answer, *Yes.*

He went across to the mini-bar and refreshed his glass. It was just after midnight in Switzerland. Andrea Nelson would soon no longer be a nuisance. He decided to refresh his drink again before he went downstairs, in celebration of another problem removed.

The reports that were coming in over the holiday were most encouraging – most encouraging indeed. With luck, within say, two years, agreement would be reached for the European Military Force. It was mind blowing what that could mean. No, he corrected himself, what it would mean. The amount of wealth created so far was as nothing compared to what would happen when huge military hardware contracts were being placed.

He had to admit to himself that he understood something of the way dictators in third world countries acted. The wealth and hence the power generated was awesome. He drained his glass and then sent a text. It was brief. *Via Condotti, Rome. No later than 4 Jan.* Within 60 seconds he had a one word acknowledgement, *OK.*

He went downstairs to the large, outdoor restaurant. There were two men at the bar with whom he'd become friendly, playing golf and drinking late into the evening. He joined them. After a drink they headed over to the BBQ. Just about everything that could be barbecued was on offer, from red meat to fancy fish. The food was unlimited, with superb side dishes and salads. With vintage wines to drink, it was, he thought, a perfect evening.

*   *   *   *

Switzerland was an oddity as far as the enforcement teams were concerned. Not being a part of the European Union meant there was rarely any requirement to operate in that country. Hence jobs were sub-contracted to other teams, depending on who was available. This operation had been given to MacGregor. He was responsible for the whole job. There were no instructions. There never were. He had been told what to do and the time factor.

The men he was using in Switzerland were relatively new and after he had been told about the presence of Richard Griffiths, MacGregor decided he would have a more hands-on role than usual. Besides, he rather fancied the idea of a few days skiing. It had been a couple of years since he'd last indulged. He thought about taking his Christmas companion but changed his mind. He wanted to ensure there were no distractions until after the job was done. The text he'd received made things easier. Trying to avoid collateral damage was such a damned nuisance.

He decided to drive and stop off in Liechtenstein en-route. He began to make a mental list of the gear he would need.

He sent a text to Switzerland. *Keep watch. Will arrive in 24 hrs.*

In reply he had a one word acknowledgement, *Right.*

* * * *

'Boss?' Peabody said into his mobile, 'MacGregor is going to Europe.'

'Do we know where?'

'We have recordings of him booking a place on the Eurostar for himself plus car. That's all. There's been no mention of where exactly he's going.'

'If you need me you know where I'll be. As soon as you know where he's going, get back to me.'

'Have you hired a car?'

'Yes. A Nissan X-trail, from Europcar. We're also booked onto the same train as MacGregor. The 08.00.'

'What about bugs?'

'We've planted a tracker under the rear but that's all. If we can, we'll get a bug inside the car.'

'Only try to do so if there are no risks. I don't want him to know we're interested in him.'

'That's what we figured. Hang on. He's using his phone in his flat. Listen in, boss.'

Peabody pressed buttons and what MacGregor was saying came loud and clear over Hunter's phone. He was talking to somebody who he was expecting to meet the following day. The conversation was one sided but it was sufficient for Hunter and the other two to learn that MacGregor was going to Grindelwald and was booked into the Hotel Eiger.

When MacGregor hung up, Peabody said, 'Aren't you going to Grindelwald, boss?'

'Yes. I guess it's one of those quirks of fate. I'm staying at the Grand Hotel Regina, not the Eiger.'

'Enjoy the après ski.'

'I'll do my best.'

The connection was broken. He was walking alongside the River Endrick, at the bottom of the hill from his parents' house. His father was with him, the dog, a golden Labrador named Winston, was sniffing the ground nearby, his tail going like an out of synch metronome.

'Work?'

'Yes Dad. Curiously enough, it's something going on in Switzerland, in Grindelwald, to be precise.'

'Coincidences do happen.'

Hunter smiled. 'They do and a lot more often than people think.'

15

It was just before midnight when Richard telephoned his cousin.

'Nick?'

'Hi, Richard. It's a bit late, what's up?'

'Something most peculiar. Have you got five minutes?'

'Sure.'

Richard brought Hunter up to speed. His cousin barely said a word until Richard finished his narrative.

'Listen, Richard, something is going on and you've obviously ended up right in the middle of it. You need to be very careful.

'Why? What's it all about?'

'You're right about something. The two men who are watching you I'm pretty certain are after the woman.'

'Andrea? Do you know why?'

'We think it's to do with her job and what's happening in the European Union right now.'

'That's more or less what I figured. Andrea's been telling me some of what's going on. Even if she's half right the corruption is staggering.'

'Yeah. Well, it's even worse than you think. Look, it'll have to wait until I get there which will be around midday. You know Jan Badonovitch, don't you?'

'Sure. He's one of your guys. I met him at some do or other.'

'He's on his way to Grindelwald. He left this morning on Eurostar.

He's got another one of my guys with him, name of Phileas Peabody. He's a SEAL.'

'Those pair are heavy duty.'

'In the meantime, I'll phone Jan and tell him what's going on. There's another man coming your way who we are certain is the boss. I'll send you a photograph. It'll be with you in a minute. Richard, let me emphasise something. Be very careful. Stay in your room if you can until we get back to you. Got that?'

'Sure, Nick. You know me.'

'Precisely. That's why I'm telling you to be very careful.'

The connection was broken and then a few seconds later a head and shoulders photograph of MacGregor appeared.

Andrea was looking over his shoulder and asked, 'Who's that? And what did your cousin say?'

'This is a bad guy and Nick said to be very careful.' Richard told her what Hunter had said.

'So what shall we do?'

'We stay here tomorrow until Nick or the others arrive.'

'Shouldn't we go to the police?'

Shaking his head, Richard said, 'To tell them what? Nothing's changed, Andrea. Not a thing. When Nick and his team get here we hand it all over to them while in the meantime, we do as Nick says and keep our heads down.'

Andrea suddenly looked at the door. 'Shshsh. What's that?'

Richard looked towards the door, his heart suddenly pounding in his ears. He stood up and walked across the room and put his head to the door, signalling Andrea to stay still. He listened for a minute or more. 'There's nothing.'

'Sorry. I thought I heard something. It must be my nerves.'

Richard conjured up a smile from somewhere. 'It's okay to be scared. If you're not, you're more likely to get yourself killed.' He looked around the room.

'Right. If these guys have done their homework, they'll have a good idea where the bed is, yes?'

Andrea shrugged. 'If you say so.'

'I do. Now, we'll use the cushions from the armchair over there, and my suitcase and clothes, and make it look like there are a couple of people under the duvet.'

'Is that really necessary?'

'Yes. You can't be too careful.'

'But if someone breaks in they'll know pretty damned quick there are no bodies in the bed.'

'Of course they will. By which time I hope they'll be too late.'

'Why? What are you going to do?'

'I am going to spend the night in that armchair,' he pointed across the room, 'placed behind the door here. To be able to point a gun at the bed, the shooter must step at least one, if not two, paces into the room. The Champagne bottle should take him down.'

'And the second man?'

'I'll deal with him if the need arises. He could be along the corridor keeping a watch. He could be behind the first gunman. He could be anywhere. Hell, they might even be so arrogant only one of them comes here.'

'Where shall I sit?'

'You'll sleep on the couch. We'll make a bed up for you. Come on. Give me a hand.'

'Richard, that's no good! You can't stay awake all night! I need to keep watch for some of the night.'

'Don't worry. I can stay awake. I've often done so in the past.'

'No! I insist!'

'Listen, Andrea. Have you ever brained somebody with a bottle?'

'No, of course not. That's a stupid question,' she spoke irritably.

'Maybe it is, but I have and it's not a pretty sight. There'll be blood and brains all over the shop if it's done properly. If you don't hit him hard enough, the man will shoot you and it'll be your guts and gore covering the walls.'

'What's your point?'

'The military tries to teach us to act fast and furious. Even so, if people hesitate, or do it wrongly, or are suddenly afraid of the consequences they screw it up. That can get you killed.'

Richard fell silent and watched as Andrea acknowledged to herself what he had said. Slowly, she nodded.

'Good. Let's sort things out and settle down for the night.'

It didn't take long. Andrea made up a bed for herself on the couch, while Richard created two humps under the duvet, which, he hoped, would fool an attacker for the first couple of vital seconds. Next, he dragged an easy chair to the wall besides the door and also brought across a footstool.

He sat down and placed the bottle on his right side, next to the chair. He watched as Andrea settled down on the settee and asked, 'Are you comfortable enough?'

'Yes thanks. You?'

They were speaking in whispers.

'Yes,' he lied. 'Now go to sleep.'

'I can't sleep,' she replied, wriggling to make herself more comfortable.

Andrea fell asleep about an hour later. Richard spent a long and uncomfortable night. In an effort not to doze off, he paced the room every 30 minutes or so. At some point he became aware that the hotel was awake, that the staff were busy. It meant the gunmen, if that was what they were, wouldn't be coming. He went across to the bed, pulled the pillows away that made one of the humps, crawled onto the bed and was asleep in seconds.

Andrea woke him with the question, 'Do you want any breakfast?' She held the menu out to him.

*   *   *   *

Badonovitch and Peabody had followed MacGregor without any difficulties. He was driving a Volvo Estate at a sensible speed of just over 130kph. Much to their surprise, he had driven most of the day. The tracker meant that they could stay well back, out of sight. In the middle of the afternoon, at Mannheim, MacGregor pulled into the forecourt of one of the huge service stations where he filled the tank with diesel.

When he went to pay at the kiosk, he didn't bother locking the car. Badonovitch had stopped one aisle across and three pumps back. Dusk was already falling, encouraged by the light rain that was threatening to turn to snow. There were no other cars either ahead or behind, although the other pumps further across were in use.

The Spetsnaz said, 'I'll bug the car, you fill up with diesel. You'll see a button so that you can pay at the kiosk or at the pump.'

'OK.' Peabody climbed down, pressed buttons and started pumping diesel.

Badonovitch looked around but nobody was taking the blindest bit of notice of them. He stepped across to the Volvo, whipped open the door behind the driver's seat and placed a bug low down on the side of the seat. He closed the door, stepped forward, looked towards the buildings and saw that MacGregor was not in sight and opened the driver's door. He stuck a second bug on the side of the dashboard, virtually invisible unless you were looking for it.

He strolled back to the Nissan. Peabody was still using the pump and looking over Badonovitch's shoulder towards the door to the station. 'Here he comes.'

Badonovitch stood with his back to MacGregor, blocking Peabody off from him. A minute or two later, Peabody said, 'That's him on his way.'

'Good. Let's get some coffee, something to eat and pump bilges.'

About fifteen minutes later they were on their way. The other car was 18 miles ahead and going steadily down the autobahn. Badonovitch was driving and he increased speed to slowly but steadily catch up with their target. An hour later, they were less than a kilometre behind and the rain was turning to snow when they heard the phone in the other car ring.

*   *   *   *

Hunter caught an easyJet flight from Edinburgh to Zurich, departing at 12.15, due to arrive 15.25. Although he was travelling light, with ski clothes and evening wear, he still checked his luggage through. It meant he didn't have to carry his stripped down Glock through security. Even with the necessary permits to carry a weapon in Europe, it still didn't allow him to take one onto a plane.

Sitting in departures, he phoned Richard.

'You okay?' Hunter asked.

'Sure, it's hardly roughing it. Room service is excellent.'

'Good. Listen, Richard. It's easy to convince yourself that every-thing is alright. That you've read the signs wrong. That there is nothing to worry about. That it is safe to go for a walk. To use the swimming pool or the sauna, and so on.'

'It's okay Nick. I hear you. We won't move.'

'Good. I'm not lecturing you. I'm just reminding you of some of the stuff you learnt in the past.'

'I appreciate that.'

*   *   *   *

'Mother,' said Maud Phillips in exasperation, 'I've told you, we are not going out in this weather.'

'But I want some fresh air,' the old woman whined, using a tone she knew only too well irritated her daughter.

It was just coming up to four o'clock in the afternoon and Maud was fed up to her back teeth. Her mother was 76 years old and acted as though she was 96. She had imaginary illnesses for which she took enough pills to stock a chemist's shop, or so Maud told herself. Christmas had been the usual boring ritual, they had exchanged a gift each, ate an indifferent meal of turkey, bought prepared and pre-packaged from a local supermarket and watched the usual rubbish on television.

Now the new year loomed and Maud couldn't wait to return to work. Her mother said something else which Maud ignored. When her mother repeated what she had to say, Maud came down to earth with a bump, looked at the old woman with annoyance bordering on dislike and then got to her feet.

'I have to go to work,' Maud announced.

Her mother looked aghast. 'But . . . But that's ludicrous. It's too late in the day. It's the holidays. You can't go.'

'I can and I will. There are a number of things I must do before Andrea gets back and this evening is an ideal time. It will be quiet and I won't be disturbed.'

Her mother looked at her daughter with dislike. 'It's a man more like. Go on, enjoy yourself. Leave me on my own. You don't care. You never have.'

Maud had heard it all a thousand times but this time something snapped. She got to her feet, her hands on her hips and looked down at her mother. 'Don't you dare speak to me like that. I've devoted my life to you. The only man I ever loved and who loved me you drove away. You have made my life a misery and I didn't have the courage to stand up to you. Now I will spend my life a lonely spinster with only you for company until you die. After that I shall be alone.'

'Typical, you think of no one else but yourself.'

Maud was about to say more but instead she turned away, too tired to argue. She was honest with herself and always had been. She recognised the fact that her mother had effectively destroyed her life. Thanks to her ability with languages – she spoke fluent German, French, Italian and Spanish, she had landed the job in the European Parliament. The salary was excellent and her pension would be more than enough for her needs when she retired. For decades their holidays were always to the same small hotel in St Ives, Cornwall, at her mother's insistence. She made a vow to herself. When she retired, whether her mother was dead or alive, she intended travelling. She would spend her time visiting countries she had only read about. It was a tantalising dream that dangled before her – and retirement was only three years away.

In the hallway, she put on her coat. Even as she did so, her heart sank. She would never leave until her mother died.

The EU building in which she worked was only 20 minutes away by taxi. It was nearly half-past four when she arrived and signed herself in. The greeting at the door was one of disinterest to which she responded with a smile and a hearty "good afternoon".

The taxi ride had managed to put the anger she felt towards her mother into some form of perspective and she headed for the lift in a better frame of mind. She was actually looking forward to working on the file she and Andrea were compiling. Its objective and the results they could achieve with it gave her focus in an otherwise hum-drum existence.

The lift came to a halt and she walked along to the offices. The main office was empty, as she'd expected. She crossed the room, saw that the door to her office was ajar and heard noises coming from within. Frowning, she reached the door and pushed it fully open.

Two men were inside. Both were strangers. One was sitting at her desk, operating her computer, the other had a filing cabinet drawer open and was rifling through the files.

'What's going on? What do you think you are doing?'

* * * *

The plane landed with a heavy bump and taxied across to the hard standing. The passengers trooped off and hurried across to enter the airport building, collars turned up against the snow that was now falling in heavy flakes. It was a long wait, but Hunter finally collected his gear and walked straight past customs and into the arrivals hall. He identified the car hire desk and went across to sign for the pre-booked Mercedes M-Class.

Once the paperwork was completed, he was directed to the car park and wound his way through the packed hall of people arriving to start their holidays. He saw the sign for the toilets and headed for them. Once inside a cubicle, he sat on the seat, opened his bag and reassembled his automatic. He quit the place and went out to the car park. Ten minutes later, he was inching the car out through the gates, the windscreen wipers going at full speed, just about holding their own against the snow. He'd programmed in the GPS and followed the instructions given by the gentle voice of an unknown woman.

According to the satnav the distance to Grindelwald was 94 miles or 151.25 kilometres. He checked the time, 16.40 precisely. That was when his mobile rang.

'Yes, Jan?'

'Boss, we got a couple of bugs inside MacGregor's car.'

'Excellent.'

'He took a phone call about an hour ago just after we left the services at Mannheim. He spoke to somebody in Switzerland. He was on speaker so we heard both sides. MacGregor asked if the woman was alone or still with the man. The answer was, still with the man. MacGregor said something like that was his bad luck and told the guy to do nothing before he got there. He was asked when that would be and MacGregor said he was going to Vaduz but would be in Grindelwald tonight.'

'Did he say why he was going to Vaduz?'

'Not really. He just said something about picking up some tools.'

'Mmm. Guns?'

'I guess so. How far away are you?'

'According to the satnav just over sixty-seven miles. What's the weather like?'

'Snowing but not bad. The roads are clear.'

'It's snowing pretty heavily here, but the Swiss are keeping the roads clear in their usual efficient fashion. I've just passed the turn-off for Lausanne which leaves me about seventy miles to go. At this rate

I'll be another two hours.' Even as he spoke a line of red tail lights appeared ahead and orange flashing warning lights came on. 'Damn. We've just come to a halt. The traffic is solid. Must have been some sort of accident.' The snow parted for a few seconds and he added, 'The lights are stretching quite a distance. So, revise my ETA. I've no idea when I'll get there. One last thing. I take it no names were mentioned?'

'Nothing.'

'Okay. I'll speak to you later.' The connection was broken. Hunter sat tapping his fingers on the steering wheel, impatient to get moving. After a few minutes he phoned his cousin.

'Richard?'

'Hi, Nick. Where are you?'

'Stuck in a traffic jam just outside Lausanne. We're beginning to move forward though it's slow. Right now I've no idea when I'll get there. We've planted bugs in MacGregor's car.' He brought his cousin up to date on what had been heard.

'So you reckon it's safe to go out?'

'Yeah. With the bugs in the car, we'll know about it if he intends to send them in. The cars are picking up speed. I'll call you later.'

The cars crawled up to 40 kph. Blue flashing lights came into view. Three cars had been involved in a pile-up. An ambulance had arrived along with four police cars. A quick glance was all he allowed himself. He knew that too many people had accidents when gawking at a car crash. Once he was past he accelerated, crossed over to the left hand lane and stayed there.

*   *   *   *

The man at the computer looked up at Maud in surprise while the other man reached into his pocket and took out his wallet.

Holding it out he approached Maud and said in French, 'As you can see, Mademoiselle Phillips, I am a police officer. My name is Inspector Henri Matteus. This is Sergeant Georges Tolbert. We are here officially. I have a search warrant which I can show you.'

Maud looked at the ID card and nodded nervously. Like most people who had never seen a police identity card the man could have been waving a child's plaything for all she knew. However, she nodded. 'Let me see your warrant.'

The inspector turned to the other man and said, 'Sergeant, please show Mademoiselle Phillips the warrant.'

The man at the computer didn't move. The inspector did. He sidled past Maud while her attention was on the other man. He clamped a hand over Maud's mouth and nose and hung on with all his strength as she struggled to break loose. It didn't take long. Her struggling ceased and she died, suffocated, in his arms.

'What will we do now?' asked Tolbert.

'We get rid of the body,' was the gasped reply.

'How?'

'How the hell do I know? Let me think.' He paused and then said, 'Down in the car park, next to the mailroom, I noticed the mail trolleys. I'll go and take a look and see if we can use one.' The mail was delivered to a room in the car park where it was sorted and then distributed, floor by floor.

'What then?'

Tolbert looked at the other man, anger welling up in him. He got his temper under control and said, 'We take it one step at a time.'

'When do we leave? As soon as you get back?' Tolbert licked his lips. Searching the offices had been one thing – murder something else entirely.

Matteus noticed the other man's nervousness and said, 'Don't worry, Georges. I'll make sure the woman compensates us handsomely for this. Trust me.'

The sergeant nodded, some of his fear being replaced by the prospect of more money.

'Nobody knows we're here and the security guards never do any rounds seeing as there's no requirement.' The two men had entered via the basement car park, using a pass key and entry code. When they'd arrived there hadn't even been a car down there. 'Give me a hand and we'll shove the old cow's body under the desk.'

Between them they stuffed Maud behind the desk, her body hidden by the front panel.

'Keep copying those files.' Matteus went quickly to the lift which was on their floor. The door opened immediately. He stepped in, used the key card and pressed the button for the basement. The lift dropped smoothly. The door opened and he paused. There still wasn't a car to be seen which was what he'd expected.

The trolleys were lined up outside the mailroom. They were two metres square and the same in height, surrounded by a blue canvas screen. An examination of the nearest trolley showed it was lined with baskets held in place with immovable aluminium rods. The second was the same and so was the third. He was beginning to panic when behind the fourth trolley he found an open trolley used for moving larger items. This one was the same size as the others but without sides. He grabbed it and was about to return to the lift when he paused. Pushing an open trolley with a dead body on it was a very bad idea.

He stepped to one of the trolleys with the canvas screen. It was held in place by elasticised cord with hooks on the end. He removed the hooks and took down the canvas. He folded it, dumped it on the trolley along with the cord and practically ran back to the lift. He arrived at the eighth floor and hurried across the open office.

'This is all I could find. We'll hide the body under the canvas. Give me a hand.'

As they dragged Maud's body out from under the desk and dumped her on the trolley, Tolbert said, 'What happens if we are seen?'

Matteus was arranging the canvas screen over the body and looked up. 'Show them our badges, tell them that we are on official business and ask to be excused. Have you got a better idea?'

'No.'

'Right. Give me a hand.'

When they had finished, Matteus stood up and looked closely at the trolley. Maud's body was completely hidden.

'Have you finished copying the files?'

'No. It'll probably take as much as another half-an-hour.'

'Leave it. I'm not staying a minute longer. Let's get going. Get your stuff together.'

In minutes they were back in the lift and heading down. The doors opened and a quick glance showed the car park was still empty.

Their car was right next to the lift and Matteus zapped it unlocked. They opened the boot and transferred Maud's body inside. Matteus returned the trolley to the mail office. He drove the car to the exit, entered the four digit pin, the barrier lifted and he drove out.

'Where are we going?'

'Antwerp. We'll take her handbag and dump the body in a backstreet. With no ID it'll be a while before she's identified.'

'If you say so.' There was no mistaking the fear in the other man's voice. Matteus didn't blame him. He was equally terrified.

* * * *

Richard and Andrea put on their ski jackets and woollen hats. They went down the back stairs, pausing at the door to the rear car park.

'I feel like a school kid sneaking out,' said Andrea.

'Yeah. Except we'd receive more than a caning if caught.'

As they stepped out into the bitter cold and heavy snow, Andrea said in mock horror, 'There was caning at your school? Mind you, I suppose it does explain a lot.'

Chuckling, Richard replied, 'Hardly. The worse thing that happened was an hour's detention reading some mind-improving book. Dickens or Trollope. Or something equally overrated.'

'Overrated? Such classic writers?'

'Who says they're classic writers?'

As they walked through the snow, arm in arm, they saw very few people out in the appalling weather. However, a couple of hundred metres from their hotel was a bar and restaurant which they discovered was three-quarters full with 80 or 90 people. At the back of the room they found an empty booth for four and sat there. The menu was extensive, the wines tempting – which they both decided to refrain from and settled for fresh orange juice instead.

They ordered French onion soup which, they agreed, was excellent. As they ate, Richard, wanting to take Andrea's mind off their predicament said, 'Tell me more about the corruption in the EU. Isn't it the sort of stuff we should be screaming blue murder about?'

Andrea nodded. 'Of course it is. I've thought time and again, if directors or employees of companies behaved in the same way they would be arrested and in prison. I've spent weeks going over past accounts. My secretary, Maud Phillips, has been a great help. We still have more to do but I think in the next couple of months I'll be able to go public with what we've got and force the authorities to acknowledge what's going on which in turn will force them to act.' She smiled. 'Maud has been a tower of strength throughout.' Andrea spent the remainder of the meal regaling Richard with stories of what she had discovered was happening within the EU Parliament.

A waitress arrived and cleared away the dishes. She returned with steak au poivre for Richard and pork tenderloin with fresh cranberry and orange glaze for Andrea. They shared a dish of vegetables.

'How's your meal?' Richard asked.

'Delicious. Yours?'

'Like only the Swiss can cook.'

'I wouldn't go that far. And you'd better not say so in the hearing of a Frenchman.'

They chatted some more and as the conversation dried up, Richard said, 'Tell me more about the goings on at the EU.'

'Did you know that MEPs are paid a daily attendance allowance? They go to the parliament building, sign a register as attending an official meeting and get paid a further three hundred plus euros. Some of them then go home. Not all and not all the time, but often enough so that prosecutions should be implemented.' Shaking her head, 'It's quite unbelievable.'

As they finished their meal in gloomy silence Richard's phone rang. 'Nick?'

'I'm in Thun. I'm twenty odd miles or so away. It's snowing pretty heavily but the roads are still passable. What's it like up there?'

'Snowing and building up. I don't know if the road is open. Want me to go and take a look?'

'Yes please. I'll head for Interlaken. I'll stay there if I have to.'

'I'll phone you back.'

'I'm just going to take a look at the road. Nick is in Thun.'

Andrea looked panicked and said, 'I'll come with you.'

Richard nodded. 'Let's get the bill.' As he stood up, he slipped the steak knife into his sleeve. It wasn't much, but it was as sharp as a razor. After paying, they went outside. It was still snowing heavily and there were no vehicles moving. The road was already covered with about half a metre of snow. While they stood there, they could see down the mountain the orange flashing lights of a snow plough gradually approaching them.

Richard took out his mobile and speed dialled Hunter.

'Nick? There's a snow plough coming up the mountain so I reckon the road is passable for now.'

'I'll give it a try. Got to go. That's Jan trying to get hold of me.'

15

'Nick, we're still in Liechtenstein. He's bedded down for the night in a hotel called Oberland.'

'What are you going to do?'

'We're booked into the Hotel Kulm. We'll sleep in shifts. If he moves we'll know straight away.'

'What about the weather?'

'Snowing like hell. What about your end?'

'Same here. I've just passed a place called Spiez. The road's passable but getting worse by the minute. I'll see you when I see you.'

The motorway ended and became an ordinary road. The snow now a blizzard and Hunter was driving slowly, his eyes straining against the virtual whiteout in front of him. There were no other cars on the road. The road became a motorway again and after only a couple of kilometres he reached the turn-off signposted for Wengen and Grindelwald. He'd just passed Wilderswil and it looked to him like he was going to make it. The car crept steadily along, the kilometres ticking away. The road was deep in snow but the 4x4 Mercedes took it in its stride. Then he reached the T junction. Right was Wengen but he turned left for Grindelwald. The road was getting steeper as he approached Burglauenen when he saw flashing hazard lights and was forced to slow down. He approached them slowly. A lorry was halfway across the road. There were no people to be seen. He stopped, put the car into park and reached for his ski jacket.

He wriggled into it and climbed out of the Mercedes. The wind had dropped but the snow seemed heavier than ever. Before approaching whatever was going on, he took his Glock out from his waist and slipped it into his jacket pocket. He jammed a woollen hat over his head and pulled it down over his ears. Placing his hand back into his pocket he gripped the gun. He was sure he was being over cautious but heroes died stupidly.

He reached the lorry and saw there was a car on the other side and that the two vehicles had collided.

He went around the front of the lorry and took a closer look at the car. It was half under the front of the other vehicle. From the tracks still discernible in the snow he could see that the car had slid down the hill, slewed sideways and hit the passenger's side of the lorry. The lorry had been forced around and was now virtually at right angles to the road. With the car sticking out, the road was impassable.

'Anyone here?' Hunter called. He was met with silence. He called out again and was greeted by the same silence. The car was a French Peugeot 207 and looking inside he saw that the airbags had been deployed. He speed dialled his cousin.

'Richard? There's been a bit of an accident and a car and lorry are blocking the road. There's nobody here and I can't see a way past. Is the snow plough on its way back down? It may be able to help.'

'It doesn't look like it. The driver parked up about ten minutes ago and I can't see him. Maybe he's just gone for a break or something.'

'Maybe. I'm about five miles away so I'm going to look for some place to stay. Where are you? Back in the hotel?'

'Heading there now.'

'In that case, you two hole up and wait until we get there.'

They said their goodbyes. Carefully, Hunter backed down the hill a hundred metres or so and turned into a driveway. He slowly drove out and headed back the way he'd come. There were no lights showing in the houses he passed although once he reached the main road there was a restaurant on his right which was still open. He crossed the motorway and headed into Interlaken. He had to admit the town was beautiful with lights glistening on the falling snowflakes – but better appreciated when warm and comfortable.

He pulled up in the car park alongside the western train station. Taking his bag, he headed for the nearest hotel, the Krebs Interlaken.

He was looking forward to a nightcap before hitting the sack. At reception, he was told there were no rooms available as due to the snow, many people were stranded in the town.

It was the same in the Bellevue and the Best Western. He finally went into the Royal St. George, near the town centre. There, he discovered they had one room left, known as a design double room, which he took at a cost of 200 Swiss francs.

He dumped his bag on the chair, thought about going down to the bar and then decided not to bother. He made himself a large scotch and soda from the mini-bar and soaked himself in the bath before falling into the king size bed.

He slept like a log.

* * * *

Richard and Andrea had returned to the hotel. Again they used the back entrance. This time they slept in Andrea's room.

In the morning, the fresh fall of snow meant they woke to a pristine landscape of white, bathed in Alpine sunshine. It was a beautiful, breathtaking scene. People were already heading for the ski lifts, eager to enjoy the thrills associated with some of Europe's skiing at its best. Others were sitting in the sun, drinking tea or coffee, savouring the day ahead.

They ordered breakfast in the room consisting of croissants, freshly squeezed orange juice and coffee.

Richard's phone rang. 'Morning, Nick.'

'Richard, are you okay?'

'Sure. This is a great hotel with all the luxuries, I'm accompanied by a beautiful woman and to top it all somebody is probably trying to kill us. A perfect holiday! Sorry!'

'That's okay. I'd be feeling the same way. Look, there's no traffic moving down here. The roads are impassable and will be until the ploughs have done their work. I asked at the desk and was told that the ploughs should have been out since first light but there's been no sign of them so far.'

'The ski lifts are already working and quite a few people are heading for them.'

'I'll get there as soon as I can.' Hunter paused and Richard could sense something was up. 'Okay, Richard, now listen carefully. We've heard MacGregor on his mobile. He did go to Liechtenstein to pick up a weapon but he's stuck in his hotel as the roads are blocked with him as well.'

'So when's he coming here?'

'We don't know. It's being reported the roads will be passable by this evening. If they are, it'll only take him about two hours to drive the ninety or so miles.'

'But that's not what the problem is, is it?'

'No. He's told the men who are up with you that if they get the opportunity they are to take care of business. That was the way he put it.' Hunter paused.

'Any more good news?'

'Quite the reverse in one way, yes in another.'

'Tell me the good side.'

'Andrea Nelson was named. You weren't, but MacGregor said that you were to be dealt with if you got in the way.'

'Collateral damage, so to speak.' Richard looked thoughtful for a few seconds and then added, 'I think the best thing for it is we do a bunk down the mountain.'

'I agree. I've been outside and it's a sod trying to walk anywhere. Be that as it may, I'll get across to the other side of the motorway and wait for you there.'

After a few seconds, Richard said, 'Okay. We'll wait until midday when this place will be heaving with people and leave then. I'll give you a call.'

Breaking the connection, Richard looked at Andrea, debated with himself how much to tell her, then made up his mind. She had the right to know everything that was going on.

'I told you a couple of Nick's men followed this man MacGregor to Liechtenstein.'

Andrea nodded, the knuckle of her right hand pressed against her cheek as she anxiously gnawed the inside of her mouth.

'MacGregor's picked up a gun. He's stuck there and probably won't get away before late this afternoon or early this evening.'

She nodded again.

'In the meantime, he phoned somebody here. He used your name. He told the man he spoke to that they should carry out the business if the opportunity presented itself.'

Andrea gasped. Thinking something might happen, being fearful something might happen, was nothing like knowing it was going to happen. She sat down heavily on the bed, her heart racing, fear gripping her throat. Throughout the period she had half believed it was all nonsense. A mistake. This man, Richard Griffiths, for some reason wanting to make her afraid.

In a quiet voice she said, 'What should we do?'

Richard sighed heavily. The idea of tearing off down the mountain, across deep snow suddenly didn't seem so attractive.

Then Andrea said, 'Richard,' her voice trembled, 'I think you'd better leave. I . . . I can take care of myself. I'll go to the police and tell them what's happening.' Her face was pasty white.

Richard smiled at her and said, 'A few points. First, the police are in Interlaken so how are you going to get there? Second, if these two men are carrying guns then believe me, the easiest thing to do is shoot somebody and get away.'

'How? Surely there are too many witnesses around for that to happen.'

Richard shook his head. 'They walk up to you, put a silenced automatic in your belly and blow a hole through your spine. You're dead in less than a minute, either from the shock or you bleed to death. Those people standing around will rush to help. They'll see the blood. They'll try and stop the bleeding. They'll wonder what happened to you. And you know what? The last thing they'll expect is that you've been shot. Here? In an Alpine resort in Switzerland?'

Andrea blanched.

'It's still my problem,' she spoke with a little more vigour.

Richard shook his head. 'No, it isn't. If you think I'm going to abandon you then think again. We Griffiths don't abandon our friends.' He smiled and added, 'Especially beautiful ones.'

Andrea couldn't help it. Tears welled up in her eyes. She took out a tissue and blew her nose. 'Thank you, Richard,' she said in a small voice.

'There's nothing to thank me for. We need to get away and we need to think of the best way to do it.'

'Any ideas?'

'Nick says that the road is impassable for now. That leaves us with skiing down the road or straight down the mountain, though we'd get less than halfway before we ran out of slope. If I remember correctly, there's a kilometre hike followed by some more slope. There's a raft of problems connected with trying that. First, skis don't like soft snow. We'll be moving slowly, the skis sinking.' He had a thought. 'However, a snowboard does work okay in deep snow. Can you snowboard?'

Andrea shrugged. 'I've done it a couple of times but I'm not very good.'

'So we rule out snowboarding. There is another problem going off-piste across farm land used mainly by cows and that is the wire that surrounds the fields. That could be hellish dangerous. So we rule that out as an option. I suppose we could try the road but until the ploughs have been it'll also be dangerous and difficult.'

'What about the train?'

Richard looked at Andrea sharply and then smiled. 'Of course. It has its own plough on the front. Virtually no amount of snow will stop it running.'

Andrea said, 'Those two men are probably thinking all this for themselves.'

'You could be right. Or they just might be the sort who react to a given situation without thinking of all the consequences. Good foot soldiers, lousy officers. Let's say we go for the train. We phone the front desk, find out the time of departure, and go there at the last second.' Richard snapped his fingers. 'The doors can be closed, in fact, that will lull the men into thinking we're not catching the train, and we jump onto the carriage at the back where the skis and sticks are carried as the train moves out.'

'I suppose it's possible,' though she didn't look convinced.

Silence reigned for a minute or so as they each thought through the ramifications of what they were going to do. On one level it was feasible, provided they had a bit of luck. On another it was impossible. The two men only needed to be between them and the station and it would all be over.

'Or we can stay here,' said Andrea.

'It's not an option. They know we're unarmed and they've been told to do the job. They'll come here. So we need to leave. Listen and listen damned carefully. If I get shot you keep going. You run like hell. Do not stop under any circumstances. Am I making myself clear?'

Nodding, she replied, 'Yes.'

'Good. You'd better put Nick's number into your phone.'

Andrea took her mobile off charge and entered the number.

Richard looked out of the window. It was mid-morning and the village was swarming with people. It should, he thought, be easy enough to stay unseen, at least until they reached the railway. That would be the dangerous time. If they were spotted and they had to wait as little as a few seconds they wouldn't stand much of a chance.

He speed dialled his cousin. 'Nick? Let me run this past you.' He briefly told him what they were planning.

'If it was me, I'd have one man at or near the train. You two appear, he comes across, shoots Andrea, probably you as well and makes good his escape. It wouldn't be that difficult. Even if the road is still closed, all they need do is take the ski lift and go over the mountain. In a couple of hours they'd be well away and just about untraceable. Getting police on the scene capable of organising a search for two killers is a tall order.'

Sighing, Richard replied, 'I know. You've said pretty much what I was thinking. But what else can we do?'

While Hunter talked Richard smiled. 'Right, you'd better get going.'

Disconnecting, Richard said, 'Get your ski things on, quick.' Even as he spoke he was pulling on his ski trousers.

Andrea was doing the same thing and at the same time, asking, 'What did your cousin say?'

Pausing, Richard said, 'He had a good idea. You know what a ski-doo is?'

'Sure. One of those things that looks like a motorbike on skis.'

'Precisely. I noticed last night where they're kept and we're going to steal one.'

16

'You ready?' Richard asked.

'Yes. I've got my passport, credit cards and cash. Maybe I'll be able to send for my stuff later.'

They had agreed that they would leave all their kit. Walking out of the hotel with a suitcase and not checking out could lead to awkward questions if they were spotted. Furthermore, they wouldn't be able to move anywhere near as fast as they needed. Finally, if either of the two men saw them with cases they would come straight at them. As it was, without the cases, the men wouldn't be aware that they were doing a bunk. Or so they hoped. Richard had already checked whether the ski-doos were available for hire which they weren't. However, he had noticed that the ignition keys were left in the machines making things easier for the staff. He unlocked the door and opened it a crack. In his hand he held the steak knife he'd pinched the night before. A quick glance left and right showed the corridor was empty.

'Let's go,' he said over his shoulder, speaking in a normal voice, stepping into the corridor towards the lift and the stairs.

Andrea hurried, caught up with Richard and walked beside him.

'Walk behind me, it's safer. Alongside each other we're a bigger target.' Richard held the steak knife in his right hand, the blade pointing towards his elbow. As they reached the lifts he saw that one was coming up. 'Come on, we'll take the stairs.'

They stepped around the corner and down the stairs. Richard

grabbed Andrea's shoulder and stopped her. It was probably instinct but he wanted to see who was getting out of the lift. He heard the door open and close and he waited a few seconds. He took a quick look around the corner and saw a man walking away from them. Richard narrowed his eyes and looked closer. There was no doubt in his mind – it was one of the two men.

'Andrea,' Richard whispered, 'go downstairs and wait for me. I'll be right behind you.' He turned back and looked carefully around the corner, his head at floor height. He saw the man, about sixty metres away, take out a gun with silencer and hold it alongside his leg. He looked about him and knocked on the door. Twice he called out room service. Next, he took out a key card and swiped it along the lock. He turned the handle and shoulder barged his way into the room.

Richard turned to find Andrea waiting at the next floor level.

'For Christ's sake, Andrea, move it. That was one of the men and he's just gone into your room. Next, he'll go into mine. That gives us a few minutes.'

They ran down the stairs. They found the basement was lacking in opulence. There were no carpets, the walls were painted a stark cream and strip lighting illuminated the area. They passed doors on the left and right. Each one had a sign painted on it. Richard translated the words in his head. Vegetables. Fresh Meat. Wines and spirits. Linen. Washroom. Then facing them, the door said ski-doos. They had so far seen nobody and their luck held long enough for them to go through the door and slam it behind them.

The room was large. Along one wall was a row of half-a-dozen ski-doos with room for half-a-dozen more. Above each one was a shelf with helmets and goggles. Along another wall were stacked dozens of pairs of skis. Richard guessed many belonged to the staff for use on their days off while others had probably been forgotten or abandoned by guests.

'Grab a couple of helmets,' Richard said, crossing to the other door. He looked through the window. As he'd hoped, there were a number of ski-doos just outside. As he looked over his shoulder to tell Andrea to hurry up she handed him a helmet. 'Thanks.' He put it on and adjusted the strap. 'You okay?'

Andrea nodded. 'I guess so.'

'Good. Now, when we walk out of this door act as though we own the place. We have the right to use the machine. We're not answerable to anyone. You got that?' As he spoke, he put the knife into his pocket.

'Yes,' Andrea replied softly.

Richard pulled open the door and stepped through with Andrea on his heels. Directly in front of him was a hotel employee smoking a cigarette. The woman looked at them both.

'Guten morgen,' said Richard, joyously, stepping across to the nearest two-seater machine.

The woman nodded her head nervously, stubbed out the cigarette in the ash can next to the door and said, 'Hullo.' She was in her late teens or early twenties and was wearing a white apron and white cotton hat showing that she worked in the kitchen.

Faking a German accent, Richard said, 'English?'

The girl nodded.

'Where? I go to England a lot on hotel business.'

'Leicester. Please excuse me. I must get back.' She hurried through the door.

'Let's get a move on. That man will know by now my room is also empty and will come looking.'

He straddled the machine, turned the key and the engine burst into life. He scanned the controls and moved a couple of switches, smiled at Andrea and said, 'Seat heaters. At least we won't have cold backsides.' Out of the exhaust pipe water vapour belched, the engine throbbing quietly. Known as SilenTrack technology, only the water vapour indicated that the engine was running.

Nodding, Andrea pulled her goggles down over her eyes, put her left leg over the back seat and sat down.

Richard engaged the gears and twisted the accelerator. A glance at the dashboard showed that the speedometer displayed a top speed of 200 kph. He had no intention of going anywhere near that fast.

They pulled slowly away from the side of the hotel. Ahead, people were walking back and forth, the vast majority of them with skis or snowboards slung over their shoulders. People were greeting each other with a nod and a smile and "Good morning" could be heard in a dozen different languages.

Richard edged the ski-doo into the main thoroughfare. There was plenty of space but he had to weave around people so could not go very fast. As they passed a group of skiers a man stepped out and looked directly at them. Recognition was mutual and instantaneous. There was no thought. Just instinct. Richard opened the throttle and the machine leapt forward. The man stepped back, Richard swerved and they passed within inches.

Richard jinked left and right. A ski school class of toddlers was in front of them and he instantly slowed down. Looking back he saw the man running towards them now about 50 metres away. He was speaking into a mobile phone.

Andrea had her arms gripped tightly around Richard's waist, her head in the middle of his back. She looked back and shouted, 'He's getting closer!'

They passed the children, Richard opened the throttle and the ski-doo accelerated from walking pace to running, to sprinting.

Looking back again, Andrea said, 'He's falling behind. He's stopped. He's bending over, his hands on his knees. It looks like he's gasping for breath.'

The mountain road was ahead. There was a flimsy rope barrier with triangular shaped red flags. There were a few pedestrians walking around the side and down the hill. An adult skier and a youngster with a snowboard also went onto the road. Richard slowed, and then stopped at the rope.

'Quick, Andrea, lift the rope.'

She climbed off the machine, darted around to the front, lifted the rope and Richard edged the ski-doo forward and stopped alongside her. Dropping the rope, Andrea sat back down heavily onto the seat. Even as she did, Richard was engaging the gears when a small eruption of snow occurred in the snow bank next to his shoulder. He looked back. The man had run hard, his breath coming in deep gasps and had now stopped. There were only a few people between the ski-doo and the gunman. The man had turned his left side towards them and had his right hand inside his jacket. The bulge in the jacket was obvious. Richard opened the throttle and the machine jerked forward. A second bullet skimmed across his right shoulder, ripped the cloth of his jacket but didn't hurt. There were two more silent eruptions in the snow bank. The first bend was a mere 50 metres ahead and a glance at the speedometer showed the ski-doo was already travelling at 80 kph and accelerating.

As they turned the bend, Richard slowed down and yelled over his shoulder, 'Are you okay?'

'Yes. What happened?'

'We were shot at,' he yelled.

'What? I didn't hear or see anything.'

Richard slowed even further and said, 'Look at my shoulder. Right side.'

Andrea looked and put her hand onto his shoulder, feeling the rip.

'That was done by a bullet. Another few bullets hit the snow bank on our left. There may have been other shots but I didn't see them.' He didn't point out the obvious. A few more inches either way and the bullet that ripped his jacket could have killed Andrea.

'Oh my God!' Andrea whispered.

'Hey, we're alright. So enjoy the ride.'

'Enjoy the ride? Are you nuts or something? Can't we go any faster?'

'This is Switzerland. The land of efficiency and money making. The snowploughs will be out. They'll have this road cleared in no time. I don't want to go tearing around a corner and slam into one. Somehow, I think we'd come off second best.'

They passed a few walkers but then the road became deserted. It was a beautiful day, the view panoramic with the mountains opposite and the Thunersee on their left. Interlaken looked like a picture postcard town, the epitome of Switzerland. They rounded another bend when Richard said, 'Listen!'

Andrea said, 'It's probably the snowplough. It'll be just ahead.'

'Is it like hell. That's coming from behind.'

Looking back, Andrea said, 'You're right!'

At that moment Richard's phone rang. He didn't bother answering it. He was too busy accelerating.

Then Andrea screamed, 'They're right behind us!'

Richard glanced behind him at the Nissan 4x4 bearing down on them.

The road had a sharp right hand bend and as they neared it, he aimed the ski-doo at the left side and leaned hard over to the right. They skimmed up the left bank by half a metre before thundering back down onto the flat. As they did, the rear of the machine slid and for one heart stopping moment Richard thought he was going to lose control. Then the ski-doo straightened, he slammed more petrol into the engine and it took off like a rocket. Ahead, the road bent to the left. This time there was no banked snow to help them. They were only metres from the bend when the packed snow in front of them erupted in small spurts as bullets hit it. He slammed on the brakes, the teeth in the wide tracks digging into the snow and ice. Their speed was dropping off fast but not fast enough.

As they hit the bend, 10 metres ahead loomed the solid mass of the snowplough. At 70 kpm they would be killed instantly.

A scream formed on Andrea's lips as Richard swung the handlebars to the right and the ski-doo went flying over the side of the road. Richard stood up and leant back, keeping the nose of the machine up. The drop was only two metres and they hit the snow and swerved

183

towards the slope. Their speed was falling off fast when they heard a huge crash behind them.

Coming to a halt, Richard looked back. The car had smashed into the plough and had folded like a concertina. Richard exhaled. There wasn't a dog's chance that either of the two men had survived – he hoped.

Turning the ski-doo down the hill they set off at a more sedate speed as the hill began to flatten. They saw a Mercedes 4x4 coming slowly towards them. Behind that were a number of other vehicles each with skis and snowboards tied to their roofs.

The road was wide enough for cars to pass and Hunter pulled over next to his cousin with a smile on his face and pressed the button to open the window. The hazard lights on the car began flashing and the other cars began to inch their way past.

'You okay?' Hunter greeted them.

'Just about. Andrea, this layabout is my cousin. Nick, this gorgeous lady is Andrea.'

'Pleased to meet you,' said Hunter.

'Same here.'

'What's going on? Why are you halfway down the mountain on a ski-doo?'

Richard gave an account of what had happened.

'Hell, Richard, you were damned lucky.'

The last car in the queue had come to a stop just before the bend. Hunter said, 'They can't get past the plough.'

Before Richard could reply, Hunter's phone rang and he put it on speaker. 'Yes, Jan.'

'Boss, MacGregor is only about ten kilometres away and has been trying to get hold of the men in Grindelwald but isn't getting any answer.'

'Jan! It's Richard Griffiths.'

'Hullo, Richard. Long time no see.'

'Jan, I think they're dead. If not dead, then they'll be seriously injured. They smashed into a snow plough at one hell of a lick. I'm just going up to take a look.'

'Okay. Nick, what do you want us to do about MacGregor?'

'Nothing. For now, just keep following him. He'll be going crazy wondering what's happening. You got his phone number?'

'Yes, as well as his service provider. We can jam him anytime we please.'

'Good.'

Richard walked up the road. A couple of cars inched past the Mercedes, the last one giving Hunter the finger. The car then stopped less than 50 metres ahead, at the end of the queue.

'Climb in,' Hunter said to Andrea, opening the passenger door. 'We may as well wait here until Richard gets back.'

Richard was back in minutes. 'The car is smashed beyond recognition. There's no doubt they must be dead. Although there's room to get past, a couple of cars have tried but they've got bogged down in the snow.'

They heard the siren of a police car and they looked down the hill. The car stopped and a police officer climbed out and waved down the cars that were approaching the mountain. Another officer was already placing marker cones across the road to stop any further traffic.

'Richard, can you and Andrea take the ski-doo and go back up to the hotel? I'll go back down and see about using the train.'

'Right. See you shortly,' Richard replied. Turning to Andrea, he said, 'I'll meet you on the other side of the plough. Okay?'

Though she was still white faced, she nodded gamely and began walking up the mountain.

Richard switched on the engine and carefully took the ski-doo over the side and down the shallow drop to the snow below. He engaged the gears and started up the slope. Under just about any other circumstances, he admitted to himself, he'd be having fun.

17

Hunter reversed a few hundred metres, came to a driveway to a house, backed in and drove out. He headed down the mountain, the road pretty much clear of snow and ice with a dozen or so cars strung out ahead of him.

He drove past the police, crossed the river Aare and went into town. He parked next to Interlaken West Bahnhoff before phoning Badonovitch. 'Where are you?'

'Just coming into Interlaken now.'

'Where's MacGregor?'

'According to the bug he's stopped about a klick in front of us. Yeah, we're getting closer.'

'What's he driving?'

'A Volvo Estate, dark blue, registration KN59KZO.'

'You the X-Trail approaching the train station?'

'That's us. MacGregor is near you somewhere.'

'Okay. Go past and stop. I'll take a look around and see if I can spot him.'

Hunter got out of the car. With his collar turned up and hat pulled down, he walked towards the train station. His phone rang.

'Boss, MacGregor's used his phone six times and is beginning to sound anxious,' came Peabody's dulcet American voice.

'His men are dead.' Hunter filled the other two in on what had happened. 'I can see MacGregor. He's using the phone again.' Hunter turned in to the station and stood looking at the timetable display board. 'If we can, we want to get ahead of him.' He didn't have to spell it out. 'Trains leave three minutes to every hour and take forty-six minutes. That's nearly an hour from now. I'll see if there's any place to park the cars long term then I'll phone Richard.'

At a kiosk displaying all sorts of Swiss treats, Hunter found a map of Interlaken. The young lady serving told him there was long term parking behind the Casino Kursaal Conference Centre. She explained how to find it. He relayed the information to the other two as he walked back to his car. Hunter found the Conference Centre and as he drove into a parking slot the other car arrived and stopped alongside. He got out, took his bag from the boot, slammed it shut and zapped the car locked. The other two did the same.

Hunter phoned Richard. 'We're about to start hoofing it.'

'I'm back at the crash site. I've been told to stay clear. They're not even letting hikers past. I took Andrea back to the hotel and she's locked herself in her room.'

'Give me a minute. I'll see if there's a way up.' Hunter took out the map of Interlaken and spread it on the bonnet of the car. There was a network of narrow back streets. 'Richard? We can go around and meet you about a hundred metres past the accident.'

'Okay. See you shortly.'

Breaking the connection, Hunter said, 'Let's go guys. It shouldn't take long. Weather like this is ideal for a pleasant stroll.' The sun was shining, the sky was blue and there was no wind, not even the gentlest of breezes.

They hefted their bags and set off. The town was busy with people enjoying an afternoon saunter along the streets, many merely window shopping, others buying last minute items for the evening revelries. The specialist schnapps shops were busy, selling liquor distilled from just about every type of fruit grown in Switzerland. The joy in the air was almost palpable as people anticipated the evening and the sheer excitement of a new year. They crossed the street and walked towards the police blockade. A few people stood around, ghoulishly wanting to see what was going on, but most stayed away. One thing about the Swiss, Hunter acknowledged, they were good at minding their own business, whether on a local basis or internationally.

They passed the road block on their left and began walking down narrow side streets where the snow was as much as half-a-metre deep.

Badonovitch said, 'Reminds me of mud runs.'

Hunter nodded. 'Me too. You ever have to do them, Phil?'

'Mud runs? Sure as hell did. Mile after mile up to your calves and knees in stinking oozing mud.'

The three men chuckled in remembrance.

'Okay, you guys?'

'Ready, boss,' said Peabody.'

'Me, Jan, Phil.'

They were in a hurry and needed to get up the mountain before MacGregor. Hunter fell into a fast gait, pushing his legs through the snow. The other two followed in his footsteps, the strain of running much reduced thanks to Hunter leading the way. Half a kilometre later Hunter fell into third place and Badonovitch took lead. Another 500 metres and Peabody moved up front.

They paused at a crossroads where Hunter checked the map. They were heading in the right direction and he said, 'About a klick.'

It wasn't long before they could see the snow plough and wrecked car. There were half-a-dozen uniformed police standing around waiting for heavy lifting gear to arrive. Even the super efficient Swiss, thought Hunter, needed time to organise wreckage clearance.

Richard was sitting on the ski-doo. Handshakes were brief. He handed a helmet to Badonovitch who climbed onto the back seat, awkwardly holding his bag in his right hand. Richard gunned the motor and they set off up the mountain. Hunter and Peabody continued walking. In less than ten minutes Richard was back, skidding to a halt. Peabody put on the helmet, sat on the seat and gripped his bag tightly as the ski-doo accelerated to 60 kph. This time Richard was back in less than eight minutes.

Hunter strapped on the helmet and as they accelerated his bag began bouncing in the turbulence. They neared the top, Richard cut the speed and they nosed onto the flat less than fifty metres from the Hotel Eiger.

'We'll abandon this thing here,' said Richard. 'I don't want to be arrested for taking it without permission, with no licence, no insurance and anything else the Swiss can chuck at me.' He parked the vehicle alongside three others and the two men strolled towards their hotel.

'The men in the car are definitely dead,' said Richard. 'I asked the cops when I was down there. They said they'll have the road cleared in the next couple of hours.'

'Good.' He looked at his watch. 'We're still the best part of thirty minutes in front of MacGregor if he takes the train. More, if he waits for the road to open and comes by car. Jan and Phil will be sitting in the bar of the hotel when he gets here and as they're ahead of him it reduces the chances of him being suspicious. I just hope he doesn't recognise them from Shacklewell.'

'Is that likely?'

'No. He was otherwise too busy and the bar was packed to the gunnels. When we get to our hotel I'll ignore you. If MacGregor does come looking for you and he tries to do the job himself it'll be easier for me to protect you.'

Richard nodded.

They reached the foyer and Richard headed for the stairs. Hunter went over to the reception, showed his passport, gave an impression of his credit card, collected his key card and also walked up the stairs.

He was unpacking when there came two taps, two taps and a single tap on the door. It was the naval diver's signal for "I have found, started, or completed work". It also meant there were no problems and it was safe to open the door. Five or more single taps meant danger. He let Richard into the room.

'Okay,' said Richard, 'care to bring me up to speed about what's happening?'

'Fancy a drink before I do?' Hunter indicated the fridge. 'The sun's over the yardarm.'

They both settled for a beer and clinked bottles. Hunter said, 'We were shoved in the deep end after the French Embassy was blown up. We found out that a man by the name of Gillespie had been involved. After we did some digging we found Gillespie was an alias for this fellow MacGregor. The more we learnt the more it seemed that he's at the heart of an EU conspiracy.'

'I know,' said Richard, 'and it looks as if it stretches all the way to the top of the European Parliament.'

Hunter nodded and took a drink of his beer. 'Correct. We had info supplied by MI5 as well as MI6. So then we were given the job of tracking MacGregor and seeing where it would lead.'

Richard nodded. 'Using your more flexible mandate?'

'Precisely. We found out MacGregor was coming here and that his target was Andrea Nelson,' he shrugged. 'It's just as well you were involved, otherwise I don't think she'd still be alive.'

'I'm pretty sure of that,' said Richard. 'Do you think there's anybody else here?'

'I doubt it. We've bugs on MacGregor and from what we've heard we are pretty sure it was just the two men. I doubt they'd want to share the price placed on Andrea's head. This boils down to the fact that MacGregor is on his own.' Hunter's phone went. 'Yes, Jan.' He put it on speaker.

'Boss, Isobel got into the hotel's booking system and sent us MacGregor's room number. We've planted bugs in both the bedroom and bathroom.'

'Good. Any sign of him yet?'

'No. He wasn't on the train and the tracker in the car hasn't moved. We asked at the desk and were told that they're expecting the road to be open in the next hour or so.'

'Has he contacted anyone? Met anyone?'

'No. His last call was about twenty minutes ago.'

'They'll probably get to the bodies pretty soon, then the proverbial will hit the fan when the police find out that they were carrying guns and that they'd been using them.' Hunter paused for a moment and then added, 'Even so, it'll probably be the morning before the police call in their top brass. After all, it's New Year's Eve and people want to party.'

'That's pretty much what we figured.'

'Okay. Let me know when MacGregor turns up. If he does nothing other than enjoy his evening, all well and good. If he looks as though he's going to start something, we lift him.'

'Roger that, Nick.'

Breaking the connection, Hunter looked at his cousin and asked, 'What do you think?'

'I think Andrea should stay in her room and I'll stay with her. Even if it is New Year's Eve we can have our own party.'

Hunter nodded. 'You're right.' Reaching to his waist, he took off the holster and Glock and handed it over. 'You take this.'

'Are you sure?'

'Of course. Andrea's the target. Not me. MacGregor doesn't have a clue who I am.'

'Okay, thanks.' Richard put it on. It would be hidden under his ski jacket when he left the room.

Hunter took a long drink of beer. 'Has Andrea told you anything about what's happening in the European Parliament? She must have valuable knowledge, the sort of info they want buried.'

Richard blew out his cheeks and shook his head. 'You're not going to believe half of what I tell you and Andrea assures me it's the tip of the iceberg.' He began filling Hunter in on what he'd learnt. It took a while, even with few interruptions. Finally, Richard shrugged and said, 'That's about all I've got so far but she's adamant there's a hell of a lot more going on than I've just told you.'

191

'I'd heard much the same when Sir William briefed me and the General.'

'Nick, what we're talking about is off the scale of common sense. Not only is it billions wasted, which is something we've known about for decades, but billions being siphoned off and used to line the pockets of thousands.'

'But there aren't thousands of people who are corrupt,' Hunter argued. 'It's more likely they are caught up in the system.'

'I couldn't agree with you more. You know, I used to like the notion of the EU. It was forward thinking at its best, ideological and fundamentally honest. It seems that slowly but surely it's become the corrupt mess it is today. Do you remember that windbag from Birmingham who was leader of the Labour Party for a few years?'

'Was that the one who walked across the stage like a prat swinging his fist and yelling "O yea" or some sort of rubbish?'

'That's the one. He was thrown out of the job and went to the EU in charge of anti-corruption. Ironically, and Andrea has documented proof, in the first year that this man took over, according to the National Audit Office, the amount of so called waste doubled. Waste is a euphemism for theft and fraud. He's now retired on a massive pension. Here's the best bit. This man once described the House of Lords as a gaggle of brigands, muggers, bribers and gangsters. He's now a member.'

Nick couldn't help grinning. 'He should be at home there, then.'

'Andrea showed me a report she's prepared. It's on her iPod as she wanted to change a few things. She can prove that one EU official, a Frenchwoman, claimed travel expenses of £465,000 over three years for meetings she never attended.'

'But surely, if she can prove it, something will be done.'

'It has.'

'Good,' said Hunter. 'And what is it?'

'The woman's been retired on a full pension and awarded a

consultancy contract dealing with manufacturing industry in France. Nick, it goes on and on.'

'Another beer? Hunter asked.

'Please.'

Hunter held out the bottle and said, 'Here's a good one told to us by Sir William. A group of businessmen would buy a trainload of butter and send it on a grand tour of Europe. Every time the train passed through the frontier of an EU country, by filling in a few forms, a huge subsidy was paid. They pocketed millions of euros with each tour. Then, when they could no longer use the same butter as it had been through the majority of the EU countries, they sold it.'

'Has the fraud stopped?' Richard asked.

'Not before they realised that carting the stuff around Europe was an unnecessary expense so all they had to do was the paperwork. It has been stopped now, though something else will have taken its place.'

'Why no arrests? No trials?'

'According to Sir William there is a raft of reasons. The first and obvious one is the amount of money we're talking about. It runs into hundreds of millions. Then the officials argue in which country has the crime been committed? Where should arrests be made? Who should be arrested? Who prosecuted? They have also argued that it is just administrative errors. No actual corruption, only mistakes with the paperwork.'

'So it goes on and on,' said Richard.

Hunter took another swig of his beer and said, 'You got it in one.' His phone rang. 'Yes, Jan?'

'He's arrived and signed in. He's just been on the phone.'

18

MacGregor paced the room, three steps one way, three steps back. Anxiety gnawed at him. The front desk had been talking about the tragedy of the two dead men. There was no doubt in his mind that they were his team. His mind oscillated between an accident and somebody killing them. But if they'd been killed, how was it done? The car had smashed into a snow plough. It was impossible to arrange something like that. What should he do? Get the hell out? Tell Jakub Kowalak that things had become too hot and that it would be better to wait for another time, like back in Brussels.

He stopped next to the fridge and took out two miniatures of vodka and a bottle of beer. He opened the bottle and took a long swig. Then he unscrewed the miniatures and poured the vodka into a glass. He took a drink of spirit followed by more beer. He exhaled with a loud, grateful sigh. The alcohol helped him to get things into perspective.

He took out his mobile, went into the contact list and speed dialled a Polish number. There was no answer. He finished the vodka and emptied the bottle of beer. There was no more vodka but there were two miniatures of malt whisky. He took those together with another beer. He made himself sip the drinks, killing time. Ten minutes later he phoned again with the same result. He finished off the whisky and beer and waited to phone a third time but his phone rang and he saw it was from Kowalak.

'Jakub?' He did his best to keep any anxiety out of his voice.

'Yes.'

'I've bad news.'

'I do not want bad news. Only good. Tell me the job has been done.'

'Er, no. The team has been killed?'

'Killed?' The incredulity in the Pole's voice was unmistakable. 'How were they killed? Who killed them?' Anger was making his voice rise.

'Calm down, Jakub, it was an accident.' He explained what had happened.

'I see,' Kowalak spoke in a more reasonable tone. 'Yes. In that case, I will get another team there.'

'I think it would be better to wait until she goes back to Brussels.'

'Nie!' Then he repeated himself in English. 'No! The contract is for her to die before she gets back to Brussels.'

Sullenly, MacGregor asked, 'What team?'

'The Kivis.'

The answer immediately lifted MacGregor's spirits. 'Excellent. They did a good job in London. Can you get them here fast?'

'They are in Chamonix so they can be there in a few hours.'

'If they get here that quick then we should get the bitch before she goes home.'

'I will make the necessary arrangements. MacGregor, do not fail.' There was no mistaking the menace in the man's voice.

MacGregor's reaction was to press the end-call button. He went across to the fridge. There was nothing he wanted to drink and so he headed downstairs to the bar.

* * * *

Hunter repeated to Richard what Badonovitch had told him. 'I'll pass the info back to Rosyth and see what they make of it. Between us, MI5 and MI6 we might get a photograph of these Kivis.'

'Who's this man Jakub? Do you know?' Richard asked.

'His full name is Jakub Kowalak. He's Polish. Sir William Summers

195

e-mailed us a copy of his file. It seems the man is not only a vicious killer but he also controls teams of killers right across Europe,' replied Hunter.

'Who does Kowalak work for? Anybody willing to pay him?'

'It appears he has only one client. The European Union Parliament.'

Richard shook his head in disbelief. 'Surely, the whole world would know about it if that was true? There's no way something like that can be kept secret.'

'This was pretty much what the General said to Summers. According to MI6, there's a small cabal at the top of the tree which means keeping secrets becomes feasible.'

'So you have to get to this Kowalak to find out who he's working for?'

'Correct. With that information we can break into bank accounts, follow the money trail and do some real damage to the whole set-up. According to Summers, if we managed all that, then we may be able to begin the process of rebuilding Europe without the fraud and corruption.'

'It seems to me,' said Richard, 'from what Sir William and Andrea have said, this is only the tip of the iceberg.'

'Maybe, but we have to start somewhere. Right, enough doom and gloom, you go and tell Andrea what we've decided about this evening while I get changed.'

'Why? What are you going to do?'

'I'm going to wander around the town, check out a few bars and have a few drinks.'

'With what in mind?' Richard asked.

'Chamonix to here is one hundred and twenty kilometres or so. That means these people, the Kivis, can easily get here tonight. And don't forget, MacGregor said he wanted them here fast. Jan and Phil will be keeping an eye on him but just two watchers isn't enough, especially if the target knows what he's doing and MacGregor's shown himself to be a professional.'

Richard nodded. He knew that a third person easily doubled the chances of not being spotted.

'You in Andrea's room?' To Richard's nod Hunter added, 'I'll come there as soon as I get changed.'

After Richard left, Hunter had a shower and changed into a black suit, white shirt and a black waistcoat. So much, he thought, for his holiday. He went along the corridor, knocked five bells and Richard let him in.

Richard sat on the sofa, looking relaxed, while Andrea was sitting in front of her dressing table mirror, looking critically at herself. It was obvious she'd been crying.

'I don't want to scare you anymore,' said Hunter, 'but we need to tell you what's happening so you're ready to react if necessary.'

Andrea took a tissue, and wiped around her eyes. 'Richard says we should stay here.'

'He's right. Has Richard told you about these people, the Kivis?'

'Yes. He said they're in Chamonix.'

Before Hunter could say anything further, his mobile rang. 'Yes, Jan?'

'MacGregor's just had another call from the Kivis.'

'What did he say?'

'He said, "No, it can't be helped. Get here tomorrow evening and we'll get the job done then. In the meantime, I'll take a good look around the town." That was all.'

'Okay. We'll stick with our original plan. If he leaves the hotel, you and Phil follow him. I'm also going for a wander. Richard and Andrea will be staying in this room.' He gave him the room number. 'I've given Richard my gun. I'll see you later.' Hunter then repeated to them what Badonovitch had said.

Andrea put her head in her hands, covered her face and said, 'Oh my God this is a nightmare from which I hope to wake at some point.'

The two men exchanged glances.

'Andrea, it's natural to think that way,' said Richard gently. 'This isn't a film. At the end of two hours it isn't going to be all over and you can go back to your normal life.'

She looked bleakly at him, desolation etched in her face. In a whisper she asked, 'What am I going to do, Richard? Tell me that. What am I going to do?'

'We need to work on that at some future point,' said Hunter. 'Right now we need to keep you safe.'

Andrea seemed to rally because she said, 'I'm not stupid. You go away and they come after me some other time.'

Hunter shrugged. 'Possibly. On the other hand, if we take care of the people who control these gangs *and* the people giving the orders, you will be safe and not have to worry about the future.'

Andrea breathed deeply, once, twice and then she nodded. 'Okay. So we'll stay here.'

'Good. In that case, I'll see you later.' He quit the room and walked towards the lifts and stairs. One thing he was sure of, Andrea was in good hands. He took the stairs. In the foyer, people were mingling, leaving, arriving, heading for the bar and the dance floor. A buffet was laid out in the restaurant, the place was buzzing and the wine was flowing. In other circumstances it was a night he would have enjoyed.

He entered the bar, ordered himself a beer, faced the room and leant with his elbows on the bar, the beer in his hand. He surveyed the room. There were very few men without female company. Most of the clientele were in groups of four to a dozen. They were all laughing and speaking in many languages, typical in a resort like Grindelwald.

To his eye, nobody looked out of place. He sipped his beer. It was local Swiss brew, not bad but too cold.

After drinking less than half the bottle in nearly 30 minutes, he left the bar and went out to the foyer. There were more people entering than leaving and as a result the room was getting packed. He went upstairs to his room and grabbed his ski jacket and woollen hat. Back downstairs he left the building through the front doors. The clear night coupled with the thick snow had brought the temperature down to minus 10° C. In spite of the cold there was the usual hard core of smokers, all freezing, stamping their feet and clapping their gloved hands trying to keep warm. At least, as Hunter acknowledged to himself, they were standing clear of the doors. Unlike their counterparts to be found in the UK and France.

He visited other bars, restaurants and hotels. Each one was the same. Everyone appeared to be having a good time and consuming a lot of alcohol.

He was half way to the Hotel Eiger when he saw Badonovitch and Peabody. They were going into a bar on Hunter's right, big smiles on their faces, a swagger in their walk. They were within three metres of him when Badonovitch pointed his index finger at the door and nodded. Hunter ignored him and then followed.

The bar was long, wide and hot and full of people joking and laughing. Hunter watched as Badonovitch shouldered his way to the bar, while Peabody stayed near the door. MacGregor staggered across the room towards the sign announcing Toilettes. He pushed past people, not caring that he was shoving them out of his way. Hunter followed in MacGregor's wake.

He was 30 seconds behind MacGregor when he went through the door marked Herren. The drop in noise level was a relief. There were ten urinals, five each side of the room and five cubicles facing him. In the middle were five wash-hand basins. Only one cubicle was occupied. There was no sign of MacGregor.

Hunter crossed the room and entered the cubicle next to MacGregor. There was a gap from the ground to the start of the panelling of about 20 cms, the panelling stretched about three metres and then there was a further gap to the ceiling of about another 30 cms.

Closing the door, Hunter stood with his head slightly on one side and concentrated on listening to the other man. He heard a sniff then a sneeze. Then he heard MacGregor open the door and walk away. He hadn't flushed the toilet nor did he wash his hands. Hunter went into the other cubicle. The man hadn't even lifted the lid. Hunter rubbed his fingers across the top and looked at the white powder. He rubbed it between his finger and thumb. It looked and felt like talcum powder. Hunter wasn't surprised to discover that MacGregor used cocaine. He went back out to the bar. It seemed even busier and noisier than when he'd left it.

MacGregor was at the bar, getting served. He took a small shot glass of clear liquid, drank it in one and followed it with a long gulp of beer. He got himself another schnapps and did the same again.

Badonovitch and Peabody each had a beer, their glasses still full. They were merely standing there, not talking, heads nodding in time to the beat of the music. Hunter looked at his watch, saw it was just coming up to 22.20 and went outside. Again, the drop in noise level was a relief. He went back towards his hotel. His breath vaporised like that of a mythical dragon, a cloud of white in the clear night air.

He had just arrived back at the Grand when his phone rang. 'Yes, Jan?'

'Nick, you saw him. He's drunk out of his mind. He's been sinking schnapps and beers all night. I'm surprised he can still stand.'

'He uses coke as well,' replied Hunter.

'That doesn't surprise me.'

'He won't be up to anything tonight so why don't you and Phil pack it in. Get an early night or go and enjoy yourselves.'

'We'll go back to the Eiger. There's some sort of folk dance going on.'

Hunter couldn't help chuckling. 'Watch out for those Swiss women with their pigtails and wide backsides. You don't want to end up wearing lederhosen.'

The hotel bar was packed. Hunter wormed his way through and looking around, saw that nobody was taking the blindest bit of notice of him.

He sank a beer and then left the room. He went upstairs and at Andrea's door he knocked five bells. Richard opened the door, standing to one side, away from the opening, his left shoulder against the wall his right arm down the back of his leg. The Glock was clasped in his hand.

Hunter stepped inside and asked, 'You two okay?'

Andrea was sitting on the sofa, watching TV. It was the BBC's annual programme, running up to midnight and a bit beyond. As the UK was an hour behind Switzerland, they still had a way to go.

She managed a smile and said, 'I would never have thought that I would be watching this drivel on New Year's Eve.'

'Look, go downstairs and join in the celebrations if you want. MacGregor is drunk as well as high on cocaine, so he's not going to be a problem.'

'Are you sure?' Richard queried.

'Positive. I'll come with you. We may as well make the most of it.'

19

Hunter's phone rang. 'Richard. Morning and a happy new year.'

'Thanks, Nick. I don't know how this will sit with you but Andrea says she wants to go skiing.'

'I see.' While they spoke Hunter was switching on the kettle. 'Can she hear you?'

'No. I'm in the heads. I know it sounds stupid beyond belief, but she's at the angry stage. You know the sort of thing. How dare these people interfere in her life. How dare they threaten her. How dare she be made to hide. And so on and so forth. She also made the point that the people coming to kill her are not due until later and aren't going to do anything until tonight.'

The kettle stopped boiling and Hunter poured the water over a tea bag in a mug. 'I must be mad but tell her okay. I'll see you later.' Hunter went into the bathroom, shaved and showered in double quick time and dressed in dark blue jeans and a black polo-necked sweater. He went below to the restaurant where a line of tables displayed a huge variety of food. He chose scrambled eggs, crispy bacon and mushrooms. With orange juice and fresh ground coffee he headed towards a table at the back of the room where he sat with his back to the wall. His phone bleeped. It was a text from Rosyth. It read – *Kivis are Estonian but no proof of any crime. They are mother, father and a son who is in his twenties.*

Hunter finished his breakfast and wandered outside. It was

another Alpine day of blue sky and sunshine. The street was packed with people jostling to get to the lifts and onto the slopes. He walked towards the Eiger Hotel, stopped at a restaurant and sat in the sun. He ordered a coffee before speed dialling Badonovitch.

'Jan? Happy new year.'

'Same to you, Nick.'

'Anything happening?

'No. He's sleeping like a baby.'

'In that case, leave him and come and have a coffee. We'll hear him if he does wake up. Come towards the Grand and you'll see me on the other side of the road.'

'On our way.'

They were with Hunter a couple of minutes later. While they waited for their coffees, Hunter told them about Andrea and Richard going skiing.

'Shouldn't be a problem,' said Peabody. 'MacGregor is in no state to do anything before tonight.'

'Hang on,' said Badonovitch, 'I can hear something.' He had an earpiece in his right ear and he put the palm of his left hand over his other ear to reduce the noise level. 'He's just getting up.' Badonovitch smiled. 'He's just groaned. Hold on!' Badonovitch pressed against the earpiece. 'He's on the phone. He just said that he'd meet them in the Eiger at around two o'clock. There are no rooms booked for them as the hotel is full.' He paused. 'It sounds as though the Kivis haven't been able to find a room anywhere. Not here nor down in Interlaken.'

'Good,' said Hunter. 'It probably means that the Kivis will want to do the job today. I've just had an idea. Why don't we be a back-up team? I'll contact MacGregor and tell him that we've been sent as well, in case something goes wrong. That there's a time constraint.'

'He's not going to like that,' said Badonovitch.

'Of course not, but I'll make it clear that this is due to Richard also being a target and that they are both now of equal importance. I'll also make it clear that his money won't be affected, unless we're needed.'

'It's a thought,' said Badonovitch. 'Will you point us out to him?'

'No. But I will be able to tell him enough about what's going on to convince him I'm part of Kowalak's organisation and that there are three of us here. Phil, you stay near the ski lift. Jan, you listen to MacGregor from the hotel. Before you go, we'll go into the heads and you can give me the Glock. Then I'll go and talk to Richard and Andrea.'

Hunter and Badonovitch wound their way through the half empty restaurant and into the toilettes. They were empty. Badonovitch carried the pistol in a bum bag around his waist where it was a damned sight quicker to get at than tucked under his armpit beneath a ski jacket. He pulled open the Velcro top and passed the weapon to Hunter who slipped it into his own bag. Badonovitch left, while Hunter waited a few more moments before following. He went across to the ski shop. The place was busy and it took nearly 40 minutes before he was served and kitted out with skis and boots.

Back in the Grand Hotel, Hunter went up to Andrea's room. 'The Kivis aren't here, so we're as sure as we can be that nothing is going to happen before this afternoon, so let's go and enjoy ourselves.'

'Are you coming as well?' Andrea asked, a tremor in her voice. Now that she was actually going to expose herself she suddenly had her doubts.

'Of course. I was coming here to ski anyway until this mess got in the way.' Hunter smiled. 'Don't look so worried, we'll keep a close eye on you. Nobody will get near enough to do you any harm.'

'Do you have any photographs of the Kivis?' Richard asked.

'Sorry, no. Right, ready? Then let's hit the slopes.'

Down on the street, Richard and Andrea headed for the ski lift with Hunter close behind. He was wearing pilot's sunglasses and his eyes never stopped moving, searching for anyone taking an undue interest in either Andrea or Richard. He saw nothing unusual as people jostled, talked loudly and called to one another.

Richard and Andrea were approaching the chair-lift with Hunter a couple of metres behind. He wanted to get closer but a number of people began to push in, shoving their way past those who were patiently queuing. Hunter was falling back. Someone jostled him in the right shoulder and tried to elbow past. Hunter turned and looked at a man he guessed to be in his early to mid twenties. Hunter stuck his right stick in the ice between the man's skis.

The man was about the same height as Hunter, fair haired, with an arrogant manner. Speaking German he told Hunter to take his stick away, or else. Looking at him, Hunter couldn't make up his mind what to do. He saw that Richard and Andrea were now about three metres away, which was too far. Hunter guessed that a man like the one he was confronting rarely had anyone stand up to him. This time, he was out of luck.

Hunter shuffled forward as did the other man. As he did so, Hunter rammed his elbow hard into the man's stomach. The man bent double, gasping for breath, while Hunter continued moving. Other people in the packed throng walked around the man, ignoring him. Hunter moved as quickly as he could, trying to reduce the distance between him and the other two. He had closed to within a metre when they climbed onto a chair and swung up into the air.

It was a few minutes before Hunter went through the turnstile and climbed onto the bench seat. Next to him was an attractive blonde lady with a winning smile.

As they swung into the air, the scenery became even more spectacular.

'Isn't this wonderful?' She said in accented English with a smile.

Guessing she was in her late twenties or early thirties, Hunter mentally cursed the situation they were in. He smiled in return. 'Yes. Where are you from?'

'Sweden. And you?'

'Scotland. I'm just here for a short break.'

'How short is that?'

'Unfortunately, I probably have to go back to the UK tomorrow morning. Something has come up at work. How long are you here for?' he asked, merely to be polite.

'A week. What a shame you are leaving so soon.'

He nodded agreement. They spent the journey in small talk and then they arrived at the lift's end. They said a polite farewell and the woman skied expertly away, towards the next lift.

Richard and Andrea were sitting in the sun at the restaurant a bit higher up the mountain, enjoying a coffee. Hunter trundled across, jammed his skis into the snow and hung the sticks over them. He sat at the next table, near enough to speak to Richard without appearing to do so. He ordered a coffee and as he lifted the cup to his lips, hiding his mouth, he asked, 'You two alright?'

'Yes,' Richard replied.

'What about you, Andrea?'

'Yes,' she said nervously, her eyes darting around, staring at people. 'No. Oh, God, I wish we hadn't come.' Her eyes began to tear up.

'Right, that's enough,' said Richard. 'Nick, we'll go straight down and back to the hotel, okay?'

'Fine with me.' Hunter replaced his coffee, untouched. He'd had enough coffee for one day.

The other two had on their skis and were starting down the mountain while Hunter was stomping his boots into their bindings. Hunter could see that Andrea was almost as good a skier as his cousin and they were moving pretty fast. Hunter was an expert and easily caught up and stayed 50 metres or so behind them. They were just off the slope when Hunter's phone rang.

'Nick,' said Badonovitch, 'I just heard MacGregor say two hours was fine and that he would wait for them in the hotel. Also, the place is crawling with cops. I heard the receptionist tell them that the two men had been staying there. The cops left and are walking around the place showing a couple of passport photographs. They asked me if I knew them or seen them before. I said no. That's MacGregor coming out of the lift now. He's going into the restaurant.'

'Right. I'll come and say hullo.' Breaking the connection, he turned to Richard and Andrea who were standing with their skis over their shoulders and their sticks dangling over them. 'Let's get back to the hotel and then I'm going to meet MacGregor.'

Ten minutes later, Hunter was entering the main entrance of the Eiger Hotel. MacGregor was sitting at the back of the bar, facing the door, a beer and schnapps on the table in front of him. The room was busy as people looked for somewhere to sit.

Hunter walked straight across to the table where MacGregor was sitting and sat opposite him. MacGregor looked at him in surprise tinged with anger.

'Go away! That's someone's seat.'

'Oh? Is this for the Kivis?'

There was probably nothing that Hunter could have said that would have shocked MacGregor more. He stared at Hunter, his mouth working, no sound coming out.

'Relax, Donald, or do you prefer Don?'

'Who ... What ... Who are you?' he managed in a strangled whisper.

'The back-up team. Or I should say, one of the team.'

MacGregor was beginning to get his wits back. He said, 'I don't know what the hell you're talking about. Go away.'

'Look, MacGregor, you do know what I'm talking about. Now speak to me or I'll contact Jakub and tell him you're not playing ball.'

MacGregor drained his glass of schnapps and took a long swig of beer. He seemed to get himself under control because he then said, 'What do you mean, back up team? I wasn't told there'd be one.'

'There wasn't going to be. However, the targets have become so important we got drafted in at the last minute. I've been told to tell you that your fee is unaffected unless we're used.'

MacGregor sat back in his chair and looked pensively at Hunter, while gesturing for another drink from the busy waitress clearing a nearby table. He didn't offer one to Hunter.

'Don't you think you've had enough?' Hunter scowled. 'You've an important operation going on and I suggest you stay sober for it.

MacGregor dished out a mouthful of abuse and when the drink arrived gulped the schnapps down followed by half a glass of beer. Hunter looked unimpressed.

'The operation is tonight. In the meantime I'll drink what I like. How do I know you're telling the truth?'

'Two of your men were killed by accident yesterday. You got here last night when you phoned Jakub and asked for another team. Jakub said he'd send the Kivis.' Hunter smiled at MacGregor as though they were buddies. 'They helped you in the embassy job in London.'

'How the hell do you know that?'

'Listen MacGregor, I know one hell of a lot. Let's just say I'm further up the command structure than you are. You have the UK. I co-ordinate action across at least six countries, sometimes more if it's needed. Switzerland is outside our normal sphere of action, hence the back-up. You got a problem with that?'

MacGregor slowly shook his head. 'I guess not. Only don't get in my way.'

'I need a coffee after last night,' said Hunter, 'would you like one?' MacGregor nodded and Hunter beckoned for the waitress and placed the order. He turned back to the other man. 'We won't get in your way. Just ignore us. When do these Kivis get here?'

MacGregor looked at his watch. 'In about an hour or so.'

'Okay. What do they look like?'

MacGregor glared. 'You'll know when they arrive.'

The waitress returned with the coffees and Hunter borrowed her pen to write his mobile on the back of the invoice. He paid for the coffees and gave her a generous tip.

'Here's my number. Let me know when they get here. Also, let me know when you're going to make your move, so that we can keep an eye on things.'

'I don't need you to keep an eye on things.'

Hunter was beginning to rethink his original impression that MacGregor was a professional. He had drunk too much and his eyes were beginning to lose focus, though he was still speaking without slurring. 'Unless you want this to be your last job you'll do as I say. It's your job. You plan it. You work it. You do it sober. Do I make myself clear?' The other man said nothing. 'Do I make myself clear?'

MacGregor nodded.

'Your two men were killed in the road accident. What happened?

'The police said it looked as though the men had decided to drive down the mountain even though the road had been closed. That they were driving too fast.'

'Is that what happened? Was there nobody else involved? Were they chasing the targets?'

'I don't know. If they were, they hadn't told me what was going on.'

'What about their weapons? I assume they were armed?'

'They must have been. Let's face it, I can't exactly walk up to the police and ask if the dead men were carrying guns.'

'Fair enough. It's also not the sort of information the police are likely to release unless they have to. Okay, it looks like there's no harm done. You move tonight and make sure there are no mistakes. You got it?'

MacGregor nodded.

'Good.' Hunter stood up and walked out of the restaurant without looking back. So far, so good, he told himself. He crossed the road, and sat at an outside dining area. When the waitress appeared, he ordered onion soup.

20

Jakub Kowalak wasn't in Poland. He was enjoying a break at his house overlooking the Mediterranean, on the outskirts of the famous village El Alamein, 65 miles west of Alexandria. It was early evening and the temperature was a comfortable 10° C. January and February was the time he liked visiting Egypt. He was away from the freezing cold that was Poland, with its temperature as low as minus 20° C, heavy snow and ice encrusted roads.

He particularly enjoyed the village with its old world feel. Of course, much of the place had been rebuilt after the famous battle between the Germans, led by Rommel and the Allies, led by Montgomery. The Allied victory was seen as one of the decisive battles of World War II and Kowalak enjoyed walking around, looking at the sites, following the action with his guide book. It was one of his hobbies. He would then stop for a drink or two at his favourite bar before returning for a late supper and some form of entertainment, though his desire for entertainment was waning and waning rapidly. He was sitting in the bar with a large brandy, soda and ice in front of him, chain smoking, thinking about his life. It was something he found he was doing more often nowadays.

Whenever he visited Egypt his wife stayed behind in Poland. She insisted she didn't like the food, the weather, or the people. He didn't bother pointing out that the food could be brought from Poland, if that was what she desired, the weather was the same as late spring in

Poland and no Egyptian entered the grounds of the villa. The reality was it suited them both. She could enjoy Poland without him and he could enjoy Egypt any way he liked. She spent time with her two sisters who were forever in the St. John's Archcathedral in Warsaw, praying for the souls of their sisters' dead husbands. The two men had died in a car accident a couple of years earlier. They had been sober, both fanatical about not drinking and driving. Unfortunately, the lorry driver in the other vehicle hadn't been so punctilious. He'd consumed the best part of a bottle of vodka when he'd ploughed into the back of their car and sent it out of control across the road into the path of a second lorry. Death had been instantaneous.

The driver of the lorry had pleaded depression and hence the drinking. He had been given a five year prison term, suspended, and banned from driving for ten years. It turned out the man's sister was married to some local wealthy businessman who had used all his influence to get such a light sentence. Although the two dead men had not been involved in Kowalak's business, they were still family. Six months later the driver was found with his throat cut in an alley near his home in Warsaw. Nobody was arrested for the crime. In the meantime, the two sisters had sold their houses and moved into the main house on the estate. It was so big, that fortunately Kowalak rarely saw them.

Thanks to modern technology Kowalak could enjoy being in Egypt while also keeping control of his business interests. Unusually for that time of the year he had two operations going on. The money he was being paid was the highest yet but on the other hand they were also the biggest jobs he'd undertaken. Before the French Embassy job he had only had to deal with individuals, issuing them with warnings or having them killed. The mass murders and destruction in London was something else. It had been a very satisfying job to take on. All expenses and additional costs were met by the client while he pocketed eight million euros.

He was now wealthy enough to retire and live in luxury for the rest of his life – but that didn't appeal. The work ethic was ingrained too deeply into his psyche. He also had three sons who had much to learn if they were to follow him into the business and be equally, or even more, successful. They were currently heading for Rome for which each of them was being paid 250,000 euros. The way he looked at it, all in all, life was pretty good. He did have one problem though, which he readily admitted to himself. His eldest son expected to inherit the organisation. His second son thought he ought to inherit, while as far as Kowalak was concerned, he knew his youngest should be the one to take over.

The eldest didn't have the drive nor the desire to succeed, the middle one wasn't ruthless enough by a long way, while his youngest son had it all.

To date, the front line teams he had used were made up solely of Estonians and Slovaks for a number of reasons. The first was because they were ruthless, secondly because they had no personal ambitions to go into business for themselves and finally, if they needed to vanish, their mother countries provided excellent bolt holes.

He looked at his watch. He didn't expect to hear anything from Switzerland for at least a few more hours. There was no doubt what had happened had been an accident. It was a nuisance that was all. The Kivis being in Switzerland was a bonus and they would get the job done quickly and professionally. He would have to make his mind up about MacGregor and soon. He was beginning to become a liability. Maybe he'd let the Kivis deal with him.

It would be a couple more days before he heard anything from Italy. He wondered how his sons were getting on – they should have already left Warsaw.

* * * *

To look at the three men, nobody would have thought they were brothers.

Marek, the oldest at 31, was pasty faced, round shouldered, had a big gut and was only 5ft 6ins tall. His head was shaven, as he had gone grey prematurely as evidenced by his bushy eyebrows.

Roch, the middle son, was red faced, stood straight and tall although his height was actually only 5ft 11ins, and had brown hair over his ears. Two years younger than Marek, he had a chip on his shoulder about which of them would take over their father's business. He thought he hid his feelings well, especially from his father.

The youngest, Casimir, had a tanned complexion. He was 6ft 2ins tall, kept fit by working out in a gym at every chance he had, was teetotal and had hair down to his collar. His eyes were brown and had a deadness about them that sent a chill through the hardest of men. At 25 he had been spoilt by his mother all his life, yet nevertheless was the most ruthless of the three.

The distance to Rome was 1,420 kms. On the outskirts of Warsaw, they stopped at a rundown industrial estate and backed the car into what appeared to be a dilapidated lock-up. In point of fact, it was lined with sheets of iron and was about as difficult to break into as a modern bank vault. There were three locks, each with a separate key. Entering without the keys would have taken a great deal of plastic explosives.

They collected explosives, detonators and timers. They already carried weapons, never travelling without them. All three used Czechoslovakian CZ83s with 15 round magazines and reasonably effective silencers. The guns made a loud cough rather than a bang. They were hidden in quick release compartments in the sides of the car's doors. The car had been extensively modified and the items they had picked up were quickly stowed away in the boot.

The snow was a nuisance rather than a hindrance, and with snow tyres on their Ford Kuga TDCi 140 Zetec 4WD the journey progressed smoothly. The car was only a couple of months old and was Marek's pride and joy.

* * * *

Macnair was sitting in his girlfriend's lounge sipping a post lunch glass of port with a contented look on his face. He gazed at the woman opposite.

Christine Woolford was of average height and build, with short hair covering her ears. She had hazel eyes, high cheekbones, and was, as Macnair often told himself, high in the bracket attractive. She had an equally happy smile.

'Thank you,' he said.

'If I'd waited for you I'd have waited forever,' she replied.

He looked a little sheepish before he nodded. 'You're probably right.'

'I guess we'd better not let anybody know I asked you to marry me. Otherwise, people will think that you're not the decisive senior officer everyone takes you for.'

Laughing, he leaned forward and topped up their glasses with the rather fine port which had been a Christmas present from Christine.

'Do you mind,' he asked, 'if we talk business?'

'No, of course not.' Lifting her glass she took an appreciative sip of her drink.

'Tell me about the political side of what's going on in the EU Parliament.'

Christine shrugged. 'Well, the real power is in the hands of the commissioners which is something you will hear time and again if you work there. They are unaccountable. They not only believe themselves to be above the law, act as though they are above the law but *are* above the law. All of which is rather scary.'

'Why did you not stand for re-election? When I asked you were pretty vague about the reasons.'

'I guess a number of things. First, I finally came to realise how deep rooted are the problems. To me, they appear insurmountable. Second, I think there are others who can do a better job than me. Younger people who should be given a chance. Then there's a third, very important factor.'

'What?'

'You.'

'Me? What do you mean, me?'

'Malcolm, this life is not a rehearsal. A contrite statement that is said millions of times as we face up to the facts that shape our lives. I don't want to be spending the majority of my time in Brussels or Strasbourg, while the man I love is in Rosyth. I want happiness and joy. I can have both with you, not without you.'

Macnair looked a little uncomfortable for a moment and then he said, 'I feel the same.'

Taking another sip of port, she asked, 'Forget the EU for a moment. When shall we do it?'

'I don't think we should have a long engagement.'

'Neither do I. I was thinking the end of the month? That'll give me time to make all the arrangements.'

'Don't you need my help?'

Christine groaned with exaggerated frustration and then smiled. 'It will hardly be a royal wedding. More a quiet do in a registry office followed by lunch and us saying goodbye and taking off somewhere for a honeymoon. About half-a-dozen phone calls to make the arrangements, followed by an invitation to various friends and relations.'

'Okay. I'll fix the honeymoon. Once,' he added hastily, as he saw Christine was about to object, 'we've discussed where we shall go.'

'I don't mind as long as it's not Europe.'

'Can we go back to the subject of Europe?'

'Of course.' She placed her glass on the table.

'What was it like to work there? To get things done? To deal with problems? To get answers from officials when you MEPs asked the right questions?'

'Lousy and impossible. Problems – they'd ignore them. Answers – few and far between. I think that about sums up the European Parliament. You know, don't you, it's the unelected European commissioners who propose all new legislation? MEPs have no say whatsoever. Furthermore, no one can remove commissioners, not even the MEPs even if a member of the commission proves to be incompetent, is guilty of lying, or of some act of misconduct. The only reason a commissioner is removed and will be removed is if he or she criticises the European Union.'

'Good God.'

'It gets worse. All laws are written in secret committee. No MEP is allowed to know who is on the committee and no MEP is allowed to know what the committee is discussing. We then have the Council of Ministers appointed by the governments of all the members of the European Union whose job it is to vote on the legislation. Each minister who is appointed to vote on the subject has that brief in his national portfolio. So for example, if the vote is something to do with agriculture then it is the Minister of Agriculture who is appointed from all twenty-seven members of the Union. The Council of Ministers meet a few times a year to sign laws already drafted by the commission. There is no discussion, no arguments.'

'But that means there is no democracy,' said Macnair.

'Correct. It gets worse. The Lisbon Treaty is a lie. It's been presented as a tidying up exercise for the European Union. It's far more sinister than that. A raft of new ministries has been proposed to effectively run Europe. Euro Police Force, Euro Gendarmerie, Euro Justice and Euro Diplomatic Corps and a Euro Armed Forces. Check out their powers. It's truly frightening.'

'Can you give me an example?'

'Europol. The police can come into your house and search your home without a search warrant and without having shown reasonable cause. You know about the European Arrest Warrant?'

'Some, though I have to confess I've taken little notice.'

'Over a thousand British people have been arrested under the guise of the warrant. A police force in say Lithuania can issue a warrant for your arrest without any form of proof of a crime having been committed. The UK police will arrest you and deport you to Lithuania where you can be thrown into some stinking jail. And by the way, I've seen their jails. It's third world country stuff. Now, there's been no evidence supplied and our courts know nothing about it. They don't even have to tell your family where you are and you can forget having an English speaking lawyer representing you. They can keep you locked up for what is deemed to be a reasonable time. There is no definition of reasonable. I know of cases where British people have been held for over eight months and then released. Can you guess why there were released?'

'Found not guilty?'

'No. Because no evidence is presented. Malcolm, I can go on and on. Take a look for yourself on the internet. Fraud and corruption is one thing. It's bad enough. This is sinister. It's an erosion of our civil liberties which is getting worse every day. And do you know what the most terrible part of it is?'

'Tell me.'

'Every law strengthens and extends the powers of the EU. Once passed, there is no going back. Forget about this government claiming they have any form of power by using the veto. It's virtually useless as the commissioners always find a way around it. A good example is what happened with Ireland and the Lisbon Treaty. Remember?'

'Yes. Ireland rejected it and that should have been the end. A second referendum was forced onto the Irish people about sixteen months later and thanks to all sorts of promises and, in my opinion, downright lies, went through.'

'Have you heard of a man by the name of Patrick O'Flynn?'

'No. He sounds Irish.'

'He is. He is also a Judge in Europe. Read some of the judgements he's handed down.' She shook her head. 'They are unbelievable.'

'I take it we're talking about the Court of Human Rights?'

'Correct. The criminals he's let loose is frightening. Vicious gangsters with a string of charges against them. These people have been found guilty in our High Courts, confirmed as guilty in the Court of Appeal, the highest court in Britain, yet released by the Court of Human Rights.'

'Are you saying he has something to do with what's going on?'

'I have no idea, but he'd be an important member of any cartel.'

They talked through the afternoon before retiring for a doze. They didn't sleep much.

*   *   *   *

Peeter Kivi was 22 years old. At 13 he reached 5ft 6ins in height and didn't grow another inch. With rounded shoulders and the beginnings of a beer belly, his face was pasty white with a square jaw and a broad nose. Beetling brows and eyes that were so dark as to be almost black gave him a brooding demeanour. Estonian by birth, he had spent the last 17 years travelling Europe with his parents. He was only 14 years old when he discovered what his parents did for a living. The knowledge both excited and pleased him. His parents didn't have an ounce of sentimentality between them and he was soon part of the team. He helped in every way he could, usually as a lookout at stakeouts or by creating a diversion. After all, who would suspect a youngster of anything linked to murder? He had killed his first victims at the age of 16.

It had been a simple operation in Frankfurt. The target was a wealthy industrialist who, following death threats, never went anywhere without a bodyguard.

It had been a cold, damp day in November. The man had been walking in a local park with his bodyguard a few paces behind, out of direct earshot. The industrialist had been on his mobile, talking animatedly, waving his arms, agitated.

Peeter had been alongside his father as they walked towards the German and his minder. As the Kivis neared their targets, the body-guard had stepped out in front of the Kivis to avoid stepping in a lump of dog turd. It was at that moment his father had been taking his silenced automatic from his long coat pocket. The guard must have realised immediately what was going on because he launched himself at Kivi Snr. His father had fallen to the ground, the gun dropping from his hand. It wasn't a conscious decision. Peeter had bent down, picked up the weapon, shot the bodyguard in the head and the target in the back.

His instinct had been to run. His father had grabbed him by the arm and made him walk away. There had been no other pedestrians which had been an important factor as to why the park and the time had been chosen.

Since then, he had killed more than a dozen people, three of them women.

Although he had been enjoying the skiing in Chamonix this job had come up and, he admitted to himself, he preferred the job to the holiday.

The family were now in MacGregor's hotel room. His mother was sitting in front of the dressing table, his father on the edge of the bed. Peeter stood by the door, his arms crossed.

'Where will we find these people?' Jaak Kivi asked.

'At the Hotel Regina at the other end of the street,' replied MacGregor. 'Here are a number of photographs of the woman.' He handed over his mobile phone and each of the Kivis looked at a number of photographs of Andrea. He took the phone back and pressed a couple of buttons. 'These two are photographs of the man, though they are not very good.'

Peeter looked at them. They were an indistinct blur. He felt a tremor of anticipation at the thought of killing him, whoever he was.

'When will you do the job?' MacGregor asked,

'I will let you know,' said Jaak. 'I want the money in my account today. The price has gone up. It is one hundred thousand euros each.'

'What? You're mad! The job isn't worth that much.'

'Then we will leave it to you. Come,' Kivi got up off the bed and stepped towards the door. His son turned, placed his hand on the knob and was about to turn it when MacGregor spoke.

'Wait! I can go as high as sixty thousand each.'

They haggled a bit further. Peeter found it difficult to keep the smile off his face when the amount agreed was eighty-five thousand euros for each kill. That was easy work for a lot of money.

The family left, the parents as stoic looking as ever, Peeter with a smile.

* * * *

When they exited the hotel, Hunter checked the time. There was about two hours of daylight left. 'Jan, come down and we'll follow the Kivis. The son is going over to the restaurant nearest the ski lifts. The parents are walking along the street towards me.'

Badonovitch came out of the hotel and sauntered towards Hunter but on the other side of the street. There were throngs of people going back and forth. Some had obviously finished skiing for the day while many others had enjoyed a long and leisurely lunch and were heading for the pistes for the late afternoon.

Hunter followed the Kivis at a discreet distance. They went to the end of the street, turned around and started back. They made no attempt to hide the fact that they were looking for someone or something. Hunter was standing looking through the window of a shop specialising in skiing paraphernalia when the Kivis passed. They took no notice of him.

A bit further along they chose a restaurant, took a table next to the street and began smoking whilst reading the menu. A waiter took their order, returning with beers and schnapps and laid the table for food. Mother and father picked up the small shot glasses, clinked them and drank the contents in one gulp. Five minutes later the food arrived and they began eating as though they hadn't eaten for a week.

Hunter phoned Richard. 'Is Andrea with you?'

'Yes.'

'In that case, say little and just listen.'

'Okay.'

'I want you and Andrea to come down and over to the patio

restaurant on the other side of the road, about 60 metres from the hotel. The one with the red and white chequered tablecloths.'

'I know the one.'

'When you get here, ignore me and get yourselves a drink. Be relaxed. Be normal. Whatever you do, don't tell Andrea that the people who have come to kill you are sitting at the restaurant opposite. The son is at the ski lifts. The parents are sitting at the restaurant wearing light grey skiing gear and red woollen hats.'

'Great,' said Richard for Andrea's benefit. 'We'll come out for some fresh air and a short stroll. It's just what we need.'

'I want you to be able to recognise them in case they somehow get to you and we're not there. These people won't hesitate to kill and you must be as prepared as possible. Phil will follow but will stay well back. Right, see you shortly.'

A waiter approached Hunter and took an order for a cheese sandwich and an alcohol free beer. Next, Hunter phoned Peabody. 'Phil? When Richard and Andrea leave to go back to the hotel I want you to close up but still ignore them. I'll get Jan to do the same. The Kivis might get impatient and try and do the job here and now.' He didn't need to spell it out. A crowded pavement, a couple of shots from silenced guns and the job was done. In the confusion and mayhem it would be easy for the Kivis to get away.

Hunter phoned Badonovitch and gave him the same instructions. His sandwich and drink arrived and he paid for them. Halfway through eating his sandwich, Hunter noticed the male Kivi sit up and look along the street. He said something and his wife looked in the same direction.

Richard and Andrea took a table a couple away from Hunter, a waiter arrived almost immediately and took their order for tea and apple strudel with cream.

Hunter phoned Richard. 'Listen and smile. You see them?'

'Yes.' Their coffees and pie were placed in front of them and Richard paid immediately.

'When you've finished, start back. Walk quickly, we'll cover you. The woman's taken out a mobile. She's probably speaking to her son. He's a few minutes away. I'd like you gone before he gets here. You okay with that?'

'Of course.'

'Good. Then eat up.' Next, he speed dialled Peabody. 'Phil? Where are you?'

'Standing at the corner of the building where the Kivis are sitting. I'm about ten metres from them.'

Hunter didn't look. 'We'll be moving in a few minutes. I'll be right behind.' He gave the same message to Badonovitch. Hunter got to his feet and walked across the road, stopping to look through the window of a shop specialising in the sale of alcohol.

Richard and Andrea stood up and began to walk quickly towards their hotel. Hunter watched the Kivis in the reflection from the window as they pushed back their chairs and followed. Badonovitch and Peabody were close behind Richard and Andrea.

The Kivis stayed back, with Hunter a mere two paces behind them, not looking their way, but fully aware of where their hands were. If they were carrying a weapon, neither made any attempt to get at it.

Two minutes later, Richard and Andrea entered the hotel. Badonovitch and Peabody followed. The Kivis went straight past while Hunter peeled off and crossed the road.

Hunter phoned Badonovitch. 'Jan? They're going back down the street. I won't go after them in case they get suspicious. You follow them.'

Badonovitch was back outside in seconds and set off after the Kivis. Hunter went the same way but at a much slower pace. His phone rang.

'Nick? They went to their car. The woman took out a handbag. It looks as though they're headed for MacGregor's hotel. Yep. Entering the hotel now. I'll go up to my room.'

21

MacGregor tried to concentrate on what the woman Kivi was saying but found it difficult. The combination of alcohol and cocaine was inhibiting his thought process. He debated with himself about telling them about the back-up team but decided against it. It implied he wasn't trusted by those further up the command and control ladder – something he didn't want to hint at to the Kivis. He recognised the fact that those who paid for his services were utterly ruthless. Likewise, he hired people who were equally without conscience. Fear gripped him and he felt nauseous when he realised what would happen if the Kivis failed. After the mess the other two had made of the operation it didn't bear thinking about.

It hadn't been his fault, he told himself. It had been an accident, a stupid accident. Hell, he hadn't even been near the place. It was unreasonable to hold him in any way responsible. But the people he dealt with were precisely that – unreasonable. He should have done more to help the Kivis. He should have found out the room numbers of the woman and the man Griffiths. He should have prepared the way. There was a lot he could have done.

He needed a drink. A large one.

Cocaine induced paranoia was taking hold. It was a fast-track to making errors. He got his mind back to what was being said.

'We will leave here and spend the evening driving around the Thunersee,' said Jaak Kivi. 'We will find somewhere to hole up. It is too dangerous to try and find a hotel, to book in and leave again in the middle of the night. The reception at the woman's hotel is manned by one person all night. Reet will get that person to open the door to her. She will kill that person, get the room numbers from the computer and we will take care of the problem.'

'What time?' MacGregor asked.

The question was greeted with silence. No answer was forthcoming. Jaak Kivi merely nodded to his family, nothing further was said, not even a goodbye, and they left.

* * * *

Badonovitch phoned Hunter and relayed what he had heard. 'We can't let them get into the hotel.' It didn't need spelling out. They would do all that they could to protect the life of an innocent person who would just be at the wrong place at the wrong time.

'I would guess they'll be back sometime around two, maybe three o'clock,' Hunter replied. 'The town will be deserted. The obvious place to park is in that corner of the car park where there's very little street lighting. Phil, we'll go back over there and take a look. Jan, you stay where you are and keep listening.'

Hunter and Peabody reached the car park. 'I thought so,' said Hunter. 'See the waste skip next to the wall? Let's take a look.'

They strolled across and looked over the rim. The skip was half filled with black rubbish bags.

'We'll dump them in here,' said Hunter. He looked around and jerked his head at two street lights. 'We'll take them out as well which will mean parking here will be even more tempting. Phil, we'll go down to Interlaken to bring the cars back.'

They decided to walk – it helped to kill time. While they did, Hunter outlined what he had in mind. Peabody made a few suggestions and they refined the plan.

* * * *

The three Kowalak brothers were staying at the luxurious Grand Hotel Plaza on Rome's Via del Corso. They had chosen to stay there because of its proximity to the intended bomb sites.

They arrived in the afternoon and booked into their executive suites. Due to Italy's financial situation, the room rates were sixty percent of the usual price. They then spent an hour wandering the busy Via Condotti with its famous Italian fashion retailers. Casimir enjoyed an excellent cup of coffee at the Caffé Greco, probably the best known cafe in the city. It was one of their targets. He visited the washroom where he established the fact that the rubbish bin suited their purpose. Next he went to a specialist shop where he purchased a mobile phone. He would only be using it once.

Marek went into a McDonald's situated near the Spanish Steps, the garish yellow M an insult to the Romans who lived in the area and the visitors who were there to absorb some of Rome's culture. A visit to the washroom satisfied Marek that the rubbish bin was ideal.

After a short debate they decided to place a third lump of plastique in another rubbish bin halfway between the Caffé Greco and the McDonalds.

They returned to their hotel where Roch and Marek went to their rooms to sleep while Casimir went for a workout in the basement. At 20.00 they met down in the bar/restaurant which boasted an extensive array of malt whiskies. Marek and Roch drank a number of them, while Casimir drank various fresh juices.

Dinner was fillet steak with all the trimmings. For the two older brothers the food was washed down with cold draft beer, for the younger, it was fizzy water.

* * * *

Hunter and Peabody had grabbed something to eat down in the town, collected the cars and returned to Grindelwald. They had arranged to meet at 01.00. Back in his room, Hunter had made himself a cup of tea. At 21.00 he went along to Richard's room and rapped five bells.

Richard opened the door, standing to one side, the Glock hanging down by his leg.

'You two alright?' Hunter greeted them.

'We're fine,' Richard replied. 'What's happening?'

'Nothing tonight. I can guarantee it. So if you want to go downstairs for dinner or go to some other restaurant, then feel free.'

Richard looked across at Andrea.

Andrea managed a tentative smile. 'You sound pretty sure.' She lifted a glass of clear liquid with a slice of lemon and clattering ice cubes and took a healthy sip. 'Gin and tonic. Would you like one?'

Hunter shook his head. 'No thanks. I'm meeting the others for a night on the town.'

Richard cast a glance at his cousin and knew that wouldn't be the case. There was no night on the town when in the middle of a major operation. He figured Hunter had said what he did to reassure Andrea. This was confirmed by Hunter's next words.

'Like I already said, nothing will happen tonight.'

'How can you be so sure?' Andrea asked, the slight slur in her voice evidence that the drink in her hand wasn't her first.

'We heard them planning with MacGregor. Trust me, you'll be fine.'

Placing her glass on the occasional table in front of her, Andrea leaned back in her chair and closed her eyes. 'I don't drink. Only an occasional glass of wine.' She opened her eyes and looked from Hunter to Richard, 'Now my head is spinning and I feel dreadful.' She paused and then said, 'Drinking never solved anything.'

'You're right on that score,' said Hunter, 'but Richard and I both understand the strain you're under.'

Tears welled up and started to trickle down her cheeks. 'God, I'm scared.'

'I've spoken to my boss back in Scotland. We know, beyond a shadow of a doubt, who is ordering and controlling the teams that are carrying out the attacks. He'll be dealt with in the near future. You can trust me on that.'

'That's all well and good,' said Andrea, 'but somebody is paying them. What's to stop whoever that is from getting others to do their dirty work?'

'To start with, they need to find people who will do the job,' said Richard. 'They also need to find people who are capable of doing the job and that they can trust. All of that is a tall order, a very tall order.'

She managed a tentative smile.

'Now, something to eat,' said Richard. 'What would you like to do?'

Shaking her head, Andrea replied, 'I'd like to go to bed. That is, if you don't mind.'

'Of course I don't,' Richard replied. 'I'll order something from room service. Nick, you want anything?'

'No, thanks. I had something down in Interlaken. I'll see you later.'

Back in his room, he phoned Badonovitch. MacGregor was still in the hotel. Peabody and Badonovitch were taking an hour about listening in while the other dozed. Hunter lay on his bed. Like military personnel all over the world, he had pretty much acquired the knack of sleeping when he could.

*　*　*　*

The brothers were in the virtually empty casino at Via 24 Maggio. Marek and Roch played roulette, Casimir played blackjack. As more patrons arrived and the noise level built up Marek and Roch steadily lost money while Casimir steadily won, playing the odds correctly. He did not take a third card if his first two totalled twelve. The house was required to take as many cards as necessary to reach a total of 17 or higher. The chance of the house exceeding 21 and busting was therefore a great deal higher than the players. When they left the casino it was after 2.00am. Marek and Roch were in foul, drunken moods having lost 11,000 euros between them. In contrast Casimir was very happy having won more than 5,000 euros.

They returned to the hotel where the two older brothers virtually passed out in their rooms while Casimir had entertainment for the night, arranged with one of the concierges. The woman was beautiful, willing and very accommodating to his needs. He didn't begrudge her the 2,000 euros fee.

* * * *

Hunter woke up at 00.45. He washed his face and changed into dark blue jeans, a black shirt and a black ski jacket. In his pocket he put a black ski mask and gloves.

His phone went. Badonovitch and Peabody were outside in their car. They'd heard nothing more from MacGregor. Pausing at the bottom of the stairs, Hunter looked towards the reception area. As he'd expected, there was nobody at the desk. Whoever was on duty would be in the back office, sleeping, available if needed. He stepped across the foyer, pushed the handle and went out into the freezing night. He stayed where he was for a few minutes, scanning the area. There was nobody about. All the bars and restaurants were closed.

Hunter headed for the rubbish skip. As he neared the car park he saw that the two street lights he'd indicated earlier had already been shot out. He also found that the black bags were stacked alongside the skip.

'You guys okay?' Hunter greeted them in a whisper.

'Sure, Nick,' said Badonovitch.

As usual Peabody grinned and nodded. They were similarly dressed to Hunter. The three of them put on their ski masks. The car park was only half full. They were standing in the gloomiest part of the area. Hunter's car was parked on one side of the skip, the rear half a metre from the edge of the container with room to walk between the car and the skip. The other car was similarly placed on the other side. If the Kivis did the logical thing they would stop in front of the skip, partially hidden by the two cars. The three men were well hidden and waited patiently for their targets to arrive. They had been in position over an hour when they heard the faint purr of a car slowly approaching.

The car wasn't showing any lights as it stopped about 30 metres away. Two minutes later it started forward again, aiming for the square created by the skip and the two cars. The car reversed into the parking slot and the engine was switched off. The occupants of the car sat there for over five minutes, proof of how carefully the family worked. Finally, the doors of the BMW opened. The courtesy light didn't come on. The two male Kivis climbed out of the front, while the mother clambered out from the back through the front passenger's side.

The three of them paused and looked around. Then Kivi senior said something and the son replied. All three carried silenced automatics. The mother whispered something to which the son replied equally quietly. The son began to walk away. Peabody came from behind the skip and stepped behind Kivi Senior. He put his hands either side of the man's head and twisted as hard as he could to the right. The crack of the spine snapping at the point where the cervical vertebrae entered the skull was sharp in the silence of the night. Peabody let the body drop to the ground.

Mrs. Kivi looked over the roof of the BMW to see a man wearing dark clothes and a ski mask. She opened her mouth to say something when a hand clamped over her mouth and her head was jerked back. Badonovitch jerked the woman's head back as hard as he could, his knee in her back. The woman arched backwards, shuddered and died.

Hunter wasn't so lucky. He had heard the scuffle and saw the son turning his head to look behind him. The original plan had been to kill the man as he passed. There was now no chance of that. Peeter Kivi was already beginning to raise his automatic to shoot Badonovitch when Hunter came around the front of the car. Kivi saw Hunter and began to change targets. He was too late. Hunter grabbed the gun barrel and silencer, twisted it towards Kivi's stomach and at the same time stunning him with a head butt to the bridge of his nose. The man's forefinger broke and the gun fired. Hunter had been careful to make sure the gun was pointing at an acute angle. The bullet entered Peeter's body just below the navel and travelled almost vertically. It

229

passed through the stomach, between his lungs, through his heart and neck and lodged in his brain, just below the top of his skull.

Hunter grabbed the front of the jacket of the dead man and lowered the body onto its back. Blood was seeping through the wound, soaking into the dead man's coat. He methodically went through Peeter's pockets and removed his passport, wallet and mobile. The other two had already done the same and had dumped the bodies into the skip.

They handed what they'd found over to Hunter who shoved the stuff into his pockets. 'Give me a hand,' he said, softly. 'I don't want blood on the ground if we can help it.'

Badonovitch took the legs, Hunter the armpits and they carried the body to the front of the skip and tossed it in. The Kivis' guns followed. When the bodies were found, the weapons would confuse matters even more. Next, they replaced the bags of rubbish. There was nothing to be seen of the Kivis.

'Check the car,' said Hunter.

Peabody looked in the boot which was stuffed with bags while Hunter searched inside the car. All he found was the mother's handbag.

'Boss, do you want us to search these bags?' Peabody asked.

'No, don't bother, it's not worth it. Look! I've found an iPad as well as a purse. Jan, you shift the Kivis' car across the car park, I'll move mine.'

It only took a few minutes, leaving the area around the skip clear for people to dump their rubbish.

'Good work,' said Hunter. 'Let's go. I'll see you in the morning.'

Hunter crossed the road to his hotel while the other two went along the back streets to the Eiger. At the front door, he checked to see that the desk was still unmanned. Satisfied, he slid in his key card, the door unlocked and he quietly entered. Crossing the foyer he went up the stairs. He stripped off and took a shower. With a towel wrapped around his waist, he helped himself to a large whisky and soda with ice, which he sat sipping for a while. He wasn't given to introspection.

He had no regrets. The Kivis could be summed up in one word, evil. The world was a better place without them. However, he did run the action through his mind. Things had gone about as well as they could have hoped. Satisfied, he finished his drink and went to bed. He was asleep in minutes.

In the morning, following a shave and a shower, with a mug of tea in his hand, Hunter phoned Badonovitch. 'Jan? Anything happening with MacGregor?'

'He's phoned the Kivis a dozen times already. The last time, he practically yelled down the phone telling them to contact him.'

'Okay, we'll let him stew a bit longer then I'll go and see him.'

Next, Hunter went through the men's wallets and the woman's purse. Between them they contained 8,000 Swiss Francs and over 900 euros. Their passports were in the name of Stolojan and were Romanian. Each of the Kivis had two credit cards and two bank cards. He'd send the lot to Rosyth. Isobel's department could strip the phones and the iPad for everything they held. That in turn could possibly lead Rosyth to the Kivis' bank accounts from where they could repatriate every bit of cash.

He phoned Richard. 'The Kivis are no longer an issue.' There was no need to spell it out.

'Good. What about the other one? MacGregor?'

'That's today's task.'

'Okay. I need to go to my room. We can talk later.' Before Hunter could say anymore the connection was broken. Hunter's phone rang a few minutes later.

'Nick? Sorry about that but I didn't want Andrea to hear me. It occurred to me last night that if MacGregor finds out his team are, shall we say, no longer operational, he'll report the fact to Kowalak. No doubt, he'll order another team into action, this time probably in Brussels. This means, even if Kowalak is taken care of, another team will need to be stopped before they get to Andrea.'

'I agree. That's why I'm going to text MacGregor later today using one of the Kivis' phones. That'll put things on hold. It should mean that MacGregor relaxes for a while. Whatever happens, you need to leave.'

'Okay. We can be away in the hour. Thanks, Nick.'

'There's nothing to thank us for. We're just doing our job. We'll have to reschedule another skiing trip.'

'That's for sure. One that's a bit quieter.'

22

The following morning, the three brothers met in the restaurant where they had a leisurely breakfast. They had plenty of time.

'Did you get the stuff from the car?' Marek asked Casimir.

'Yes. It's in my room.'

'Good.' Looking at his watch, he said, 'We'll meet in the car park at 11 o'clock. Casimir, you set the timers for 12.15. That gives us time to get out of Rome before the city goes mad.'

Roch nodded while Casimir sighed in exasperation. 'We've already decided that,' he said.

'It's always good to double and triple check. Now, I think I'll have a pastry and another coffee.' He beckoned for a waiter who took his order. Roch asked for the same thing while Casimir left the table to return to his room. Once there, he screwed the detonators into the explosives and set the timers. A flick of the switch on the base and the bombs would be set to go at 12.15.

* * * *

Hunter had finished his breakfast, gone for a brief walk and double checked the road down the mountain was still open.

Back at the hotel he met up with Richard and Andrea and accompanied them to Richard's car. He smiled when he saw it.

'The Austin-Healey? A bit cramped and uncomfortable for a long journey, isn't it?'

Richard grinned back. 'Only for an oldie like you.' He put their cases in the boot and Andrea climbed into the passenger's seat. As the two men scraped the snow off the car and the frost off the windows, Hunter said quietly, 'Keep the gun. You probably won't need it, but just in case. I wouldn't let Andrea know you've got it. When it comes time to go back to the UK take the gun apart and get rid of the pieces.'

'Right.' They shook hands and Richard climbed into the car.

Hunter went around to the other side and bent down to speak to Andrea who opened the window. 'You okay?' He gave her an encouraging smile.

Andrea's smile was a bit wan. She nodded. 'My instinct is to go to the authorities and tell them what's happening. Get them to protect me. After all, that's what they're there for.'

Hunter nodded. 'Andrea, that's your prerogative and we won't try and stop you. All we can do is tell you the way we see it. Right now, all you're doing is getting out of here. If you want to go back to Brussels then Richard can take you.'

'I'm due back. I have a job to do.' The worry and fear was etched in her face.

'Andrea, Brussels is only a job. Go ill for a few days. Send an e-mail saying you've caught a cold or the flu. Just give us time to remove the risk.'

'Nick, you can't know that's what you'll do. That's why I want to go to the police. Explain it all to them.'

'What will you tell them? How can you convince them that the danger is real?'

Sighing, she shook her head. 'I have to think about it.'

'Richard, you'd better get going. Now it's stopped snowing MacGregor might decide to come for a walk and the last thing we want is for him to recognise you.'

'Okay. I'll talk to you later.' Starting the car, Richard drove slowly away.

Hunter watched them go. The road down the mountain had been ploughed and salted but even so, an Austin-Healey wasn't good on icy, slippery roads.

Hunter took out Reet Kivi's phone, switched it on, waited as it logged in, put it on text and sent a message:- *Job done. Left for important meeting. Will speak in 3 days.* He didn't send a name. Minutes later his own phone rang.

'Nick?'

'Yes Jan.'

'MacGregor's still in his room. He's just got a text.'

'I know. I sent it.' Hunter told him what he had written.

'What now?'

'Now I need to talk to MacGregor. I want him out of here as soon as possible. I'm coming across to the hotel.'

On his way to the hotel, Hunter stopped at the post office, bought a padded envelope, put in the booty they'd lifted from the Kivis and posted it special delivery to Rosyth. At the Eiger, Hunter went into the bar where he used the house phone.

'MacGregor? The job's done. Care to come down to the bar and we can celebrate?'

'I'll be there in a couple of minutes.'

'I'll set them up. What do you want? A Swiss boilermaker? Or a shot and a beer?'

'A boilermaker, preferably with bourbon.'

'It'll be waiting for you when you get here.' Turning to the barman, Hunter said, 'A half litre of the lager and a double shot of bourbon, please. Leave room in the glass for the bourbon. I'll have a ginger ale.'

The drinks were served, Hunter paid for them and then poured the bourbon into the beer. He took the drinks to the back of the room and sat at one of the tables, facing the door. He took off his ski jacket and put it on the chair next to him. He had his bum bag around his waist. MacGregor joined him minutes later.

Sitting opposite Hunter, MacGregor picked up his glass and took a long swallow. 'Ah, that's better,' he said wiping the back of his right hand across his mouth. 'I needed that.' He looked at Hunter with suspicious eyes and asked, 'How do you know the job was done?'

Hunter smiled and said, 'I saw it.'

'Oh? Where was it and what happened?'

'Don't you know?' Hunter feigned surprise.

'No. I keep away from the actual operation but stay in the locale to see nothing goes wrong.' He frowned. 'What about you? Surely you don't get involved with your teams, seeing as you claim to run a number of them?'

Hunter laughed and replied, 'Hell, no. But this time, as I was on the scene, I wanted to see what they did and how well. I have to admit they were slick.'

'Oh? What happened?' MacGregor took another long drink, his glass now only a third full.

'I don't know how they arranged it but they went in through the back door at about ten to three. Less than twenty minutes later they came back out with the bodies slung over their shoulders. The old woman brought their car around and minutes later they were gone.' Hunter shook his head, awe etched on his face. 'Slick as anything.'

MacGregor drained his glass and smirked. 'They're a good team. I guess I can tell you now. They did the embassy job.'

'They did? That took a lot of nerve.'

'I sorted out the explosives side of things but they shot the two members of staff. You remember the one at the Thames and the one around the corner from the embassy?'

'Of course I remember. Again, both were slick.'

'Not only do they get the job done but they're no trouble. They just get on with it.'

'That's what you want. Okay, you get the message?'

'What message?' Frowning, MacGregor waved to a waitress to take his order. When she arrived he asked for the same again, but Hunter declined.

As the waitress left Hunter said, 'I'm keeping a clear head. I'm out of here this afternoon.'

'What message?' There was exasperation in his voice when he asked again.

'Have you heard of The International Force Against Terrorism?'

'Those morons? Who hasn't? Useless idiots.'

'I wouldn't dismiss them like that. I know they've had a lot of success with some of the operations they've pulled off. Don't forget something.'

'What's that?' As he asked the question the waitress returned and placed both glasses on the table. MacGregor took a mouthful of bourbon, washed it down with a gulp of beer and then poured the liquor into the other glass. He asked again, 'What about them?' he took a large swallow.

'I had a text from Kowalak. He said that they've been given the case dealing with the embassy job. He thinks they're on their way here.'

MacGregor's face turned an unhealthy pallor. 'Christ! How can he know that?'

'How the hell should I know? Don't forget something. They shoot first and don't ask any questions after. And no matter how stupid they are, I'm not hanging around to meet any of them. I also think it's a good time to get the hell out of here before the hotel starts asking where Ms Andrea Nelson and friend have got to.'

Draining his glass, MacGregor said, 'I'm going as well.'

'Right decision.' Hunter looked around and lowered his voice. 'Are you carrying?'

'What?' MacGregor looked startled. 'No. I leave all that to my team.'

'Take a look.' Hunter ripped open the top of his bum bag. The butt of the automatic showed for a fleeting second and MacGregor's eyes bulged. 'You'd better come with me. We'll meet at three o'clock outside here.'

Nodding, MacGregor said, 'I'll drive my own car.' Even as he said it, he turned to beckon the waitress over.

'Don't,' said Hunter. 'If you're going to drive you need to remain sober.'

MacGregor continued with his gesture, the waitress approached and he ordered the same again. He turned back to Hunter and said nothing. His look said it all.

'Alright, here's what we'll do. I flew here and then came by train,' he lied. 'This was the way I was going to leave. Instead, we'll take your car. Give me the keys.' He held his hand out, MacGregor looked closely at him, shrugged, reached into his jacket pocket and handed them over.

'It's the Volvo at the end of the car park with British number plates.'

'Right. It's coming up to eleven o'clock. We'll go at two. You can enjoy a drink now.' Hunter spoke lightly, a half smile on his face.

By way of an answer, MacGregor raised his beer glass and drained it with a satisfied sigh.

Hunter walked outside. The street was heaving as people headed for the slopes and a day of fun and frolics.

* * * *

The three of them strolled separately along the Via Condotti.

Casimir placed his package in the bin in the Caffé Greco. Marek put his package in the McDonald's and Roch placed his in the rubbish bin in the street. All three began to make their way back to the car park. They didn't hurry, although each of them wanted to run and run fast. They kept glancing at their watches. The minutes seemed to be ticking by faster than normal.

They arrived at the hotel at the same time and went inside. They had checked out of their rooms earlier and now collected their luggage from the concierge, gave a tip and carried their suitcases out to the car. They needed to act as normally as possible.

Marek drove, his hands clenched tightly around the steering wheel. He was going too fast along the streets and having to slam the brakes on at the lights.

'Slow down,' said Casimir, who was sitting alongside him. There was no response. 'Slow down!' he roared.

Marek jerked and took his foot off the accelerator. 'What . . .'

'For Christ's sake, slow down. You just jumped that red light,' said his younger brother, looking as though he hadn't a care in the world. 'It's just coming up to a quarter to twelve so we've plenty of time. Take it easy.'

Marek gave Casimir a venomous look and slowed down to just under 50 kph.

* * * *

'Nick, have you seen the news?' The General's voice was so sombre it sent shivers down Hunter's spine.

'No, sir. Why? What's happened?'

'There have been three bombs in Rome. In one of the busiest parts of the city. There are literally hundreds dead and God alone knows how many injured. To say it's carnage is the understatement of the year.'

'Has anyone claimed responsibility yet?'

Macnair sighed. 'Yeah. The usual fanatics but mainly Islamic fundamentalist groups from just about every Islamic country in the world.'

'Do you think one of them is responsible?'

'Not according to MI6. Summers is just off the phone. He's as sure as he can be that it's this Pole, Jakub Kowalak.'

'Do we know where he is?'

No. We're still looking. What we do know is that he has a place in Poland. That's the reason I'm calling. I want you to go and take a look. By the way, I got your text. Good job.'

'Thanks, sir. I posted their stuff special delivery this morning.'

They said their goodbyes. Hunter noticed that the street was quieter than normal and he could see the bars were full of silent people, watching large screen televisions wherever they were to be found.

He speed dialled Badonovitch. 'You heard about Rome?'

'Yeah, Nick. We're watching it now. Bloody hell, it's bad. The murdering swine that did this . . .' he paused. 'We've got to find them and find them fast.'

'I got a message from the General that MI6 are convinced it's this man Kowalak. MacGregor and I are leaving at fourteen hundred.' He went on to explain what he was intending they do.

'We'll be looking forward to it,' said Badonovitch.

Hunter arrived back at his hotel. There were few people about. There was nobody at reception and he could hear a sombre voice speaking in German on a television somewhere in the back. He got to his room and switched on the TV. One commentator was comparing the atrocity to 9/11. Then 2,977 victims had died along with 19 hijackers. It would be impossible for the number to be that high but there was the chance of there being at least 500 deaths. On top of that were the injured. Thousands of people whose lives had been changed irrevocably. Hunter flicked across the channels, looking to find the newscasters who could shed the most light on events. There was nothing other than pure speculation. Then he hit a newsreader on the BBC. An EU spokesman was being interviewed in Brussels. He was talking about the call by members of the European Parliament to create a single European Military force in Europe. To strengthen the borders. To stop this kind of carnage in the future.

Hunter watched the news for the best part of an hour. His feelings oscillated between murderous rage and deep sorrow. Hatred washed through him.

23

Jakub Kowalak smiled in satisfaction as he watched the scenes unfolding on the television screen in front of him. His sons had done well and were already heading back to Poland. His paymasters would be pleased. He had also received word from Switzerland that the matter there had been dealt with satisfactorily. This meant that all-in-all things were looking pretty good. He let himself dwell again on the thought of retirement and handing over the reins, but only for a few seconds. Not only would he be bored out of his mind but there was still the question of succession. He shook his head. He was going round and round with no answer in sight. This meant that the status quo would remain.

The heat of the day was settled at 19° C as 14.00 approached. He decided to go for a walk around his extensive grounds of three hectares.

The gardens were well set out, in three tiers. The one nearest the door was a lawn as smooth as silk. Next came a series of flower beds that gave such a divergent beauty to the area and finally came the orchard of orange trees. They were picked and despatched to a local factory where they were squeezed and the juice pumped into plastic bottles. Even the property he owned was making money! He liked to think of the journey he had made since the fall of the Berlin wall and the end of communism. It had been a close call in a few instances, but he'd finally got there. He'd won through because of his ruthlessness. He never hesitated to pull the trigger, no matter who the target was.

The FBI agent in Washington had been close to identifying him as the man who had killed the senator from Arkansas. He had gone to the man's house and killed the agent's two young children and his wife while he waited. The agent had walked into his kitchen, stopped in horror at the sight of his family, looked at Kowalak and died with a bullet between his eyes. He had nostalgia for the old days, when he had been in the front-line. Now he left it to others, orchestrating his teams around Europe, controlling, ordering, and counting his wealth.

He reached the edge of the orange groves, picked an orange, peeled it, halved it and then started on each segment. It was ripe, juicy and sweet. As he ate, he cast a satisfied eye over the trees. He continued meandering around his grounds. He reached the whitewashed perimeter wall and looked it over. It was three metres high, had three strands of razor sharp wire across the top and a movement sensor should anybody succeed in cutting the wires. There were also four armed guards patrolling the grounds at any one time. It took 12 men to guard the place 24/7 but they were well worth it.

He approached one of the guard shelters. It was four metres square, with an inner closet that housed a toilet and wash-hand basin. In the other corner was a coffee machine and small refrigerator holding fresh milk and cold drinks. There was a table and chair under a window, alongside the door. A panic button was next to the door. If pushed, sirens would ring all over the grounds and house. If the noise didn't frighten an intruder to death, the guards would do the job. The Pole always looked after those who worked for him. That, coupled with a significant salary, meant he could expect and receive loyalty.

On seeing Kowalak, the guard stiffened as though at attention and all but saluted. They each carried an AK74, the replacement for the more famous AK47, both designed by Mikhail Kalashnikov. The production numbers were mind numbing with the best part of 100 million AK47s in the world, while there were a mere five million AK74s.

'Sir.' The guard nodded to him. Like all the guards the man was Polish and the two men spoke in their native tongue.

Kowalak nodded back. 'I take it all is quiet.'

'Yes, sir.'

They exchanged pleasantries for a few minutes and then Kowalak moved on towards the second guardroom. The first guard would not warn the others that their boss was on the prowl – he knew better.

Generosity was one thing. Ruling his empire with a fist of steel quite another.

* * * *

Hunter was standing next to the Volvo when MacGregor appeared, a bag in each hand. Opening the boot, MacGregor slung the bags in and slammed the lid shut. For a moment, Hunter thought that the other man was sober until he had a closer look at his eyes. MacGregor got into the passenger side, twisted the handle that operated the back of his seat and eased himself back. He closed his eyes and was snoring only seconds later. He did it all without saying a word. Shaking his shoulder, Hunter tried to wake him up. The man was out for the count.

The sky had become overcast again and light snow was falling. Looking to the north where the weather front was coming from, the bank of thick black cloud promised a lot more snow.

Badonovitch and Peabody were standing together a few cars away and Hunter went across to speak to them. 'Did Jan tell you what we're doing?'

Peabody nodded. 'With the lake over three hundred metres deep and already having over three hundred thousand tonnes of weapons and explosives left over from World War II sitting at the bottom I don't think a body is going to make much difference.'

'On the outskirts of Thun there's a small marina. Even though some boats are lifted and stored ashore, most are left where they are for use on a sunny day in winter.'

'So we borrow a boat and dump him in the lake,' said Badonovitch.

'Yes.'

Already the snow was beginning to fall heavily.

243

'Let's go before the roads become impassable again,' said Hunter.

Hunter went for the Volvo, Badonovitch took Hunter's car and Peabody took the third. Hunter started the car, put it in gear and drove slowly out of the car park. He kept the car in first gear, even though the street was empty of pedestrians and the roads only just beginning to accumulate any snow.

He had the windscreen wipers going full tilt, the windscreen and rear window were heating up and the heater was going full blast. The car's temperature was beginning to creep up to comfortable. He tried the brakes. The snow tyres did their job and the car slowed, the wheels gripping the road. Hunter reached the bottom of the mountain and turned left onto the N6 motorway for Spiez and Thun. The snow on the ground was thickening but the car was handling it with no difficulties and he wound the speed up to 50 kph. The road became just two lanes but as he approached the sign for Krattigen on his left, the motorway re-emerged in the gloom. He glanced at MacGregor and shook his shoulder. No reaction.

Hunter turned off the motorway at Spiez, and took the road that followed closely along the southern shore of the lake. Apart from the purr of the engine and the swishing of the wipers the only discordant noise in the car was that of MacGregor snoring. As they approached Thun, Hunter saw the sign for the Strandbad on his right and slowed down. A few hundred metres further on he saw the turning he wanted, indicated right and turned off the main road. The other two cars were right behind him. On the whole journey they had seen only two cars going the other way and none going in their direction. He parked close to the water's edge where a row of boats were lined up, each with a waterproof cover. By now the weather had deteriorated further and it was snowing heavily. When the three men climbed out of their cars they had on their ski jackets with their hoods pulled over their heads.

'Jan, you take the end boat on the right, Phil, you start on the left and I'll start here in the middle. Look under seats and in lockers. One of these boats is bound to have keys hidden onboard.'

Both men nodded and went down to the wooden walkway running alongside the lake. The boat Hunter chose had a cover threaded with extra flexible steel wire rope and locked with a padlock. He went back to the Volvo and searched in the boot for the wheel changing kit. Inside the kit he found the spanner, on the end of which was, in effect, a chisel. Back at the boat he shoved the spanner through the u-bend of the lock, braced one end against the deck and jerked hard. The lock popped open and he quickly pulled back the cover and clambered onboard. Five minutes later he was as sure as he could be that there were no keys hidden in the boat. He climbed out, replaced the cover and rammed the lock back into place. It looked as though it hadn't been touched.

He had just done the same to a second boat when Peabody called out in a loud whisper.

'Boss! I've found some keys.'

'Good.' Hunter hurried to join the other man. 'What about fuel?'

'I've just checked. There's plenty.'

He turned to Jan who had just joined them and said, 'You two take some of the rope off the boat and tie up MacGregor. Gag him and bring him down here. I'll warm the engine through.'

Hunter stepped onto the bow of the boat and made his way to the stern. The craft was a Maxum 1800MX. It was about 5.5 metres long and just over two metres wide. It was basically a water skiing or wakeboarding craft. Hunter put the key into the ignition, turned it and watched the dials flicker into life and saw that the battery was fully charged. A further twist and the engine burst into life. There was one instrument he was particularly pleased to find and that was an echo sounder. Perched on the instrument console as an add-on was a compass, which would make things a lot easier in the dark.

'Boss,' Badonovitch yelled, 'MacGregor's vanished!'

* * * *

It seemed to Peter Waterfield that he had never been happier. No, that was the wrong word. Elated would describe his feelings more accurately. Already, the screams and demands for a unified military force across Europe were gaining momentum. He looked at his watch and yawned. Jet lag was a sod.

The judicious payments that had been made to various reporters and newspaper editors across the continent were paying off in a big way. Not surprisingly, the television channels were filled with the events in Rome. The deaths had been unfortunate but necessary just like the French Embassy. There was no other way. Europe had to be made to face the reality of its porous borders. Like many people who were responsible for the kinds of acts that had taken place, Waterfield lied to himself that there had been no other option. The fact that he and the others were driven by pure greed and hunger for power was never acknowledged, particularly to themselves.

The newspapers had article after article, comment after comment, all claiming that the only way to solve the problem was by forming a Combined European Force.

Waterfield was in his office. The Parliament building was virtually deserted as there was still one more day of vacation remaining. The others would be along shortly and they could discuss what their next move should be. How soon before the next atrocity? It couldn't be too long but on the other hand, not too soon either. It was all a matter of balance – on the right scale and with the correct moves, a bit like a game of chess. Each move a step towards their ultimate goal.

His office was large, fitted out to a luxurious standard. He had just made some fresh coffee and he walked across to the machine to pour himself a cup. His was a corner office, proof that he was a senior member of staff, an important person in the EU hierarchy. It was pitch black outside, the heavy snowfall blocking out the street lights and lights from other empty offices.

He lived 40 kms away. However, on this dreadful night he was intending to stay at the Regent Contades – the Concorde Hotel, less than a kilometre away, where the bureaucrats had an arrangement to be given a room if needed. Pausing with the coffee pot in his hand, he changed his mind. He bent down to the cupboard underneath and took out a bottle of fine French wine, a Chateau Lafite. He pulled the cork and with a satisfied sigh poured himself a glass. Sniffing the wine, swirling it in the glass, he took a great deal of satisfaction at the fact that he could easily afford such a fine drink. Though, he had to admit to himself, even he wouldn't have bought the bottle of 1787 Chateau Lafite that had sold at auction for $160,000. Of course, it would be kept in a display case. It was probably undrinkable. He knew that unless the cork was changed every decade or so, it could dry out and air could seep in. Then, over time, the wine would change to vinegar. It was one thing to have an expensive, drinkable wine, but a ludicrous keepsake, no.

He took a mouthful, savoured it and swallowed. A second and a third quickly followed. It was then he heard his secretary's outer office door open and footsteps on the parquet floor. The door opened and Jacques Dupuis entered, immediately followed by Gunther Friedmann.

'Good evening, my dear Peter,' the Frenchman greeted him.

'Good evening, Jacques, Gunther. Can I get you something to drink?'

Dupuis smiled. 'If I am not mistaken that's a Chateau Lafite. I'll take a glass of that please.'

'Of course. And Gunther, what can I get you?'

The German chuckled. 'As this is a great celebration, I too shall have a glass of wine.'

'Are you sure?' Waterfield frowned. 'Don't forget your ulcer.'

'For one evening it is forgotten.' He rubbed his hands together. 'Have you been listening to the news? The yells for a unified border force? It is happening all over Europe. It is within our grasp.' He clenched his fist in front of him. 'Then think what we will be able to do!'

The other two chuckled with satisfaction.

Waterfield poured the wine and reached down into the cupboard for a second bottle. Opening it, he said, 'I'll let it breathe for a few minutes. Have you heard from Enrico or Patrick?'

Friedmann answered, 'Yes. They both said they will try to be here but this weather is so bad they may not make it.'

'And Anicka?'

Dupuis answered, 'She won't be coming. She's snowed in.'

Waterfield nodded. 'In that case, let us get down to business. First of all, I believe the operation with regards to Miss Nelson has been successfully concluded.'

'Yes,' replied Friedmann, 'I had a message from Poland yesterday. It didn't go quite as we'd hoped.'

There was a quickening of interest around the table.

'Oh, nothing to worry about, I assure you,' Friedmann continued, waving a podgy hand in the air.

'What happened?' asked the Judge.

'It seems our Miss Nelson became involved with an Englishman by the name of Richard Griffiths. As a result, the team that was sent in were unable to make the thing look like an accident.'

'But she is dead?' Dupuis interrupted.

'Oh, yes. I have been assured of that.'

'Why has there been nothing in the news about it?' Waterfield asked.

Friedmann smirked. 'The bodies have yet to be found. In fact, the probability is they never will be. It will be a mystery which will be forgotten in days especially after what has happened in Rome and will be happening in Madrid. The deaths of two people is, by comparison, not very newsworthy.'

'Good,' said Dupuis. 'An accident is difficult to stage. I was always concerned that with the procedures and scientific methods available to the police they would establish her death as murder. That would have created a lot more fuss than her going missing. What about this man Griffiths? Will there be any problems about him vanishing?'

Friedmann shrugged. 'We have no way of knowing. We do not know who he is. We won't know until somebody comes forward looking for him. I don't think it's a subject to concern us any further. Let us move on.'

It was Waterfield who asked, 'There have been no further expenses, apart from payment to the Pole, I take it?'

Both men shook their heads.

'Good.'

'What about the Madrid job?' Dupuis asked.

Before Waterfield could reply his mobile rang. He saw it was the judge. 'Yes, Patrick?'

'Peter, I'm turning round and heading back home. I've managed at most two kilometres. Any further and I'll be stuck.'

'In that case, we'll see you when we see you.' He broke the connection and passed on the message.

'Back to the Madrid job,' said Dupuis.

'Yes, everything has been arranged,' said Friedmann. 'I have spoken to Herr Kowalak and emphasised the situation.'

'He has agreed the date?' Waterfield asked.

'Yes.'

'And they have the right people?' Waterfield persisted.

It was the sort of question that irritated the German and so he replied with some annoyance. 'Of course they have. Kowalak has not let us down yet and he is insistent that everything is in place. Now, gentlemen, I suggest we leave it at that.' The German looked at his watch. 'It's only just six o'clock and I want to get home if I can.'

'Would you like another glass of wine?' Waterfield asked.

Shaking his head, Friedmann replied, 'No, thank you. I fear that last glass is already playing hell with my ulcer.'

'I'll come with you,' said Dupuis. 'I'll take the Metro.'

'No more wine?'

'No, thank you, Peter. I have a guest coming for dinner.'

'In this weather?'

'She lives less than a hundred metres away.' His smirk said it all.

The two men departed and Waterfield sat nurturing another glass of wine. He was going through the sequence of events they had planned. With the Madrid atrocity, carried out by Muslim fundamentalists who will have sneaked past Europe's border controls, the cry for a unified force to protect Europe will be overwhelming. Especially when they show that the people responsible for protecting Italy knew about the possibility of the attack and hadn't passed the information to the relevant authorities in Spain. That was a fire they would be stoking, and stoking it well.

He drained his glass, thought about having another and decided against it. It was damned annoying that he'd opened the second bottle. He managed to stuff the cork back in and put the bottle in the pocket of his jacket. He put on his overcoat and hat, and picked up his overnight bag. He didn't bother switching off the lights when he left. Saving energy was for the peasants. Outside, it had stopped snowing. There was a hush across the city that came only when the snow was thick and deep. The clouds were clearing fast and a half moon was beginning to show at the edge of one of the high rise buildings that made up the parliament. He looked about him. The grandeur of the complex never failed to impress him. Like so much that went on in the EU Parliament there were a vast number of secrets that nobody dared mention if they wanted to keep their highly paid jobs and their huge pensions. One such secret was the cost of building the complexes in Strasbourg, Luxembourg and Brussels. At nearly ten times the original quoted price for each building, many people had made vast fortunes. In some ways it had been the start of the corruption that has since become endemic and ingrained in the psyche of all those who believed they ruled Europe.

The walk through the snow was both invigorating and tiring. He would sleep well that night. Luckily for him he had no such thing as a conscience.

24

Badonovitch and Peabody were already jogging through the snow. MacGregor's tracks were easy to follow. He had vanished behind the boathouse but in less than a minute the two men caught up with him.

Peabody used the flat of his hand across MacGregor's neck to stun him. They tied and gagged him and Badonovitch slung him across his shoulders. He trundled back to the lake. Halfway there MacGregor came to and began frantically struggling. They dumped him unceremoniously on the walkway and Hunter leapt ashore.

Placing his foot heavily on MacGregor's chest he pushed down and said, 'Keep still.'

The man stopped wriggling. His face was beginning to get covered with snow and he shook his head.

'Jan, put that weight on the boat, will you?'

There were a number of concrete weights dotted along the walkway, used by the boats when they were floating stationary in shallow water. Badonovitch picked one up, stepped onto the bows of the boat and then into the cockpit, placing the weight near the stern.

'When I told you TIFAT operatives were coming, I lied. We're already here.'

At that MacGregor wriggled even more, bucking, pulling frantically at the ropes.

'Phil, give me a hand and we'll put him into the boat.'

'Sure boss.'

Between them they virtually threw MacGregor into the stern of the boat

'Phil, tie the weight to his legs. Jan, we shouldn't be more than half-an-hour. Let go the ropes will you?'

Moments later, Hunter had the boat in astern and he gently turned the wheel to port to send the stern to starboard. Once clear of the other boats he put the gears into neutral, then ahead and increased power. The boat moved gently forward and up to the narrow entrance to the lake where Hunter began to increase speed. The depth sounder showed the water was six metres deep and shoaling.

'Phil, take the wheel will you, and head south-east. Keep an eye on the depth gauge.'

Hunter stepped across to MacGregor who had stopped wriggling but now started again. Hunter untied the gag.

'What is this?' MacGregor asked, hatred in his tone, fear in his eyes.

'I told you. We're from TIFAT. You're responsible for the explosion at the French Embassy which killed a hell of a lot of people, maimed and injured a lot more and killed five teenagers. You're a vile, cowardly piece of dog excrement.'

'That had nothing to do with me. I swear it didn't. Nothing. I don't know what you're talking about even. Please, you've got to believe me.'

Hunter shook his head. 'MacGregor, we know you were responsible. We know you were using the name of Victor Gillespie. We've been recording you for the last few days as you tried to kill Andrea Nelson and Richard Griffiths. You brought the Kivis to do the job. They didn't. They're dead. We killed them.'

MacGregor looked at Hunter in utter astonishment. 'You . . . You're lying. I know you are.'

Hunter shrugged. 'Believe what you like. We know that you report to and take orders from Jakub Kowalak. We'll be talking to him soon.'

MacGregor's forced laugh of derision sounded hollow. 'You won't get near him. Not in a million years.'

Hunter bent down and grabbed hold of MacGregor's lapels and half lifted him up. 'Listen, he's nothing but a coward and a thug surrounded by cowards and thugs. He was responsible for the explosion in Rome that's killed the best part of five hundred innocent people. Men, women and children. I will get him. I will ensure as painful a death as I can and then I will get the paymasters, whoever they are.'

Looking at Hunter in absolute terror, MacGregor managed to say, 'A million pounds. I'll give you a million if you let me go.'

Instead of replying, Hunter turned to Peabody, 'What's the depth of water Phil?'

'A hundred metres and falling fast.'

Turning back to MacGregor, Hunter said, 'As soon as we get back ashore, I will be sending your credit cards and bank cards to our technical department. Your house back in the UK has already been raided and information lifted from your computers and whatever else they found. They will have every asset you possess in our coffers within forty-eight hours.'

MacGregor was shaking his head. Mentally he was in that place of limbo where people denied their imminent death.

'Depth?' asked Hunter.

Peabody glanced from the compass to the echo sounder. 'Two hundred and seventy metres.'

'That'll do.' Hunter bent down, grabbed the weight which was fixed to MacGregor's ankles with a metre length of rope and dumped it over the side, into the lake.

'No!' MacGregor screamed. 'You can't. You . . .'

Hunter grabbed hold of MacGregor's coat with one hand and dragged him so that he was sitting up. Putting his face close to the other man he said, 'You've destroyed lives, wrecked families, left people with injuries that they will never recover from. You are the sort of filth that needs exterminating like a bug that spreads a virulent disease. I just wish I had the time and inclination to make you pay more.' With that he put his left hand under the man's legs and heaved him after the weight. 'Let's get back ashore,' he said to Peabody

The snow had been building up the whole time they'd been on the lake and it was now approaching blizzard strength. Peabody followed the reciprocal heading and about 15 minutes later they saw the first of the entrance buoys to the marina. Shortly after that they were back alongside, the boat was tied up, its cover was in place and the three men were ready to leave.

'This is no good,' said Hunter. 'This weather is hellish.'

'What do you suggest, Nick?' asked Badonovitch.

Hunter replied, 'Take all the gear out of MacGregor's car and put it in mine. We'll leave his car here. There's a pretty decent hotel in the centre of town. We can go there for the night and see how things are in the morning.'

The snow brought an early dusk and although sunset wasn't until 16.50 it was already pretty dark.

Minutes later, the other two were following Hunter into the town. They passed the railway station which was deserted, followed the road around, went across the River Aare next to the large supermarket and turned right for the hotel.

Rooms were available and they booked in, arranging to meet in the bar later on.

25

Hunter, Badonovitch and Peabody shared one of many similar characteristics – when ordered on an operation they were impatient to get going. If, however, patience was needed when actually on the job then they had it in spades. Sitting around in a Swiss hotel did not come under that category.

They had just finished breakfast and were sitting at a window looking at the weather. The snow had stopped, there was no wind and the square they were looking out on was superbly peaceful.

Peabody asked, 'What are we going to do?'

'Can you guys check the roads while I phone the General? Take a look and see if the ploughs have been out and then check the internet and see if the motorways are clear.'

Hunter went up to his room and speed dialled Rosyth.

'Hullo, sir? Have you got anything for us?'

'Yes. Sir William has been in contact. Kowalak has an estate just outside Warsaw. We'll be taking a closer look later today once the weather has cleared up over the city. Cheltenham is working on it.'

The General was referring to the UK Government Communications Headquarters at Cheltenham in Gloucestershire. It was the centre of the UK's SIGINT – signals intelligence – operations. It could listen in to practically every transmitted signal anywhere in the world. But that wasn't enough. There were many billions of messages being sent around the world everyday – from mobile telephones, faxes, landlines, e-mails and texting. The communication carriers were satellite transmissions, public telephone networks and microwave links. Collecting and recording all of that data was all well and good but it needed to be analysed. Software had been designed to control the download and dissemination of the intercepts so that certain words triggered their systems to start identifying where the signal originated and what it meant. The collection and analysis network was known as ECHELON and was a network operated on behalf of five signatories, the UK, USA, Australia, Canada and New Zealand. Hunter knew that although originally established during the Cold War, the system was now used in the hunt for terrorists, drug dealers and gathering information about the political and diplomatic plans of certain states.

The European Parliament had tried on numerous occasions to get ECHELON closed down on the basis of human rights and the right to privacy. So far, they had come nowhere close to succeeding. This was mainly due to the Americans, Canadians, Australians and New Zealanders telling the EU Parliament where to go. The UK, as usual, was ready to cave in to the demands of Europe. For now, they were hiding behind the skirts of the other four countries.

The reason the personnel from TIFAT were able to use their mobile phones and laptops whenever they wished with impunity was because of certain software designed by Isobel's team at TIFAT. Any transmissions they made were scrambled at source to a degree that made deciphering them impossible. It was unique and on the open market would have been worth millions of pounds.

'We are sending you details of the place.' The anger in the General's voice was palpable as he went on, 'We learnt yesterday and it was confirmed today, that the three sons had been in Rome when the explosions occurred. There can be no doubt that they had something to do with what happened.'

'I look forward to meeting them,' Hunter said.

'Right now they're holed up in a city called Brno in the Czech Republic. That's about three hundred and fifty miles south of Warsaw.

According to the text they sent their father they intend staying there for the next two days.'

'Do we know exactly where they are?'

'Not yet. If push comes to shove then you'll have to head for Poland. In the meantime, Sir William is again using every contact he can. The Czech Security Information Service can't be trusted for a number of reasons. One being, we believe some of their senior officers are on the payroll of the people in the EU Parliament.'

'Okay. How far away is Brno?'

'As near as dammit, six hundred and fifty miles.'

'We could do it in the time, I suppose, but it's hard to tell with this weather.'

'I've taken care of that. I've spoken to Markus Maurer and explained the situation to him.'

'What can Markus do?'

Markus Maurer was the head of the Swiss Federal Intelligence Service. TIFAT had recently prevented two dirty bombs from being taken across Europe, through Switzerland and into France and possibly the UK. At the time, one of the bombs nearly exploded in Switzerland but was made safe by Hunter. As a result co-operation between the Swiss FIS and TIFAT was at an all-time high.

Also, at that time, there were around 2,000 extremists living in Switzerland of which half were thought to be violent. In an effort to keep things under some semblance of control the FIS had embarked on an operation to collect information about foreigners who were living in the country. Nearly 200,000 people had been targeted and as a result numerous terrorist attacks had been stopped before any damage or deaths occurred. After 23 successful operations civil liberties raised its ugly head. The FIS had not bothered to observe the correct legal procedures and as a result much of the information collected was ordered to be destroyed, following a ruling by the Swiss Parliament and enforced by a federal judge. Instead, the information had been uploaded to TIFAT and was available whenever the FIS required. Under the strict letter of the law and the orders given to FIS no law had been or was being broken. Under oath, the head of FIS had been able to swear that they no longer held the information.

Hunter was aware that, as with many of the Intelligence Services across Europe, there was a great deal of co-operation, albeit unknown to the vast majority of politicians. After all, politicians were incapable of keeping a secret – any secret, even one in the national interest.

'He's arranged for a police helicopter to pick you up at Thun airport. It'll be waiting for you. It'll take you to Basle where I've arranged for the hire of a private jet with a company called Executive Services. It's a Citation and should get you to Brno in less than two hours. Markus has confirmed there'll be no security checks.'

The General didn't need to spell it out. It meant there would be no problem in carrying their weapons with them.

'What do you want us to do with the Kowalaks? I take it we're after as much info as we can squeeze from them?'

There was a pause on the line before the General said, 'Correct. It's imperative that we find out the reasons behind the attacks, and more importantly, if any more are planned. Have you seen the press recently?'

'Only some news last night about Rome. Even the French Embassy attack has been relegated to a footnote.'

'Yes, well, there's now a swell of opinion that is building up hour by hour for a unified border force to protect Europe. Political control of that force will be with the European Union Parliament. Hence, although Islamic fundamentalists are not being blamed *per se*, organisations outside our borders *are* being blamed. That's drug runners, people smugglers, anarchists as well as fundamentalists.'

'And the solution is a national border force around Europe. What will change from what we have now?'

'Very little, except for one thing.' Macnair stopped speaking.

'What's that, sir?'

'I've only just thought of it. The control and purchase of equipment.'

He paused and then said, 'No. I'm going nuts. Even that lot wouldn't do it.'

'Who wouldn't do what?'

'I need to think this through. Nick, get hold of these Kowalaks, get every bit of info you can from them and make sure they won't be standing trial. At the moment we don't know where Jakub Kowalak is but somebody in his organisation does. Stop them in anyway you can and, most importantly, find out who's behind their activities.'

'Roger that, sir.'

26

Badonovitch and Peabody returned to the hotel to tell Hunter that the roads were already being made passable and that they could leave at any time. He brought them up to speed on what the General had been saying and they went back to their rooms to pack their bags.

Down in the lobby, Hunter asked the receptionist, 'Can you tell me where the Europcar office is please?' He asked in German.

She replied in English. 'Yes, sir. It's out along the Gwattstrasse, about two kilometres past the train station.'

'Thank you.'

Settling their bill, they went out to the cars. Although the square was still covered in snow it was not difficult to get out to the road. They headed back the way they'd come and in ten minutes were at the Europcar office. They dealt with the paperwork needed to hand over the cars and while they did, a taxi was ordered. The Flugplatz Thun was only four kilometres away. When they got there a police inspector was waiting in the reception hall.

'Commander Hunter,' he held out his hand, 'I am your pilot. Heinz Gutter.'

'Hullo, Heinz. Please call me Nick. This is Jan and this is Phil.'

They shook hands.

'I understand that I am to take you to Basle.'

Hunter nodded and said, 'That's correct.'

'Follow me, please.' As they went out through the door, the pilot said, 'I know something of what happened when those bombs were on the train. Switzerland owes you a great debt. I have been told to tell you that if there is anything you need, you have only to ask, anything at all.'

Hunter didn't take praise easily but smiled and shook his head. 'Just the helo ride will do.'

'Are you alright for weapons?' Seeing the wary look on Hunter's face he added hastily, 'Sir, I have various automatics onboard the helicopter which I am authorised to give you. No paperwork. You just have to say.'

'Can you spare a Glock? Also some ammunition.'

'I'll give it to you after we arrive at Basle.'

'Thanks. It's much appreciated.'

They climbed onboard and put on headphones. The pilot began to wind up the engine and as he did so, said, 'Flying time will be forty minutes.'

The helo lifted gracefully into the air with its characteristic pitch forward and skywards swoop. The ride was breathtakingly beautiful, the countryside bathed in bright sunlight reflecting off the pure white of the snow. They could see that an effort had been made to clear the roads, but the traffic was only crawling along, even on the motorway to Bern.

Off to the left they could see the Swiss capital, like a picture post-card of what a city should look like in winter. The helicopter turned slightly to starboard and headed directly north. In front was the majestic beauty of the Sonnenberg mountains and the pilot turned the helicopter further to the east to go around the peaks. As soon as the mountains were behind them Basle loomed ahead. Instead of going over the city the helicopter turned west and went around it. The pilot used his radio and then said to his three passengers, 'We're cleared to go straight in. Landing in five minutes.'

They passed over the south-western end of the airport, went into a hover and landed as light as a feather on the ground near a single storey building. The pilot switched off the engine and they sat still for a minute as the rotor blades wound down.

The pilot took off his headphones and said over his shoulder, 'If you feel under your seats you'll find some boxes.' As they did, the pilot continued, 'If you open the smaller boxes you will find ammunition, nine millimetre Parabellum. Each of the cardboard boxes holds fifty rounds. The Glock is in the other box.'

'Thanks,' said Hunter, 'and thanks for the ride.'

'It's a pleasure, sir. I think that's your plane waiting for you over there.'

They each took a box of bullets. Hunter couldn't help thinking the inconsequential fact that the name Parabellum was derived from the Latin, *Si vis pacem, para bellum* – If you seek peace, prepare for war. This was the motto of the German company Deutsche Waffen und Munitionsfabriken where the bullets had been designed as far back as 1902 by George Luger.

All four climbed down, handshakes were brief and the three men walked across to the Citation jet. A man wearing a uniform with two stripes on his sleeves greeted them.

'My name is Hans Anders and it is my pleasure to fly you to Brno. My co-pilot is just completing the pre-flight checks which means we should be away in ten minutes.'

'Thanks,' Hunter replied. They followed the pilot up the steps and into the luxurious interior of the aircraft.

'Once we take off we'll offer you fresh coffee, tea, sandwiches, and alcoholic drinks.'

'Okay. And thanks again,' said Hunter.

The Cessna Citation Mustang had five leather seats the size of armchairs.

As they sat down and buckled up, a warm female voice said, 'Welcome onboard, gentlemen.' The engines began to wind up, the noise a muted sound, barely intrusive. 'Our flight time is one hour and thirty minutes at a speed of three hundred and ninety knots and a cruising altitude of twenty nine thousand feet. You know the drill in the event of a possible crash. Bend down and carry out the normal procedure of kissing your fundamentals goodbye. Anything else is a waste of time.'

The three of them chuckled.

Peabody said, 'That's the first time I've heard a proper instruction in the event of a crash.'

Within minutes the plane was in the air, and thirteen minutes later the co-pilot came out of the cockpit and into the lounge.

Hunter had to acknowledge to himself that the tall blonde was as attractive as the dulcet tones of her voice.

Smiling, she said, 'Can I get you something? Tea? Coffee? A drink?'

Coffees all round were requested. Excellent soup and beef sandwiches were distributed and then the co-pilot returned to the cockpit.

After eating, they settled down to sleep. Badonovitch and Peabody were soon dozing while Hunter sat for a while thinking about what they needed to do.

*   *   *   *

Jakub Kowalak was torn between two emotions. The first was satisfaction as plans to carry out the bombing in Madrid were progressing well. The second was anger and concern in equal measure. He should have heard from MacGregor. It was their standard operating procedure and had been established some time ago. It could only mean that something had gone wrong. The question was what? Kowalak was sitting in the shade, looking out at the Mediterranean, wondering what he should do. If the team had failed, then the probability was that the woman Nelson was still alive. But if she was, where in hell was she?

Ever cautious, he decided to take some action – just in case. To date, he had never failed to complete a job successfully and he had no intention of allowing that to change now. He sent a brief text to his contact in Brussels and then took the phone apart. Using a pair of pliers, he destroyed the whole thing, before dumping it in a wastepaper bin. He was only too well aware of the capabilities of the English GCHQ supported by ECHELON.

* * * *

The aircraft landed with something of a thump as a sudden down draft caught it when they were a couple of metres above the runway. It taxied to one side of the airport, came to a halt and the pilot joined them. Opening the door, he lowered the steps and the three of them exited the plane. They gave their thanks as they departed and went quickly across the tarmac to the only door in sight. They went through, and approached a counter with a uniformed official behind it. He asked to see their passports, welcomed them to Brno and waved them through a side door. They stepped into a bustling terminal.

The Europcar kiosk was across the hall and they threaded their way around the other passengers to the counter. While Badonovitch arranged the hire of a BMW X5, Hunter phoned the General.

'Sir? We're in Brno.'

'Good. Isobel's team have been into every hotel booking and registering system in Brno. We haven't found the name of Kowalak, however we have found three men travelling together with the name of Stawiki. Polish. They arrived yesterday and are staying at the Comsa Brno Palace Hotel. You three are also booked in.'

'Right, sir. Is there anything else you can tell us?'

'Yes. William Summers called a few hours ago. There's a rumour out on the streets that there's going to be another atrocity.'

'Where?'

'That's just it, we don't know. We think it's going to be either in Germany or Spain, but that's about all we've got. Keeping the lid on the info is proving difficult to say the least, while at the same time the politicians are screaming blue murder for action.'

'What sort of action?'

'They don't say.'

'Sir, was there any hint of anything going to happen at the embassy or in Rome? Any rumours?'

'No, nothing. I asked Summers the same question.'

'So where are these rumours coming from?'

'No one knows. It's okay, I'm ahead of you. The rumours are stoking up the demand for the EU border force to be created. An attack, which we fail to prevent, will be further proof of the need for one.'

'Who will be carrying out the attack? Do we know?'

'The rumour is that it's going to be Islamic fundamentalists.'

'Suicide bombers?'

Macnair gave a heavy sigh. 'Probably.'

'Damn.' The most deadly enemy to face was one who was not only unafraid to die, but welcomed death.

'I'd better go. We've got a car and should be in the city in half an hour or so.'

They were given directions to the car park and went outside into the early evening air. It had been snowing just as badly as it had been in Switzerland. However, Czech efficiency for clearing the roads and making them passable was nowhere near the capabilities of the Swiss. Hence, after collecting the car, a 30 minutes drive into the city took the best part of an hour and a quarter.

They arrived at the Comsa Brno Palace Hotel, in the centre of the city, next to the Cathedral of St Peter and St Paul. The hotel's outside facade was in sharp contrast to the modern chic look of the interior. Hunter thought to himself that it wasn't the sort of place where he would choose to stay, but it was reputed to be one of Brno's better hotels.

It was just 18.30 when they checked in. With an American, a Russian and a Brit, it was easy to act as though they didn't know each other. They dumped their bags in their rooms and went downstairs to wander around the public areas, checking out the hotel's amenities. There was no sign of the Kowalak brothers.

* * * *

'Richard, I must get back. If we leave in the morning, I can be back home by tomorrow evening.'

They were spending a second night in Strasbourg. Richard had managed to persuade Andrea to stay away from Brussels for an extra day at least. The journey had been tedious, as the beauty of a snow covered landscape was lost when driving across it. The motorways had been relatively clear, but there had been far too many idiots speeding past without a thought for either their own safety or, more importantly, the safety of others.

Richard wasn't one to hang about, but even so the journey, 180 miles, which should have taken about three hours, ended up being over five hours. They had holed up in the hotel Regent Petite France, located in the centre of Strasbourg in the heart of the Petite France district of the city. The hotel was the height of luxury, usually frequented by members of the European Parliament and their officials. It was a converted 17th century mill which boasted an excellent cuisine and a stylish "Champagne Bar".

They had dumped their bags, had a quick shower and gone down to the bar. Richard had ordered himself a whisky and soda and a gin and tonic for Andrea. A few more drinks, an excellent but overpriced dinner washed down with too much wine and they had slept fairly well, despite the obvious worries. During the day they had explored the city, not that either of them had found much of interest.

Now they were back in the hotel bar, dinner an hour or so away, glasses of white wine in front of them.

'Andrea, I really don't think that's a good idea.'

'I'm going and that's all there is to it.'

'Okay, I can't stop you, but it's dangerous. Wait until we hear what Nick has to say before we do anything.'

Obstinately, she shook her head. 'I'm going to the authorities. I'll tell them,' she paused, 'I'll tell them someone is out to kill me. They can protect me, find who's responsible and arrest them.'

'How?'

'I don't know how and I don't care. I do know this doesn't happen to someone because of their job. Not someone working for the EU Parliament.' She drained her glass and said, 'I've been giving it a great deal of thought. I'm going home. You can take me there or I'll catch a train first thing in the morning.'

Richard beckoned a waiter over, ordered more wine and then turned back to Andrea. 'I'll take you. I can't stop you. But I will say it loud and clear, you're making a huge mistake. Nick isn't some paranoid idiot. He's damned good at what he does and he has contacts and resources through TIFAT that you couldn't conceive of.' Richard paused, sighed and then said, 'I wasn't going to tell you but there was an attempt on our lives two nights ago. Nick and his team stopped it.'

'What do you mean, they stopped it?'

Richard was about to tell her but changed his mind. 'Never mind,' he muttered.

Andrea gave Richard an incredulous look and after a few seconds, said, 'Are you mad? Is this some sort of stupid game you're playing?'

It was Richard's turn to look incredulous as he slowly shook his head. 'No, this isn't a game and you didn't think it was either when we were at Grindelwald.'

'Maybe. But I've told you, I've had time to think since then and I think this needs to be handled by the police.'

'Andrea, for crying out loud, have you forgotten everything that's happened over the last few days?'

'Of course not. I am going back to Brussels to sort out the mess from there.'

Although he tried, Richard could not persuade Andrea to change her mind. Dinner was a strained affair and when they went to bed they were barely speaking.

27

Having drawn lots for the rota to have dinner, at 20.15 Hunter was the first into the long, narrow restaurant with its single row of tables down each of the walls. The restaurant was busy and the waiter had tried to show Hunter to a table near the door. However, Hunter had insisted on sitting at the far end, so he could watch the entrance. He skipped a starter, had steak for his main course and didn't bother with a third course. He drank water and dawdled over a cup of coffee. He finished at 21.30 and stood up to leave as Badonovitch walked in.

They strolled past each other with a pleasant nod and a smile, the nod a signal that the brothers hadn't been seen by either of them. A shake of the head would have meant the opposite. Hunter went through the foyer where Peabody was sitting in a corner with a *New York Times* in his hands and a cup of coffee on the table. The two men didn't even glance at each other.

Hunter went through to the bar. At 22.30 he went out to the foyer and sat where Peabody had been sitting. Peabody went in to dinner and Badonovitch went into the bar. Minutes later, three men came through the front door. Two were loud, jovial and had obviously been drinking. The third was silent, wary, his head swivelling back and forth as he looked carefully about him. His eyes lingered on Hunter before moving on to a group of four men who were heading for the bar. The two men who had been drinking followed in the wake of the other four whilst the third man headed for the lift.

One of the men looked over his shoulder and called out, 'Dobranoc, Casimir.' He was ignored.

Hunter knew about six words in Polish. One was *dobranoc*, meaning good night. Getting to his feet, he also went into the bar. The two men were standing at the bar, ordering drinks. Hunter wandered across and stood near them. They spoke heavily accented English to the young lady serving them. Both ordered large malt whiskies.

Badonovitch, who had been sitting at a nearby table stood up and crossed to the bar. He too ordered a malt whisky. He turned and smiled at the other two and spoke in Russian.

They looked at him in some surprise and stopped smiling. The man who replied was pasty faced with a large gut and a shaven head. He stood a couple of inches shorter than Badonovitch. He spoke Polish, Badonovitch shrugged, turned to the bar and lifted his glass, taking a sip. The two went back to talking to each other.

Badonovitch stayed where he was, sipping his drink, straining to hear what was being said. Which wasn't difficult as the two of them weren't exactly keeping their voices low.

Just then, the third man entered and walked quickly towards the bar He was wearing his padded jacket and was obviously about to go back outside. Hunter went back to the foyer and ended up near the door. He speed dialled Peabody.

'Phil? The three men we're interested in are in the bar. Have you eaten yet?'

'No. But I can leave it.'

'Don't do that. We don't know if they've eaten and if they go into the restaurant I'd rather you were there to keep an eye on them.'

'Okay.'

Hunter broke the connection and put the phone away. As he did, the third man stalked out from the bar and headed towards him. Hunter stepped outside, into the freezing air, and walked quickly towards the corner of the building. He was only wearing his dark jacket, trousers and open-necked white shirt and immediately began to feel the cold. He stopped at the corner and watched as the man came outside and went down to the street. The lights on a parked car flashed and he opened the boot. He reached inside and took out a small bag, slammed the boot shut, flashed the lights again and headed back to the hotel. Hunter watched him go. As soon as he was out of sight Hunter went down to take a look at the car. The car was reputed to have the longest name in the industry – a Ford Kuga TDCi 140 Zetec 4WD. Hunter's teeth were beginning to chatter and he went quickly back into the warmth of the hotel. An idea was beginning to form.

In the bar, he got himself a whisky and soda and stood nursing the drink while his shivering faded away. The two Poles were sitting at a table with Badonovitch at the one next to them. The two men finished their drinks, stood up and walked out of the room. Hunter watched them head towards the lift area, put his glass on the bar and hurried after them. When they stepped into the lift, so did he. As was normal in such situations he gave a brief smile and a slight nod. The two men ignored him.

Looking at the control buttons, he saw that they were headed for the same floor he was on. The lift went quickly up, stopped and the doors opened. Hunter stepped out and turned right towards his room, feeling in his pocket for the key card. The other two went left. Hunter stopped at his door and made a bit of an issue about unlocking it, enabling him to watch as the men went into their rooms which were next to each other. Opening the door, Hunter stepped inside, waited a few moments and then went back out and along the corridor. He checked the numbers on the doors and then returned to the lift. He went back downstairs and into the bar.

Peabody was still in the restaurant. Hunter phoned him. 'Have you finished eating?'

'Just.'

'Okay. In that case, my room in fifteen.'

'Okay, boss.'

He phoned Badonovitch and said the same. Next, he went to the front desk.

Smiling at the concierge he said, 'Do you speak English? Or German?'

The man smiled back and said, 'Both, sir. Along with Russian and Polish.'

'I am always in awe of people who have such language skills.'

The man shrugged. 'Thank you, sir.'

Taking a 200 koruna note out of his pocket, about nine euros, Hunter slipped it across the counter and said, 'I need a favour.'

'Yes, sir?'

'Nothing much. I've lost the key to my briefcase. Can you get me a pair of pliers so that I can force the lock? I've stupidly done it before,' he shrugged and looked sheepish, 'and I've found a pair of pliers works best.'

'Certainly, sir. I'll have them brought to your room immediately.'

'That's alright, I'll wait here.' He slipped another 200 korunas over and said, 'Give this as a thanks to whoever gets them.'

Hunter wandered across the foyer and sat in a corner. The concierge picked up the phone, pressed a few buttons and spoke into the receiver. A man appeared in minutes and delivered the tool. Hunter noticed the concierge didn't part with any money. Hunter returned to the counter, collected the pliers, thanked the man, crossed to the lifts and went up to his room. Badonovitch and Peabody joined him a few minutes later.

'Jan, how sure are we that they are the people we want?'

'I pretended I didn't understand Polish. They were talking about what they were going to do with the money that had just come their way. It was from a job they had done in Rome.' Badonovitch narrowed his eyes. 'They clinked glasses and the one with the hair said something like all those deaths were worth it. Then the other one said it came in at about fifty euros a life. At that they both laughed.'

The anger and hatred in the room was palpable.

'They also said they were leaving in the morning. The bald one wants to get back to Warsaw and the roads are reported as being clear but with snow forecast in twenty-four to thirty-six hours.'

'Okay. Here's what we're going to do. Phil, their car is outside. Do you know how to dismantle their brakes so that they become ineffective after they've been used a few dozen times?'

Peabody nodded. 'Open the brake reservoir and turn the float upside down, which will stop the brake warning light coming on. Then slacken the opposite connections on the pipes of both systems.'

'Good. Take this.' Hunter handed over the pliers. 'Slacken the connections just enough so that no fluid is leaking but will start oozing out whenever the brakes are used. We'll also put a tracker and bug into the car.' Looking at his watch, he added, 'It's half past midnight. We'll go down in half an hour. I'll come with you.'

It was a slow thirty minutes. When the time came Hunter put on his ski jacket while Peabody went to his room and got his.

The two men went down the stairs, paused at the bottom, saw that the foyer was now unmanned and went out into the street. It was bitterly cold and although the area had been cleared of snow, there was ice underfoot which was treacherous.

At the car, Peabody took out his universal lock opener, aimed it and waited almost 60 seconds for the zapper to go through thousands of signals until the lights flashed and the doors unlocked. He opened the car bonnet and got to work.

Hunter stood 50 metres away and kept watch on the hotel. Peabody completed the job and closed the bonnet. He placed the magnetised tracker under the front wheel arch and the bug he stuck to the underside of the steering wheel. He locked the car and they both returned to the hotel.

At 06.00 Hunter was up, shaved and dressed with his bags packed. He went downstairs to the restaurant where he was the only person there. He wandered to a long table displaying an array of dishes, both hot and cold, and settled on scrambled eggs, bacon and toast and coffee. When Hunter stood to go back upstairs Peabody arrived. The SEAL took his time having his breakfast and then, when he'd finished Badonovitch came in. It was while he was eating that the Kowalaks arrived. The two drinkers from the night before were bleary eyed and looked the worse for wear, whilst the third was alert and in good humour. He was making fun of his brothers' distress in return for which he was being bombarded with insults. Badonovitch ignored them.

The two who were suffering took mounds of food while the other brother settled on a reasonable selection of cold meats and fruit. They were sitting at a table two removed from Badonovitch when he heard the sober one say that they would be leaving at 09.00.

Although he had finished eating, Badonovitch loitered over his coffee, listening intently to what was being said although he learned nothing more of value. When the three men got up to go, he stayed where he was for a few minutes then went back upstairs and reported to Hunter.

At 08.45 the three TIFAT men checked out and went down to their car. They were wearing snow boots and ski trousers as well as their ski jackets. They didn't expect to be in the car very long. They were parked 100 metres from the Ford and although they couldn't see the car they could see the front of the hotel. It was 09.18 before the Poles appeared.

The voice-activated bug went into operation as soon as the men climbed into the car. They had been arguing from the time they left the hotel and were still at it.

'What's happening?' Hunter asked.

'One of them is saying he's driving as the other one is still drunk from last night,' translated Badonovitch. Suddenly there was silence and the bug stopped transmitting.

They saw from the screen that the Poles' car was moving and they followed. Peabody was driving. He kept a few hundred metres back, out of sight, following the tracker. At the first garage they came to he pulled in and Hunter went into the shop and bought brake fluid.

273

According to the satnav the distance to Warsaw was 463kms with a suggested time of about five hours. The roads were clear of snow and had also been well gritted. The Ford got on to the E50 toll road and headed north-east towards Olomouc, 80 kms away.

They were less than halfway to Olomouc and the roads were mercifully empty when the car in front slowed down. They had closed up to within only a few hundred metres with no other vehicle between the two cars. There was a signpost indicating a turn-off to the right for Vyskov. The car was now crawling along at less than 20 kph. Peabody had also slowed right down, letting the other car pull ahead. The brothers took the turn-off and went down onto a two lane feeder road. They kept going until they came to a track, turned onto it and come to a halt.

Peabody drove past; Hunter glanced right and saw that the back of the Ford was visible from the road. A few hundred metres further on, around a bend, was a parking place and Peabody drove into it. The three men grabbed their coats, checked their weapons and walked back towards the other car. Hunter had the brake fluid in his pocket.

As the team neared the lane they could hear the Kowalaks yelling at each other. The engine was still running, the exhaust creating a cloud of condensed vapour.

Hunter took the driver's side, Peabody the front passenger's and Badonovitch the passenger seat behind the driver.

There was no hesitation. No niceties. No asking any of the men to step out. They flung open the doors and jammed their pistols into the side of the head of each of the men. They rammed the guns in hard, pushing the Poles' heads over to one side. There were loud expletives from all three. Badonovitch told them to shut up or they would be shot. He had to say it twice before the message penetrated the brain of the bald man.

'Nice and easy,' said Hunter, 'because believe me, I will kill you.' He reached in and switched off the engine.

The driver spoke harshly in Polish. There was no sign of any fear.

Badonovitch translated. 'He says they don't understand English. That we are making a big mistake.'

'I see,' said Hunter, acting as though he was thinking it over. 'If they don't speak any English we may as well kill them now.'

The man in the back seat was the red-faced drinker and Hunter said, 'Jan, get him out.'

Badonovitch slammed the butt of his Glock onto the knee of the other man with all his strength. The man screamed in pain as a loud crack indicated that his kneecap was probably broken. He jammed the gun back into the man's head and told him to unbuckle his seatbelt and get out. The man did as he was told, his hands shaking with fear. Badonovitch put his pistol to the back of the man's head and pushed him forward, along the track.

'I'll take it, Jan,' Hunter said.

'Are you sure, boss? It will be my pleasure.'

'I'm sure.'

Hunter and Badonovitch changed places. Hunter pushed the man harder and he stumbled. The snow was up to his knees and his trousers were soaked, his teeth chattering from a mixture of cold and fear. 'I will ask you one more time. Do you speak English?'

'Nie! Nie!'

'Ask his brothers,' Hunter ordered Badonovitch.

There was a short, sharp exchange of Polish and Badonovitch said, 'They said no. The driver said that they will kill us for this.'

Hunter had the gun at the base of the man's neck, angled upwards. He pulled the trigger; the bullet went through the man's spine, up through his pallet and exited through the top of his head. The angle meant there was no blood splattering over Hunter. The body toppled forward and was half buried in the snow. The silenced weapon had barely made a burp in the deep stillness of the day.

The two Poles sat frozen in shock. Whatever they had expected it wasn't that. They were the ones who killed people, not the other way around. The front passenger fumbled with his seatbelt and leant out of the door. Peabody stepped back just in time as the man vomited up his breakfast. He kept vomiting until all that was left were dry heaves.

The brother in the driver's seat hadn't moved. He was shaking. Badonovitch thought for a second it was with fear.

Slowly, the man turned his head to look at Badonovitch and in a low voice dripping with hatred said, 'I will kill you.' It was a matter-of-fact statement, said in such a way that it was obvious the man believed what he was saying.

Peabody grabbed the passenger by his collar and dragged him out, letting him collapse into the snow. He jammed his foot into the back of the man's neck and said, in English, 'Spread your arms out.'

The man did as he was told. 'I guess they do speak English after all,' said Peabody.

'It looks like it.' Hunter bent over the dead body and frisked his pockets. Tucked under his left arm he found a Czechoslovakian CZ83 automatic and in his inside pocket a passport in the name of Roch Kowalak. He also lifted a mobile phone. 'Phil, turn your man over.'

Peabody took his foot off the man's neck and kicked him in the side. 'Keep your hands above your head and roll over.'

The man did as he ordered. Peabody knelt alongside him and removed another CZ83, a passport and phone. He looked inside. 'His name is Marek Kowalak.'

'Get him to put the body in the boot,' said Hunter.

Hunter went around the car and said to the third man, 'Undo your seatbelt and climb out.'

He received a string of abuse in reply in a mixture of Polish and English. Badonovitch took his pistol from the man's cheekbone, raised it as high as the roof would allow and brought it down as hard as he could on the man's temple. The man went out like a light. He reached in, undid the seatbelt, grabbed the man's arm and pulled him out, in to the snow. He reached under the man's jacket and removed an automatic, passport and mobile. 'His name is Casimir Kowalak.'

Peabody had kicked Marek to his feet and pushed him stumbling to the dead body. 'Drag him to the back of the car.'

Marek reached under the armpits of his brother and with a great deal of gasping and struggling, dragged the body to the boot of the car. Hunter had opened the boot and shifted the men's bags around to make more space. With a great deal of effort Marek stuffed the body inside the car. Peabody prodded Marek as far as the back seat. 'Get in,' he ordered. As Marek put his foot inside the car Peabody hit the back of his head a skull crushing blow and pushed the unconscious body into the car. In the meantime, Hunter had opened the bonnet, tightened the pipe connections and refilled the brake fluid. He dropped the bonnet shut. Badonovitch had dragged Casimir around the front of the car and stuffed him into the front passenger's seat.

'Jan, go and fetch our car. We'll go along this track and see where it leads. Looking at this snow I'd say nothing's passed this way in the last couple of days.'

Peabody got into the back and Hunter climbed into the driver's seat. The engine burst into life, he shifted into first and nudged forward. According to his watch the whole affair since they had pulled up at the parking place had taken less than nine minutes. They were in luck. Half a kilometre along the track they came to a dilapidated barn. They drove up to it and stopped outside the doors. One door was hanging off, the other upright. Peabody got out, crossed to the barn and pulled the doors open. The building was about 40 metres long and empty apart from a rusting plough parked in one corner. Hunter drove the car inside and switched off the engine. They dragged both men out of the car and dumped them next to each other.

Peabody went outside as the other car approached. Badonovitch manoeuvred the car so that it was facing back down the track. Hunter stayed in the barn, guarding the two men, while Peabody went outside for a handful of snow. He came back in and dropped the snow on Casimir's face. He had to do it three times before the man groaned and opened his eyes. Badonovitch had been doing the same to Marek who took longer but finally he also regained consciousness.

Casimir lay still, glaring at Hunter. Then he moved his head and looked around him. 'If you didn't have a gun I would kill you,' he spoke calmly to Peabody.

Peabody looked at Hunter who nodded. Peabody walked across to the Ford and put his automatic on the bonnet. He stepped back to Casimir and said, 'Okay. Get up.'

Casimir looked at him for a few seconds and then warily started to get to his feet. He stood up and put his hand to the side of his head, giving his temple a gentle rub.

His brother said something in Polish.

Badonovitch translated. 'He said to kill him.'

The man lashed out with his foot, aiming it at the American's crotch. Peabody had been expecting it. It was so obvious a move Casimir might as well have sent a text message.

Peabody stepped left, put his hand out and continued the swing of the leg, lifting it up past shoulder height. The Pole was flung high into the air and landed on his back, his head hitting the dirt with a heavy thud. He lay there for a few seconds, a dazed look on his face.

'You're a gutless piece of dirt,' said Peabody. 'You kill women and children. You blow them up with no warning. You wreck lives and ruin families. You are a typical coward who needs wiping off the face of the earth. Get up and fight like a man.'

Casimir got slowly to his feet, his hands clutching into the dirt. Peabody saw what he was doing and knew what to expect. As the Pole threw the dirt, Casimir stepped forward, and at the same time went into a series of choreographed katas. Peabody had raised his arm across his eyes and protected them from the dirt and now backed effortlessly around the barn as the other man tried to land a blow. Countering the katas was child's play as Casimir came at him as hard and as fast as he could. In spite of the cold, the Pole was sweating, breathing heavily, his movements becoming slower, more laboured.

Peabody saw the other man glance at the bonnet of the car. Again, he'd been expecting it and allowed himself to be manoeuvred until the Pole was within an arm's length of the bonnet and the Glock. Casimir made a lunge for the bonnet, reaching for the gun. Peabody stepped in fast and slammed the cutting edge of his hand across Kowalak's arm. The bone broke with a loud crack. The Pole screamed and collapsed to the ground, clutching his arm.

Peabody looked down at the man and said, 'I thought you were going to kill me? But then you fight like a girl, don't you? Except most girls have more guts than you.'

In reply, he received a torrent of Polish.

Badonovitch said, 'I won't bother translating but let's just say he is not being very complimentary about your parents or your colour.'

It was then that the bald brother asked two questions they should have asked from the start. 'Who are you people? What do you want?'

Hunter stood looking down at them both. 'My name is Commander Nicholas Hunter, Royal Navy,' he spoke formally. 'I am a senior officer with an organisation known as The International Force Against Terrorism. Perhaps you have heard of us?'

'What do you want?' asked Casimir.

Hunter said, 'Information.'

'What information?' Marek looked at his brother who sat holding his arm, his face drained of colour.

'To start with, we want to know where we can find your father.'

Marek replied. 'We don't know where he is.'

'Okay, we can do this the hard way or the easy way. What's it to be?'

'You are officials. I demand you arrest us and let us see a lawyer. I demand you prove whatever you think we have done in a court of law,' said Casimir.

Hunter shook his head. 'First, we know you are responsible for the explosions in Rome. We heard your two brothers talking about what you did and how much you were paid for the job. They also said there was another job coming up soon though they didn't say what it is. Perhaps you can enlighten us?'

Casimir shook his head. 'We don't know. Our father hasn't told us.'

'I'll ask you again. Where is your father?'

'We don't know I tell you,' Casimir shouted.

'This is your last chance. You will tell us. You'll tell us the easy way or the hard way. Either makes no difference to me.

28

Hunter gave no warning. He raised his Glock and shot Marek through the ankle of his left foot. The shock lasted about a second and then the man began to scream.

'Phil, you'd better go outside and keep an eye on things, will you? We don't want to receive any unexpected visitors.'

'Roger, boss.'

Hunter walked across to Marek who had his hands clutched around his ankle. 'Shut up,' Hunter yelled, 'or I'll put a bullet in your other ankle.' He pointed his gun at Marek's other foot and the man managed to stop moaning, dry sobs now wracking his body. 'Where's your father?'

'I tell you,' Marek gasped, 'I don't know.'

Hunter looked across at Casimir. 'You? Are you going to tell me?'

'I do not know. All we know is that he is in Egypt.'

'Where? My patience is running out and you had better tell me and tell me now.'

Casimir shook his head.

Hunter looked at Marek who, in spite of the freezing temperature, was sweating, agony and fear on his face. 'I'll ask you again. Where is he?'

'I don't know. We have never been there. It is a place our father goes to when he wants peace.'

'Somebody must know where that is.'

There was no reply. 'Okay. The hard way.' Hunter's second shot blew Marek's knee apart. Marek screamed loud and long, ending in a sob, tears rolling down his cheeks.

Hunter turned to Casimir and said, 'Now tell me where.'

'All I know is it is in or near Alexandria. I swear that is all we know.'

'Who knows where in Alexandria?'

'His brothers. Our uncles. They're in Warsaw. At the family estate.'

'The family estate is two houses and a mansion. Is that correct?' Hunter asked.

'Yes,' gasped Marek.

'Where do your uncles live?'

'They have a house each. Our father and mother live in the main house.'

'What about guards? Are there any?'

'Yes, yes. Oh God.' His hands were on his knee, the blood seeping through his fingers.

'How many?'

'It depends. Two on the gate at all time and four are reliefs.'

'Are there guards inside the houses?'

'No. Please, do you have something for the pain?'

Hunter ignored the request. 'Then where do the other four live?'

'In a building out the back.'

'What's the new job he's planning?'

'We don't know,' said Casimir. 'He hasn't told us.'

'I don't believe you.' Hunter put his foot on Marek's shattered ankle and yelled, 'Where is it?'

'We don't know I tell you,' screamed Marek, who started to sob.

'Which country is it going to happen in?'

The man shook his head. 'We don't know.' He could barely get the words out.

Hunter nodded and said, 'I shall now blow apart your other knee.'

'No! No! I swear we don't know. I swear it.' He began to sob.

'What about you, Casimir? Do you know?'

282

'No! I swear I don't. Our father never tells us anything unless he has to.'

Hunter's instinct was to blow each man's ankles, knees and elbows apart and let them die in agony. But at the end of the day it wasn't the sort of thing he could do. Without warning he shot each man through the forehead.

'Jan, help me drag the bodies under the car. We'll torch it. Leave their guns and passports. We'll take their mobiles and send them to Rosyth.'

They dragged the bodies to the car. Badonovitch removed the bug and the tracker while Hunter searched Marek's body for a cigarette lighter. He found one and then shoved the body under the car. Next he opened the boot, dragged out a suitcase and lifted out a shirt. He shoved the case back into the boot and slammed the lid shut. He opened the petrol cap, stuffed the shirt into the tank and then pulled the soaking cloth half out. 'Ready to go?'

'Ready when you are, boss,' Badonovitch replied.

'Okay. In the car.' Hunter held the lighter at arm's length and touched the shirt. The petrol burst into flame as Hunter turned and ran like hell. He threw himself into the BMW and Peabody took off with a jerk. The petrol tank exploded, a fireball of flaming petrol hitting the walls of the barn. It took a few seconds but then the barn became engulfed in flames.

The team got back to the road, turned left and followed the signs for the E462. Looking back, a black cloud of smoke was rising into the air.

They drove in silence for a while until they saw a sign indicating a service station ahead. 'Let's get a coffee and something to eat,' Hunter suggested.

Peabody turned off the motorway.

They bought coffees and sandwiches which they took out to the car. Once on the road again, Hunter phoned the General and told him what had happened and what they had learnt.

'Damnation! So there is something else going down. Nick, well done to the three of you but we must find out what's going to happen. I'll get Isobel to concentrate her efforts around Alexandria. She may come up with something useful. In the meantime, talk to the brothers. I'll have another private jet waiting for you at Warsaw.'

'Any chance of any help from the SB?' Hunter was referring to the Security Service of the Ministry of Internal Affairs.

'I'm not sure. I'll have to ask William Summers. From the talks we've held recently, I doubt it. He's convinced that many of the security services personnel, especially at senior levels, are somehow either colluding with what's going on or are merely ignoring it.'

'Does he know the head of the SB?'

'Yes. He's had very little to do with him but he says he's heard nothing good about the man. I don't need to tell you to be careful. A neutral force we can handle but one that's actively working against us is something else. We know what they're like in Eastern Europe, even after all this time. They'll shoot first and say sorry afterwards.'

'Where's this estate of theirs?'

'Isobel is sending you the details in the next few minutes. We've got satellite photos of the area which are pretty detailed thanks to clear skies.'

They said their goodbyes. The phone had been on speaker and Peabody summed up the situation.

'Boss, it's in and out and damned fast at that.'

According to the sat-nav it was about seven hours to Warsaw.

* * * *

Richard and Andrea did begin speaking again but not until after they'd been in the car for an hour or so. Andrea offered the olive branch with an apology which Richard gladly accepted. Of course, he then spoilt it.

'Andrea, I know what you said, but please wait a few more days.'

'Richard, how many more times? No, I am not waiting a few more

284

days. I am terrified something has happened to Maud and I must do all I can to find her. The only way I can do that is to go to the authorities. I know there are problems with the Parliament but I don't think they're as bad as you and your cousin have been painting them.'

Richard glanced at her, and then concentrated on the road. There was nothing more he could say. Strasbourg to Brussels was 290 miles as near as dammit. Richard took his time. Although the roads were clear enough, they were still treacherous in places and besides which, he was in no hurry. They stopped at Luxembourg for a snack and a break just after midday, and then at Namur around 15.00. They arrived at their destination a few minutes before 17.00. Andrea's building had underground parking and Richard drove down the ramp. The place could hold about eighty cars and was half full. Strip lighting lined the roof, casting deep shadows in places. There was nobody in sight. Andrea indicated a parking place next to a VW Beetle. 'That's my car. Please stop there.'

Richard reversed into the spot Andrea indicated, the rear of the car close up to a breeze block wall. He looked around. There was a line of pillars supporting the roof, about 10 metres apart. 'This is pretty big, how many apartments are there?'

'Fifty.' Her answer was sharp but there was also sadness in her voice.

For the sake of something to say, to delay the inevitable, he asked, 'Which floor do you live on?'

'The third, flat three zero two. I have a lovely view of the building opposite.'

In the far corner was a double door. He looked at her and said, 'Well, this is it.'

She nodded. 'Yes. Thanks for everything. If you don't mind, I'd rather you didn't come in.'

Richard nodded. 'I don't mind.' It had been a pleasant interlude, a holiday romance, even if it had turned into something far more deadly. It was now time to get back in harness and get to work.

'Bye then, Richard.' Andrea leaned across and kissed him on the cheek.

Richard opened his door and said, 'Let me get your stuff.' He went around to the back of the car and popped the boot. Being parked so close to the wall made it awkward but he reached in, dragged out Andrea's suitcase and extended the handle. He slammed the boot shut and then trundled to the front of the car dragging the case behind him.

'Thanks, Richard.' She kissed his cheek again. 'Bye.'

'Bye, Andrea. And good luck with your battle against the forces of evil.' He smiled to take any sting out of his words.

She smiled back, turned and walked away. Richard stood watching her go. As she reached the door, she opened her handbag, took out a card and swiped it along the lock. She looked back at him and waved before going through the door.

Richard waved back and as he did he saw a movement out of the corner of his eye. A figure had appeared from nowhere and was going towards the ramp. It was pure instinct. The man hadn't been in sight and yet he suddenly appeared. If he lived there and had been sitting in a car for some reason, he would be going to the door to the building. He wouldn't be heading for the ramp. Also, the only place he could possibly have come from was from behind one of the pillars.

'Excuse me!' Richard called out, taking a couple of paces, 'Excuse me!'

The man turned and Richard saw that not only was the collar of his coat turned up but he was also wearing some sort of mask. Even as the man was raising a silenced gun to point at him, Richard was throwing himself back, behind the nearest car. A bullet hit the car's bonnet. Surprisingly, the car's alarm didn't erupt with its cacophonous noise and flashing lights.

Richard lay on the ground and looked at where the man had been standing. The man's feet were coming his way. Richard crabbed his way to the Austin-Healey and wrenched open the driver's door. There was no internal light, thank goodness. He frantically felt around the space behind the seat for his bum bag but couldn't find it. One option was to climb into the car, start it and go hell for leather at the man and the ramp. His chances of making it were minuscule. A few well aimed shots would take him out.

Now he could hear the footsteps. The measured tread coming towards him sent shivers of fear along his spine. Move! He told himself. Move or in the next 30 seconds you're dead.

He looked under the vehicles again. The man was half a dozen cars away and closing. Richard turned, bent double and ran. He was grateful he was wearing soft soled shoes. He knew he couldn't keep running so what was there left to do?

He looked back and as he did so he saw the gunman drop to the floor. At that point he had a modicum of luck. He found himself next to a Mercedes van. It was at least ten years old and had a tow bar fitted to it. Richard stood, grabbed the door handle and stepped up onto the tow bar. The van moved slightly under his weight. He prayed it wasn't enough for the man to notice.

The measured tread continued in his direction. Richard couldn't see the man. All he had to go by was the footsteps. The feet stopped moving. Richard wasn't sure but he thought the man must have been only a couple of metres away. There were another two steps and a shuffle. The man was on Richard's left. At that moment the silenced automatic came into sight. It was being swept in a narrow arc. As the man's arm and then his side came into view Richard stepped down and launched himself.

The gunman's reactions were incredible. He must have noticed movement out of the corner of his eye and was already turning to face Richard who was still a pace away. From what Richard could see of his assailant, he appeared to be thin and wiry and a couple of inches shorter than Richard.

Richard was focused on the gun. If it pointed at any part of him, even his arm or shoulder, and was fired, it would all be over.

Desperation coupled with his Bartitsu training gave the concentration he needed. He gripped the barrel with his left hand and the man's fist with his right. A shot was fired and missed. With the adrenaline coursing through him at that moment he felt no pain. Richard twisted with all his strength and the man's fist opened and he let go of the automatic. The barrel slipped through Richard's fingers and the gun flew away.

Richard was half turned from his assailant who wrapped his arm around Richard's throat and began to strangle him. Richard grabbed the man's arm and was bending it away from his neck when the man clamped his other arm across his wrist and pulled it back. Richard was being strangled to death. His lungs were bursting and spots were floating between his eyes.

* * * *

Andrea let herself into the building and pressed the button for the lift. The middle one of the three was at car park level and the doors slid open. She stepped inside.

Although she looked to be in control of her emotions it was far from the truth. She was nervous and fearful at the same time. The interlude in Grindelwald had begun so promisingly but then had deteriorated into a nightmare. Richard had been fun, intelligent and considerate. It had been just what she'd needed.

Then the actual threats to her life. Then the shootings as they'd taken the ski-doo and run for their lives. If it hadn't been for the crash, God alone knows what would have happened.

The involvement of TIFAT had reinforced the seriousness of what they were facing. It was then, she was now certain, she should have gone to the police and explained what was happening. Asked for help and protection. Had an escort back home and then given the information to the local police authority. Perhaps even to Interpol.

Now she had the fear of what had happened to Maud. She just wouldn't have vanished like she had. It wasn't in her character. Maud was a loyal fighter and was as determined as she was to put the spotlight on the corruption that was pervading the EU Parliament.

The lift arrived at her floor and she stepped along to her door and inserted the key. As soon as she was inside she would phone the police. She inserted the key, turned it and reached for the door handle. Twisting it, she pushed the door open and stepped inside. She was bending to pick up the pile of mail on the floor when she sniffed the air. There was a faint smell of gas. How peculiar, she thought and took the few paces across the hall to the door leading to her kitchen/diner. She twisted the handle and pushed the door open further. It was stiff. She looked down and saw that a rubber seal had been placed under the door.

* * * *

Richard knew he had less than a minute. He arched backwards, and did the unexpected. His attacker's head was close to the back of Richard's neck. Richard bent his arms backwards. His left hand grabbed the man's hood, his right hand grabbed his ear. Without pausing, Richard bent his body forward and dropped heavily to his knees. The man flipped over him to land with a heavy thud on his back.

At that moment, the shock of the explosion registered. Richard was gasping for breath, his lungs heaving, but he knew he had no time to indulge himself by taking long and grateful gulps of air. He clasped his hands together and brought them down with all his strength onto the bridge of his assailant's nose. The man screamed in agony as his nose broke and flattened across his face, blood soaking into his mask.

For all that, the killer still had the presence of mind to roll towards his automatic that was an arm's length away. He had his hand on the weapon when Richard dropped onto his back, grabbed the man's forehead and heaved back with all the strength he could muster. The snapping of the gunman's spinal cord was a loud crack in what had become the deathly silence of the car park.

Richard grabbed the gun and ran towards the doors to the building. He fired half a dozen shots and shattered the lock. He dragged the door open and stepped through. Reaching the lifts, he hesitated, changed his mind and then looked around for the stairs. He could hear the faint sound of the lift descending. Above it, he could hear the screaming of the fire alarms and he paused. His initial reaction had been to get to Andrea's apartment, but then common sense kicked in.

He had no illusions that Andrea had been blown up and was dead. Nobody survived a blast such as that. There was nothing to be gained by becoming involved. If only half of what Andrea had told him was true, then to get mixed up in the officialdom of the EU and the European Arrest Warrant combined with the new legal act imposed by a Labour Government in line with European legislation would be a tragedy to say the least. He knew that under the new act, anyone arrested could be held in prison, without charge, for as long as the authorities took to bring a prisoner to trial. That could easily run into more than a year. As the jury consisted of a gaggle of judges and not made up of a panel of his peers, his chances of a fair trial were negligible. That was assuming he lived long enough to be tried – which was doubtful. The last thing those in power wanted was for him to get on a stand and tell the world what he knew.

Reluctantly, he returned to the car park and ran across to where the dead man lay. He grabbed him by the shoulders and dragged the body out of sight next to the wall. He reached into the man's pockets and extracted a wallet which he opened. It contained a few euros and a credit card. He flipped open the side of the wallet and looked at the ID card in shocked horror. The identity card showed the man's name to be Henri Matteus, his occupation – an Inspector in the Belgian Federal Police.

Richard knew that if he was caught he would never see the light of day again. He found the man's gun, wiped it clean of fingerprints and placed it next to the body. He decided to take the wallet with him and shoved it into his pocket. That could delay identifying the body for a few hours at least. He'd get rid of it later. Climbing into his car, he drove sedately out of the car park and up onto the street. It was deserted. The explosion had been at the front of the building, on the other side. There, the blue loom of flashing lights and the sound of sirens could be seen and heard. Richard, with a heavy sigh, turned away from the growing crowd and slowly drove off.

He looked at his watch. It was 17.16. Less than twenty minutes to cause such devastation. One thing he'd noticed and he thanked God for, was the fact that there had been no security cameras either in the car park or at the entrance.

In the relative safety of his car and as the adrenaline rush faded he felt his throat. It hurt and swallowing was painful. He was also experiencing anguish and sorrow. Not to mention guilt – he should have prevented Andrea from returning. Even as the thought took hold he realised how stupid it was. All he would have succeeded in doing was delaying the inevitable.

He debated with himself what to do and where to go then decided to head for the A10 autoroute. He got onto the autoroute and shortly afterwards he passed the sign informing him he was entering France. Stopping at the first service station, he climbed out of his car, zapped it locked and went into the building. He found the Toilettes and went inside to wash and tidy his clothes. Looking in the mirror he saw a haggard face blearily looking back at him. In a cubicle he took out the wallet he'd lifted and went through it carefully. He took a note of the man's full name and ID number along with his credit card details. He wiped the wallet as best he could to remove any fingerprints and as he left the Toilettes, he dropped it into a rubbish bin. Next, he went out to the restaurant area, got himself a burger, some French fries and a cup of coffee. Sitting at a table he looked at the food and thought he wasn't hungry. He began to eat the food but swallowing was too painful. Sipping his coffee was bad enough, but at least he managed to drink that. While he sat there, he knew of only one man he could trust

291

and whose help he could use – whose help he needed. Two minutes on his mobile and he had the number he wanted. He dialled it.

'HMS *Cochrane*, can I help you?' asked the pleasant, competent voice of the operator.

'Good evening. Can I speak to General Macnair, please?'

'I'm not sure the General is available, sir. May I take a message for him?' The dulcet voice of the female operator rankled with Richard and he replied irritably, 'No, you can't. It's imperative that I speak to him now.'

This time there was more steel in the voice. 'I am sorry, sir. I cannot locate the General at this moment.'

'Sorry. Sorry.' Richard said, contritely. 'Please don't cut me off. Do you know Commander Hunter?'

'Who?'

Richard gritted his teeth at the games played by TIFAT in the name of security. Sighing, he said, 'My name is Richard Griffiths. I am Nick Hunter's cousin. Please give the General a message. It is of vital importance that he contacts me. Here is my number.' He relayed his number to her. 'Tell him I am in France and this is an emergency.'

The girl spoke in a doubtful tone. 'I'll do my best, sir, but I can't guarantee anything.' She kept up the fiction that the General was possibly unobtainable, like all well-trained switchboard operators the world over.

'Thank you.' Richard sat back, suddenly exhausted, the trauma of the last hour or so draining him of energy. His thoughts turned to Andrea. He was furious with himself. He should have insisted they stay away. He should, he thought bitterly, have kidnapped her and faced the consequences afterwards. Even as he thought it, he told himself not to be so damned stupid.

He was taking another sip of coffee when his phone rang. 'Hullo?'

'Richard? It's Malcolm Macnair.'

'General! Thanks for getting back to me so quickly.'

'You said it was an emergency.'

Taking a deep breath, Richard replied, 'Andrea Nelson has been murdered.'

'What! What happened?'

Richard ran through the details, starting with her insistence to return to Brussels to find her missing secretary and ending with the death of the inspector and the explosion.

'I'm not surprised there are police officers involved. What are you going to do?'

'I'm on the A10 autoroute about an hour and a half from Calais. I thought I'd go there and take the train to Folkestone.'

'Can you get to Gatwick or Heathrow and fly here tomorrow morning?'

'Yes. Why?'

'Her death shows that there are others who had been given the job of killing her. Furthermore, the explosion is proof that they didn't care who else died in achieving their objective.'

'They could have just shot her. This man Matteus only needed to have waited in the car park.'

'Except for one important factor. Her obvious murder would mean an investigation. We'll wait for the report, but I suspect the police inspector was smart enough to try and make it look like some sort of accident.'

'Like a gas leak?'

'Probably.'

'Things like that just don't happen. Any competent investigation will show that.'

'You're right of course. But what if the investigators are also part of it? After all, we have no idea how far and wide these things go.'

'True enough.' Richard sighed. 'If they can do it, they would want Andrea's death to look like an accident. Me on the other hand . . .' he trailed off.'

'Precisely.'

'The thought had already occurred to me. They probably already know who I am. Hell, that puts others in danger.'

'Maybe. They can booby-trap your car and your house but to do so takes more planning and more effort than a bullet, whether from a sniper or a close encounter in a crowd. Your death won't cause anything like the furore of Andrea's murder and it will fade away into the mists of time.'

'For that read a couple of days.'

'You being here is about the safest place I can think of right now, at least until we get this mess cleaned up, unless you've a better idea.'

'How about the Maldives?'

'There is that. On the other hand, you can help us go through what we know and maybe it'll help us to get to the bottom of who's responsible.'

'You're right.'

'I'll meet you at Edinburgh Airport.'

'I'll text you when I'll be arriving.' They broke their connection and Richard checked the times of the trains. There was a Euro Tunnel Shuttle train at 20.50. He looked at his watch and saw it was 18.03. He could just make it or he'd have to catch the 21.20. Crossing time was 35 minutes. He returned to his car, pulled forward the back of the driver's seat and found his bum bag. He strapped it around his waist. There was a certain comfort to be had knowing the Glock was available in seconds.

A police car pulled up behind him, its lights flashing.

29

The team were on the outskirts of Warsaw, at the western edge of the city in an area known as Bemowo. Hunter was in the front passenger seat, Badonovitch was driving while Peabody was dozing in the back. Details of the location of the Kowalak estate had been transmitted to them from Rosyth and the satnav was pleasantly insistent as to which route to take. According to the gadget, they were only 10 kms away. It was 20.15 local time when Hunter's phone rang. Looking at the display he saw that it was the General. He put the phone on speaker.

'We've arrived, sir.'

'Good. I'm afraid I have some bad news. I heard from Richard. Andrea has been killed. It appears she was blown up when she tried to enter her apartment.'

'What was Richard doing taking her back to Brussels? He was meant to keep her away until we sorted out this mess.'

'It wasn't his fault. It seems she insisted.' Macnair repeated what Richard had told him.

When he'd finished, Hunter said, 'You're right. I guess it wasn't Richard's fault. The police inspector's involvement is even more proof of how wide, deep and rotten things are.'

'I've been on to MI6 and asked them if they knew anything about the explosion. They said they'd heard a report that it had been a gas leak and that at least six, possibly as many as ten, people have been killed. The situation was still being investigated. The usual mixture of facts, media fiction and political lying will no doubt have the whole story swept under the carpet in the next forty-eight hours. Back to the matter in hand. What's the weather like?'

'It's been snowing, then it stopped for a while but it's back with a vengeance.'

'Okay. Let's hope it doesn't prevent you driving. I've got another Citation hired from midnight at the Frederic Chopin Airport. It's a Citation Three. It's bigger than the last plane and it has a range of over 2,000 miles with a cruising speed over 540 mph. It means you won't have to land to refuel and all that will entail. It'll save a few hours and as we don't know what we're dealing with every hour counts. You can get access to the jet at anytime during the night. However, the airport is shut from 23.00 until 05.30. Aircraft arriving late are allowed to land especially if the delays are caused by the weather. What it means is that you can go to the airport and get on the plane but you can't take-off before 05.30. Incidentally, we picked up some phone transmissions between Alexandria and Warsaw. They were too short to pinpoint on the Egyptian end but we are positive they were made to Kowalak's estate.'

'We'll ask the brothers very nicely where Jakub is,' said Hunter, sarcasm dripping from every syllable. 'I take it we'll have to go through security?'

'I'm afraid so.'

'In that case, we'll ditch everything. That's us less than three kilometres away. I'd better go.'

'I'll speak to you later.'

Hunter looked at his iPad and said, 'Jan, according to the map Isobel's sent, there's a side road about 500 metres from the grounds of the place, around the back. I'll direct you. We can park there.'

*   *   *   *

Richard Griffiths was gripped by fear and panic raised its ugly head. His instinct was to drive away as fast as possible but commonsense prevailed. He would never make it. He thought about grabbing for his automatic but dismissed the idea. They could just as easily be ordinary cops and not connected with what was going on, merely obeying orders to arrest him. Opening the door, he slowly got out. If they took out their guns he was in serious trouble but they didn't.

The officer to the left wished him a good evening.

Richard replied in French. 'Is there something wrong?'

'We wish to check your equipment.'

'I see. If I may take the papers out of the glove compartment?'

The man nodded and Richard opened the driver's door and leant in. Relief flooded over him. Opening the glove compartment he took out his original registration document plus his insurance and handed them over. While the officer checked them, the other one went around the back of the car and looked at the GB sticker, compulsory in much of Europe. Richard didn't need to be told what to do. He opened the boot, rummaged around and took out a warning triangle, reflective jacket and two breathalyser kits.

'Snow chains?'

Richard emptied the boot and lifted the cover to the spare tyre. Taking out the chains he showed them and received a nod in return. The officers looked at each other, shrugged and without another word, walked back to their car. Richard repacked the boot, as angry as hell. He knew the French police picked on UK drivers because much of the stuff he'd shown wasn't carried in British cars. The on-the-spot fines were rumoured to finance a great deal of the French Police Forces' budget. He got back into the Austin-Healey and sat there for a few minutes. The relief he was feeling was overwhelming and he needed to compose himself before he drove away.

From the glove compartment, he extracted a Swiss army knife and cut up the identity card and credit card of the Inspector. He then drove across to the garage forecourt where he filled up with fuel and was soon back on the autoroute. The speed limit was 130kph and even though the road was clear he was careful not to exceed it.

He decided he'd spend the night at the Travelodge at Ashford and go to Heathrow first thing in the morning. While he drove, he dropped the plastic pieces one-by-one out of the window. Then he thought about the instructions he'd had from his cousin regarding the automatic. He pulled open the bum bag, took out the Glock, thumbed open the magazine, opened his window a couple of inches and dropped the bullets at intervals onto the road. These were followed by the mag. He took out the knife again and pulled open the screwdriver attachment. He fumbled with the gun but couldn't see what he was doing. Cursing, he saw there was a services 20 kms ahead. He'd stop there, dismantle the automatic and also ditch its parts along the road.

* * * *

Thankfully, it had stopped snowing, the storm that had been ravaging the area having scuttled across the sky to leave a cloudless, dark, moonless night. Hunter switched off the satnav as the voice began to go berserk with her orders to turn around and directed Badonovitch to the side road which turned out to be a track around a copse of trees. Badonovitch drove carefully along the track for about 100 metres, and although the snow was about 30 cms deep it was not proving an impediment.

'This'll do,' said Hunter.

Badonovitch turned the car and switched off the engine. Hunter was studying the map of the estate.

'There are a number of buildings. There's the main house, what looks like a stable near to it and another two houses close together a few hundred metres from the mansion. Rosyth has confirmed that the two brothers live there.' He studied the pictures for a few more seconds and said, 'There are a few outhouses as well. See here?' He pointed and showed the picture to the other two. 'One of them will house the guards.'

He looked up at the wall. It was about three metres high with broken glass embedded in the concrete along the top and a strand of wire running the length of the wall.

'Kowalak takes his security pretty seriously,' said Hunter.

'That wire is probably some sort of alarm,' said Peabody. 'But he's made a mistake.'

Hunter said, 'That's for sure. That oak is too near the wall. He should have had it cut down.' Hunter changed the iPad setting to real time satellite images, the clear skies proving to be a godsend. By making adjustments, he was able to superimpose an infra-red picture onto the other one. It showed stationary heat spots at the three houses, as well as two smaller dots walking back and forth near the main gates, which were about 700 metres from the houses. 'Three fires and two guards,' said Hunter. 'Both near the gates.'

'Shall we take them out first?' Peabody asked.

'Yes,' was the stark reply. 'Jan, when we go in, you take care of those two. Then come back to the buildings and stay outside. Cover us. If they're really smart, they'll have interconnected alarms that can be set off from different places throughout the grounds and in the houses. Check comms.'

They each switched on their communications transmitter/receiver sets. They hadn't used them in Grindelwald in case MacGregor or one of the Kivis had noticed. Using a mobile was one thing – dozens of people at the resort had been doing it at any one time – speaking into your wrist with an earplug in was something else.

Satisfied the sets were working, they climbed out of the car into the freezing night. They were dressed in their ski trousers, jackets, snow boots and ski masks. Each man checked his Glock, and put spare ammo in his pockets.

'Ready?' Hunter asked. 'Good. Let's go.'

They crossed to the tree and stood looking up at it for a few seconds. The nearest branch was a metre higher than the wall, hanging over it into the grounds. One side of the tree was caked in snow, the other side was bare. The remainder of the branches hung heavily, weighed down by the snow, an occasional lump dropping from the tree.

'Jan, bring the car over and park it just here. We'll climb onto the roof.'

Badonovitch backed the car up close to the tree. He opened the driver's window, stepped up onto it and then onto the roof. The branch was just out of Badonovitch's reach.

'Let me get up there,' whispered Peabody.

They swapped places. The branch was just within Peabody's reach and he grabbed it and swung himself into the V of the branch and the tree trunk.

Badonovitch went next. The SEAL leant over, took his hand and pulled him up. The Russian straddled the branch and edged his way along and across the wall. The snow on the branch fell to the ground. Once over the wall, he lowered himself down and dropped into the snow. Hunter was already straddling the branch and inching forward. Seconds later, he joined Badonovitch, closely followed by Peabody.

Hunter checked his watch. Lights were still showing in the two houses which were about 80 metres away on their right. The main house was in complete darkness. He checked the iPad.

'The two men are still at the gates. The other three dots have faded slightly, presumably because the fires are dying down.' There was a sea of white stretching across the grounds with a few white lumps of some sort of plant scattered across the vista.

'We'll stay close to the wall,' Hunter said in a low voice, 'and work our way around to the rear.'

The three of them carried their weapons, walking slowly around the perimeter with the wall on their right. Hunter kept glancing at the iPad but the dots hadn't changed except the three superimposed on the houses had faded a little more.

They came to the end of the wall and turned left. There were no lights to be seen in the houses. They turned their attention to the outhouses behind the dwellings. There were four of them. Each one appeared to be large enough to hold at least three cars. When they reached a position where the first building hid them from the nearest house, Hunter signalled to the other two to stay where they were while he slipped across to look inside. The walls appeared to be made of wood. There was a side door which was unlocked. He entered and found two cars, as well as a work bench along one wall. There was nothing of interest and he returned outside. He darted across to the second one. It too was constructed of wood. He went inside and found nothing but a pile of logs.

The third shed was made of stone and had a heavy, locked door. Hunter waved Badonovitch across to him and then reached into his pocket and took out the lock-gun. He carefully examined the lock and changed the attachments on the end of the gun. He placed the muzzle of the gun into the lock and pressed the trigger. There was a low buzz, barely discernible even in the hush of the night, which lasted nearly a minute before the lock clicked and the door opened.

Hunter slowly pulled the door towards him. It was heavy and he realised it was made of steel. When the door was sufficiently ajar, he sidled inside. It was pitch dark. Unlike the other outbuildings which had windows and a degree of visibility, here he could see nothing. Stepping further into the building, he took out his mobile phone and switched on the torch. He recognised the smell that permeated the atmosphere – gun oil. There were numerous tools lying on the workbench and he lifted a small screwdriver which he put in his pocket. There were three shelves holding cans of different sizes and shapes as well as various other bits of gear. At the end of the workbench he found a rack of AK74s. There was a metal cupboard with a handle which had a built-in lock. The lock-gun had it opened in less than ten seconds. It was packed with blocks of plastic explosives, detonators and timers. On a bottom shelf he found half a dozen transmitters used to set off explosives from a distance. He pressed a button on the side of one of the transmitters, which checked the battery power, and was relieved to find it fully charged.

He went back to the door, opened it and said quietly, 'Jan, this place is full of weapons as well as plastic. I've found some transmitters and I'm going to set a charge.'

'Roger that, boss,' Badonovitch whispered.

He spent less than five minutes setting the plastic. He married up the detonators to the remote and then went back outside.

The fourth and final building was about 20 metres away. Badonovitch pointed and whispered, 'Footprints.'

'I see them.' There was a path trodden through the snow from the door of the building and heading towards the side of the main house.

They went back to the wall where Hunter took out the iPad to check on the infra-red spots. The two that had been at the gate were walking towards the side of the house. 'Down!' Hunter whispered into his microphone. Even as he spoke, he was dropping to the ground. The other two were a split second behind him. Luckily, the snow made it impossible for anyone to see them unless that person came close enough to step on them.

Hunter saw the door of the building swing open and a man appeared, quickly followed by a second. A light was on in the building and it spilled across the snow. The door closed just as the two from the gates appeared. They greeted each other in voices that easily travelled across the bleak landscape. They exchanged a few words and the two from the building followed in the footsteps of the guards from the gates.

When the men were out of sight, Hunter whispered, 'What did they say?'

'One of those who came out said to make sure the other two relieved them on time. Then he added that they weren't to drink all the vodka.'

'Jan, you carry on to the gate and take care of those two,' said Hunter. We'll take out whoever's in the hut.'

Badonovitch moved quickly to the side of the mansion. Hunter watched him on the iPad walk directly towards the main gate.

'Let's go,' whispered Hunter.

They darted through the snow, Hunter in front, Peabody at his left shoulder. 'You take the left, I'll take the right,' said Hunter. 'Ready?'

'Yep.'

Opening the door, Hunter stepped inside. It was a room with six beds along the furthest wall, a couple of armchairs and a table with six chairs around it. Four were occupied. The men had a bottle of vodka on the table in front of them, along with cans of beer. The room was thick with smoke, each of the men with a cigarette in his hand.

Three didn't react, one did.

The three men who sat and looked at the intruders were shot through the forehead and were dead before they realised what was happening. Peabody had killed the two on the left. Hunter shot the one furthest to the right but the fourth man's reactions were incredible. He had thrown himself off his chair and towards one of the beds before Hunter could change aim. But even as the man reached for the holster hanging on the end of the bed, Hunter fired twice. Both shots hit their target – one in the chest, the other in the side of the head.

They quickly looked around the place. It wasn't much more than a dump. They found two toilets and two shower stalls. At one end was a kitchen with a cooker that looked as though it hadn't been cleaned in a decade and a fridge in which all they found were cans of lager and bottles of vodka. Next to the sink was a coffee machine with dirty mugs stacked up alongside.

Badonovitch arrived back then and said, 'Okay, boss. They thought I was one of these guys until it was too late. I dragged the bodies to one side in case anyone drives in.'

Alongside each bed was a locker, which contained spare magazines for their weapons and wads of Polish zlotys. The weapons they left, the cash they took.

Now that there were no guards around, Hunter checked the last outhouse. It was stacked full of gardening equipment. Alongside one wall was an aluminium ladder. He hoisted it onto his shoulder and returned outside.

'Jan, can you take this back to where we left the car?'

'Right, boss.' He lifted it onto his shoulder and went quickly around the perimeter to the spot where they had climbed over the wall. Hunter and Peabody followed but stopped when they were at the back of the two houses. Badonovitch was back in minutes.

'Jan, you stay here and cover us. Phil, you take the house on the right, I'll take the one on the left. Jan, here's the remote. Don't hesitate to use it if you need to. We can't be sure what will happen if there's an alarm system.'

'Hard and fast, boss,' said Peabody.

'Yeah. We've no choice. Okay, let's go.'

They only had the one lock-gun. Hunter used it on both houses, each lock taking about ten seconds to open.

Hunter and Peabody opened their respective doors a few inches and felt along the tops to see if they could feel any type of alarm. Then they ran their hands down the side of the door. There was nothing.

'Ready?' Hunter asked, speaking into his wrist.

'Ready.'

Both men pushed open their door and stepped inside.

Hunter found himself in a kitchen. It was large, well kitted out with a six plate oven, a large fridge/freezer, a coffee blender and a microwave.

The bleeping and flashing light showed the security pad on the wall beside the door. He figured he had two minutes, maybe three, before it burst into life. He darted across the room, pulled open the door which led to a corridor and stepped through. At that moment a figure loomed up in front of him, like a dark ghost in the grey of the night.

The alarm had yet to go off so the figure Hunter was confronting reared back in shock. They were two metres apart. Hunter stepped forward two paces and hit the person with a hard knock using the butt of his Glock. Bending over the body, Hunter saw that it was a woman. He checked and found she was breathing steadily. Hunter figured that though she was unconscious, she could wake up at any moment. The safe thing to do was put a bullet though her head. Instead, he dragged her across the polished floor and through a door on the right. It was a large room, well furnished. He saw that the curtains were controlled using rope pulls. Even as he grabbed one and pulled it down the alarm erupted into life. The noise was deafening.

30

Now it was a race against time. Peabody was in the corridor of the house which stretched about 20 metres to the front door. There were two doors either side of the corridor. He looked through each one. All four rooms proved to be empty. At that moment the lights in the house came on. He was at the bottom of the stairs when a man appeared at the top with a gun in his hand. The point of being there was to question the two brothers about the exact location of Jakub Kowalak, not to kill them. Peabody didn't know who the man was and he didn't want to do it but he had no choice. He shot the man twice. The man went flying backwards.

The stairs were wide. The right side ran along the wall while the left side was open to a banister. There was a balcony running around three walls of the house. Peabody ran up the stairs, taking them two at a time. There were three doors leading off the balcony, one was open, two were shut. Peabody guessed the dead man was in his late twenties, maybe early thirties. Not the man he wanted. He saw that the walls were lined with wood, pictures hanging about every metre. The door immediately on his right opened. A man stepped out with a gun in his hand. He looked to be in his fifties, had grey hair and a pasty slab of a face.

Peabody was better prepared for problems than the other man. The SEAL swept the man's gun to one side and smashed him across the side of the head, just above his ear, with the butt of his gun. It was one hell of a blow. The man collapsed, pole-axed. Damn! If the man was one of the brothers it would be some time before he could be questioned.

A door on the other side of the balcony opened and someone stepped out. The person was wearing a dressing gown, had curlers in her hair but most importantly had a gun in her hand which she was pointing at Peabody. He flung himself to one side and fired four shots through the banisters at the woman. Two rounds hit one of the uprights of the wooden banisters and blasted it apart. All four bullets hit her in the chest and she went down. The SEAL stayed where he was, looking about him to see if there were more surprises in store.

There were none. After 30 seconds he got up and checked each of the bedrooms. All were en-suite, all were empty.

*   *   *   *

Badonovitch waited patiently, expecting trouble to come from the main house. He didn't have long to wait. Two minutes after the alarm went off a number of people came stumbling out of the house heading quickly in his direction. He thought there were three individuals but then spotted the fourth.

Each of them was armed.

One yelled, 'Cyryl, you and Feliks take the other house. Krzysztof we will take this one.'

'Boss, Phil,' Badonovitch whispered, 'four baddies. Two to each house. I'll deal.'

The transmission wasn't acknowledged.

Two ran past where Badonovitch was lying in the snow. They didn't bother to be careful. They didn't follow the most basic of procedures. They just ran for the back doors of the houses. Taking out two of them would be child's play, three a bit of a stretch, four was asking for trouble. Even these clowns, Badonovitch acknowledged to himself, had a good chance of putting a few bullets his way.

Two men went through the kitchen door of the first house; the other two men were nearing the second house. Badonovitch made his move. Even as he did, silence descended like a blanket. Someone had turned off the alarm. He ran to the first house and went through the door into the kitchen. Both men had their backs to him and were now carefully approaching the door opposite. It was a turkey shoot. Two slugs into the back of the man on the right. Two more into the back of the other man. Both shots were either side of their spine, close together and just slightly lower than their shoulder blades. Both men died instantly. Badonovitch didn't wait to find out the result of his action. He was already through the door and running like hell towards the second house.

At the door, this time, he paused and looked in. The lights had just come on and the house was lit up like an operating theatre in a hospital. He could see the back of only one man. He was standing at the door opposite. He was looking into the corridor which Badonovitch could see ran the width of the house. The Russian ran towards the target, ten paces away. The man was turning his head as Badonovitch reached him. Two torso shots and a third in the head killed the man. He didn't slacken his pace. Stepping into the corridor he saw the second man was at the door on the right, his hand on the handle, turning it.

The team had a significant advantage over the Poles. Everybody they encountered apart from each other, were enemy. For the Poles, they couldn't be sure who they were confronting. The alarm going off could just as easily have been a mistake or a problem with the mechanism – or just about anything other than intruders. Which meant that they had to be careful, hesitant, unsure. This meant they died.

Badonovitch fired twice. One body shot, one head shot. It had turned out a turkey shoot after all. 'All down,' he whispered into the transmitter.

*   *   *   *

Hunter had trussed up the woman so that she couldn't move. Next, he stepped into the corridor, ignoring the cacophony created by the

308

alarm system. He opened the door to each of the other three rooms and checked they were empty.

He stepped across to the stairs and stood with his back to the wall, looking upwards, scouting out the area. There was a balcony that ran around three sides of the house. He ran up the stairs, keeping as close to the wall as he could. Speed and surprise was what was wanted. His head was just above floor level when a door on the other side of the balcony opened. A man stepped out. He was about 50, bleary eyed, wearing pyjamas.

He stood there, looking around him, befuddled. Hunter reached the balcony and began to run around towards the man. The Pole seemed to come to life, stepped back and slammed the door shut.

Suddenly, it was silent.

Hunter kept running and slammed into the door with his right shoulder mustering every ounce of force that he could. The lock broke off and Hunter went flying into the room.

The bedroom was large. There was a bed along the wall opposite, a double wardrobe on the left, a dressing table and chair and a door on the right. There was no sign of the man but the door was closed. His target hadn't been carrying a gun when he'd come out onto the balcony, and Hunter was as sure as he could be that he hadn't had time to pick one up. After all, who would have a gun lying around a bedroom, especially if you felt safe in your own home protected by guards? But, he acknowledged to himself, he might be wrong.

Hunter stopped next to the door, kicked it and at the same time stepped to the side, the wall protecting him. The bullets exploded through the door, slamming into the wall opposite. It took less than three seconds for thirty rounds to be expended and the gun clicked on empty. Hunter stepped into the room. It was a bathroom. The bath was directly in front of him, a toilet on the right and a shower on the left. The man was standing between the door and the bath about two metres away.

With a snarl, the man raised his right arm, swung it back and went to throw the gun at Hunter. Hunter shot him in the left knee and the man collapsed, screaming. Hunter took three paces across the tiled floor and shoved the muzzle of his Glock into the Pole's face. The man stopped writhing. There was no hint of fear in him. He said something in Polish.

'Speak English!'

'English? You are a dead man but you don't know it. After you leave I will track you down to the ends of the earth. You will regret coming into my house. You will regret what you have done to me.' His accent was heavy, guttural, but understandable. Sweat was pouring from the man's face. He was obviously in agony but he wasn't going to show it. Hunter acknowledged that the Pole was a brave man – though that didn't make him a decent one.

'Where's your brother?'

There was more than surprise on the man's face. There was incredulity mixed with the pain. 'My brother?'

'Yes. Jakub!'

'I don't know.'

'Yes, you do. Your nephews told us to ask you as they didn't know.'

'My nephews? What have they to do with this?'

'Where is he?'

'I don't know I tell you!'

Hunter grabbed the man by his uninjured leg and dragged him towards the door. The man made a feeble effort to kick at Hunter with his other leg but ended up yelling in pain. He began struggling, putting all his energy into the leg Hunter was gripping. It was proving difficult for Hunter to keep hold of him. He was aware that time was running out. It was possible the alarm system was linked to a local police station, or there were more of the Kowalaks' men somewhere in the area also linked to the alarm. Just then, a telephone began to ring. At that time of night it could only mean that somebody was checking up. Hunter dropped the leg he was holding, stepped back and using his gun, hit him across the side of his temple. It was just hard enough to daze him, not to make him unconscious. The struggling stopped.

Hunter crossed to the door, stopped, knelt down and carefully looked out. There were two other doors. One on his left and one on his right. Both were closed. He needed to check each room. Scuttling along the balcony, he reached the door on the right. He stayed low, twisted the handle and flung the door open. Nothing happened. He lay on the floor, looked carefully inside and saw that the room was a mirror image of the other one, except it was used by a woman. The bathroom door was open, the room was empty.

That left one room. He carried out the same procedure and found it was also empty.

'Nick,' Peabody transmitted, 'I found one of the brothers but he'll be out for the count for some time.'

'Okay. Can't be helped. I've got the other one.'

'I'm going outside to keep watch.'

'Roger that.'

Hunter grabbed Kowalak's leg, dragged him across the balcony and as the man began to feebly struggle, shoved the body head first down the stairs. It stopped halfway down and he needed to give it another shove. Kowalak had stopped struggling and Hunter dragged him into the kitchen. He got a bowl of cold water and flung it over Kowalak's face. The man began to splutter and opened his eyes.

Hunter bent down and grabbed hold of the man's pyjamas in one hand and shook him. 'Where's your brother?'

The reply was a disjointed mumble in Polish.

Hunter used his comms, 'Jan, I need you.'

Badonovitch was watching the other house and he hurried across to Hunter.

'Where's Phil?' Hunter asked.

'Gone to the corner to keep an eye on the main house and the gates. We heard the phone. I guess somebody was checking up. If there's no answer they'll probably come running.'

'That's what I figure.' Hunter nodded at Kowalak. 'Ask him if he knows where Jakub is.'

Before Badonovitch could say a word, the man let loose with a torrent of Polish.

'He says that his men will be here any minute and that he will enjoy seeing us die slowly and painfully.'

'These people are morons.' Hunter summed up. 'You'll be dead before they get here,' he addressed the Pole. 'Where's Jakub?'

Again he was treated to another mouthful of Polish.

'He said he'd never tell us and followed it with a mouthful of abuse a lot of which had to do with your parents.'

'I'll ask you again one last time,' said Hunter. 'If you want to live, tell me where your brother is?'

Badonovitch shook his head. 'He's still claiming he doesn't know.'

Peabody transmitted, 'Incoming!'

'Damn!' was Hunter's response. Without hesitating he shot Kowalak in the left ankle. The man screamed. 'Where is he? I will blow out your other knee and ankle if I have to.'

'I don't know!' This time he spoke English.

'It's up to you.' He placed the silenced muzzle against the man's knee. 'Where is Jakub?'

The man jabbered in Polish.

Hunter looked at Badonovitch.

'He says in some estate to the west of Alexandria. He swears he is telling the truth. That you must let him live.'

Hunter looked at the man and shot him between the eyes.

Peabody said, 'there are three cars coming up the drive. One minute away.'

'Let's go!' Hunter said.

The three ran towards where the ladder had been placed.

Halfway there, Hunter stopped and said, 'You two go on and get the car started. I'll see to things here.' He dropped down into the snow. The other two kept going.

Hunter could see that after their mad dash up the drive, the men were more circumspect. They were walking slowly, guns out, focusing on the houses. They couldn't miss the open doors and the lights on in the kitchens. They had ignored the mansion house and Hunter supposed that was probably because nobody was there. A head count showed there were ten of them. Hunter waited patiently. Some of them passed the outhouse where the explosives were stored. A couple approached the building where the guards had been. One of them looked inside and called out something. Whatever he said caused the others to stop. It couldn't have been better.

Hunter almost burrowed himself into the ground. He had his left hand over his head and the remote in his right, aimed at the shack. He pressed the button. The explosion was huge, the shock waves washing over him, the noise disorientating. He stayed where he was for a few seconds. Then he looked up and climbed to his feet. There was nothing left of the building containing the explosives, while the other outbuildings had been smashed to pieces. The rear of the nearest house began to collapse while the roof of the other house was beginning to sag. There was no sign of the men. Hunter turned and ran for the wall. He reached the ladder, climbed it, got onto the branch of the tree and worked his way to the trunk. He hung down, dropped onto the car and then onto the ground. He climbed into the back, Badonovitch engaged the gears and they left. He drove sedately along to the road but once there the Russian wound the car up to 100 kph. There was no other traffic on the road.

Hunter said, 'We'll take the Glocks apart and get rid of them. I lifted a screwdriver back there.' Hunter went to work. It only took a couple of minutes. He threw the pieces out of the window one by one. Then he handed the screwdriver over to Peabody who did the same with the other two weapons.

'I feel naked without a gun,' Badonovitch summed up the feelings of the other two.

'It can't be helped. If the police are as corrupt as the General

313

thinks, then our warrant cards allowing us to be armed won't be much good. Jan, stop there, by that building site. We'll ditch our clothes and put on something more respectable.'

Badonovitch pulled over, the three men clambered out, opened the boot and hoisted out their cases. It was freezing cold but they quickly stripped off and put on clean shirts, trousers and jackets. The clothes they'd been wearing they stuffed in a skip on the edge of the building site. It began to snow as they climbed back into the car. It wasn't heavy, just enough to keep their speed down.

By then it was 02.30 and rather than telephone Macnair at that late hour, Hunter sent him a text. Two minutes later Hunter's phone rang and he put it on loudspeaker.

'Commander?'

'Yes, sir.'

'I got your message.'

'I'm sorry we didn't find out where exactly Jakub is but we can go to Alexandria and try and find him.'

'That won't be necessary. We had an intercept a couple of hours ago. Isobel's lot have been working on it and are pretty sure they know where to find him. The info will be with you later. You'll be met at Alexandria by a man by the name of Samuel Wilson. He knows where the place is and he'll also have the equipment you'll need.'

'That's a relief.'

Fifteen minutes later they saw the first sign for the Frederic Chopin Airport and twenty minutes after that they were parking in the multi-storey car park. When they walked into the departures hall they heard an announcement in Polish, repeated in English, that the airport was closed due to the weather and flights would start again at 07.00 when the runways were expected to be clear.

Hunter went across to the Europcar desk where there was a young man sitting on an uncomfortable seat, dozing. Hunter woke him up, told him where the car was, handed over the keys and gave him a 200 zloty note. It was near enough £40 and more than he earned in a day and so he was happy to have the car collected from the car park and taken to the hire car compound.

The team made their way to the departures gate. They informed the officials who they were, their names were checked off against a list and they were allowed through. The influence of using a private jet wasn't to be underestimated. Once through security, Hunter crossed to the information desk and asked the way to the jet. The attendant made a phone call, a young lady appeared and they were escorted through a side door and across the tarmac to the Citation. As they approached, the door opened.

The co-pilot introduced himself, welcomed them onboard, explained that they would leave at 06.00 before the airport was officially opened and to help themselves to tea, coffee, snacks and drinks. He would be in the cockpit with the pilot.

'Thanks,' said Hunter. The three sank wearily into their seats. 'Anyone want anything?'

'Yes,' Badonovitch replied. 'A bath, a large drink and a bed. But I'll settle for this.' He twisted a handle and the seat reclined all the way back. The others did the same. Sleep came quick and easy.

They didn't take off at 06.00, or 07.00, or 08.00. However, they were finally 'wheels up' at 09.23 and heading south. DTG was 1,515 miles and would take three hours and a few minutes according to the co-pilot's announcement. The three of them shaved, washed and tidied themselves up. Then they sat down to a breakfast of orange juice, packed sandwiches and coffee.

31

Macnair met Richard at the airport. They shook hands and the General asked 'Good flight?'

'Okay. Breakfast was indifferent and the coffee virtually undrinkable, but apart from that it was most enjoyable,' Richard grinned.

'One thing I can assure you of is decent coffee. How's your throat?'

'Not bad. Swallowing is a discomfort rather than painful.'

Macnair led the way to the short term car park, paid the fee and a few minutes later they rolled out of the building and headed towards the A8. As usual, it was busy and it wasn't until they were on the M9 that the General could put his foot down. The Mercedes responded like the thoroughbred it was and accelerated to 85mph with barely a change in the quiet tone of the engine. In minutes they were at junction 1A and heading for the Forth Road Bridge.

'I'm really sorry about Andrea,' said Macnair.

Richard sighed and nodded. 'She was a very nice woman.'

Macnair glanced at his passenger. 'Were you two serious?'

'No, not at all. It was a case of ships that pass in the night and all that. But even so,' his hands clenched tightly, 'I'd like to get my hands on those responsible. And I don't mean the corrupt cop.'

'We're working on that right now. Nick's made a lot of progress. The man responsible for the actual attacks is a Pole by the name of Jakub Kowalak. What we are not sure of is who the paymasters are, though we have our suspicions. Right now we're examining certain facts that have come our way. Once we're satisfied we'll make our move.'

'Arrests and trials?'

Macnair couldn't help it. He chuckled. 'Hardly. The people we think are involved wield a great deal of power in Europe. There's a cabal at the centre of the EU from which spreads an insidious and deadly poison. We think it's possible the whole structure will implode unless something is done to cut out the criminal elements at its heart.'

'If it implodes, will that be such a bad thing?'

'Not as far as I'm concerned. What about you?'

'Originally I was all for it, but gradually I've come to change my mind. In hindsight we shouldn't have gone in. I'm a Europhile, but it doesn't mean I want to be ruled by Europe. Our trade agreements were one thing, where we are now is quite another. However, the economy is in a bad enough state and this would make our MPs' expenses scandal look like the theft of a piggy bank.'

'I agree. I hope you're not beating yourself up over Andrea?'

'No. Whenever she'd returned to her place she would have been killed. So whether or not I'd kept her away for a few more days was irrelevant. The callousness of these people is unbelievable.'

'Frightening, more like,' said Macnair. He turned towards the gates of HMS *Cochrane*. There was an unarmed sentry standing there who nodded to the two men and opened the barrier. What was not on show were the three armed guards inside the reinforced shack, watching events on the screens that lined the perimeter fence. TIFAT had been attacked once. Thanks to intelligence received, the attack was easily thwarted and the attackers killed. However, they wouldn't be taking any more risks and relying on information received to stay safe. The cameras surrounding the grounds were also linked to pressure pads and infra-red beams. Macnair parked outside the main block and led the way up to his office. He phoned Isobel and asked her to join them and then started making the coffee. It was ready just as Isobel walked through the door. Introductions were brief.

Macnair poured three mugs and placed milk and sugar on the table. Isobel took hers black. Richard took only milk.

'What have you got for us?' Macnair asked Isobel.

'Thanks to the information we've acquired so far, we've been able to concentrate our energies in certain places.' She shook her head. 'We've uncovered massive frauds at all levels. I'll tell you just a few of them, otherwise we'll be here all day.' She took a sip of coffee. She began running through various scams she had discovered. 'The Common Agricultural Policy is a good place to look. Google "fraud" in the Ag policy and you'll be shocked what you discover.'

'Such as?' The General asked.

'Such as olive groves which have a huge subsidy supposedly growing in a car park. Or the fact that olives grown on a waste dump were claimed to be organic. Fifty percent of Portuguese claims for suckling cows were found to be fictitious and there was a so-called error rate for forage and crop acreage in Luxembourg of 89%. That meant subsidy claims were nearly double the legitimate figure.' She went on, presenting fact after fact. 'One last statistic. This is the EU's own figure. Or I should say they have been forced to admit that one euro in every five given in aid is stolen by corrupt officials.'

'If the EU admits to that,' said Richard, 'then the figure is more than likely to be double.'

'That's incredible,' said Macnair. 'Surely, someone has to write-off such a huge amount and justify any action they take.'

'Correct,' said Isobel. 'Whenever an official wishes to purchase something, such as a computer system, two things are obvious. First, that they pay well over the market price for whatever they are buying and second, the person making the purchase is the same person who approves it. This means that there are no checks of any description.' Isobel went on to explain how other scams were worked, each one adding to a massive total.

'I don't understand something that's pretty basic,' said Macnair. 'How is it all of this isn't public?'

Isobel replied. 'It is, only nobody is listening. What I've told you is documented. Books have been written on the subject and names have been named. Do you know what the EU Parliament does? How they get away with it?'

Both men shook their heads.

'Ignore it. Make a noise about some other subject. Divert attention. Of course, the worst thing of all is the way the laws are written without a democratic discussion.'

'According to Andrea, it's a farce,' said Richard. 'The laws are written by the commissioners. They are not discussed properly or argued about by the elected MEPs and they go through on the nod. Any argument from the floor is quickly put down. If you consider that well over 70% of UK law now comes from the European Parliament you can see why many commentators are yelling about the destruction of democracy in Europe.'

'That's a powerful statement,' said Macnair.

'Malcolm, it's the way it is. I had no idea that things had become this bad. Like the vast majority of people I accepted the EU Parliament for what it was. I know,' she waved her hand as though warding off a pesky fly, 'that there's been plenty of warnings. I know the signs have been there for the last twenty years, but I chose to ignore it.'

Richard slowly stood up and went across to the coffee pot. He waved it in the air. Both accepted a refill. 'It's unimaginable,' he said, as he sat back down

'You're not telling me all the employees and all the MEPs are crooked,' said Macnair.

'Certainly not,' replied Isobel. 'Many do a good job. An honest job and within the law. They merely implement those laws and follow the rules. The problem is the laws and rules have been manipulated to make life sweeter for the people working there.'

They talked a lot longer, and then Macnair said, 'What we're looking at is far worse than corruption, fraud and embezzlement. We're talking murder.'

'Have either of you heard the news in the last hour?' Isobel asked.

Both men shook their heads.

'The authorities in Brussels are claiming that the explosion was caused by a gas leak.'

'What?' Richard almost yelled. 'You have to be kidding! Anyone with the smallest amount of expertise will know that some form of explosive was used. Probably PE.'

Macnair shook his head in sorrow and said, 'Richard's right. Experts will have examined the site and they'd know instantly it wasn't a gas leak. What about the dead man? Anything said about him?'

'He's been identified as a police inspector. They're claiming it was merely a coincidence he was there,' replied Isobel. 'He was to meet an informant in the car park though what it was about nobody knew. It's been reported that he was a very able man and an excellent officer who must have been ambushed. Maybe by the informer he had gone to meet.'

'What about the fact that he was armed?' Richard asked.

'Operational requirement for personal protection. They went on to say that he was obviously bushwhacked.'

'We know it's rubbish,' said Richard, 'so they damn well do as well.'

'Of course they do,' said Macnair in a harsher voice than he'd intended.

'By the way, Isobel, I wrote down the inspector's name and credit card details. I thought it might help.'

'Good,' said Isobel. 'Let me have them and I'll see what we can do.'

Richard handed over the piece of paper and Isobel phoned her department. She read out the information to one of her staff and replaced the receiver.

'Thanks for that. It'll save a lot of time and energy tracking down what we need to know,' said Isobel.

They continued with their discussion. In less than 15 minutes the phone went and as Isobel was next to it, she answered.

'General Macnair's office.' There was a pause before she said, 'Thanks, Leo. See if there's anything else.' She hung up the receiver. 'The policeman was nearing retirement, divorced with three children scattered around Europe. Here's the interesting thing. He had a very active bank account.'

'Active?' Macnair queried, 'How?'

'A lot of money has been going in and a lot out. The money out has been transferred to a bank in Bermuda.'

'How much are we talking about?' asked Richard.

'Ten thousand euros a month for the last three years. Before that it was five thousand euros for two years. Not bad savings, wouldn't you say?'

It was Richard who asked the all important question. 'Where did the money come from?'

'We're working on it and it shouldn't be too difficult to track.'

'What a sodding mess,' said the General.

32

Nick, Jan and Phil were woken up when the co-pilot made his announcement.

'Gentlemen we are approaching Borg El Arab International Airport. We are landing at Borg El Arab as the El Nouzha Airport is closed for renovations. The time there is now 13.15, one hour ahead of Polish time. You may like to know that after the freezing cold of the North the temperature in Alexandria is a pleasant thirteen degrees centigrade. I trust you enjoyed your flight. Thank you.'

They put their seats in the upright position and looked out of the windows as Alexandria came into sight. The plane touched down and rolled to its allotted stand. The co-pilot came out of the cockpit, opened the doors and watched as the three men went down the steps. They crossed the concourse to a door where a young lady was waiting for them. She welcomed them with a smile and a greeting and led the way past customs and to the security kiosk. They showed their passports, they were stamped without query and they went through into arrivals.

They had hardly stepped into the hall when a man raised his finger to them and they crossed over to him. He looked to be in his early thirties, dressed in a lightweight, cream coloured suit and a blue open-necked shirt. He shook hands with each of them and introduced himself as Samuel Wilson. The three of them replied using their Christian names only.

Hunter asked, 'Do you know where we're going?'

'Yes, sir, El Alamein.

'I thought Kowalak's place was somewhere near Alexandria?'

Wilson shook his head. 'It's closer to El Alamein. I have a car for you. It's a consulate car. A bit dilapidated I'm afraid, but with diplomatic number plates. When we leave, if you follow me, I can show you to your destination.'

'Thanks.' Diplomatic number plates had a big advantage. They would not be stopped and searched by the police. On the other hand, the car would draw attention to them. On balance, the plates would probably be an advantage.

'I take it you're with MI6?'

'Yes. Most of the embassies have one of us nowadays. As you know, there's been a lot of trouble out here and it has still not quietened down completely.' They exited the building. The relative warmth of Egypt was a pleasant change after Poland.

'We're twenty-five miles away from the city. We're not going into Alexandria but around it.' As they spoke they headed for the car park about 200 metres away. 'I've got Glocks. I'm sorry, but there are no silencers.'

Hunter looked at the other man with a certain amount of amusement. 'You're well stocked considering you're the consulate.'

'All new. The officials usually honour our diplomatic status but the rabble doesn't. We've had some trouble in a few parts of the world so now we are able to at least put up a token resistance.' Wilson's cynical tone said it all.

'Whose stupid idea was it?'

'It came from the brain of our famous schoolboy, the Foreign Secretary. What the hell we're going to do against a mob when we're armed with a few automatics is beyond me. Can you see one of the secretaries shooting anybody? The Foreign Office hasn't a clue. Anyway, I'd better get off that hobby horse. Here we are.'

They were on the ground floor of the multi-storey alongside a battered looking Ford Explorer.

'It's done over 350,000kms but still goes well enough. That's my Focus. I'd better give you this.' He reached into a pocket and took out a wad of cash. 'Here's ten thousand Egyptian pounds, as near as dammit, a thousand quid in real money.'

'Do I sign for it?' Hunter asked.

Wilson smiled. 'That won't be necessary. We'll stop and sort out the equipment in a quiet spot I know. Here are the car keys.' He handed them over to Hunter who unlocked the car and the three men climbed in.

The car started sweetly enough and they rolled out behind the Focus. About half-an-hour later Wilson turned off the main road and onto a side road that vanished straight into the desert. During their journey there had been few cars on the road, though a fair number of lorries, many tilting to one side or the other as their springs had given out.

A kilometre down the road they stopped. Wilson opened the boot of his car and reaching inside opened a tin box. 'Here you are. Three Glocks and two boxes of ammo. Here's the piece de resistance. Or should I say pieces. Three Kevlar vests. Not the latest polymer, I'm afraid, but still pretty useful. Oh, and a pair of binoculars.'

'I take it the vests are protection in the event of an attack on the consulate?' Hunter asked wryly.

'You got it.'

'Thanks.' He looked at his watch. It was 14.15. 'What time is sunset?'

'About 17.10, or thereabouts.'

Hunter leant against the side of the car. 'Do you know anything about Kowalak? His movements? What he does?'

Wilson shook his head. 'Sorry, no idea. I was told to give you this stuff and show you where the man can be found, but that's all. There hasn't been time for anything else.'

'Okay. In that case, when we get there, point us in the right direction and let us get on with it.'

'I had a message from London. I'm to do everything I can to help.'

'Thanks. Have you been told anything at all about what's going on?'

Wilson replied, 'Nothing.'

'We are as sure as we can be that there's going to be another attack like the ones in Rome and London. Where and when we don't know. However, we are sure of the identity of the man organising it all.'

'Kowalak?'

'Precisely. We know he's the brains behind the atrocities but he's not the paymaster. That's who we want to get our hands on.'

'Presumably it's Muslim fanatics of some sort. There are enough of them around.'

Hunter shrugged. 'It could be. That's why we need to interrogate Kowalak. We'd better get going. One more thing, can we stop in El Alamein? We need to buy some clothes.'

Sure. There's a shopping precinct in the middle of town.'

When they got to El Alamein they parked the cars and walked along the busy street. There were shops on both sides catering for just about anything anyone would want. There was an abundance of cafes with tables and chairs blocking the pavement all of which were occupied. They found a clothes shop and went inside. They were soon done and left with a bag holding light brown chinos and safari jackets. Wearing the gear they had with them would be too noticeable. The clothes would also help them to blend into the countryside.

They returned to their cars and continued through the town. The road led them up to a rise that overlooked the Mediterranean. There was a parking place for visitors to stop and enjoy the spectacular view. It was protected with a metre high wall to lean on and to prevent people plunging 50 metres down to the sea.

'See that white building over there?' Wilson said, pointing back the way they'd come. 'The one with the red tiled roof? About two kilometres away.'

Hunter placed the binoculars to his eyes, adjusted them and brought the building into sharp relief. 'Looks to be a fair size.'

'It is. I checked with the town recorder for houses. It has six bedrooms and cost three million dollars. Kowalak's had this place about six months. Before that he had a smaller house closer to Alexandria.'

'Okay.' Hunter pointed up the steep hill behind them. It was bare and covered in rocks. 'We'll go around and take a look. I don't want anybody seeing us scrambling up there. The car's out of sight here, so we'll leave it.'

There had been some traffic passing but it had been light. Hunter turned to Wilson and stuck out his hand. 'Thanks Samuel, we'll take it from here. Give me your mobile number in case we need any help. Also, don't go further than El Alamein. If we have to get out in a hurry it will be useful to have somebody with diplomatic immunity with us.' Hunter keyed Wilson's number into his mobile.

'What are you going to do?' If Wilson was in any way nervous, he wasn't showing it.

'No idea. We need to get a close look at the place. Try and find out what Kowalak's movements are.'

'Right. I'll see you later,' said Wilson, returning to his car and heading back to El Alamein.

The team quickly changed into their new clothes, putting on the Kevlar vests under their jackets and adjusted the Glocks under their arms. They walked around the hillock where they found a path leading to the summit. From there they moved forward slowly and carefully. If Kowalak was serious about his security he'd have someone looking their way on a regular basis and three men standing in view would set the alarm bells ringing.

Using the binoculars, Hunter carefully scanned the area, segment by segment. The swimming pool was empty but he identified a jacuzzi next to it with steam coming out of the sides of a cover. The gardens were layered, with two expanses of lawn easily an acre each. Shrubs grew around the lawns, evidently carefully tended. There was a large shed with an open door with an unoccupied chair outside.

Hunter handed the binoculars to Badonovitch. 'What do you see in the far corner of the wall?'

The Russian looked closely and then said, 'There's some sort of small building. A man has just come out. I think he's carrying an Uzi. If that is a guard hut then there could be one in each of the other corners.'

Badonovitch handed the glasses over to Peabody who also carefully examined the area. 'I concur it's an Uzi,' he said.

Twenty minutes later the sun dropped over the horizon and dusk fell fast.

'Let's go,' said Hunter when it was fully dark. The three men stood, dusted down and walked back to the road.

When they returned to the car, Badonovitch asked, 'What now?'

'I'd like to know how many there are in the grounds.' Hunter took out his mobile and speed dialled Macnair. 'Sir?'

'What have you got?'

'We've confirmed the place. There are armed guards patrolling it.'

'How many?'

'Can't tell. Can we have a satellite image of the area?'

'Sorry, no. The system we use is down for some sort of automatic maintenance done by onboard computers.'

'Damn!'

'MI6 picked up some intel. We are as sure as we can be that the next attack is in two days time. We *think* its Madrid, but we can't be sure.'

'Have you got GCHQ locked on Kowalak?'

'We did have. He's hardly made contact with the outside world. It seems when he's on holiday it really is a question of doing no business.'

'Then presumably he knows nothing about his sons and what happened in Poland?'

'We don't think so. Not yet anyway.'

'We want Kowalak shaken, gutted by what's happened to his family and his organisation. If he's scared then he could be panicked into helping us.'

'Possibly. However, he doesn't strike me as the sort of man who panics easily. Besides, if he isn't answering his phone and I presume he isn't using his computer, how will we get the message to him?' Macnair paused and then answered his own question. 'Actually, I have a way. A very simple one.'

'How?'

'I know Chuma Hamadi who is the head of the Egyptian Security Forces. Their job is to help protect foreign embassies, riot and crowd control and to arrest fundamentalists. There was one man they couldn't touch. An Imam. I arranged for him to have a car accident for which Chuma was particularly grateful. I'll get hold of him and ask him to send someone to give the news to Kowalak. I'll tell him it needs to be around what, 22.00?'

Hunter agreed and they said their goodbyes. He then told the others what Macnair had said. Hunter's phone beeped.

'Yes, sir?'

'It's all fixed,' said Macnair. 'A couple of policemen will deliver the message around 22.00.'

33

As it was, they didn't have to wait that long. It was just after 21.00 when a police car pulled up at the gates, sirens blaring and lights blazing. Hunter was on watch on the hillock while the other two were dozing in the car with the seats slung back. He stayed watching the compound and after about ten minutes he saw the police car drive back out through the gates, this time without lights and sirens. He went down the path and thumped the roof of the car. Both men jerked awake. Hunter climbed into the back.

'Let's go, said Hunter to Badonovitch who was behind the wheel. 'The police arrived fifteen minutes ago.'

Badonovitch started the engine and headed down the hill. There were houses with gardens each side of the street, average structures of three or four bedrooms. Some had lights on, some were in darkness. In spite of the police car's flashing lights and blaring sirens nobody seemed to have come onto the street – Egypt was the sort of country where it was better to mind your own business.

The team turned left off the main road and found the gates about 100 metres in front of them. They then turned right and followed the road that ran alongside the estate's wall. There were no street lights and no houses in the immediate vicinity. The three men climbed out of the car to take a look around when the peace of the night was shattered by a loud yell followed by a voice ranting loudly in Polish.

'It sounds,' said Hunter, 'as though he's having a tantrum.'

Badonovitch said, 'It sounds as if he's yelling curses mixed with a lot of profanity.'

Peabody had walked further along the road and then came back. 'Nick,' he said softly, 'there's a side gate. It doesn't seem to be alarmed.'

They checked their communications and Hunter said, 'Okay. Let's take a look.'

Abruptly the yells and curses stopped. They reached the gate and Hunter looked closely around the edges of it. Then he examined the lock. It was worn, with the tongue able to move a couple of millimetres back and forth. In theory, it meant that no alarm would be of any use as the gate could move and the alarm erupt. He prodded the gate which moved a few degrees. Nothing. 'Let's go.'

They had their Glocks in their hands. Hunter twisted the handle of the gate and gently pushed. It opened with a loud squeak. Luckily, there were more yells coming from the house but even so they stopped, knelt on one knee and waited to see if anyone approached. Nobody did. Then, they heard something being smashed.

'What's he saying?' Hunter whispered.

Badonovitch cocked his head to one side and frowned. 'He says somebody is going to pay. He wants to know where his lazy, good for nothing brats are so that they can take care of things.'

'Which means,' Hunter whispered, 'that either the General didn't tell the security chief about Kowalak's sons, or the chief didn't pass it on, or the policemen forgot. Whichever way, I'll enjoy telling him the bad news. You two follow the wall to the left, I'll go this way.

They moved out.

Hunter reached the first sentry box. It was empty. He was about to carry on when he saw a flicker and a cigarette lighter burst into flame. Then the tip of a cigarette glowed red. The man was about eight metres away and looking towards the house. Hunter quickly stepped up behind him. The deaths in London and Rome, coupled with the shattered lives of so many people came to mind. He used the edge of the pistol grip. The blow was as hard as Hunter could muster. It crunched in the back of the man's head. The man shuddered for about two seconds then his legs folded underneath him and he dropped down dead. Hunter grabbed the body by the collar of its jacket and dragged it behind one of the bushes lining the lawn. He paused for at least two minutes while he scanned the route ahead of him and on either side. He saw nobody. He continued around the perimeter of the grounds. He could see the corner of the wall and a second sentry box. From there he could see the main gate as well as the front door. The door was wide open. Light spilled across the turning circle of the drive. Nobody was visible but he could clearly hear voices.

Badonovitch was near the sentry box on the other side of the main gate. He could see the open door and moved to come at it from an oblique angle. The pleasant aroma of the orange grove was marred by the faint smell of cigarette smoke. He pulled a few oranges off the tree next to him and stood alongside the door. He threw an orange onto the ground just ahead of the box. There was no reaction. He did it again, throwing the orange onto the ground with more force.

The guard called out in Polish, 'Who's there?'

In reply, Badonovitch threw a third orange. There was a faint scraping noise followed by a hacking cough as the man stepped through the door, drawing on his cigarette. The guard was an arm's length away. Badonovitch made the same move as Hunter. He smashed the butt of his Glock down onto the back of the man's skull. Like Hunter he used all the force he could muster and like Hunter's target, the man fell dead.

Peabody was nearing the box behind the house, in the farthest corner. He could hear voices inside. It sounded like two men only. There was a great deal of agitation in their tone. A light came on in the box and one of the men spoke harshly. The light was immediately switched off. Seconds later a lighter was clicked into flame and a cigarette was lit. Just then more yells could be heard coming from the house, although only faintly due to the distance. With the noise in the house there would be no better time. Peabody walked to the door, knelt down, looked carefully into the space and confirmed there were two men, both drawing on their cigarettes. They were standing only a couple of metres away, looking at each other and seemed to be arguing. They were side on to Peabody. He fired twice in quick succession. Both shots were through the targets' temples. Although the shots were sharp in the night there was no abating of the yells coming from the house. Peabody continued around the wall until he met the other two.

'Okay?' Hunter asked. 'We heard shots.'

'There were two of them. I didn't have any choice.'

'No problem. From that distance I doubt they would have heard anything at the house. Phil, you go to the front door and keep it covered. Jan, go clockwise around the house and I'll go anti-clockwise. Try and look through the windows. Kowalak must have other guards to relieve this lot.'

The other two acknowledged their instructions. Hunter got to the corner of the house and started along the wall. There were two windows on that side of the house, each dark, each uncurtained. Carefully, he looked inside each one. They served the same room. It looked like some sort of lounge. At the next corner, he was looking at the front of the house and the driveway. There was no sign of Peabody.

He started along the front towards the open door. Halfway towards the door he came to a lit window and looked inside. A man was sitting on a settee with an Uzi next to him. From the shadows being cast from a corner of the room and the way the man was staring in that direction he was obviously watching television. Hunter wondered why the man wasn't with Kowalak in the kitchen but then Hunter couldn't blame him. Who wanted to be on the end of Kowalak's tirade? He ducked down and went past. He paused at the door, there was nobody in sight and he slipped across to a second window. Inside it was dark and he could see nothing. A few more paces and Badonovitch came around the corner and joined him.

'Anything?' Hunter whispered.

'So far the only place I've seen anyone is in the kitchen. Kowalak's there with two other men. He's pacing up and down, yelling into the phone. He knows about the compound but he definitely doesn't know about his sons. He said he's going to kill the little swine when he gets hold of them. The two men are carrying Uzis. That's all I've seen.'

'There's a guard watching TV in a room on the left side of the hall. He's got an Uzi next to him. Let's go.'

At the front door they paused. The stairs were on the right, while there was a closed door on the left leading to the room where the armed man was sitting.

'Okay. We'll check upstairs first. We don't want any surprises.'

Hunter went through the door like a wraith, Badonovitch on his heels. Hunter covered the right, Badonovitch the left. The hallway was empty. There was a second door along on the right and another door facing them. From the noise that was coming from there, it obviously led to the kitchen. The stairs were about two metres wide with a wall on each side. Hunter took the steps steadily, one at a time, his right side dragging along the wall. He was looking up, while Badonovitch covered their backs. Apart from the incessant noise from the kitchen there was nothing more to be heard. They checked each of the six bedrooms. They were all in use as none of the beds were made. All the rooms were empty.

They went back downstairs. Things had quietened down and then they heard a voice yelling a name. Badonovitch said, 'Its Kowalak yelling for somebody.'

They heard the same voice again and Badonovitch said, 'I think he's yelling to somebody in the garden.'

'Phil,' Hunter whispered into his microphone, 'get around to the back. If he sends somebody to find one of his men we don't want him getting back to the house.'

'Right.'

'Let's make a start on the room there,' whispered Hunter.

The sound of gunfire came from within the room.

34

Hunter opened the door and walked into the lounge. The film showing on the television was an old war movie, the actors speaking in dubbed Polish. The man looked up. He was the only person there. He was sitting halfway across the room that was littered with furniture, half facing the door, the huge TV screen dominating the corner on the left. There were three settees, half a dozen easy chairs and a wall lined with the sort of bar found in a public hostelry. Behind the bar the wall was lined with bottles and optic dispensers. The man's expression changed from surprise to shock.

Badonovitch stepped from behind Hunter and said in Polish, 'Don't move or you are a dead man.'

The man looked at the Russian, Hunter stepped around the furniture, neared his quarry and was about to hit him when the man dived for his weapon. Hunter had no choice. He shot the man in the middle of the chest. Though the gunshot was loud it was no louder than the TV.

Badonovitch stood at the door and looked towards the kitchen. The door remained shut. The two men went back into the hallway and Badonovitch checked the room on the right. It was empty. There was another door opposite and he crossed the room to find it was a large lounge. He returned to the hall.

'That leaves only the kitchen,' Hunter said softly.

They paused at the kitchen door. A voice yelled out and carried clearly to where they were standing.

'He's yelling different names. Hang on. Another man is saying something I can't quite catch.'

The kitchen had gone quiet. Neither Hunter nor Badonovitch needed to be told what was happening. The fact that something was wrong had finally occurred to the two Poles. That meant there was no time to waste. Hunter grabbed the door handle, twisted it and shoved the door open, hard. It slammed back against the wall. The two men in the kitchen had been looking at the back door. They turned round like startled rabbits to stare in shock as Hunter and Badonovitch stepped through the doorway.

The older of the two men wasn't armed. The other one had his Uzi tucked under his arm.

'Don't try it,' Hunter yelled.

Whether or not the man understood him, or whether or not he was too stupid to understand, he began to raise his Uzi. Badonovitch had stepped to one side of Hunter and had a clear view of the man, while Kowalak stood between Hunter and the gunman. Badonovitch fired three shots into the torso of his target. The body slammed backwards into a fridge and collapsed in a pool of blood.

Kowalak stood with utter horror on his face and then made to reach for an Uzi that was on the unit to his right.

'Don't!' Hunter yelled. 'Don't!'

The Pole looked at Hunter with a mixture of perplexity and surprise. He then looked at the kitchen door and towards the door just behind Hunter.

'They're not coming,' said Hunter, using a steady voice. 'They're dead.' He was aware that a matter of fact statement in times like the one they were facing worked wonders. It kept the enemy off balance. The last thing Hunter wanted was to have to take action against Kowalak before he'd told them what they wanted to know.

Peabody appeared at the back door. 'The other one won't be coming back.'

Hunter nodded. 'Keep a watch on the main gate in case of any unexpected visitors.'

Peabody nodded and like a wraith vanished into the night.

Kowalak again looked at the weapon so near to his hand. He seemed to be debating with himself whether or not it was worth the risk to grab for it. This showed more stupidity than bravery. Then he lost the chance. Badonovitch stepped across the room and removed the temptation.

Hunter walked slowly towards Kowalak. The man was facing him, a sneer on his heavily jowled, slab of a face.

'How much?' The Pole asked in accented English.

Hunter ignored him and just kept walking until he was less than a metre away. Stopping, Hunter stared into the other man's eyes. He thought of the death and misery the man had caused.

Hunter normally had his feelings under control. This once he allowed them to get the better of him but only for a few seconds. He slammed the palm of his hand into Kowalak's nose, flattening it. An upward thrust would have sent the cartilage into his brain, killing him. Kowalak staggered back, his hands to his face, blood oozing between his fingers. Then, with a force similar to that displayed by a footballer, Hunter kicked Kowalak in the lower belly. He'd planned a kick in the crotch but he needed the Pole to talk. Kowalak collapsed with a scream, tears rolling down his cheeks.

'Where's the attack on Madrid going to be and when?'

The Pole managed to turn his face towards Hunter. 'What . . . What are you talking about? What attack? When? Who are you?' The questions came out in an incoherent mumble.'

Hunter stood looking down at the Pole. 'Jakub, tell me what I want to know or you'll regret it. I've been told to stop the attack. To do so I need to know exactly where and when it's planned.'

'I don't understand what you mean,' Kowalak gasped. 'These are my men. They are here to protect me from unscrupulous criminals. I have been threatened more than once. Now you are here. You prove the need I have for protection. Who do you work for?' As the pain receded even a little, so the Pole's chutzpah grew.

There was no harm in telling him but as he was about to do so, Hunter had an idea. 'You know who I work for.' He left it at that.

The other man looked perplexed. 'What the hell are you talking about? I don't know who.' He broke into a torrent of Polish.

Hunter let him have his rant. When he stopped speaking Hunter said, 'We were sent by your paymasters. The people who order you to carry out the atrocities you in turn order to be committed.'

The look on Kowalak's face told Hunter that shock was following shock. Keeping the man off balance was half the battle. He'd rather get the information he was after without resorting to violence.

'What . . . What do you mean?'

'I told you. The men in charge aren't happy with you and sent us to take care of things.'

Kowalak lay quietly for a few seconds, evidently thinking through what he'd just been told. Then his expression turned to one of scorn. 'Go back to Brussels and tell your masters, *our* masters,' he corrected himself, 'that I am not some idiot they've been dealing with all these years. They thought they were so very clever in keeping their identities hidden from me. I spit on them.' Which he did, aiming at Hunter's foot.

Hunter moved his shoe and the man missed. Hunter said nothing as he registered what was being said.

'I tell you, go back. I knew their identities one week after they first hired me. They are idiots. Children playing men's games. I have carefully accumulated all the information I need to send each of them to prison for the rest of their lives. Tell them that. Go back and tell them that for what they have done all jobs are increased in price by 50%.'

Hunter nodded, looking pensive. Then he shook his head. 'It won't matter. You'll be dead.' So saying he pointed the Glock at Kowalak's crotch. 'Only it won't be a pleasant death.'

'Wait! Wait, I tell you. If you kill me then the information I have will be sent to every newspaper, every broadcaster and every police force in Europe. It is all arranged. If I die I take those clowns with me. Except they will have a living hell, while I will no longer be here. These people are cowards. Frightened of their own shadows. They think themselves so clever, so ruthless. They are nothing. Nothing!' He was yelling and screaming now.

Hunter shook his head slowly as though he'd considered the matter and dismissed it. 'I think I'll shoot you. I'll be following orders. We'll earn the ten million we're being paid and I can forget about those, as you say, clowns in Brussels.'

'Wait. Ten million? I'll make it twenty. Paid tomorrow. My sons will arrange payment. You can trust them.'

Hunter frowned and said, 'You mean you haven't heard?'

'Heard what?'

'Your sons are dead.'

The shock left the man rigid, his mouth agape, his breath coming in sharp gasps. For a moment Hunter thought Kowalak was going to have a heart attack. After a minute or two the man got himself under control and said the same as many people did when they heard such terrible news, 'I don't believe you.'

Hunter shrugged and said, 'You've been unable to get hold of them. You never will. We killed them on orders from Brussels.'

There was no sorrow in the man, merely hatred and a desire for vengeance. 'I want those people dead. I will pay thirty million euros to you to let me live.'

Hunter frowned and looked puzzled. 'You do know about what happened to your estate in Poland, don't you?'

'Yes,' was the harsh reply. 'Many of my people are dead. I will find out who did this and get my revenge. I promise you that.' Under any normal circumstance what Kowalak was saying would be a farce. It was as if part of his brain had shut down. He wasn't able to acknowledge the fact that he was lying on his kitchen floor, his guards dead and guns pointing his way.

Hunter said, "Tell me who you want us to take care of. If I think it's

338

a goer, we'll do a deal at thirty million. And by the way, that's pounds, not euros'

For an instant, Kowalak looked as though he wished he hadn't offered so much but then Hunter saw the man's expression change and then shut down. It was as easy as reading a book. If Hunter did as he was asked there would be no thirty million. Kowalak would have them killed.

'You know who they are!' Kowalak yelled. He wiped his nose with the back of his sleeve. The blood was beginning to dry.

Hunter shrugged, stepped back and aimed the Glock at Kowalak's crotch. 'Wrong answer. I need to compare names.'

'Wait! Wait!' he followed the yell with a torrent of Polish.

Hunter looked at Badonovitch who shook his head. 'Just ranting and raving,' said the Russian.

'Kowalak, you've got ten seconds to start telling me what I want to know or we're out of here.'

'Alright. Alright. The man I want you to kill is named Peter Waterfield, he is the President of the Internal Audit, Administration and Personnel Department. I took my instructions from him.'

'And the other names?'

The Pole looked embarrassed for a couple of seconds and then mumbled something.

'What did you say?' Hunter asked, his anger building by the second.

'I said that was the only name I have.'

'So much for dealing with idiots and children playing at adult games.'

Some of the Pole's bravado returned and he said, 'It was not necessary to learn more. I had enough to protect me.'

'You are quite correct,' said Hunter. He appeared to think for a moment and then said, 'You lying down there is ludicrous. If we're going into business together, I think you should sit up here.'

Awkwardly, Kowalak scrambled to his feet and staggered across the kitchen. Ignoring the dead body and the pool of blood, he sat on a stool and leaned forward. His hand shook slightly as he opened a bottle of

Zubrowka vodka that was in front of him and poured a shot – a large one. He didn't offer any to his guests. Hunter knew something about the drink. He could see the blade of grass in the bottle which came from bison territory in Poland. For this reason it was called bison vodka. At 80 degrees proof it was a drink Hunter had tried only once.

Kowalak emptied the glass in one gulp and poured a second one. This time his hand was a little steadier. 'We have a deal?' He looked at Hunter with narrow eyes.

Hunter nodded. 'Probably. You know that the Madrid job has been cancelled, don't you?'

The Pole looked at Hunter in surprise. 'But I have heard nothing!'

Shrugging as though he couldn't have cared less, Hunter said, 'It's none of my business. I was told to take care of you and that was all. It is, I understand, some sort of cleaning up operation. What it's all about and why I neither know nor care.'

The Pole's hand tightened around the glass and he looked as though he could crush it. His hatred for the men in Brussels was all encompassing.

'A lot of work has gone into the Madrid attack. I have pressed all the buttons, made all the moves. The men and means are in position. Stopping them is impossible. They won't back down. Not now. They want to do the job. They are not being paid to do it. For them it is a holy jihad. You must know that.'

Hunter frowned. 'Where's the target?'

'The American Embassy.'

If he was shocked, Hunter didn't show it. Instead, he said, 'We might be able to stop them.' Pensively he stroked his chin. 'Do you know where they are?'

Kowalak looked at Hunter suspiciously. 'Why try and stop them?'

Hunter shrugged and then replied, 'Because we're being paid to stop it, for a very large fee. Don't ask me the whys of any of it, just the how. Which is something you know all too well. Who are they? How many of them are there? How are they going to do it?'

340

Drinking the rest of the vodka in one gulp, Kowalak poured a third glass. If the alcohol was having any effect, Hunter couldn't see it. This time though, the glass was left on the surface. As the Pole sat staring at the glass, Hunter realised the man was drunk. Kowalak had obviously been drinking heavily before they'd intruded.

'Who they are I don't wish to know. Only that they will do the job. What I do know is that there are possibly eight of them in five cars. They also have all the plastique and detonators they need,' he paused, then added, 'as well as guns.'

Before Kowalak could say anymore, Hunter interrupted and said impatiently, 'Do you have some means of contact?'

Kowalak shook his head. 'No. It was agreed that once the whole thing was set up they would just get on with it. It's safer that way. That is something you should know.' He was now becoming bleary eyed as he tried to stare at Hunter.

'In that case, when is it going to happen? We might be able to stop the attack as it takes place.'

'It is tomorrow at midday. I tell you, it can't be stopped.' There was now suspicion lurking behind his eyes. It was gripping him tighter by the second as he realised that Hunter should have known some if not most of what he was saying.

'I suddenly don't like you,' Kowalak announced.

Hunter wondered for a moment if the man was just drunk or border-line psychotic. He'd shown no feelings of any sort about his sons, and what had happened in Poland had already faded into the background. Hunter couldn't help asking, 'Don't you care about your sons?'

'Bah!' Kowalak waved his hand in front of him, as though dismissing them from his thoughts. 'They were fairly useless except for my youngest. Casimir was all man.' Tears of self pity welled up in the man's eyes as he focused his hatred back at Hunter. 'And you killed him.'

'I told you, it was orders. Something you understand only too well.'

'Yes, I understand them,' he was slurring his words. He reached for his drink and took a mouthful.

Hunter was sorry that the man probably wouldn't understand what he was about to do. 'Kowalak! Kowalak!' he spoke harshly.

The man looked at him, his eyes squinting as he appeared to be trying to focus on Hunter.

'Have you heard of an organisation known as The International Force Against Terrorism? Based in Scotland?'

'Something, yes, but I don't remember. Don't they, they look at things and report? A talking shop I think it is called.'

Shaking his head, Hunter replied. 'No. They kill people. They track down the scum and kill them.'

'Them! I know them! Pansies all of them. Morons.' Another torrent of Polish followed.

Badonovitch translated. 'It seems we are a bunch of useless idiots. A few more things along those lines and we prefer sheep to women.'

The language that Badonovitch was using finally penetrated the drunken Pole's mind. Shock left him rigid for a few seconds, then he said, 'You are these men? You are from . . . from Scotland? Not from Brussels?'

'Correct,' said Hunter. 'We now have what we wanted.'

'But our agreement. The money I can pay you. I will pay you.'

'Thanks, but no thanks. I'm only sorry we don't have the time available to watch you suffer after what you have done to so many innocent people. The lives you've wrecked and all for more money than you can spend in a lifetime.'

'I tell you . . .'

Whatever he was going to say was lost when Hunter, pointed the Glock and sent the first bullet into the man's lower belly. Kowalak screamed, flew backwards off the stool and smashed onto the floor. He was moaning in agony, blood pouring between his fingers. The bullet had erupted out of his back, severing his spine. Hunter knew that Kowalak would live for about five minutes in agony, before he died. The Pole had no more strength than to whimper, his hands clutched tightly around his stomach.

'What now, Nick?' Badonovitch asked, ignoring the dying man.

'We'd better search the place. You make a start. Computer stuff is what we want.' He used the comms set. 'Phil, stay where you are, just in case any others arrive. I'll give the General a call and tell him what we've found out.'

Turning his back on the dying Kowalak, he speed dialled Macnair who answered immediately.

'What have you got? I hope it's good news.'

'I know the name of one of the paymasters. A Peter Waterfield. He has some long and fancy title.'

Macnair sighed, 'Why am I not surprised?' As the question was rhetorical, Hunter didn't bother replying. 'Is it Madrid?'

'Yes, sir. The attack is at midday tomorrow and the target is the American Embassy.'

The General showed no emotion. He'd been expecting something big. 'Do you know who is carrying out the attack and how?'

'Islamic fundamentalists. Kowalak said five cars are being used with as many as eight people.'

There was silence for a few seconds before Macnair asked, 'Is he telling the truth? Or is he just playing with you?'

Hunter half turned and looked at the Pole. He was in time to see the man gasp and die.

Hunter had already asked himself the same question. 'I'm afraid he won't be answering any more questions.' There was no need to elaborate. 'I'm sure he knew what was happening even if he didn't know any of the details. He said that he arranged the cars, explosives, dets and guns. Apart from that, he was insistent that he didn't know the details of how the job was going to be done.' Silence reigned again for a few seconds and then Hunter asked, 'What do you want us to do, sir? Go to Madrid? Right now there can't be any suitable flights from Alexandria.'

'Yes, there is. I've kept the Citation on standby. Get to the airport ASAP while I warn the aircraft company that you're going to Madrid and to file a flight plan.'

'I take it we'll be met when we get to Madrid?'

'Yes. I'll see what I can arrange.'

'Sir, what about the Spanish Police? Are they going to be informed about what's going on?'

'Yes, I've no option. I'm not going to keep anything secret if lives are at stake. I'll contact the head of their National Police Corps. They're the lot responsible for handling terrorism and immigration along with crime in urban areas.'

'Do you know the boss?'

'I met him once. Name of Hilario Clavet. He's a commissioner.'

'Any good?'

What Hunter really wanted to know was whether or not the man could be trusted.

Macnair sighed. 'Nick, I'm sorry, but I don't know any more. He hasn't been in the job long and if you'd asked me that a fortnight ago I would have said yes. Now, I've yet to figure out who we can trust. This is so much bigger than I first thought. If you'd asked me at the start, I would have told you it couldn't get any worse. But I would have been wrong.' Macnair paused and then added, 'Wrong like I've never been before.'

'What about the Americans? Are you going to tell them what's going on?'

'No.' The General went on to explain his decision.

'That makes sense. Sir, I've been thinking about this five car business. I've never been near the embassy. Is it possible to attack from four directions at once?'

'No. It would mean the embassy standing alone with four roads surrounding it.'

'Then I wonder what their plan is?'

On that note they said their goodbyes. Hunter checked his watch. As was usually the case, he was surprised at how little time had passed and so much had happened.

35

In Brussels the time was 21.34. The meeting had been going for nearly an hour. In attendance were Peter Waterfield, Jacques Dupuis, Gunther Friedmann, Enrico Maimone, Patrick O'Flynn and Anicka Kadlec, their new member – the Director General of OLAF.

The delicious irony of the woman's position was not lost on Waterfield. Her power was absolute when it came to fraud and corruption within the European Union. Her department worked outside of Brussels and outside of Strasbourg as all those working within the EU Parliament were honest and trustworthy. He loved the irony of the thought. Hence there was no need for her department to investigate anybody working there – there was far too much to do around Europe.

The success of the department was a farce considering the number of fraudulent cases there had been and the amount of money recovered. An amount boasted by OLAF. Waterfield dwelled on the thought that since 1999 there had been 3,500 investigations resulting in the recovery of 1 billion euros. The total number of years given out in prison sentences was a pathetic 900.

Waterfield looked at Kadlec and somehow managed not to squirm. She was short, round faced, carried too much weight, had lank hair and wore thick rimmed glasses. She had never married but to the best of his knowledge wasn't a lesbian. What she was, they all agreed, was what was known as a professional virgin. It was, after all, the rudest thing they could say about her, even if it was utterly meaningless. Like many of the men in the parliament, he was a sexist of the first order. Hence, he belonged to that school of thought which said an attractive woman could not hold high office. She couldn't be beautiful as well as intelligent. To be effective and be in charge she needed to be less than appealing. Kadlec was proof of that – if proof was needed.

One thing had been confirmed at that very meeting. There had been a rumour in the upper echelons of management that Anicka Kadlec knew all there was to know about the senior members of staff over whom she wished to have more power. She had spent the previous 30 minutes showing the others in their exclusive club some of the information she'd garnered over the years.

It brought uneasy smiles and chuckles from the others. Waterfield wondered what she had on them. It was a scary thought. On the other hand, she was now a part of the team. A part of a cabal that already held sway over the EU and whose power would increase significantly over the next few years. Then he corrected himself. A few months would be more like it the way things were shaping.

The clamour for more border controls organised and controlled on a European wide basis was getting louder by the day. A European military would start to evolve soon. He knew its growth would be rapid. Astronomically so, with what they planned. If it didn't happen fast enough in accordance with the timetable they planned, then all hell would break lose. They would see to that.

Waterfield asked, 'Any word on Madrid?'

'How in hell,' asked O'Flynn, in his usual blunt fashion, which was at odds with his demeanour when sitting on the bench with his judge's hat on, 'would we be knowing that?'

Waterfield recognised the fact that it was a stupid question. He put it down to nerves. The rules had evolved over the previous decade and now were automatic. Wind Kowalak up using significant sums of money and let him loose on the target. Like a modern missile. Fire and forget. London and Rome were both prime examples of the technique.

'I apologise,' Waterfield managed to smile. 'You're right. This is such a huge step after what has already happened I guess I'm a little nervous.' As soon as the words were out of his mouth he regretted saying them – there was no room for weakness. Or more to the point, there was no room to display any weakness. 'This final act will help to consolidate power in our hands.'

Kadlec said, 'I would not put it as strongly as that. I must also correct you on what you just said. It is not a huge step. It is the last planned small step that may or may not have brought us to the end of the road. If not, we keep taking those small steps. I have a number of proposals that we can discuss at a later date if the act committed in Madrid does not finally ensure a European wide defence force.' Her smile reminded Waterfield of a crocodile about to clamp down on its victim. 'However, I am confident it will. I have had a private word with a number of influential people here in Brussels, as well as some of the higher political echelons of the member states. As a result, I am as sure as I can be that the necessary legislation required to implement our plan will be passed. They will include,' she paused for effect, 'an agreement to standardise all military hardware across the EU. What's more, all purchases will be made through our offices here.'

Their dreams of even greater power and wealth were dangling in front of them. A frisson of anticipation swept through the room. The deaths of more people, possibly even hundreds of people, were insignificant when compared to what would be the result. They had already rationalised among themselves that the deaths and injuries incurred between London and Rome were fewer than happened on the roads of Europe in a month.

'Do any of you know,' asked Waterfield, 'what went wrong in Switzerland? How was it that the woman Nelson wasn't killed and we had to have the job done back here?'

The others exchanged glances but nobody answered. None of them had an inkling as to what had gone wrong. There was no post operation briefing or analysis. As it was, the job was done one way or the other and that was all that mattered.

'All I can say,' said Friedmann, 'is that on one level this is a better method of ensuring her death. We have made it clear that it was due to a gas leak and most of the media went along with it. There are a dozen parties around Europe who are demanding a full enquiry which we will give them.'

'What are you proposing?' asked Waterfield.

'I will recommend that Judge Patrick O'Flynn head up an enquiry and report his findings in say the next six months. By which time nobody will be interested, life will have moved on and we can ignore the findings.' Friedmann raised his glass in salute to the judge and took a healthy drink of wine. He did his best to ignore his ulcer.

It was Dupuis who queried, 'What was the final death toll at the apartment building?'

Friedmann looked at a sheet of paper in front of him and replied, 'There were five men, six women and, I am sorry to say,' though he didn't look or sound apologetic, 'four children under the age of ten.'

'And injured?' Kadlec asked, her look fixed on Friedmann.

'In total eight seriously and nine or ten with minor injuries.'

The woman nodded. 'All very acceptable in the circumstances.'

Waterfield raised his glass, another one of his better vintages, and said, 'Here's to success.'

This time they all raised their glasses and drank. Waterfield couldn't help watching Maimone drain his glass. The man had said he was going to stop drinking, but seemed incapable of doing so. His alcoholism had too great a hold. At times like this he doubted whether the Italian should be one of them. He conveniently forgot that it had been Maimone who had invited Waterfield to join them.

*   *   *   *

It had been simplicity itself. Hunter and the team had met up with Wilson and given him the guns and vests. He hadn't asked any questions and Nick hadn't volunteered any information. It was, as ever, the way of clandestine ops. Handshakes had been brief, the return to the airport uneventful and they had ditched the car without any hassle. They had been escorted to the plane. There had been no customs and no security – an arrangement made by Macnair and Chuma Hamadi.

The plane was in the air by 00.35. Hunter had a long briefing with the General and then the three of them settled down to sleep. At a speed of 500 knots, they would be landing about 03.45 local time, or perhaps a little later. Luckily, Madrid Barajas Airport was open 24/7, even if very few aircraft landed after midnight and before 06.00.

Head winds delayed them by 20 minutes then, with one thing or another, they didn't arrive at the airport terminal until 04.20. They stayed on the plane and slept for two hours. When they eventually left the plane, they were met by a young lady and escorted into the main building. They went through customs and passport control in minutes and wandered out into the arrivals hall. There was one individual, dressed in a suit, waiting for them.

Just like in Alexandria, greetings were brief. His name was Mike Tattler of MI6. Again, the team used only their Christian names. They went out into the bitter cold and climbed into the Mercedes belonging to MI6.

'Have you been told anything?' Hunter asked.

'No, sir. I had a message from Sir William himself.' There was awe in the man's tone. He had never spoken to the head of MI6 who lived and breathed in a rarefied atmosphere well above that of a mere agent. 'I was told to give you every assistance. I have weapons in the boot as well as comms gear.'

'Glocks?' Hunter asked with a slight smile.

'Yes, sir. Where are we going?'

Hunter shrugged and said, 'In to the city. We're waiting for instructions from my boss.'

The agent looked to be in his mid to late twenties. Hunter could see that the man kept himself in good shape and from the alert way he was constantly checking what was going on around him, took nothing for granted.

'There's something you need to know,' said Hunter. 'We now know that the next atrocity, like those in London and Rome, is going to be here. Actually at the American Embassy.'

'When?' Tattler asked in a shocked voice.

'Today. At midday, to be precise.'

'My God!' Then he got himself under control and, in a steady voice, asked, 'Do we know how it will be carried out?'

'We think it will be five cars carrying explosives with possibly eight men.'

'That sounds enough to level the whole area, not just the embassy.'

'You're right,' replied Hunter. 'At first we thought it might be some sort of simultaneous attack around the building, but we know that's not possible. What we think is that they intend making the embassy the focal point, but will detonate the bombs anywhere as long as they get near to the place.'

'What are we going to tell the Americans?' Tattler queried.

'If you were told that an attack by terrorists driving cars packed with explosives was to take place today at noon, and you were the target, what would you demand happened?'

'Huh! That's easy. That the road is closed and no cars allowed.'

'So would I. That's logical. Why?'

'What do you mean, why?'

'What I said. Why would you make such a demand?'

Tattler glanced at Hunter as though he'd gone nuts. 'Obviously to protect the embassy. To save lives.'

'British lives.'

'Of course, British . . .' he trailed off. 'Hell! I see.'

'What do you see?' Hunter asked.

'If we block off the road and stop any cars going near the embassy the terrorists will scatter.'

'What if they have a contingency plan to do just that? How about one car aimed at our embassy. Another at France's, another at Italy's and so on. So we have two objectives and that is to stop the bombing and kill the bombers. In that order.'

'Bloody hell, sir, how are we going to do that?'

Hunter sighed. 'I'm damned if I know right now. One thing TIFAT is doing, in conjunction with your lot, is running all arrival tapes through a face recognition system to see if we can identify anyone who has flown into Spain in the last week. It's one hell of a big task. The programme began last night and is still running. If we had more time it could be useful, as it is, there's hardly any time left.'

There was genuine anguish in the agent's voice when he said, 'Why can't they just live in peace? I don't care how a man or a woman prays. I say, let them enjoy their religion and everything associated with it. Just leave us alone to enjoy our lives the way we wish. Which isn't killing others.'

'The vast majority of people all over the world agree with you,' said Hunter. 'Whether they are Christians, Atheists, Buddhists, Muslims and all the rest of the religions, they agree with that sentiment for peace and tolerance. The trouble is there are minorities who are spoiling life for everyone else all over the world, especially in Europe'

'Huh! Nothing like the Islamic fundamentalists are trying to do.'

'Unfortunately, they are not the only ones. We have Judaism fundamentalists and Christian fundamentalists who all have one thing in common. They hate those of different faiths. The problem in this case is the Muslims are not the planners. They are being used. Oh, I admit, they are willing participants, but the men behind the whole thing are truly evil. These men are not doing what they are doing from any form of belief. They are doing it for power and wealth.'

Tattler again glanced at Hunter, a deep frown etched across his face. 'Then who's doing it? If we know, why don't we go after them?'

'We don't know all the players yet. However, before we do anything we have to take care of this major problem. And right now we've no way of solving it.' Hunter rubbed his eyes. Catnapping was all well and good, but a proper sleep in a bed made all the difference – even for hardened men.

'Sir, we're approaching the city centre, where do you want to go?'

'To the American Embassy. We'll take a look around and try and work out some sort of strategy.'

'Presumably GCHQ and ECHELON are at work,' said Tattler.

'Yes. This area is targeted. Nothing can or will be said using a mobile phone that we don't hear. Key words will trigger recordings and operatives will listen in. A massive effort has gone into finding these terrorists under the guise of a major and important exercise. We don't want the news being broken to the media if we can help it.'

'Even with a blanket of secrecy,' said Tattler, 'I'm surprised something about what's going on hasn't leaked to the press.'

'The lid won't be kept on things for long, but that's not the point. Stopping this atrocity is all that matters for now. The rest can wait.'

Tattler indicated right and pulled onto the Calle de Serrano. It was a wide thoroughfare, one way, with the American Embassy on the right as they passed. There were five lanes as well as parking on both sides of the street.

Hunter blew out his cheeks. This was going to be a damned sight more difficult than he'd originally thought.

'There's a Starbucks just along here, we can go there if you like,' said the MI6 agent.

'Please. We could use a shot of caffeine.'

The two men in the back grunted their agreement. As Tattler pulled up outside the Starbucks, Hunter's phone rang.

'Sir?'

'Ah, Nick, we have, I think, what we can call good news. Or at least helpful news.'

'Yes, sir?'

'GCHQ picked up a number of transmissions about an hour ago. Cheltenham honed the area down to within two kilometres of the

352

embassy. What we now know is that they intend using four cars, not five. Somebody was ranting and raving at the lack of explosives. They were speaking Persian and we are certain, from their accents, that they're Iranian.'

'Is the time scale still the same?'

'Yes. It was emphasised as being midday.'

'What's the score with the Spanish police?'

'I'm still trying to get hold of Commissioner Clavet. There are already police vehicles with armed men in that vicinity because of the number of embassies in the area. So there'll be nothing suspicious if there are a few more than normal. Once I get hold of Clavet I'll get back to you.'

'I have an idea,' said Hunter slowly. 'There's one thing we can do, but we must plan it to the minute. We need the Spanish police otherwise it won't work.'

36

Mohammed lit another cigarette. He didn't offer one to the woman. 'We will wait here,' he said.

'We cannot park here,' she replied.

He immediately bristled. 'Do not tell me what I can and cannot do,' he said through clenched teeth.

She looked at her brother-in-law with contempt. She was aware how he felt about her but it was nothing like her hatred of him. He was stupid, ignorant and easily manipulated. She may have become a Muslim comparatively late in life but she had loved her husband and had embraced his faith wholeheartedly. Her husband had brought her to the ways of Allah while his death, at the hands of the Americans, had brought her to holy jihad. Like many people who converted to their faith, she was more passionate and committed than those born to it – no matter what faith. Now, at last and quite soon, she would be reunited with him. In the meantime, she would suffer the fool sitting next to her. He had done his best to undermine their marriage and as the eldest son of three, with their father dead, he expected the other members of their family to do as he ordered. Faakhir, her husband, had refused.

She dwelled on the memories of their meeting. It had been in the university of Leeds. Faakhir had been the only member of the family to go to university, first in Tehran and then with a scholarship to Leeds. At least, that was what she had thought at the time. In fact, it turned out he had been sent there by the Mullahs in Iran to prepare him for battle against the infidel West. By becoming steeped in the ways of the western world, he would become a planner, a general, leading the Iranians to great things. He had believed it with a passion and never wavered. It hadn't taken long for her to believe it as well.

Then, back in Iran, on the night she had announced her pregnancy to Faakhir, had come the rocket attack. They had been so happy for those few minutes before the bombs started exploding. American made, Israeli launched. He had been killed and she had lost the baby. It would have been a boy. At the memories, she could not help feeling her eyes begin to water.

With her red hair and pale face she was ideal camouflage. Nobody would suspect the man she was sitting next to was a Muslim. It made their task all the easier.

Now, she'd had enough. She turned to him and said, 'We are on a holy jihad and you are too stupid to know what you are doing.'

He looked at her in shock. No woman could speak to him like that. He was about to slap her when she spoke.

'This is a parking zone for permit holders only. Walking towards us and only six cars away is a man in uniform checking for permits. If we stay here it could become awkward.'

He looked at her and said nothing. She looked back at him and said nothing further.

Reluctantly, he turned on the engine and pulled away from the curb. He hadn't looked to see that the road was clear and there was a screeching of tyres and the sound of a horn.

Mohammed looked at the woman driving the other car and jerked his middle finger at her. It was a western gesture he liked to use.

* * * *

In Starbucks, the four of them had double espressos as well as a plate of muffins. The premises were half full, though many other customers entered to collect their takeaways as they headed for work. Hunter still had his mobile to his ear.

'A car pile up?' said Macnair. 'It would have to be planned to the minute.

'I realise that. I think it could work because the street is one way. We'll need at least four cars, preferably more and we need to have the accident at, say, 11.50 or 11.55.'

'If we want to trap them it needs to be 11.55, otherwise they'll be able to turn off long before they get near the embassy. Mind you, that's assuming they stick to the original timetable.'

'There are a lot of assumptions in this kind of op, sir, but we have no choice.'

'You're right.'

'Sir, when you get hold of Hilario Clavet don't mention to him about the EU side of things. He doesn't need to know. Besides which, it'll take too long to explain and will only complicate matters.'

'I agree. So that we have the same story, I'll tell him we know it's an attack by Al-Qaeda and that we've only just confirmed it.'

'Sounds good in theory but it doesn't work. What are we doing here if we've only just found out about the attack?'

Macnair was silent for a few seconds. 'You've been hunting down the leads we've had. It looked like Madrid but we couldn't be sure. What the hell, I don't care what he thinks. The important thing now is to stop it happening. If he wants an argument later he can have one.'

'It'll be his bosses who'll scream the loudest. They'll want to make political capital out of it. Especially,' said Hunter in a bleak voice, 'if one of the cars explodes.'

'Naturally, that's only to be expected' said Macnair, cynicism dripping with every word, 'After all, they're politicians. Wait a moment.'

Hunter could hear the General speaking on his intercom. Then he heard, 'Thanks, put him through.'

'Nick, that's Clavet on the other line. I'll ask him to meet you. That'll be better than you going to them. Where are you?'

'We're half a kilometre from the embassy at a Starbucks,' Hunter replied. 'There is one very serious problem.'

'What's that?' Macnair asked.

'Shoot-to-kill. The police will want to make arrests. If they try, then I think we can expect at least one or more bombs to explode. If the bombers have prepared for the possibility of being intercepted then setting off the explosives will take about a second.' Then he added, 'Maybe two or three if we're lucky.'

'You're right. I'll see what the commissioner has to say. The one thing we can hope for is that the attackers won't be expecting you. That should add a few more seconds to the time scale.'

'Finding them will still be difficult. If they become suspicious and are trapped in a traffic jam, they'll just blow up the cars where they are.'

'We have no choice. I'll get back to you just as soon as I've spoken with Clavet.'

About 15 minutes later, a car with flashing lights and a two-tone horn pulled up outside the coffee shop. The four men watched as one man climbed out leaving a driver. The man was in uniform. He entered the premises, looked about, saw the four of them and crossed to where they sat.

'My name,' he announced, 'is Commissioner Clavet.' His face was austere and Hunter wondered if they were going to have trouble. 'Hilario Clavet. Which one of you is Commander Hunter?'

Hunter stood and offered his hand. The other man shook it with enthusiasm and a half smile. Hunter felt a great deal of relief.

'It is indeed a great pleasure to meet you,' said Clavet, a smile on his face. 'Your reputation goes before you.'

'Sorry?' Hunter looked surprised.

'Yes, yes. Those of us with the job of keeping Europe safe know about what happened when we were targeted with those dirty bombs. You and your men saved Europe from destruction. I have read the report. Without your intervention,' he shook his head, 'God alone knows what would have been the outcome.'

'Thank you for that, sir. Let me introduce my team. This is Jan Badonovitch.'

357

The commissioner shook Badonovitch's hand with equal enthusiasm, 'If I remember correctly, you were also there.'

'Yes, sir, I was.'

'This is Phil Peabody. He's new to the team.'

The men shook hands.

'And this is Mike Tattler, attached to the embassy.'

'How do you do, sir,' said Tattler.

'Commander . . .'

'Please call me Nick.'

'And I am known as Hil,' he said in English with barely an accent. 'Often referred to as Over The Hill by my English speaking junior officers.' It was obvious that he didn't mind.

Clavet waved to the waitress behind the counter and indicated fresh coffees all round. He grabbed a chair from a nearby table and sat at the end of the table, looking bleakly at Hunter.

'Care to tell me what's happening?'

'What did the General tell you?' Hunter countered.

'That there is definitely going to be a bomb attack in the city and that you know about it. Is it true?'

Hunter nodded. 'I'm afraid so.'

'And you're sure?'

'Yes. There is no question about it.'

'Do you know when and where?'

'Midday, here.'

'What? Are you sure?' There was shock in Clavet's voice.

'Yes.'

The commissioner looked at his watch and said in a whisper, 'That's only an hour and forty three minutes away. Why here?'

'The target is the American Embassy.'

'We must stop them.' It was a statement of such obvious fact that nobody said a word. 'We can close the road. Prevent them from getting anywhere near the street. Evacuate the buildings. If the embassy is their target . . .' he trailed off as the obvious struck home.

Hunter didn't need to say a word. He was sure the man had just arrived at the same conclusion they had hours earlier.

In a whisper, Clavet said, 'They can then go anywhere and set off the bombs. Or they can come back another day. Catching them today is the only chance we have of stopping them.'

'Hil, I want to ask you something,' said the Hunter. 'You said stop, not arrest. Can you spell out what you mean?'

Anger washed across the police officer's face. 'We stop them permanently. A trial gives these people a platform from which to spout their hatred. It foments trouble when we have enough as it is.'

'What about your superiors? Presumably it's the Minister of the Interior you answer to.'

'No. It is in fact the Director General.' Clavet managed a bleak smile. 'However, I have operational control. I will make my report after the event.'

'Any particular reason?'

'Yes. Those milksops will want the terrorists arrested, put on trial and political capital made of it. What they won't acknowledge is the danger our men and the public will be in if we try to make the arrests. You know as well as I do the terrorists will be able to set off the explosives with the flick of a switch.'

'In that case we will give you all the help you need. If,' Hunter looked at the other man with narrowed eyes, 'you had said anything else I would have withdrawn my men. We don't and won't, take unnecessary risks.'

The commissioner nodded. 'I was told pretty much the same by General Macnair.'

Hunter said, 'It all comes down to timing. These men are loose in the city with cars packed with bombs. If they do the same here as in Rome they can set them off anywhere and kill and maim a lot of people.'

'I know that.' The worry lines were etched deeply into the commissioner's brow.

Hunter knew that what they were facing was the nightmare every senior cop in the world prayed would never happen. No matter how much you trained, nor how much you planned, you were never ready for the shock of reality. One of the biggest problems of the lot was reaction time. 'We have a couple of advantages. The first is that the American Embassy is the prime target. Therefore, they will do everything they can to reach it. Secondly, we know when they're going to make their move.'

The commissioner nodded.

Hunter went on to describe his idea for a staged accident to which Clavet nodded as Hunter made each point. 'I've also been going over and over in my head as to when we should stage the incident. It has to be in time to stop the cars getting too close to their target but not too soon so that they can turn down a side road and get away. We're sure that if they have the slightest inkling something is wrong they'll set of the bombs. Which means the accident has to be as realistic as possible.'

'I can arrange that. All we need is six men yelling at each other with a policeman trying to keep the peace.'

'Have at least one woman. Somebody who can be shrill and domineering,' said Hunter.

'Yes, that makes sense,' replied Clavet. 'If the Iranians are anywhere nearby, they will love it. More proof that men in the West are weak and pathetic. No woman would be allowed to speak to a man like that back in their own country. They will probably find it highly amusing. And I have just the person.'

'Good.' Hunter's phone rang. 'Sir?'

'Nick, we've picked up a number of intercepts from four different phones. These people don't seem to have any concept of security. What's more, voice analysis suggests that three of them are barely out of their teens. This is confirmed by what they've said and their talk of how proud their families will be. The fourth man appears to be much older and is the leader. We have used Kowalak's phone number and sent the man a text. In it we've said that if the bombs explode within fifty metres of the embassy, one million euros will be paid to each of the families of martyrs who are making such a great sacrifice in the name of Allah and his prophet, Mohammed.'

'And they've accepted it?'

'There's more. We emphasised the need to explode the bombs at noon, when all true Muslims will be reciting their *Dhuhr* prayer. That it is of huge significance according to the will of the great Ayatollah. Then, the final straw was us saying that special prayers would be said for them across the Islamic world as word of what they will have achieved spreads.'

'They believed it?' Hunter asked.

'It looks like it.'

'Have you been able to pinpoint their locations?'

'We know where they are when they are using their mobiles but they're continuously on the move.'

'Do we know how they are going to get together? That type of close timing is virtually impossible. Two cars can marry up easily enough, a third makes it problematical and a fourth is difficult to say the least.'

'We've a bit more good news. They are going to meet in the parking lanes further along the street from where you are. That's all for now. Is Commissioner Clavet with you?'

'Yes, sir. Do you want to talk to him?'

'No. That's okay. Is he co-operating?'

'Yes, sir.'

'Good. Good luck.'

Hunter told the others what Macnair had said. 'Their belief in the afterlife and all that entails is absolute. We know it's all encompassing, which is why these people are so dangerous. Their concentration on the time factor will be a distraction to what's going on around them. Hunter looked at his watch and saw it was 10.53. 'Hil, can you get things organised?'

Before the commissioner could answer, Hunter's phone trilled again. 'Sir?'

'We are pretty sure that each of the cars has two people in them.

The passenger will be controlling the explosion. The driver will be concentrating on getting them there at the right time.'

'That makes things easier.'

'Agreed. Four parked cars with two men of swarthy complexion in each shouldn't be that difficult to spot.'

'Thanks, sir.' Again Hunter relayed the information.

'I'll get everything organised my end,' said Clavet. 'What about weapons?'

'No problem,' replied Hunter.

The commissioner smiled. 'That's what I thought you'd say.'

'Do you have any trained snipers?'

'Of course. I have four officers here in Madrid. They use the British Accuracy International L96A1. All four are excellent shots. I have seen the results for myself.'

'Target shooting?'

'Yes. To date there has been no requirement to use their skills.'

'Can you get them into locations high enough for them to see the cars parked along the lanes?'

Clavet frowned for a second and then nodded. 'Yes. I can think of places on both sides of the street.'

'Good.' Hunter went on to explain what he was thinking. 'Is there anything else? Anything we've forgotten?'

'Yes,' said Clavet. 'Communications.'

'We have sets for us,' said Hunter. He looked at the transmitter and gave the frequency showing there.

Clavet wrote it down and said, 'I'll radio you as soon as I can.'

'Nothing more?' Hunter asked. The others shook their heads. 'In that case, we'll get going.'

Even as the team stood up to leave, Clavet was using his mobile phone and issuing instructions.

37

Outside the coffee house they split up. Hunter and Tattler crossed the road, while Badonovitch and Peabody stayed on the side they were on. Both sides of the street were lined with small boutiques and shops – everything from fresh vegetables to expensive jewellery. They passed the American Embassy and continued sauntering along, looking into the shops, checking each car.

About a kilometre past the embassy Badonovitch grabbed Peabody's arm and stopped, looking into a shop selling leather goods. He pointed at an item and said, 'Three cars ahead, two men in a silver Ford.'

Peabody was far too well trained and experienced to look. Instead, he said, 'Linda might like the handbag.'

'That's a good idea. Let's go in and take a look.'

They entered the shop and were immediately pounced upon by a young woman.

She said something in Spanish and Peabody replied in English. She switched to the same.

'Is there anything I can help you gentlemen with?'

'Yes,' replied Badonovitch, who suddenly had an idea. 'The shoulder bag in the window, can I see it?'

He was standing next to the window, pointing at the bag, looking at the car. The two men in the car were nervously looking around. Their heads weren't still for a second. They looked to be in their late teens or early twenties and they both had swarthy complexions.

Peabody was standing next to him and softly said, 'Bingo.'

The sales assistant looked at him with a puzzled frown as she took the bag from the display unit. 'Sir?'

Peabody smiled and said, 'Nothing. Do you want the bag?'

Badonovitch replied, 'We'll take two.'

If he was surprised, Peabody didn't show it as the penny dropped. He smiled; it was a damned good idea.

The girl's smile widened as she took a second bag down from the shelf. The bags were brown leather, about 25 centimetres long, a similar depth and six centimetres wide. She was about to wrap the bags in tissue paper before placing them in a garish paper bag with the name of the shop on its side when Badonovitch stopped her.

'That's okay. We'll carry them.' The Russian handed over the cash and slung the bag over his shoulder. He then adjusted the length of the strap so that the bag was next to his hip. Peabody did the same.

The girl couldn't help but look surprised but said nothing. The two men thanked her and left. They strolled past the car and glanced in.

'Nick, we have one,' Peabody spoke into his transmitter. 'It's the silver Ford a couple of cars behind.'

There had been a brief debate about whether or not to use their communications sets or rely on their mobiles. As co-ordination was key and being spotted by their targets highly unlikely, they decided it was best to use the sets.

'We've got one too. Also a silver Ford.' Hunter looked at his watch. It was 11.38.

'We're outside a coffee shop. We're going inside,' said Peabody.

They entered the coffee place, ordered Americanos at the counter, paid for them and took them across to a table next to the window. They took turns going to the toilet and came back quickly with their guns in their bags.

'Phil, you stay here. Move when you think the timing is right. I'll go further along the sidewalk.'

Peabody nodded and took a seat at the window where he could keep an eye on the car.

A glance at his watch told Badonovitch it was 11.53. As he stepped outside there was an almighty crash and looking to his left he saw that cars were braking to a halt. The traffic quickly backed up. Sirens could be heard and police cars began to descend on the area. The passenger in the car they were interested in climbed out and craned his neck to see what was going on. He looked at his watch and then bent down to speak to the driver. A phone rang and the man took out his mobile and answered it. There followed a heated, one-sided tirade by him and then the call was disconnected.

Badonovitch hurried along the sidewalk. He'd gone about eight cars when he saw the second one. Two men, nervous, looking around, pointing, both talking at the same time. As he walked past the car, he was close to it and looked down into the driver's lap. He couldn't identify it but the man was holding an automatic. Badonovitch looked at his watch, 11.56.

Speaking into his transmitter, he said, 'One of the men here has a gun. The others could also be armed.'

It was 11.58. It was time to take action.

Hunter said to Tattler, 'Mike, you take out the car we just passed. I'll go and look for the other one.' He didn't wait for a response but walked briskly away. Nothing. Nothing. A possibility. No, that was a man and a woman. Nothing. Nothing. Damnation, where the hell were they? A glance at his watch showed it was 11.59.

Hunter paused and looked around. If there was a fourth car in the vicinity he couldn't see it. He looked behind him. It was sheer luck, just sheer luck. The woman passenger had climbed out of the car he had just passed and stood on tiptoes to try and see along the street. She was an attractive, fair skinned redhead. Stupidly, she still had her automatic clutched in her hand. She seemed to wake up to the fact and turned to get back into the car. As she did, she saw Hunter looking at her and at her hand. She was four metres away. It was impossible to miss the weapon. She seemed to realise that fact and began to raise the gun at him. She was too slow.

Hunter had been standing with his right hand under his jacket, clutched around the Glock. He didn't hesitate. He drew and fired three rounds. They all hit her in the chest and she went flying backwards.

Before she hit the ground Hunter was dashing to the car. He bent down and didn't hesitate for a moment. He fired two rounds into the terrorist's head.

Badonovitch had his hand in his shoulder bag when he stepped to the car. He didn't bother taking his weapon out of the bag. He fired through it. Two bullets went through the passenger's side window into the man's head followed by two shots into the driver's head. Neither of the men knew what was happening. One second they were alive, the next they were dead.

Peabody stepped in front of his target. He snatched his hand from the bag, raised his Glock, saw the shocked incomprehension on the faces of the two men and fired. Two rounds into the passenger's head, two into the driver's. Both were dead in less than two seconds.

Tattler bent to the side window on the passenger side. A bullet slammed into his chest and sent him flying backwards across the sidewalk to end up crumpled against the wall of a fresh vegetable shop.

Hunter saw the car suddenly jerk and pull out of the parking lane. It went through gaps in two lanes of traffic and smashed to a halt in the side of a car directly in front of it. He had seen what had happened but was too far away to do anything about it. He flung himself to the ground, expecting an explosion at any second.

It didn't happen. He stayed where he was for about ten seconds then quickly leapt to his feet and carefully approached the car. He looked through the shattered windscreen. Both men were hunched forward. The backs of their heads were missing.

The snipers, wherever they were, had done a good job.

He turned to the MI6 agent. He looked to be in a bad way. Sighing, Hunter stepped across to the prone body. Tattler was slumped with his back against a box of carrots. His head was bent forward. He was breathing slowly.

Hunter said into the comms set, 'Man down. Hil, get us some help as quickly as you can.' As he spoke, Hunter felt in the agent's pockets and lifted his car keys and put his Glock in his pocket.

'It'll be with you in two minutes,' said the commissioner, 'I have half the city's emergency medical teams here, just in case.'

Seconds later, two men with a stretcher and a doctor with a stethoscope around his neck arrived. They took charge. At the same time police officers wearing protective uniform were carefully approaching the cars to deal with the explosives. Commissioner Clavet appeared.

He was all smiles as he held out his hand. Hunter shook it and reciprocated with an equally wide grin.

'My friend, I do not know what to say. Spain is indebted to you and your men.'

'Just doing our job,' said Hunter who was reluctant to accept praise.

Then the commissioner's demeanour turned sour. 'I suggest you and your men get the hell out of Spain, before the Director-General gets here.'

'Oh, why?' Hunter was somewhat taken aback.

'He's the type, in order to justify his existence, who will demand an enquiry. He will want you kept here to answer questions like why weren't these people arrested and put on trial as expected of any civilised country? I can hear him now. Nick, the man is the worst kind of political appointee. He is out of his depth, self-centred and has an ego the size of Mount Everest. I'm not saying you won't be released but it'll be days maybe even a week or two.'

'I get the picture. What about Mike?'

'He has diplomatic immunity. Besides, he didn't actually fire his gun.'

'If you look, you won't actually find one. I've got it. I'll return it to the embassy along with ours.'

'Good. Leave it to me to come up with some sort of suitable story.'

'Your powers-that-be will know soon enough that we were behind today's events but we can let General Macnair fight any battles that come our way. What about you?'

Clavet chuckled. 'I'm going to let the politicians scream blue murder about today's events and then I shall enjoy taking apart whatever idiot arguments they use. Now, let me wish you a pleasant journey. I have much to do.'

Handshakes were brief and Clavet walked away. The team went across to Tattler's car and removed their bags.

'Where to now, Nick?' Badonovitch asked.

'To the embassy. We need to let the Ambassador know what's happened and return the Glocks.'

The roads were jammed, car horns were blasting and irate people were standing in the road yelling at each other. It didn't take the team long to walk to the embassy situated at Torre Espacio. There they hit a problem. They weren't allowed in to see the Ambassador.

Hunter phoned Macnair and explained what was up. Minutes later a harassed looking man appeared, escorted them around the security systems and up to the Ambassador's office.

The man was dismissed, leaving the three men with the Ambassador.

'Ma'am,' said Hunter, 'I've been instructed by General Macnair to bring you up to speed on events.'

She waved a manicured hand in front of her and replied, 'I've heard most of it.' Her smile was genuine and warm. 'I'd like to extend my thanks for what you did.' She was in her fifties, smartly dressed in a business suit, with brown hair going grey. Although a little overweight, she was an attractive woman. Hunter noticed the wedding ring on her left hand. 'The Spanish are in TIFAT's debt which is never a bad thing.'

'We've brought back your Glocks,' the three men reached under their jackets and placed the guns on the desk, while Hunter took Tattler's out of a side pocket. 'Also, here are Mike Tattler's car keys.' He explained where to find the car.

'Thank you.' The Ambassador looked at the Glocks with distaste. 'I appreciate the necessity for them but I hate weapons.'

'Is there any word on how Mike is doing?'

'As of a few minutes ago he was still alive.'

'Thanks. We'd better go,' said Hunter, standing up.

'Thank you again,' she rang a buzzer and the door opened. 'Tim, please see these gentlemen out.'

In the street, cars were backing up in all directions and they decided to walk to the railway station. From there they would take a train to the airport to fly back to Scotland. At the station, they entered a restaurant and found a table. Weariness was creeping in after the huge adrenaline rush of the morning's events. The waitress took their orders for something to eat while Hunter phoned Rosyth.

'Sir? We're at the railway station. There's a train in fifty minutes to the airport and an evening flight to Edinburgh.'

'Sorry, my boy, but I have something else for you to do. I want the three of you in Brussels. Do you still have the automatics from the embassy?'

'No, sir. We returned them.'

'Never mind. Take the overnight sleeper. I'll speak to Sir William and have you met at the station. I'll make sure you'll get what you need. I'll also give you a full briefing tomorrow morning.'

'Right, sir.'

Hunter relayed the information to the other two. 'After we've eaten we can go and buy some clothes.'

*   *   *   *

Waterfield had finished his late lunch. He was in a good mood expecting to be told at any minute about the explosions in Madrid. He relished the idea of the American Embassy being destroyed. After this, the question of whether or not there should be a European wide border force would no longer be asked. Instead, there would be a demand for such a force and he, with the help of the others, would make sure it happened.

The next couple of years were going to be interesting, exciting and, significantly, rewarding. He drained the last of a glass of red wine and contemplated having another. He decided against it.

He was sitting in a restaurant less than a kilometre from his office. Unusually, he was alone. He wanted, even needed, an audience. Someone to hold forth with. In reality boasting of his achievements for the United Kingdom in particular and Europe in general. Those who knew him were aware of his requirement for continual praise and having his ego massaged. He was surprised to see Gunther Friedmann waddling his way towards him. The man dropped into the chair opposite.

'Good afternoon, Gunther, may I get you a drink? A glass of wine or an aperitif of some sort?'

'Nein. I do not wish for a drink. Have you heard the news?'

'What news? What's happened?'

'Madrid . . .'

'Oh, the bombing? No, I've not heard. Perhaps you can tell me.'

The German leant forward and stabbed the table with his left index finger. 'There have been no explosions. The terrorists were stopped before their bombs could be exploded.'

The blood drained from Waterfield's face. 'Are you sure?'

'What do you mean, am I sure?'

'Keep your voice down. We don't want everyone in the restaurant to hear you.'

The place was packed and a couple of people had looked their way.

'What happened?' Waterfield asked.

'We know nothing!' Waving his hand in disgust, Friedmann slumped back in his chair, caught the eye of a waiter and beckoned him over. He might have an ulcer, but right then he needed a brandy.

'Make it two,' said Waterfield conjuring up a smile. When the man had gone, Waterfield asked, 'What have you heard?'

'There were four cars, packed with explosives, headed for the American Embassy. They were stopped, the terrorists were killed and the explosives dismantled.'

'How did the Spanish police find out what was happening?'

'They didn't. I've spoken to one of my contacts in Madrid. The whole thing was as a result of TIFAT being involved. The Commissioner of Police in Madrid told the media that they owed a great deal to the men of TIFAT, for their bravery, resourcefulness and a load of other things which I can't remember.'

'Damnation!' Just then the drinks arrived and Waterfield nodded his thanks to the waiter. After he had left, Waterfield said, 'One of the first things we need to do is get TIFAT disbanded once the border force is established. We can argue that there is no longer a requirement for such an organisation. We can make a great fuss about the fact that they do not arrest people but murder them.'

Friedmann took a sip of his drink, seemed to be more settled and nodded. 'Ja. It will be a great pleasure to get rid of them. They have had too much freedom to do as they wish for too long.'

Although Waterfield's demeanour was pleasant enough, inside he was seething. It wasn't a step back, but on the other hand, it wasn't a leap forward like he had hoped for. He would have to arrange another atrocity. What he needed to do was contact Kowalak.

'Gunther, leave it to me.'

'What?'

'I'll sort out something. A phone call and Kowalak can see to it. If not Madrid, then we can hit Bonn. It shouldn't take him long to make the arrangements.'

Friedmann nodded, took another sip of his drink, grimaced as it burnt its way over his ulcer and set the glass down. 'I shall tell the others. They will be relieved.'

'Good. Fine. Is that brandy not agreeing with you?'

'No. My ulcer. You know what it's like when I get upset.'

'Only too well. My dear Gunther, don't worry. I'll sort it out.'

'I had better go.' He stood up. 'I am meeting my wife.' He inclined his head and left the restaurant.

Waterfield saw that his glass was empty and ordered a second.

Once he had downed it he felt better. His nerves were once more under control. He paid for the meal and returned to his apartment. He tried to contact Kowalak but couldn't reach him. Over the next two hours he took calls from Dupuis, Maimone, O'Flynn and Anicka Kadlec. To each of them his message was the same. They weren't to worry. He would sort it out.

*   *   *   *

Nick Hunter and the team booked themselves first class on the overnight sleeper, departing at 18.00. Next, they dumped their bags in a left luggage locker and wandered around the streets of the city looking for a men's clothing shop – it didn't take long to satisfy their requirement for clean clothes.

The journey to Brussels proved to be a pleasant interlude. They enjoyed a decent meal, a few glasses of wine and then a glass or two of malt whisky. It was an ideal way to unwind after the last few days, even though they knew there was more trouble ahead.

In Brussels, they were told to wait in the restaurant at the station where they would be met by one of MI6's people who would supply them with equipment. They had a late breakfast of barely edible croissants and indifferent coffee. Half an hour later a woman walked in, looked around, and headed straight for their table. She was in her mid-thirties, had brown hair, of medium height, plain faced and of average build. She was an ideal MI6 operative – lost in a small crowd.

'Commander Hunter?' She looked at Hunter.

He stood, offered his hand and said, 'Please, call me Nick. This is Jan and Phil.' The two men waved hullo as the woman sat down.

'My name is Carol.'

'Can I get you a coffee, Carol?' Hunter asked.

'That's okay, thanks.' She placed a bag alongside her chair. 'I travelled by train from London and I'm awash with the stuff. Everything you asked for is in the bag. I've been told that I'm to stay in the city in case you need me. There may be things you want me to take back to London. Is that right?'

Hunter nodded.

She handed over a business card with only her name and phone number on it. 'Call me and I'll come immediately. Sir William emphasised the importance of it, so day or night is fine.'

Hunter nodded. 'Okay, thanks.'

She stood up, smiled and walked away.

They hired a Mercedes and drove away from the station. Badonovitch was in the back and opened the bag. 'Glocks, silencers, bugs, trackers and an eavesdropper.' The latter looked like a torch, six inches long, and one inch in diameter. The parabolic microphone was the latest in that type of technology and not yet available on the open market – it was still the plaything of the security services. It could be aimed at a window and any conversation inside the room was immediately heard and at the same time, recorded.

* * * *

Waterfield awoke with the mother of all hangovers and didn't get to his office until after 10.30. He told his secretary that he didn't want any calls and spent the morning watching various news broadcasts about what had happened in Madrid. The scream for TIFAT to be held accountable was loud and clear along with the demand for a European Defence Force. In spite of his headache, Waterfield was more than satisfied with the outcome. At lunchtime he didn't bother having anything to eat. He decided that the hair of the dog was needed and poured himself a large brandy.

He had his glass in his hand when his mobile rang. He took it from his pocket, looked at the number on display, didn't recognise it and frowned. He pressed the receive button.

'Hullo! Yes, what do you want?'

'Now, now,' said Hunter, 'not so rude.'

'Who is this?'

'My name doesn't matter. But I have some information I need to pass to you.'

'What information? And how did you get this number? It's private.'

'How I got it doesn't matter. I have phoned to give you some important information. Two days ago a man by the name of Jakub Kowalak was killed. Along with his three sons and sundry other personnel belonging to his organisation.'

The blood drained from Waterfield's face. 'What . . .' the word came out in a croak, 'Why are you telling me this?'

'Oh, you know only too well, Mr. Waterfield. You paid Kowalak to attack the French Embassy and set off the bombs in Rome. You also paid for him to arrange for Muslim fundamentalists to attack the American Embassy in Madrid which was prevented.'

Waterfield tried to hold the phone steady.

'Who . . . Who are you? What do you want?'

Hunter's chuckle sent a wave of fear washing through Waterfield.

'What do I want? Why, nothing. You and I are going to meet very soon. When we do, you will tell me precisely what I want to know. You will answer all my questions which I shall enjoy asking. Then,' Hunter paused, 'I shall kill you.'

Waterfield pressed the end call button and threw down the phone as though it would bite him. He sat paralysed with fear. He could think of nothing except that voice and the words. He didn't know how long he sat there. He stared straight ahead, barely breathing. Then, at some point, he found he was able to move his hands, his head. On unsteady legs he headed for the door. He collected his coat from the coat-rack, told his secretary he wasn't feeling well and left. He passed numerous people as he walked along the corridor and into the lift but didn't acknowledge any of the them. He went out into the freezing cold, his coat over his arm. A taxi was outside and he climbed in. He gave his address and sank back. What could he do? What had gone wrong? These and many other questions sped across his mind. He had answers to none of them.

38

Hunter couldn't help grinning at the other two. 'I enjoyed that,' he announced.

They were sitting in the car, opposite Waterfield's apartment. They watched as the man climbed out of the taxi and rushed across the pavement to the main entrance. He lived on the second floor of a ten storey block, each floor having four apartments, each apartment three en suite bedrooms, an opulent kitchen and dining room. There was also a large lounge with another room off which Waterfield used as a study. They knew all this because that morning they'd been inside and placed bugs in all the strategic locations. While they'd been there, Hunter had switched on Waterfield's computer, logged in to a remote access account which gave Isobel in Rosyth full control. In five minutes his mobile had rung. Isobel had confirmed that they had hacked in and copied all the files they could find.

'Right,' said Hunter, 'I'll stay here if you two would like to go back to the hotel. It's 14.00, so if nothing happens come back around 19.00.'

They were staying at a budget hotel about five kilometres away. It was more than adequate for their purposes as well as being the only hotel in striking distance. The two men climbed out of the car and said their goodbyes.

Hunter's phone rang. 'Sir?'

Macnair gave a sigh and said, 'I'm sorry Nick, but I've just had word from Sir William that Mike Tattler died an hour ago.'

'Damn!' He paused and then asked, 'How has Isobel and her gang been getting on tracking down the money?'

'She's just told me. The info was on his computer. It was password controlled but she said Leo created a back door and went in that way. We've discovered Waterfield has accounts scattered across the world.'

'What about investments?'

'We're working on those but he seems to have preferred cash.'

'What about the names of any of the others?'

'We're getting somewhere, though nothing we can say is definite yet. They've been extremely cautious as well as clever. Have you put the frighteners on Waterfield yet?'

'Half an hour ago.'

'Right. Keep the pressure up,' said Macnair before he disconnected.

Hunter was listening to Waterfield but all he heard was him walking around the place, his feet clattering on the wooden floor. Then came the sound of glass on glass and Hunter presumed the man was drinking.

The afternoon dragged. Just after 19.00 the other two returned.

'Mike Tattler died,' Hunter greeted them.

'He was a nice guy,' said Peabody. It was as fitting an epitaph as any.

All three had friends and colleagues who had died – it was the nature of what they did. Even so, it was not something you got used to. What it did though, was stoke up the anger to administer justice – their brand of justice.

'We'll give him another thirty minutes,' said Hunter. 'If he hasn't contacted any of the others I'll phone him again.'

Twenty minutes later, the General phoned again. 'Nick? Isobel is sure that she has identified all of Waterfield's accounts.'

'How much are we talking about?'

'Thirty two million plus change.'

'Hell! That's incredible!'

'Don't forget, it's been going on for over fifteen years.'

'When are you going to raid the accounts?'

'Isobel is working on it now. She said they needed about twenty minutes. They will hit all six banks simultaneously.'

'I'll phone him then.'

It was just 20.00 when Hunter phoned Waterfield's home number instead of his mobile. It rang and rang. Finally, Waterfield answered with a tentative, 'Hullo.' His voice was a croak. He cleared his throat and in a much stronger voice said, 'Hullo.'

'Mr. Waterfield, I thought I would call and let you know that you have less than twenty-four hours to live.'

Waterfield was gasping for breath. For one moment Hunter thought the man might have a heart attack, but he recovered.

'I don't know who you are but I will pay you one million euros to leave me alone.'

Hunter's laugh was genuine. 'Don't speak to me like I'm a fool. After what you and your vile cronies did? Besides, you don't have a million euros.'

'I have far more than that,' there was a vestige of hope in the man's voice. 'I can pay you more. Say five million.'

'No.'

'Ten! For God's sake, ten million euros! Think what you can do with so much money.'

'Waterfield, you haven't been listening. You don't have that sum of money. In fact, you have nothing.'

There was something in Hunter's voice that caused Waterfield to say, 'What . . . What are you talking about?'

'I'm hanging up now. I will phone you in five minutes.'

'Wait! Wait!'

The receiver was on loudspeaker and they could hear Waterfield babbling, still asking Hunter to wait, unaware that they were no longer connected. Then Waterfield stopped.

They heard him rushing across the room. Badonovitch said, 'He's just gone into his study. Yep, he's at the keyboard of his computer.'

Waterfield couldn't stop his hands from shaking. In fact, his whole body seemed to be in some sort of uncontrollable spasm. His fingers wouldn't work the keyboard properly and he had to stop what he was doing. He got to his feet, went across to the drinks cabinet, poured himself a large brandy and drank it in one. He poured a second and went back to sit at his desk. The spasms had stopped. The alcohol was giving him a false sense of bravado.

'I'll show them,' he said out loud. 'Nobody does this to me.'

He went into his account in the bank in Luxembourg. His eyes goggled as he saw that it was not only empty but it was 49,999 euros overdrawn. His overdraft limit was 50,000 euros. The shock sent him into spasm again. He wanted to scream. Like all bullies, Waterfield was a coward at heart. He could dish it out, but he couldn't take it.

He started going through his other accounts. The next was in Switzerland. He typed in the account number and his password. He was sure his money would be there. After all, the Swiss were well known for their secrecy when it came to banking. They could be relied upon. His eyes goggled at the screen. It wasn't possible! The account was empty! Empty! But there had been over ten million Swiss francs in it, when he had checked only a few days ago. It was one of his pleasures – to log into his various accounts and gloat – particularly after a new payment had been made.

The Bermuda account was empty, so was the Singapore account, so was the Lebanon account.

Waterfield didn't make it to the wastepaper bin. He was sick all over the floor. He vomited up the alcohol he'd been drinking followed by his dinner. When there was nothing left he vomited bile. He couldn't stop heaving. He was on his hands and knees. He stopped and collapsed onto the floor, moaning. He couldn't help himself. Over and over he asked himself what he could do. His brain wasn't functioning. It was as though he was in a fog, lost, wandering around looking for a way out.

He managed to get to his feet. His clothes were covered with vomit and he staggered into his bedroom. There, he tore off his clothes and threw them into a corner of the room. He went into the shower and turned it on. He stood there for some time letting the water cascade over him. Finally, he began to think more coherently – he needed to speak to the others. He got out of the shower and put on jeans, a shirt and a sweater. He crossed the room, sat on the side of his bed and lifted the extension to his house phone.

He dialled Jacques Dupuis. The phone was answered.

'Jacques, I need . . .' He stopped speaking. It was a recorded answer telling him to leave a message. He tried Gunther Friedmann. The phone rang and rang. No answer.

Panic was beginning to set in as he pressed the buttons.

'Enrico? Enrico? Thank God! Enrico, I need your help!'

'Peter? Do you know what time it is? I am about to get ready for bed. I want an early night as I am away first thing in the morning for a breakfast meeting.'

'Enrico, please, forget about bed. I tell you I need help.'

The panic in Waterfield's voice finally got through to Maimone. 'What are you talking about? What do you mean you need my help? What's happened?'

'I . . . I have had a phone call. Two calls. The man who phoned told me that Jakub Kowalak was dead and so were his three sons along with others in his gang.'

'What?' Maimone's voice faltered. He cleared his throat and said, 'What do you mean? Dead?'

'For Christ's sake, Enrico! What do you think I mean? They're dead. But . . . But that's not the worst of it. The voice said that he was going to kill me as well. In the next twenty-four hours.'

'Go to the police. Tell them some maniac has threatened you. Demand protection. They will have to give it to you. Now, I want to go to bed.'

'Wait! Wait, I say. There's more!'

'What do you mean, there's more?' The exasperation was clear in his voice.

'I have no money.' It was such a stark statement that the man on the end of the phone said nothing for nearly half a minute.

'What do you mean? What do you mean you have no money? You have millions. Like me. Like the others.'

'It's all gone, I tell you. My accounts have been raided. Stripped bare. I have no money.'

The phone went dead. 'Hullo? Hullo? Enrico?' No answer. Nothing. Waterfield jiggled the phone. He got the dialling tone and redialled. Still no answer. His guts hurt, his mouth was dry and he couldn't prevent himself from starting to shake all over again. He phoned the Judge. It went straight to an answering machine. It was then that Waterfield remembered O'Flynn was yet again in the South of France at some sort of legal conference.

That left only one person to call. He dialled Anicka Kadlec. The phone rang and rang and he was about to hang up when she finally answered. 'Anicka? Thank God.'

'Hullo? Who is this?'

'It's me. Peter. I need your help.'

Warily, she said, 'Help? To do what? What sort of help?'

'My life has been threatened. A man phoned me. He said . . . he said he was going to kill me in the next twenty-four hours.'

'Go to the police. Only don't bother me.'

'Wait!' He realised he was speaking into a disconnected phone. Slowly he replaced the receiver. He had never known such despair. Such fear. He felt his mind clouding again. Thinking was becoming more difficult. Fear not only had him by the throat, it was squeezing the life out of him. What could he do?

His phone rang.

'Peter?'

'Enrico? Thank God.'

'Peter, get hold of yourself. I have checked my accounts. Nothing is missing.'

'I tell you all my money is gone. I have received threats to my life.'

'I have already told you, speak to the police. As to the money, mine is still here so I do not know what has happened. Perhaps it is a computer glitch at your end.'

'What do you mean a computer glitch? Don't be so stupid.' Waterfield's voice was shaking in time with the receiver at his ear.

Maimone said, 'Wait until tomorrow. Things will be better then.'

The line went dead and Waterfield looked at the phone as though in a trance. Better tomorrow? Didn't the man understand what was happening? What was he talking about? Waterfield stepped to the drinks cabinet, poured himself a large brandy and took a large gulp. It hit his stomach and he retched. He kept it down and after a couple of minutes he took another slug. With the glass in one hand and the bottle in the other he staggered up the stairs to his bed. Thanks to more alcohol he passed out.

* * * *

Hunter phoned the General, 'Sir, did you get the numbers?'

'Yes. We're running them through the system now. Here you go. Jacques Dupuis, Gunther Friedmann, Enrico Maimone, Patrick O'Flynn and the last one is Anicka Kadlec. We'll find out their addresses. Your ploy to panic the man seems to have worked. Like you said, there was nowhere else he could go except to those who are part of their organisation.'

'Good. Thanks, sir. Goodnight.' The connection was broken.

Hunter looked at the other two. 'Let's call it a night. Although we've bugged Waterfield's car and put the tracker in we'd better keep watch.'

Badonovitch had the first watch, Hunter the middle and Peabody the morning.

It was just after 06.00 when Waterfield made his move.

Peabody phoned Hunter. 'Boss, that's Waterfield out of bed. He's having a shower.'

'Thanks. Let Jan know, will you?'

Hunter lay still for a few seconds and then, with a groan, threw back the duvet and climbed out of bed. He wondered where Waterfield was going. The rooms weren't en-suite so after shaving he went out and along the corridor for a shower. He was dressed and ready to go when his phone rang.

'Boss? That's him leaving now.'

'Right, meet us outside. Have you told Jan?'

'He's waiting.'

Outside it was still dark. Sunrise wasn't until 08.45 and right then the time was just coming up to 06.50 It was freezing cold after a cloudless night. The streets were virtually deserted. In another hour they would be packed solid, but right then travelling around the city presented no problems.

Waterfield got out of the city and headed north-west on the A10. If he stayed on the road he'd hit Oostende. If, when he got there, he hung a left he'd be heading south-west to Calais. Hunter wondered if he was going back to the UK.

The A10 soon turned into the E40 and shortly after that Waterfield turned off onto the B401 and headed for Ghent. An hour after he'd left Brussels he was pulling up in front of a detached, imposing looking house on the edge of the city. It was only 07.22 and, Hunter thought, a bit early for making house calls.

They passed the house and saw that Waterfield was sitting in his car opposite the gates. The team went a few hundred metres further on and then parked.

Peabody said, 'That's Maimone's place.'

Peabody turned the car and drove back towards the house. They were in a salubrious part of the city, driving along a boulevard with trees on both sides. The houses were imposing, each in their own grounds, many with swimming pools and tennis courts.

Fifty metres from the house, Peabody pulled over and switched off the engine. The house had a low wall, barely a third of a metre high. Waterfield was clearly in sight, still sitting in his car. A short while later the front door opened and a woman came out with two teenage children.

The teenagers got into a car while the woman walked across to Waterfield who was climbing out of his. The team could see them talking. After a couple of minutes she turned away, walked to her car, climbed in, started the engine and drove sedately out of the driveway. She and Waterfield waved to each other as he walked up the drive to the front-door. He rang the doorbell. Waterfield rang it a second time before it was opened by a man. Waterfield shouldered his way past and into the house. The door slammed.

Peabody aimed the eavesdropper at the house. He pressed the receiver to his ear and said, 'Waterfield is going on about his money. Maimone has just said that none of his is missing. I've lost them. They've gone into the back of the house.'

Hunter broke the connection and said, 'Phil, you stay here and let us know if the wife comes back. Jan, let's go house calling.'

The two men climbed out of the car and crossed the road. As they did so they pulled on flesh coloured rubber gloves of a type worn by surgeons. At the door, Hunter rang the bell. After a few seconds he did it a second time.

The door was flung open and an angry man stood there. In French he asked, 'What do you want?'

Hunter answered him in English. 'You.' As he said it, he thrust his way through the door, pushing Maimone in front of him. The Italian stumbled.

'What are you doing? Get out of my house! Get out now before I call the police!' His voice was loud and shrill.

Waterfield came to the door at the end of the short corridor and looked to see what was happening.

'Jan, bring him with you.' Hunter took the half dozen paces to where Waterfield was standing and said, with a pleasant smile on his face, 'I've been looking forward to this.'

Hunter slapped Waterfield across the face with an open palm.

Waterfield put his hand to his cheek and said in a terrified voice, 'You! You're the man who threatened me. Enrico! This is the man I told you about.'

'I do not care who he is. Get out or I shall call the police.'

The Italian was a little taller than the Russian. He had a bushy black moustache which didn't hide his nicotine stained teeth. In his left hand he was holding a lit cigarette. He went to put the filter tip in his mouth when Badonovitch slapped his hand hard and the cigarette flew from his hand onto the carpet.

'What? What do you think you are doing? Get out I say.'

Hunter and Badonovitch exchanged shrugs and Badonovitch swiped the back of his hand across Maimone's face. The slap was loud and clear in the quiet of the house. The man stepped backwards, his hand to his cheek, tears forming in his eyes.

'Go through there,' said Badonovitch, jerking his head at the door through which Hunter had just stepped.

The Italian didn't move but merely stood there, his hand on his cheek. Badonovitch grabbed the front of Maimone's shirt and dragged him along to the kitchen.

The two EU members stood there, frozen to the spot. Hunter looked around. The kitchen was large and immaculate. A dishwasher was churning away in a corner and a coffee maker was creating fresh coffee next to the sink. Hunter wandered across to the machine, found a mug on the draining board, picked it up and waved it at Badonovitch who nodded.

Hunter busied himself for a couple of minutes pouring two coffees, both with milk, no sugar.

39

'Help yourself if you would like some,' he said to the two men, waving at the coffee machine. Taking a sip of his, 'Very good,' he said.

'You said…,' Waterfield spoke in a croak. He cleared his throat and said again, 'You said you were going to kill me.'

Hunter smiled, if the rictus on his face could be deemed as such. 'I am. Today. But first I want to know what you are doing here.'

Shaking his head, Waterfield said, 'Nothing. Nothing. Enrico is my friend. I came to speak to him. That is all. Please … Please don't kill me.'

Hunter shook his head and said, 'Sorry, that's not possible. You have been tried *in absentia* for crimes against humanity the penalty for which is death.'

'What? What are you talking about?' Maimone asked.

'The atrocities you have committed. The latest being the attacks in London and Rome. All those deaths. Then the attack you tried to pull off in Madrid. All paid for by you. Oh, and Dupuis, Friedmann, O'Flynn and Kadlec. We mustn't forget them. We will be speaking to them pretty soon.'

'I will pay you whatever you want, anything,' said Maimone.

Hunter seemed to be thinking about it before he said, 'Let's take a look on your computer. Check out how much money you have.' He finished his coffee and swilled the mug under the tap.

Maimone nodded eagerly and led the way through the back of the kitchen to a large, book lined room. At the far end, the whole wall was triple glazed glass, overlooking a well kept garden. A substantial desk with a computer was in the corner. He walked towards the desk and as he sat down he turned to pull open a drawer at his right hand. It was something in his demeanour that alerted Hunter who had been right behind him and was standing on the other side of the desk.

Placing his left hand on the desk, Hunter vaulted over it and rammed his feet into the chest of the other man who went flying backwards off the chair. Hunter opened the drawer and lifted out an Italian Beretta Centurion. Pressing the magazine catch on the left side of the butt, behind the trigger, he removed the mag. There were bullets in the magazine and one in the chamber. Hunter removed it by hauling back on the slide. The shell ejected onto the floor.

The Italian lay where he was, scowling at Hunter.

'Get up, and get on to your computer. There's something I want you to see.' The man didn't move. 'Shift it!' Hunter shouted.

Maimone clambered to his feet and sat at his desk.

'First, I want you to go on the internet.'

'What? What are you talking about?'

'Type this address.'

Maimone didn't move. Hunter grabbed him by the hair and shook his head. Maimone screeched in pain. 'We can do this the easy way or the hard way, it's entirely up to you.' He gave the address and the Italian, with shaking hands, tapped it into his computer.

'Now press enter,' Hunter ordered.

Maimone did as he was told. The word "connected" came back within seconds.

'Now we wait.'

'What . . . what for?' Maimone asked.

'Sit!' Hunter ordered Waterfield, indicating a leather sofa next to him. He did as he was told and sat on the edge of the cushion. Waterfield's hands were shaking.

Silence blanketed the room like a shroud. Hunter wandered around the room looking at the books, noticing that there were

French, Italian and English titles. Badonovitch stood stoically at the door, his left hand under his jacket, gripping his automatic. The two EU men were like rabbits caught in headlights, swivelling their faces between Hunter and Badonovitch.

It was ten minutes later when Hunter's mobile indicated that he had received a text message. It said "done".

'Okay, now, I want you to take a stroll around your bank accounts. Let's see how much you have.'

'I need my notebook. It is in the same drawer.'

Hunter reached under his jacket and took out his Glock. It was the first time he had shown the two men that he was armed. 'Take out the notebook and start going through your accounts.'

The Italian sat at his desk and began pounding the keyboard, referring to notes in a small leather book. When he entered the first account he said, 'Like I checked last night. There's . . .' his jaw dropped as he watched the figures flash from 3,445,367 euros to a string of zeros. 'What . . . what is going on? What's happening?'

He glared up at Hunter who merely shrugged nonchalantly back at him. 'I think you will find that is the case with all your accounts.'

Maimone opened the next account to see the same thing happen, then a third. The man panicked as he went through all seven accounts. Each time he opened the account it emptied before his eyes. He seemed to have aged ten years when he reached the end and looked up at Hunter. 'Who . . . Who are you?' He managed to ask.

'My name is Commander Hunter, Royal Navy. However, I am currently attached to The International Force Against Terrorism and we have been investigating you scum. You arranged the murder of Andrea Nelson, a friend of ours who had been trying to prove how corrupt an organisation you have in the EU Parliament. There are all the other deaths you have arranged for which you have been found guilty. Sentence is now to be passed.'

'Wait!' yelled the Italian. 'Wait. I have cash in my safe in the corner. A million euros. You can have it all. Only . . . Only don't kill me.'

'What do you think, Jan? Is his life worth a million euros to us?'

The Russian seemed to give it some thought and then said, 'No, I don't think so, boss.'

'I agree.' Without hesitation he turned and shot Peter Waterfield through the centre of his forehead. The man flew backwards, blood and brains splattering across the floor and the cream coloured wall.

The Italian's mouth hung open. He looked up at Hunter and said, 'No . . . No . . . It's not possible. No . . .'

Hunter shot him through the forehead also. 'We'll leave the money in the safe, his wife and kids will probably need it.'

They searched the house looking for anything they thought might be useful. They found some zip drives in a drawer and Hunter stuffed them into a pocket.

'Ready?' Hunter asked.

Badonovitch nodded and both men went out through the front door and crossed the road. Peabody started the car and sedately pulled away from the curb. They were headed back to Brussels.

Hunter phoned Macnair. 'Sir? We're just going back to Waterfield's place to see if there is anything there that's useful. I'll then get hold of the woman from MI6 and give her the stuff. Any word on where the others are?' Hunter asked.

'Yes. We know that Judge Patrick O'Flynn is in Cannes for the debate or whatever they are proposing about the European Arrest Warrant. The woman, Anicka Kadlec, is in Brussels, we have yet to find Dupuis and Friedmann.

'They'll surface sooner rather than later when they learn that Waterfield and Maimone are dead.'

They got back to Waterfield's apartment and searched the place thoroughly. All they found was a number of zip drives and memory sticks. He lifted a computer bag and shoved them in. Once they left the apartment, Hunter phoned Carol and they arranged to meet back at the railway station.

Hunter went in alone and met her at the booking office. He handed over the bag. 'Take these for your lot. There'll probably be more tomorrow.'

She nodded. 'I'll be back this evening.'

'Right, let's find this woman Kadlec's place,' Hunter said.

The Director General of the Office de Lutte Anti-Fraude, OLAF, lived on the south side of the city at Ixelles Elsene. It was an area populated by many employees of the European Parliament.

The nearest street parking was a few hundred metres from her building. It was too far for the eavesdropper to be effective. Instead, Hunter strolled over the mainly cobbled streets to the front door. There was a call-button system for the eight apartments in the block. Hunter pressed the button alongside Kadlec's name. There was no answer. He did it a second time. Nothing. There was no lock on the door so he opened it and stepped into the foyer. It was unmanned. He took the stairs up two floors to the apartment and let himself in using the lock-gun.

The door led straight into the living room. There was a coat-stand just inside on the left, a settee and two worn looking armchairs. A television set stood in the corner and there were three doors leading off. The one on the right led to a bedroom, the one in the middle opened onto a small kitchen with a table just big enough for four to sit around and the third door led to a shower room and toilet. Overall, the place was cramped, untidy and worn. It didn't look like the sort of place somebody with large sums of money would inhabit. Unless she was hiding the fact that she had accumulated significant wealth. There wasn't even a computer. He spent a few minutes placing bugs and then left.

'Where now?' Badonovitch asked when Hunter got back to the car. 'The Judge's.'

It was less than two kilometres away on Rue Alphonse De Witte. The building was a six storey, nondescript looking sandstone building. They found a parking slot almost opposite the front door. Hunter stepped across the pavement to the building. According to the call-button system, the judge was on the ground floor. He pressed the button twice and received no reply. The door was locked and he again used the lock-gun. The door to the judge's apartment yielded to the gun and Hunter went in. He was surprised to find that the Judge occupied two floors.

The first floor consisted of three large rooms, opulently furnished with a kitchen and a separate dining room. It was obvious that two of the rooms weren't used. Upstairs there were four bedrooms, all en-suite. Three didn't look as though they'd ever been used. It seemed that the Judge lived a lonely and private life.

In the corner of the lounge was a large, antique looking desk on which sat a computer. Hunter turned it on and once it was powered-up opened the remote channel to give Rosyth control. The receive message came back and while the computer was being accessed Hunter searched the desk drawers. He found nothing. No zip drives, no memory sticks and no computer discs. His mobile beeped and he signed off the remote connection. He then placed bugs in every room, even those that weren't in use. An examination of the kitchen and the fact that the fridge contained only sour milk suggested to him that the Judge didn't eat at home very often, if ever.

Their next port of call was at a house to the north-west of the city near the beautiful Parc Elizabeth. The street was Avenue du Duc Jean, Ganshoren. The house was terraced, three storeys high with further rooms in the roof. From outside it looked like the dwelling of a wealthy man. The kind of place that a man like Gunther Friedmann would occupy. The street was quiet, with very few pedestrians.

There were plenty of parking places along both sides of the street as well as along the middle where Badonovitch parked. A quick glance in both directions showed there was nobody around and Peabody used the listening device. In seconds he announced there was somebody in the house.

They were just down the road from a restaurant called Le Grand Duc and Hunter said, 'Why don't you two go in there and get something to eat? I'll stay and keep watch.'

Peabody and Badonovitch got out and went along to the restaurant. Five minutes later Hunter decided that the gods were smiling on them. The front-door opened and a fat woman emerged. She looked both ways, then turned right and walked away. He aimed and listened to the eavesdropper for a few minutes before deciding the house was empty. He got out of the car and made his way into the restaurant where he joined the other two sitting next to the window.

'Did you see the woman?' he asked.

'I did,' said Peabody. 'Jan was getting some coffees.'

'It doesn't sound as if there's anybody there so I'm going to knock on the door.'

Hunter went to the house and rang the doorbell. No answer. He waited a minute or so and tried again. Still nothing. Using the lock-gun he had the door open and was inside a few seconds later. He found himself in a short corridor. There was a door on his left, a door in front of him and a set of stairs on his right. Just before the stairs was a coat-rack and umbrella stand. Half-a-dozen coats hung on the hooks and three umbrellas sat in the stand.

He stepped through the door on his left. It was a lounge, well furnished, yet comfortable with a pleasant feel to it. There were family photographs on just about every surface that could hold a frame. Hunter picked one up and looked closely at it. The woman appeared to be a younger and thinner version of the one who had left the house. There were two girls and a boy standing next to her. He placed a couple of bugs in the room then went into the corridor and through to the kitchen a part of which was a large dining area. It was well used, there was a pleasant smell of cooked food permeating the area and a glance in the fridge showed it to be well stocked. Again he placed a couple of bugs.

On the next floor was a lounge overlooking the avenue and at the back of the house was a study. A sideboard in a corner of the room was groaning under the weight of bottles of alcohol. Next to the window was a desk on which sat a laptop. To his surprise he found that it was still switched on. He pressed the enter key and as the screen came to life he saw that it was showing a list of ingredients for baking a cake.

He gave access to the computer to Rosyth and began to search the desk drawers. All he found was a box of computer discs. A flip through showed that only some had been used. These he stuffed into a pocket while the remainder he replaced. His phone beeped, he logged off and then placed bugs around the room. He went up to the third floor where he found two bedrooms and a bathroom with toilet and then up to the roof space. Here there were another two smaller bedrooms as well as a shower room and toilet.

After planting more bugs he started down the stairs.

'Boss,' came through his earpiece, 'the woman is coming down the street with a bag of shopping in her hand.'

Hunter paused at the front-door. 'How far away is she?'

'About two hundred metres. She's stopped. She's talking to some-body who has just come out of a house. She's not looking your way.'

Hunter opened the door, stepped out and slammed the door shut. He crossed the road and climbed into the back of the car.

Frau Friedmann stood talking to the woman for a further ten minutes in spite of the cold. Then she turned and walked towards them. They watched as she stopped outside her front door and let herself in. They could hear her moving about the house. The phone rang and she answered it. The bug planted on the bottom of the unit picked up the conversation from both ends. It was Friedmann saying he would be home late as there was a meeting he had to attend. His wife accepted it with a sigh and asked if he would want dinner. He replied that he would.

The team then drove to the eastern side of the city to an area known as Evere. Dupuis lived in a small, detached house on the Clos de l'Oasis. It had a minuscule lawn in the front and space for parking a car. The eavesdropper indicated the place was empty.

Hunter entered the house. The hall was only a couple of metres long with a door on either side. The door on the left led to a small, poorly furnished lounge and the door on the right to a well furnished study, complete with two walls of leather bound books. There was no sign of a desk or computer but then he saw the wheeled desk chair in a corner of the room and noticed the tracks in the carpet. They stopped in the middle of the wall in front of a double door, waist high cupboard. He crossed the room and pulled the doors open. A flap came down, creating a work area. There was the computer. He switched it on and while it was powering up he searched the room but found nothing of interest.

When the computer was fired up he connected Rosyth to it and while the downloading was taking place he searched the rest of the house. He found a small kitchen which appeared to be well used, with a table just big enough to seat two.

Upstairs were two bedrooms, only one of which was in use, as well as a bathroom. He was planting the bugs when he received the bleep that Rosyth was finished. He returned to the computer, logged off, put the room back the way he'd found it and left.

A couple of hours later, while he was in his hotel, Hunter's phone went. 'Sir.'

'The bugs have been picking up what's being said and the transmitters have forwarded it to us. Most of it's drivel, but it sounds as though they're planning a meeting tonight. They are going to use a room in the parliament building. Wait a minute. There's another call being made.'

It was a few minutes before Macnair came back on the line.

'That was Dupuis screaming at Friedmann that Waterfield's and Maimone's bodies have been found. He wants to know what's happening. Hang on. There's something else. That's interesting. Friedmann has told him to calm down and think rationally. He said that they had been together in Maimone's house. He's asking wasn't it more likely that they were killed by an armed burglar than anyone else? Dupuis seems to be getting himself under control. He's admitting that the chances of the deaths being in any way connected to them are remote. They're agreeing to continue with the meeting. Friedmann just said that it is more important than ever. Ah! Room 147. I think that's the ground floor of the Louise Weiss building. I'll check it. That's all for now.'

When Macnair phoned back, he said, 'Yes, it is the Weiss building. It's a peculiar looking building. It's often said that it looks unfinished. You won't be able to get any bugs planted because we can't get near the place.'

'Okay, thanks, sir.'

*   *   *   *

In many respects it was almost inevitable that Anicka Kadlec took control of the meeting. The other three had just about fallen apart. The contempt she felt for them she kept well hidden. It wasn't time yet to make her move. There was far too much at stake. With them removed she would have absolute control and would be able to pick her own people for the roles she had planned. As it was, she had to listen to them frantically discussing the deaths of Waterfield and Maimone.

The room they were occupying could easily seat 20 around the heavy wooden table in the centre of the room. Like everything else in the EU parliament, it was fitted out with only the finest of furniture. The coffee machine in the corner produced some of the best coffee in Belgium, if not Europe.

Only Kadlec had a cup in front of her.

The anguished bickering went on for a few more minutes until Kadlec slapped the table a number of times with the palm of her hand. The three men stopped talking and looked at her expectantly.

'Good. Now, let us be sensible. Let us look at the facts and come to the correct conclusions. First, what do we know about the murders of Peter and Enrico?'

'Only what we have heard on the news. That it looks like an

opportunistic burglary that has gone wrong. That the burglar was armed and shot them.'

'Why should we disagree with the findings?'

The three men exchanged sheepish glances. The reality was, nothing else made any sense. They were aware that if the crimes they had committed were known to the authorities then arrests would have been made. As the boss of the European Anti-Fraud Office was seated with them, nothing along those lines could be expected.

She made that even clearer when she said, 'Gentlemen, I know of no investigation going on into our activities. If there was I would be bound to know about it. Is that not so?'

The three men nodded. They had been working with very tight security and no hint of what they were doing had leaked. The results of their activities were known but not their involvement. Their operation was made even more secure by having Anicka Kadlec on their side. There was also another important fact in their favour. Fraud and corruption was so endemic, stretched so far and wide, that stopping it was a near impossibility.

'Good,' said Kadlec. 'If you wish to mourn the deaths of Peter and Enrico I suggest you do it in your own time. We have work to do.'

From the looks on their faces, Kadlec didn't think there would be any mourning at anytime. 'What do we know about what happened in Madrid?'

The men exchanged glances and shook their heads. 'Nothing. Only what the press have reported. The Commissioner of Police in Madrid made a statement in front of the cameras.'

'I haven't heard it,' said Friedmann.

'He said that due to careful and organised police planning and investigation they had been able to learn about the attack. He said that they had also had some luck thanks to information passed to him via a mole in the Iranian Parliament. He also went on to say that TIFAT played a vital role in stopping the explosions and without their assistance many people would have died and been injured. Also that a great deal of damage would have been the result. He went on in that vein for some time.'

'Blaming the Iranians,' said O'Flynn, 'plays into our hands.'

'How so?' asked Dupois.

O'Flynn replied, 'We insist on an enquiry to make sure nothing like this happens again. Plenty of noise but getting us nowhere. However, a powerful message will be sent out as a result of the inquiry which is that we need a united border force and as soon as possible a united military.'

'Good,' said Kadlec. She sneezed. She did it again.

'Are you alright?' O'Flynn asked.

'I think I'm going down with a cold or even flu.'

She could see that Friedmann and Dupuis were beginning to look more upbeat. The fear and panic that had been blanketing the meeting was rapidly vanishing. The thought of the future was beginning to outweigh all other considerations.

Friedmann said, 'Of course, the deaths of the other two have been as a result of a burglary. It stands to reason as the only explanation.' Nods all round greeted the German's statement.

O'Flynn said, 'Are we going to replace them?'

'Who with?' Dupuis queried.

'On the British side there's that Welsh Labour MEP, Clive Jones. He's about as corrupt as they come according to the reports I have on him in my office,' said Kadlec.

'No, said Friedmann. 'I do not trust him nor do I think he would contribute anything that would be of any use. He is not known as the Welsh Windbag for nothing. He would never keep things secret.'

The others nodded.

'Good. In that case, let me give you my thoughts,' said Kadlec. 'It is too early to think about replacements. Our usual business will continue. I have looked at our operation in great detail and it is obvious that we do not need to do anything more than the occasional minor adjustment. I think we should leave things as they are and concentrate on getting the parliament to pass a law applicable to all member states that a European Border Force should be created as soon as possible. We will then follow that up with a requirement for all equipment to be the same across the whole of the EU. That the standardisation of all equipment would be cheaper in the long run and it would make the movement of military personnel across borders that much easier.' She let out several sneezes.

'I think there are many senior military figures who will protest,' said O'Flynn.

In spite of only just having joined the group, it was Kadlec who replied. 'Not if we dangle big jobs with fancy titles. Of course, such positions would need to have a suitable salary and pension to reflect the huge increase in responsibility.'

The others agreed. They judged everyone else by their own standards. The notion of honour and duty was alien to them.

Kadlec continued, 'Let us turn to more important matters. There is the question of the Pole.'

40

The eavesdropper, which was on loudspeaker, picked up every word as clearly as if they were in the room.

'So that's what it's all been about.' Hunter spoke with a mixture of awe and hatred in his voice. 'To embezzle vast sums of money when a European wide military force comes into being.'

'Can it be done?' asked Badonovitch.

'Easily,' replied Hunter. 'You've seen how much these people have stolen over the years. Think how much more would be available if they had access to funds twice or three times greater. Perhaps even more.' Then he added, 'Also, let's not forget, military organisations responsible for buying equipment are about the most inefficient in existence. It was interesting that now they've concluded Kowalak is dead how Kadlec volunteered to find a replacement who would run the operation exactly as before.'

'What was also interesting,' said Peabody, 'was how quickly the other three accepted her offer.'

'I suspect they don't want to get their hands dirty with that sort of detail,' Hunter said. 'Right, let's get down to it. We know Friedmann drives into the parliament every day, and although his three offspring work with him they live very near here. So he'll be alone. I think we should set a half kilo surprise which we can explode when he's clear of the houses and other cars.'

'Dupuis?' Peabody queried.

'How about the same?'

The other two exchanged glances, shrugs and nods.

Hunter speed dialled Rosyth. 'Sir? Can you ask Isobel to strip out the accounts of Friedmann and Dupuis tomorrow when I phone?'

'No problem. What are you up to?'

'We're going to set some PE. I want them off balance and one way to do that is to telephone them in the morning before they leave for work. Tell them to check their accounts and if they want the money back they are to do what I tell them. I think, somehow, they'll comply.'

'What about the judge and this woman Kadlec?'

'I intend a personal visit as neither owns a car.'

'Right. In that case, goodnight. I'll speak to you tomorrow.'

They returned to their hotel for a few hours until finally the time dragged round to 02.00. They left the hotel, drove to Friedmann's house and parked a few hundred metres away. Badonovitch stayed in the driver's seat while Hunter and Peabody walked to the house. It was a clear night, freezing cold, with a heavy frost and ice on the road. The houses on both sides of the street were in darkness. Using a silenced Glock, Peabody shot out the street light that illuminated the outside of the terraced house. Friedmann's car was an expensive Mercedes, parked a little further along the street. Hunter placed the PE in the opening between the windscreen and the bonnet. He taped the plastic into place and pressed the electronic detonator into the plastic. It took him less than 30 seconds.

Next, they drove across the city to Evere. Dupuis' car was in his drive. The street was dark, the nearest streetlight a good 100 metres away. Again, it took Hunter no time at all to plant the explosives and return to the car.

'Right, back to the hotel.' They knew that none of the four people went to work before 10.00. The judge only went to his chambers on three days, the rest of the time he was supposedly discussing and examining cases and how the laws of Europe affected the criminal.

A few hours later, just after 08.00, Macnair phoned Hunter. 'Commander, we've just picked up Friedmann getting out of his pit. He's told his wife he won't be leaving until 10.30 or thereabouts.'

'Good. Thanks, sir. Anything about Dupuis?'

'Nothing as yet. He's still sleeping the sleep of the good and the just.' There was no mistaking the sarcastic anger in the General's voice.

'Sir, I'll phone just before I call Friedmann.'

'Okay. Isobel is standing by ready to transfer the money.'

Hunter met up with the other two in a pleasant restaurant across the road. 'Dupuis isn't up and about yet but Friedmann is. Jan, you take the tram to the Da Vinci station at the Evere Shopping Mall. As soon as we know what Dupuis is doing we'll let you know.'

They finished breakfast and while Badonovitch went to catch the tram, Hunter and Peabody returned to Friedmann's house where they sat and waited patiently. The rush-hour traffic thinned out.

At 09.56 Hunter phoned Friedmann.

'Ja?' The voice was harsh, disgruntled at being disturbed at that time.

'Mr. Friedmann,' Hunter said in a pleasant and upbeat voice, 'I am your worst nightmare come to life.'

'What? What rubbish is this?' Friedmann's voice was shaking with anger even after so few words.

'Mr. Friedmann, I suggest you log on to your computer and check out your international bank accounts where you have been hiding the money that you have embezzled from the European Union.'

The silence on the end of the phone was broken by the gasping of a man finding it difficult to breath. Hunter sat listening to Friedmann, enjoying the sound.

After nearly a minute a strangled voice asked, 'What? What did you say?'

'I said check your accounts. I'll stay on the line while you do so. When you have finished I shall tell you where we should meet so that we can rectify the situation. Oh, if you don't want it rectified then hang up. If you do, then stay on the line.'

Hunter could hear the squeaking of a chair as it took the brunt of the German's obese body. Faintly, in the background, he could hear the tapping of keys, then a cry, as though Friedmann was in pain. There was more tapping followed by a moan of even deeper anguish, then silence except for the clack of the keys. Like before, as Friedmann accessed each account Rosyth stripped it bare.

Finally, a whisper came over the phone. 'Who are you? What do you want? Where is my money? What have you done with it?'

'It's available. We have need of your services. Nothing too onerous. If you want to see your money again then head for the A10. There's a service station not far out where we can meet and I can explain what we want done. Of course, there is no need to tell you not to contact the police. After all, you're the criminal. Now hurry up.'

It took Friedmann less than five minutes to come hurrying out of his house. He climbed into his car, pulled away from the sidewalk, almost causing an accident with a car passing along the street, and turned left. He drove too fast, breaking the speed limit almost all the way to the A10.

Five kilometres further and there was a sign for the services. Hunter dialled Friedmann and said, 'Park at the edge of the car park away from other cars. I will phone you when to get out and meet me in the restaurant.'

The answer was a croak. Friedmann pulled into the car park, paused, saw there were plenty of empty spaces over to his left, away from the other cars and drove there.

When he stopped, Hunter phoned again.

'Friedmann? You have been found guilty of embezzlement as well as murder. We know that you were responsible for the bombings in London and Rome and the attempted bombing in Madrid. The penalty is death. Goodbye, Friedmann.'

The explosion was loud and reverberated across the empty space. Hunter and Peabody drove sedately away as people poured out of the services building to see what had happened. The Mercedes was a burning inferno.

Hunter's phone went. 'Yes, Jan?'

'He's still in his house, though I just heard him on the phone telling someone that he was leaving in ten minutes.'

'Right. If you're all set, I'll phone him.'

'I'm ready.'

Breaking the connection, Hunter telephoned Dupuis. When he answered, Hunter said, 'Mr. Dupuis?'

'Yes.' Nothing further.

'Mr. Dupuis, please get on your computer and go through the various bank accounts you possess.'

There was silence for a few seconds and then the Frenchman said, cautiously, 'What are you talking about? Why should I go through my bank accounts? What accounts? I only have one here and one in my home town.'

'Tut, tut, Mr. Dupuis. I am talking about the accounts you hold in countries around the world where the balances amount to nearly thirty million euros. There is also your involvement in the bombing of the French Embassy in London and the killing of all those people in Rome. Luckily, we prevented the explosions in Madrid.'

The silence was absolute. Then, in a strained voice, Dupuis said, 'What . . . What are you saying?' He had the presence of mind to add, 'I don't know what you're talking about.' The tremor in his voice revealed his anxiety.

'Are you at your desk?' Hunter asked. 'Because if you're not or don't log into your computer in the next 60 seconds I will disconnect and you will be arrested within the hour. Is that clear?'

There was no answer, but Hunter could hear the keyboard being tapped. The tapping became more frantic. Nothing was said and then, after nearly three minutes a strangled voice said, 'Who are you? What do you want?'

'Who I am is not important. You have just seen your money vanish before your eyes. I want to return the money to you but I have a little job for you to do. I won't talk about it over the phone. Go out to your car and I will give you further instructions.

Peabody was connected to Badonovitch. 'Jan says he's come running. He's getting in his car. He says its all clear.'

Hunter speed dialled the Frenchman. When his phone was answered Hunter said, 'Mr. Dupois? The penalty for what you have done is death. Goodbye.'

Peabody said, 'Right, Jan.' There was a short pause. 'Jan says there's not enough left to fill a rubbish bin.'

Hunter nodded. That left two of them. Phoning Rosyth, he said to Macnair, 'Sir, that's Dupuis and Friedmann dealt with. Is the judge still at home?'

'Affirmative. He doesn't seem to be doing anything. No phone calls, nothing.'

'What about the woman?'

'Nothing. It's so quiet she must be in work.'

'In that case, I think it's time we visited the judge.'

When the connection was broken, Hunter said, 'Right, Phil, we'll meet Jan and then go and see how the judge is doing. I'm rather looking forward to our chat.'

They picked up Badonovitch at a tram station and headed out to Ixelles Isene. Parking was a problem but they got to within a kilometre of the judge's apartment.

'You guys wait here,' said Hunter, climbing out of the car. He switched off his mobile before approaching the front door, used the lock-gun and opened the door. He crossed the foyer and had the apartment door unlocked in no time. He put the lock-gun in his pocket, drew his Glock and slowly opened the door. There was the faintest of squeaks. Hunter stepped inside and closed the door behind him. He stood still, listening intently. He heard movement in the kitchen, and then O'Flynn coughed, followed by what sounded like a newspaper rustling.

Hunter walked towards the doorway and stopped to look at the judge sitting at his table with a mug of coffee near at hand. Hunter decided to say nothing and to wait for the other man to notice him.

O'Flynn picked up his mug, raised it to his lips, saw Hunter, jerked violently, spilt the hot liquid over himself and let out a shriek.

'Who . . . Who are you?'

Hunter stood staring at him. He said nothing.

'What do you want?'

Still nothing.

'Say something blast you, before I call the police.'

Shaking his head, Hunter said, 'You won't be doing that, that's for sure.'

'For the love of God, tell me what you want.'

'Oh, that's simple enough, I want you.'

'Me? What the hell are you talking about?'

'Stand up. I want us to go through to your study. I want you to switch on your computer.'

'What for?' O'Flynn made no move.

Hunter, beginning to lose patience, took the four steps that separated them and hit the judge across the side of the head with the butt of his Glock. Not hard but just enough to make the man yelp.

'Get up if you want to live!'

O'Flynn stood up on shaky legs and went through to his study.

'Now switch on your computer.' While the man did so, Hunter speed dialled Rosyth and was put through to Isobel. 'Ready? We're starting now. We'll go through the judge's accounts one by one.'

On hearing the words, the judge looked at Hunter who ignored him.

Hunter said to O'Flynn. 'Go to your account in Switzerland first. If you don't have the number I can give it to you.'

O'Flynn frowned and then took a notebook out of his desk drawer. He referred to it, his fingers hovered over the keyboard and then he pressed the necessary buttons.

After a few seconds, Hunter said, 'What does it say?'

'What? What do you mean?'

'How much is showing in the account?'

'Not . . . Not much,' he spoke hesitatingly.

Hunter gave an exaggerated sigh and said, 'Isobel, how much is there? Thanks. O'Flynn, you have more than eleven million Swiss Francs in the account. Am I right?'

O'Flynn looked at Hunter in horror and then back at the screen.

'Am I right?' Hunter yelled.

The judge jumped and nodded.

'Isobel, hit it. Watch the screen, judge. Watch it carefully.'

The judge stared at the screen in horror as he saw the numbers vanish and be replaced by a zero.

Looking up at Hunter, he said, 'What... What's happening?'

'Before we get to that, let's go through the other accounts.'

Hunter refused to say a word until eleven accounts had been emptied of a total of around 33 million euros.

As he watched, the judge went whiter and whiter. 'What . . . What's going on? I demand to know!'

'You can demand all you like. My name is Hunter and I am a Commander with The International Force Against Terrorism. You have been found guilty of fraud, theft and embezzlement. Also for planning and ordering the deaths of hundreds of innocent people in London and Rome. Then there was the attempt you made to blow up the American Embassy in Madrid. As a result you have been found guilty and the penalty passed is death. Do you have anything to say before the sentence is carried out?'

The judge's complexion grew worse. His breathing became haggard. He suddenly gasped for breath, half rose to his feet clutching at his chest and collapsed over the computer. Hunter checked. O'Flynn wasn't breathing and his eyes were wide open. He had obviously had a heart attack. Hunter hoped it had been painful, although the suffering hadn't been for long. Five down with one to go.

41

It took less than 15 minutes to get to the vicinity of Anicka Kadlec's apartment. They were close enough to listen on the transmitter to anything that happened in the apartment. They didn't require a relay from Rosyth.

The place was completely silent.

It was Badonovitch who summed up the situation. 'The transmitter isn't working. It's never this silent. There's always background noise.'

'You're right,' said Hunter.

'What shall we do?' Peabody asked.

'I'll go and pay a visit and wait for her to come home.'

'Do you want one of us to come with you?' Badonovitch asked.

'No. I'll be okay.' Hunter got out of the car and walked over the cobbled stones towards the apartment. As he approached the building, the main door opened and a woman came out. It wasn't Kadlec. He didn't approach the door, but walked past and kept walking until the woman was out of sight. He then turned around and walked quickly back to the door. Using the lock-gun he opened it, ran lightly up the stairs to the second floor and paused outside the door. He leant towards the door and listened carefully. Dead silence. He unlocked it, turned the handle, slowly pushed the door open and walked in.

He wasn't prepared for what faced him.

She'd had a lousy night. Between coughing and sneezing and feeling sick, she'd hardly slept at all. In the early hours of the morning she'd given up, climbed out of bed and sat in her lounge. She'd poured herself a large whisky, for medicinal purposes and lit a cigarette. The latter had caused her to cough heavily and she'd had to stub it out. The whisky had slid down easily. She had sat there, gloating. Everything was going far better than she had hoped. With Waterfield and Maimone dead she would soon have control of the milksops who were left. How on earth had such pathetic individuals been able to achieve so much? Where on earth had they found the backbone? Not only did it beggar belief but it also meant that they would be easy to deal with. She already had the contacts to replace the teams that had been controlled by Kowalak. She also had in mind two replacements for Waterfield and Maimone. Again, they would be her people.

Seeing that her glass was empty, she had boiled the kettle and made herself a hot whisky toddy with sugar. She had sat down and looked around the place. The first thing she was going to do was find a better apartment. She had helped to establish her place in the pecking order of things. It had been her who had arranged the bombing of the Nelson woman's place after Waterfield had admitted that he couldn't get hold of the Polish thug. She had told herself that she was highly satisfied with the way things were turning out. With these pleasing thoughts she had fallen asleep. She had woken with a start, saw that it was 09.30 and had moaned out loud.

She had got to her feet, gone unsteadily across to the sink and had poured herself a glass of water. Three glasses later she had been feeling a little better. The sand pit dry feeling in her mouth had gone. She had put on the kettle, spooned two teaspoons of instant coffee into a mug and had taken the milk out of the fridge. She had added three teaspoons of sugar, poured in the water, added milk and had sipped the coffee gratefully. She had needed that. She had been pleasantly surprised to find that she wasn't feeling as rough as she had been. Maybe, she had thought, the hot toddy had been effective after all.

She had pottered around the kitchen, put some bacon in a frying pan, waited a few minutes before adding an egg and had put on some toast. When her breakfast was ready, she had eaten it unhurriedly. After eating she had moved across to an easy chair, sat down, closed her eyes and had drifted off into that world of nether-land, neither awake nor asleep – a pleasant place to be where your dreams could be controlled and enjoyed.

It was just after noon when she fully came to and struggled out of her chair. She had a long hot shower and washed her hair. She had decided not to go to work and had dressed in faded jeans, a white blouse, a warm sweater, and socks and slippers.

She had made herself something to eat at lunchtime, baked beans on toast and another fried egg. She had little food in the apartment as normally she couldn't be bothered cooking for just herself. Besides, she ate an excellent, subsidised lunch in the parliament. One thing about the place, they knew how to look after their staff. In her 30 years of public service she had never known anything like it.

The blue light flashing above her door warned her that there was somebody outside. When it came to her personal safety, she wasn't a novice. The job she had was the sort that could and did create enemies. Probably not the sort to harm you physically, but certainly ones to denigrate you at every opportunity. Even so, there was no guarantee that she wouldn't be attacked so she'd taken precautions.

What was alarming was that the bell downstairs hadn't rung.

She had reached under her chair, found the small deadbolt and had slid it open. The automatic had fallen onto the floor. It was a SIG P225, one she'd had for the best part of a decade. It was well used and well maintained. She had been a member of a gun club back in Czechoslovakia when she was a child, taken there by her dear father. She had continued with her hobby after her country split in two and the Czech Republic was formed back in 1993. She had been given the SIG as a 40th birthday present by her now dead brother.

She had pushed the armchair about a quarter turn so that it was facing the door and had sat down. She had held the silenced automatic pointed at the door.

The door had opened and a tall, dark haired, good looking man had entered the room and had stared at her. If he had been shocked or even surprised he hadn't shown it. He had merely raised his hands to shoulder height and stood in the doorway.

'Who are you?' She asked in French.

Hunter replied in English. 'A visitor.'

She didn't hesitate. She fired a round that scraped along Hunter's left biceps. He grimaced, she smiled. 'Let me ask you again. Who are you?' She altered her aim to his leg.

Before she opened fire he said, 'My name is Commander Nicholas Hunter.'

'Commander of what?'

'Not of, in. In the Royal Navy.'

The reply caused her to frown. 'The Royal Navy? What are you doing breaking into my apartment?'

'Right now, I am on secondment to another organisation.'

'Which is?'

Whatever she was expecting, it wasn't the reply she got.

'I am attached to The International Force Against Terrorism.'

Silence reigned for more than a minute as she mulled over what he had said. Then she asked, 'Do you know who I am?'

'Yes. You are Anicka Kadlec. You are the Director-General of OLAF, the EU anti-fraud office.'

'I don't understand. Why are you here?'

'You are part of a group who have committed fraud, embezzlement and many murders.'

Again, whatever she had been expecting, it wasn't that. 'How? What? What are you talking about?' She realised that killing the man wasn't much of an option. If she did, she knew enough about TIFAT to appreciate she wouldn't live very long. She needed to find a way out of her situation and find it fast. One option was to phone the police. Have him arrested. Stepping outside the bounds of his authority. A thought took hold. It was perfect. She would show that

TIFAT was a rogue organisation. That it needed to be disbanded. That a European wide military organisation was more important than ever. Then she had an inspirational thought. The notion was beginning to excite her.

She smiled. 'Please, take your hands down. Thank God you're here.' She placed the gun on a side table. 'I was going to contact you as the only people I was sure I could trust.'

Hunter's face remained an impassive mask.

'Please come in and take a seat.'

He sat down opposite her, a couple of metres away.

'Let me get a plaster for that wound.' She stood up, went through to the bathroom and lifted out a first aid kit from the bathroom cabinet. Returning to the other room, she saw that Hunter had removed his coat and rolled up his sleeve. It was barely more than a scratch but it was seeping blood. She peeled the back off a plaster and put it over the wound. Hunter nodded his thanks, rolled his sleeve back down and replaced his jacket.

'I have something I must tell you,' Kadlec said. 'Just before Christmas I was asked by a group of men to join their organisation. To the best of my knowledge there are, or I should say, were, five members. Two are dead. One was an Englishman by the name of Waterfield. Peter Waterfield was a commissioner and President of the Internal Audit, Administration and Personnel department.'

Before she could go on. Hunter said, 'He died with Enrico Maimone. Jacques Dupuis and Gunther Friedmann are also dead from unnatural causes and Judge Patrick O'Flynn died of a heart attack.'

She couldn't help it. The look of shock on her face was impossible to hide. She conjured up a smile from someplace and nodded. 'Good. They deserved it. Have you any idea how much they have embezzled from the European Union? Have you any idea how many deaths they are responsible for?'

'We have a pretty good idea.'

'Did you know about their involvement in London and Rome?'

Hunter nodded.

She could see that he was wondering what the hell was going on. It was time to put him out of his misery.

'They asked me to join them. I resisted at first. I, like the rest of my colleagues, pretended nothing untoward was going on. Self delusion is a powerful enemy of the truth,' she said pontifically.

Hunter nodded and said, 'I couldn't agree with you more.'

'I came to realise that things were really out of control and decided to do something about it.'

'So what did you do?'

'Just before Christmas I told them that after much consideration I had decided to join their little band. It was the only way I could think of to get the information I needed.' She paused.

'What happened?'

Shaking her head in incredulous disbelief, she said, 'I knew things were bad, but this was horrendous. I had no idea how far and wide things went. The depth of corruption is impossible to gauge. I learnt of the police involvement and I think some agents in Interpol are also a part of it. If so, who could I trust? I became aware that if I tried to do anything I would be lucky to live. So I thought of you. TIFAT is one organisation I felt I could trust. In the right quarters you have an extremely good reputation. I was expecting to attend a meeting with the others inside the next twenty-four hours and anything I learnt I was going to pass to you.' She had a further flash of inspiration. 'I have only been associated with them for just over two weeks and already I have over two and a half million euros in my account. Where it all comes from I don't know, but it's there. I was going to use it as proof that what I am telling you is the truth.'

* * * *

Hunter sat frowning. He didn't believe a word of it but the trouble was it sounded so plausible. At the back of his head was the thought that she might have been telling the truth. After all, she had only just

411

joined them. She had not been responsible for the atrocities that had been committed. With the story she told, in a court of law, the probability that she would be acquitted was very high.

'I see,' Hunter said.

'What happened to the others?'

'Let's just say they were in the wrong place at the right time and leave it at that. Let me ask you something. What are you intending to do with the money you've been paid?'

She looked at him with revulsion. 'I don't want it. It's blood money. I shall have to do something about it but I don't know what.'

'Please give it to some suitable charities.'

She seemed to think about it before nodding. 'Yes. That is a good idea. I will make the arrangements. I have the details on my iPad and will see to it today. I must ask, did you have anything to do with the deaths of the others?'

Hunter shook his head. 'No. In spite of what you may have heard, we don't operate in that way. All we do know is that they were killed by an off-shoot of the murder teams they've been using. In the mean-time, the teams appear to have gone to ground. As long as they stay there, then there are no problems. If they resurface we may be tasked with dealing with the matter. Although, to be honest, I doubt it.'

Her frown was genuine. 'Why do you doubt it? Surely, it's the sort of thing you should be involved in?'

'No, not really. National police forces need to take over. Probably Interpol as well. Maybe even the security forces of the EU countries such as MI6 in Britain. I just don't know.'

'So what's going to happen now? To me?'

'I'll report to my boss. It's up to him.' He raised his hand, palm outwards and said, 'Don't worry. You're quite safe. Nothing will happen to you. You're the Director-General of OLAF, it's your job to stop the fraud so you just need to take control of your department and track down as many people on the take as you can.'

She shook her head. 'Just need to? That's a tall order but I will ensure we do our best. We must prevent further corruption, then, over time, what's happening now will wither on the vine.'

Hunter nodded as though the idea was a new one and he agreed with it. 'We also think that's the only position to take. We'll see if we can give you any information that might prove useful. What about any of the other commissioners? Are they involved do you think?'

'There must be some. Not to the depth and level of the other five, but some of them must be on the take otherwise some of the things that have happened couldn't possibly have been kept secret.'

'Again, we agree.' He stood up and held out his hand. 'May I say it's a pleasure to meet you? Good luck in your job of cleaning out the stables. It's a big task.'

'I know, but somebody has to do it.'

'You're quite right. No doubt we'll meet again sometime.' Hunter exited the door and went downstairs. He couldn't help thinking that it was somewhat unusual, to say the least, for an official in the European Parliament to have a Swiss SIG at her disposal.

When he rejoined the other two, Badonovitch said, 'Phil replaced the batteries in the receiver and we got most of it. How's the arm?

'Okay. Did you believe her?' Hunter asked.

'No,' said Badonovitch.

'Of course not,' said Peabody.

'No, I didn't either. It's up to the General what he wants done. It's time to head back.'

*　*　*　*

Richard and Macnair were sitting in the wardroom, both with glasses of whisky on the table in front of them. They'd been discussing what to do about Anicka Kadlec.

'Here's Nick,' said Richard, as his cousin strolled into the room.

Hunter crossed to where the other two were sitting. 'Can I get you anything?' They both asked for a whisky and soda. He went to the bar and ordered five large whiskies. He signed for the drinks, put the whiskies on a tray, and got a bowl of ice, a jug of water and some soda.

Badonovitch and Peabody came in and sat with them. The drinks were very welcome, water and ice added by the two NCOs, while the other three added soda and ice. They raised their glasses, said cheers and drank appreciatively.

'What are we going to do about the woman?' Hunter asked.

'We'll monitor things for as long as the batteries last,' said Macnair.

'Then what?' Hunter asked.

'I'm not sure. Pass it on to MI6 and let them deal with it. We already have other operations beginning to pile up and I can't spare the manpower. You know, she *might* be telling the truth.'

Richard pursed his lips and said, 'No, she isn't.'

Macnair sighed. 'You're right. Damnation! It's true she didn't have anything to do with the atrocities, and embezzling a couple of million doesn't deserve the sort of justice we dole out. Maybe she's learnt her lesson and will stay on the straight and narrow.'

'In that place?' Richard asked, incredulity in his tone. 'I doubt it.'

'One can but hope,' said Macnair.

'I see that the media is sniffing around,' said Hunter. 'That may help to force the authorities to do something about it.'

'For now,' said Macnair. 'Many in the Parliament will deny it all and keep denying it until along comes the next salacious event and the media loses interest. A detailed report of the actual frauds we know about will be given to every MEP. There are enough eurosceptic parties in the Parliament who should be able to make enough noise to force improvements as well as better controls. That's up to the politicians.'

'Then God help us,' said Richard.

'Sir William is putting it all in a report for the Prime Minister. What happens then is anyone's guess.'

'What about us?' Hunter asked.

'No official mention and not in the written report,' said the General. 'However, the Prime Minister will get briefed in private, along with the Foreign Secretary and the Home Secretary. Richard, I've been meaning to ask you. Have you seen any of the corruption yourself? In your business activities?'

'Personally no, not in Europe. My division is world-wide where in many places bribery is rife. Oil is mainly in the third world,' he shrugged. 'I don't have to spell it out. I'm not trying to be holier than thou but if the French, the Germans and the rest are using bribery to get contracts then we'll be doing the same. Otherwise, we'll be left out in the cold.' He took a drink of whisky and added, 'Which is why we need root and branch reform though under the current set-up I can't see it happening.'

* * * *

Nearly two months later Richard was in his office. Spring had officially sprung, as he liked to think of it, when he took a call from General Macnair.

'Malcolm. What can I do you for?'

'Morning, Richard. I have some news for you about Europe. MI6 has been keeping an eye on things and it seems that Anicka Kadlec has a contact in the Czech Republic who is going to take Jakub Kowalak's place. I suppose she doesn't want to wait any longer before she gets her snout in the gravy train. Anyway, a few days ago this contact killed three people.'

'Good grief! Who was killed?'

'A woman and two men who only joined the parliament last summer. They knew each other. The woman was in OLAF, one was in transport and energy and the third was with the agricultural commission.'

'What happened?'

'We are not one hundred percent sure but from what we can gather they got together one evening and swapped stories about what was going on. The woman became incensed and put together a comprehensive dossier which she took to Kadlec. As a result, Kadlec arranged for the three of them to be killed.'

'How? Shot? Blown up? What?'

'A car accident. A heavy goods vehicle hit them head on. They died while the lorry driver escaped with minor injuries. He's been arrested. We have it on good authority that he'll spend at most a year in jail.'

'A year? For three deaths?'

'I'm afraid so. He will be paid one hundred and fifty thousand euros for his trouble.'

'Bloody hell.'

'It seems the system is still rotten to the core. The trouble is, I suppose there's one head left on the hydra.'

'Can you do anything about it?'

'No. Nick's away and besides, we've sailed as close to the wind as I'm prepared to allow.' Macnair sighed. 'It's up to the powers-that-be to sort out any more of the mess. Sir William knows the score and it's up to him.'

'What about these pan-European armed forces they're still screaming blue murder about?'

'That's political and as such I think there's an inevitability to it.'

They talked a while longer and then Richard said, 'Malcolm thanks for all that. I'll no doubt see you sometime in the future.'

Richard got to his feet and drifted across his office to the coffee machine. He pressed the right buttons and made himself an Americano. Sitting back down at his desk he contemplated the stack of files in his in-tray and the lack of files in his out-tray. There was only one thing for it. He was still owed about five weeks leave. It was time, he decided, to cut off the last head of the mythical beast.

42

It didn't take long to discover where the next European Parliament major event was to take place. It was a debate on climate change and would be held in Monte Carlo. There would be the best part of two hundred delegates, mainly from the EU but also from China, India, Brazil and the USA.

The Director-General of the Office de Lutte Anti-Fraude would also be there.

Richard didn't bother staying in a hotel. Instead, he hired a 40ft cruiser and sat in the marina, looking at the place where Anicka Kadlec was staying. Although it was warmer at the Mediterranean than in Brussels, it wasn't that pleasant for March. There was a sharp wind blowing from the north, and rain clouds gathering over the hills, which was helpful. Bad weather usually meant people were less alert, more concerned with keeping dry and warm. He had a plan of sorts. He wondered if he'd get the opportunity to carry it out. If not, then it would keep for another day. He had both the time and the burning desire.

As well as the delegates, there was an overwhelming coterie of press, with each country having broadcasters as well as newspaper reporters in attendance. They weren't staying in the same salubrious establishments as the delegates – they had budgets. If the report he had seen was correct, the cocktail party to be held on the first night, was costing in excess of 40,000 euros. What the money was being spent on was beyond Richard's comprehension. He put on a warm jacket, went ashore and wandered around the streets. He approached Kadlec's hotel where a man in uniform gave him a half-hearted salute and opened the door. Bellhops were standing around, waiting to be of assistance.

Richard handed over his coat at the cloak room, gave the girl ten euros, pocketed the ticket and walked towards the bar. It was full of delegates, talking loudly to each other, mainly in English. In parliament they only spoke their own national language, as policy dictated. It also meant that there was a requirement for over 950 translators to deal with the many different languages. Richard found it ironic that the United Nations of 193 member states made do with six official languages.

Like the people there, he was dressed smartly, in his case wearing a dark grey suit. He wandered through the crowds, nodding a greeting here and there, oblivious to those who wished to be friendly and talk to him. It took nearly 15 minutes but he finally saw her. She was standing with three men and appeared to be enjoying herself as they laughed and joked. Richard felt the anger building up, turning to hatred. He wanted nothing more than to kill her – slowly and painfully. He realised that he was staring at her and turned away. A waiter was working his way past holding a tray full of flutes of champagne.

With the glass in his hand he didn't feel quite so conspicuous. A number of people approached him and tried to engage him in conversation but after a few minutes of his company they drifted away. He was unreceptive and uncooperative. Kadlec stayed with the people who appeared to Richard's jaundiced eye to be sycophants and so he had no opportunity to approach her. Shortly afterwards, the delegates began to drift away into the dining room to enjoy a superb buffet.

Richard joined them. Afterwards, he couldn't remember what he'd eaten. His attention had been surreptitiously focused on Kadlec as he tried to find the opening he wanted. It was with much regret that in the middle of the afternoon, when the opportunity he was looking for hadn't presented itself, that he returned to the boat. He sat at the lower console with the heater on, a coffee in his hand, contemplating his next move. It would have to be the cocktail party. A little while later he went below to the master bedroom and got a few hours sleep.

When he awoke, he had a shower and got dressed. The cocktail party was scheduled to kick-off at 19.00. He was aware that at such events most people didn't begin to arrive until around 19.30 or even later. It was only a short walk to the hotel, the wind had dropped and the temperature had risen by a few degrees to give a warm, pleasant evening. As a result, he didn't need an overcoat. Wearing his dinner jacket, wing-collared dress shirt, bow tie and maroon cummerbund, he looked like he was part of the event – that he had every right to be there. This proved to be the case as when he arrived, nobody asked to see an invitation.

The bar was heaving and it took him the best part of ten minutes to find her. Again, she had a small number of people with her, smiling and nodding at whatever she was saying.

Looking at her, Richard decided that she was too ugly to look attractive. Wearing a low cut, gold and black, floor length dress, she had done her best. It must, he thought, have been hard work. Then he told himself to concentrate on the matter in hand. He wandered around, exchanging banal comments with other guests. Although it was only 19.50, many were already three sheets to the wind. He could tell that some of the attendees were busy lining each other up for some late night entertainment – he didn't think it would be a game of Scrabble. Finally, he stood in a corner, ignored, with his glass on a ledge in front of him. The vial he took out of his pocket contained a colourless liquid known as Epinephrine – adrenaline mixed with a few drops of ricin.

Richard had bought the first drug from a reputable chemist on the basis that he needed it to treat the potential cardiac arrest of his aged father. The second drug he cooked up himself. It had been an easy, but time consuming process, extracting the poison from the seeds of castor sugar. The drugs, when mixed together, were untraceable, tasteless and deadly with no known antidote. He wandered back into the party, saw that Kadlec's glass was almost empty and made a beeline for a waiter who was about to hold out to her a tray with glasses of champagne.

He made it. He swept up a glass off the tray and said, 'Allow me.' He gave his most ingratiating smile and held the flute of champagne out to her. It was the one he'd been carrying in his other hand. Such a switch went unnoticed in the bustle and hubbub of the party. She smiled her thanks and Richard lifted his glass again and clinked it against hers. She took a mouthful. Richard took a sip, managing somehow to keep the smile plastered on his face.

'This is a very pleasant event,' he said loudly. He had manoeuvred himself so that he was next to her.

'Yes, it is. What is it you do?'

Her coquettish smile nearly had him reaching for a bag in which to vomit.

'Me? Oh, I'm in computers. My company has been awarded a contract to replace the current system. As a result, I've been sent here to show the flag, as it were. What about yourself?'

She seemed to straighten up as she replied in a condescending tone, 'I am the Director-General of OLAF.'

Richard looked puzzled and asked, 'What's OLAF?'

'It is the Office de Lutte Anti-Fraude. I am responsible for investigating any fraud and corruption that takes place within the EU which has its origins within the parliament.' She took another mouthful of wine.

It was enough. 'In that case you'll be very busy. Now, please excuse me.' As he walked away, he saw out of the corner of his eye that she was already talking to somebody else.

Richard left the hotel, satisfied with what he had done. He knew that in about eight to ten hours she would suffer abdominal pain and vomiting – very much as if she had food poisoning. Diarrhoea would come next and shortly after that the diarrhoea would turn bloody.

Damage to major organs would follow and the spleen, kidney and liver would start collapsing. Death, if she was lucky, would then occur within a few hours. He hoped she would be unlucky. Death could then take as long as 24 to 36 hours. During that time she would be on painkillers, requiring stronger and stronger doses.

He stood leaning on a low fence, looking at the marina, enjoying the beauty of the boats berthed there, none of which appeared to be worth less than half a million euros. One vessel, berthed at the end of the walkway, he guessed, must have cost at least $20 million. Either it belonged to a Saudi Arabian Sheikh and hence a prince of the Saudi royal family, or to a Russian oligarch, grown rich on the fraud and corruption that was to be found in the former USSR. He wondered if the scale of organised crime in Russia was as great as it was in the EU. He decided it was. Not even the commissioners and the rest of them could match what was happening on the other side of the long border between Russia and Europe. He took the vial from his pocket, poured the remainder of the contents into the sea and then also dropped the vial.

The splendour of the place suddenly became enhanced as a full moon rose over the horizon, bathing the area in white light.

A voice next to him said, 'Isn't it beautiful?'

He looked at the woman standing next to him. She was very attractive and looked to be in her early to mid forties. She was wearing a low cut evening gown that showed off her figure in a tantalising way that had Richard's imagination working overtime.

'Yes, it . . .' he croaked, cleared his throat, and said, 'Yes, it is.'

'Are you a part of what's going on back there?'

'Not really. I dressed up like this to go to the casino but after about ten minutes I left. Gambling isn't my thing.' He grinned. 'Then I walked into that lot and decided to join them. After all, my taxes are being squandered in there. But after a couple of drinks I decided I'd had enough. I'm just contemplating where to go and eat. What about you?'

421

She smiled. 'I'm part of it but I hate the whole shebang. I detest the people that are there. Do you know what they remind me of? It's a book. Take a guess.'

Richard frowned and then inspiration struck. '*Animal Farm*?'

'Precisely. Do you mind if I join you for dinner? My husband is in there now, getting blind drunk. He won't even notice if I'm gone. And even if he does, he won't care.'

Richard bent his arm and held it out for her to slip hers through. 'I do know of a rather pleasant restaurant a few streets back. Let's see if we can get a table.'

As they strolled along, she said in a pleasant Welsh lilt, 'My name is Meredith. Meri for short. And yours?'

'Richard. Richard Griffiths.'

'Where are you staying, Richard, Richard Griffiths?' She said, with laughter in her voice.

'On a boat in the marina.'

'What's it like?'

'It's a she. She's new, plush, expensive and I've only hired her.'

'I love boats. Can we go onboard after dinner?'

He looked and nodded. 'Of course. But only if you're in no hurry to go anywhere.'

'Oh, I won't be. Not until the morning, at any rate.'

Richard smiled.

Epilogue.

General Macnair phoned Richard in London a few days later. He got right to the point. 'I suppose you were in Monte Carlo for the EU event?'

'Ah, yes. Why?'

'You've heard about the death of the Kadlec woman?'

'Yes. What a tragedy.' There was no attempt at hiding his pleasure or his satisfaction at the verdict. Death by unknown causes but possibly food poisoning. The fact that nobody else had suffered suggested she must have eaten something from a source other than what was served at the hotel.

'Yes,' said Macnair, with a great deal of cynicism in his voice. Then he laughed. 'I'm glad you and Nick are on the side of the angels.'

'Why do you say that?'

'Heaven help us if you weren't.'

Richard chuckled. 'By the way, I haven't told anyone yet, but after a great deal of thought I've decided to go into politics.'

'You? In the House of Commons?' There was no disguising the incredulity in Macnair's voice. 'Sorry, Richard, but I just can't see it.'

'Nor me. No, I'm thinking about where the real seat of power now lies, in the European Parliament. After all, something between seventy and eighty percent of all laws come from there with no debate and no argument. As a result, I believe Europe is being destroyed as a trading block. Which means we're digging a grave so deep, unless we stop digging, the UK will be a third world country in the next decade or two.'

'Now there, I agree with you. Good luck.'

MAYHEM

A Nick Hunter Adventure

Israel faces imminent destruction, nuclear Armageddon. A series of kidnaps, bombings and senseless murders have left her isolated from her allies and threatened by enemies of old. Unknown to all but a few, the situation has been orchestrated by multi-millionaire Zionist, Samuel Dayan. His vision of a Greater Israel will be carved from the charred ruins of the Middle East.

But Dayan is up against the international anti-terrorist organisation, TIFAT, and our hero Nick Hunter. To the age-old struggle of Good against Evil, author Paul Henke adds state-of-the-art communications technology and computerised warfare. In a desperate race against time, Hunter and his team of hand-picked specialists deploy satellite intelligence and high-tech weaponry to track Dayan to his lair.

The plot twists and turns in a series of setbacks, betrayals and mind-blowing developments. Myriad minor characters deserve story lines of their own.

Relentlessly building the tension, Henke strips his hero Hunter of all resources but those within himself – knowledge born of experience and the inability to give up. Hunter simply must not fail.

CHAOS

A Nick Hunter Adventure

Ambitious Alleysia Raduyev has inherited the family business – the largest crime cartel in Georgia. Operating on the classic theory of supply and demand, she caters for her customers' every desire – narcotics, arms, prostitutes, forced labour. Her payroll has extended to include lawmakers and law enforcers. No one is safe from her tyranny and oppression.

Power base secured, Alleysia moves on to her next objective – the formation of a super crime cartel, whose actions will result in global chaos. As a deterrent to those who would oppose her, she chooses the ultimate weapon – three nuclear warheads.

Desperate to prevent a new, anarchic world order, the West declares World War III against the cartels and their terror organisations. As violence escalates, the now battle-hardened troops of TIFAT are pitched against the massed forces of evil.

Spearheading the battle is Lt Cdr Nick Hunter, the fearless explosives and diving specialist seconded to The International Force against Terrorism.

Paul Henke's latest TIFAT novel is a clarion call to the Western world as it comes to grips with the realities of modern terrorism.